Dawn of the Forsaken

by Kyle Michelle

Cover by Kyle Michelle

ISBN: 979-8-9921360-0-5 (Paperback)

ISBN: 979-8-9921360-1-2 (Hardback)

ASIN: B0DWZRFMV5 (eBook)

First edition 2025

For Eli, who believed in my dreams from the moment we met and allowed me a safe place to let them come true.

For my sweet baby girl, I will always encourage you to follow your *own* dreams, no matter how small you think they are.

And, for anyone too afraid to follow their dreams *because* you think they're too small...take the leap. No dream is too small and it's never too late. Your dreams are worth pursuing.

APHRIA

The Sea
of
Leski

Lost
City of
Perpet

Snowed in
of Gra

Quartz Wall

Forbidden City
of Fahal

Eld

The Chasm
of
Whispers

Bay of
Souls

Quartz Wall

Trench of Ardinn

Sacred City
of the
Goddesses

Temple

Quartz Wall

Abandoned
Docks

Shal

Quartz Wall

Western
Tower

Realm Gate

Vilquin
Ocean

Marsa

Delbrook
Ocean

Meobith

Bayra

Derst
Sea

th

Kingdom
of Odrera

Forest of Truth

Realm Gate

Eastern
Tower

Lake Eavain

The Cottage

Lake
Brecken

The River Vesta

Peham

City Wall

Halor

City of Naver

Vilquin
Ocean

Author's Note

This book contains fictional depictions of violence and gore, death, mentions of rape, physical and emotional abuse, mentions of depression, strong language, and sexual interactions. Please note that this book is intended to be an adult fantasy book, and may not be suitable for younger readers.

May 19th

20 Years Prior

The Start

She had to keep running.

She couldn't recall how she got down to the dungeons as quickly as she did, but the minute she saw the black mist creeping towards the castle lawn, she knew she needed to get Lianna to safety.

She hadn't expected the mist to move as quickly as it did, and had started to panic when she found that they couldn't escape through the main gates, or even cross the city. They were surrounded. The only other way out of the kingdom was through the old tunnels that ran under the castle. After the war, everyone forgot about the escape route, thinking it had been destroyed. But, she had been secretly clearing them out over the years. Just in case.

The tunnels stretched on for miles and there were countless passages to take, with no distinct markers to keep anyone from getting lost. The longer they stayed in the tunnels, the quicker she ran, trying to outrun the darkness from swallowing them up, until she saw the small hole allowing moonlight to pour in and illuminate a way out, right to the realm Gate, and straight into Peham. Human territories.

Crossing the realm Gate was forbidden.

One wrong step in their territory, and they could find themselves in immense danger. But she knew this was the only way for Lianna to be safe from *her*. Was she really going to give up her child to the race who hated them the most? Would Lianna even survive her childhood if anyone were to discover her true heritage or her rare gifts?

And, now, she didn't have time to wonder about her daughter's fate. This was the only way. She ripped the amulet from around her own neck and clasped it on Lianna. She furrowed her brows in concentration and cast a spell on her tiny body that would conceal the rare gifts she possessed until she was able to break the tether on them one day.

Maybe she would be ready by then.

She could only hope.

Any small protection she could give her child to keep her from harm, she would do it, even if it meant sacrificing her own safety. Despite the fact that they were after both of them, with their rare gifts and secret heritage so unknown to the realms, Lianna was the one that they desired, that much was clear. If what she had suspected was true, Lianna would be the key. She needed to be hidden.

She squeezed through a makeshift hole in the wall and ran across the stretch of land to the decomposing bridge that separated the Fae realm and the humans. She crept into the quiet town on the other side, finding the familiar house and praying the family she knew from another life would keep Lianna from harm. Laying her on the steps, she tucked the handwritten letter into her blanket and kissed her daughter on the forehead before turning to run back to the dangers of the Fae realm.

She only took a moment to look back when she heard the door creak open and saw a young mother with a baby on her hip peer into the dark night. *Amara.* Tears filled her eyes as she watched Lianna get scooped up from the step by the female she once knew so well, and brought into the warmth of the house, catching a glimpse of her child for the last time.

PART ONE

The Five Years
Before

Chapter 1

May 19th
Age 20

A cool, sticky breeze blows from the water to my spot at the edge of Lake Carsin. My chin rests on my knees that are firmly pulled to my chest, my eyes red and swollen, and my cheeks streaked with dry, salty tears. The typed letter loosely dangles from my fingertips, threatening to slip from my grasp and into the crystal water that lightly laps my bare toes. Before it can fall, I adjust my hold on it and bring it in front of me, reading the words I've read too many times already:

"LIANNA,

MY NAME IS DRAKE, THE KING OF ODRERA, KING OF ALL FAE. I AM ALSO YOUR TRUE FATHER. THIS MAKES YOU A PRINCESS OF ODRERA, WHICH IS YOUR TRUE HOME. I KNOW YOU DON'T KNOW ME OR ANYTHING ABOUT WHERE YOU'RE FROM, BUT YOU NEED TO COME HOME. NO MORE PRETENDING TO BE A HUMAN. IT'S ABOUT TIME YOU STARTED EMBRACING YOUR FAE HERITAGE, ONCE AND FOR ALL. THE EVIL THAT CHASED YOUR PARANOID MOTHER AWAY YEARS AGO, AS SHE STOLE YOU FROM ME, IS STARTING TO STIR ONCE MORE. IN HER MIND, SHE BELIEVED YOU WOULD BE SAFER IN THE HUMAN REALM INSTEAD OF IN THE KINGDOM WITH US, WITH ME.

SHE WAS WRONG AND SELFISH.

SINCE SHE LEFT, HOWEVER, I HAVE NOT BEEN ABLE TO LOCATE HER. MY ATTEMPTS TO FIND HER HAVE BEEN FUTILE. FOR ALL WE KNOW, YOUR MOTHER IS DEAD. BUT PERHAPS YOU HAVE THE SKILLS I DO NOT POSSESS.

I'M CERTAIN YOU ARE POORLY MISINFORMED ABOUT YOUR OWN KIND, SO LET ME EDUCATE YOU ON SOMETHING THAT YOU WILL BE DEALING WITH QUITE SOON. WHEN YOU TURN 25 IN A FEW SHORT YEARS, YOU WILL REACH YOUR MATURITY AND CEASE TO AGE. IN ADDITION, ANY "PROTEC- TION" I'M SURE YOUR MOTHER PUT ON YOU WILL FADE AND YOU WILL BE IN GRAVE DANGER. THE HUMAN REALM WILL BE FAR TOO DANGEROUS FOR YOU, AND THOSE YOU'VE COME TO LOVE. NOT ONLY THAT, BUT I'M SURE THAT YOU HAVEN'T BEEN PROPERLY TRAINED WITH YOUR POWERS. WE CAN HELP YOU HERE. I HAVE TRAINERS READY TO TEACH YOU ALL YOU NEED TO KNOW ABOUT THE MAGIC WITHIN YOU. MAGIC THAT ODRERA NEEDS TO SURVIVE.

IT IS TIME FOR YOU TO RETURN HOME TO YOUR SISTER AND I. I'M SURE THAT COMES AS A SHOCK BUT, YES, YOU HAVE AN OLDER SISTER. HER NAME IS MARIAH AND SHE IS MY HEIR, MY JEWEL. I NEED YOU HERE TO HELP HER RULE OUR KINGDOM WHEN I AM NO LONGER ABLE TO.

NOW, I'M NOT AN INSENSITIVE MALE, SO I WILL MAKE YOU A DEAL. SPEND THE NEXT FEW YEARS IN THAT MORTAL TOWN OF YOURS WITH THE HUMANS YOU HAVE GROWN FOND OF. BUT, WHEN YOU TURN 25, YOU WILL RETURN HOME. THERE IS NO OTHER CHOICE IN THIS MATTER. AS YOUR FATHER AND KING, I DEMAND IT. AND IF YOU DO NOT COME, I WILL SEND SOMEONE TO RETRIEVE YOU.

BECAUSE OF HOW UNEDUCATED YOU ARE WITH TRAVELING THROUGH OUR REALM, I'LL GIVE YOU SIX MONTHS FROM YOUR 25TH BIRTHDAY TO MAKE IT HOME TO ME.

-FATHER"

I sigh and fold the letter back together, nestling my chin back on my knees. I want to cry more, but there's nothing left. No sadness, no anger, no fear. There's only emptiness.

The letter arrived this morning as my family and I sat down for my birthday breakfast. We watched the strange male nervously stroll up our walk to the front door and knock repeatedly until someone answered. Living in the small town of Peham, we know everyone that resides here. So, naturally, all of our guards went up when this strange male came to the door requesting me by name, and subsequently calling me "the Princess".

Though him calling me that was extremely unsettling and a lot to unpack, it was how he looked that made me anxious. What I originally thought was a cloak turned out to be a pair of brown wings that wrapped and melded around his skin, unable to be used. They covered the majority of his body, only leaving his neck, feet, wrists, and hands exposed. And, wrapped around each of his wrists were thin bands of quartz. At first glance, they looked like dainty pieces of jewelry. But, when I looked more intently at him and saw the harsh bruises around the edge of those bands, I knew they were a form of shackles. And I was almost certain that if I could see his ankles, matching bands would be there as well.

He didn't speak again after his initial greeting. He simply handed me the letter and turned to leave. I watched him take a few steps down the front walk before he stopped abruptly, his hands twitching at his sides. He quickly turned to face me, and his eyes darted from side to side, keeping him aware of everything and everyone around us. As he closed the distance between him and I, the fear that rippled off of him settled heavily on my own skin. My eyes shut tight as he brought his face right next to mine and spoke in a whisper so quiet that a human never would have heard it.

But I'm not human. I'm fae, hiding here with my adoptive family.

"She lives," he hissed, pulling away just as quickly as he appeared. And, when I opened my eyes again, he was gone. I scanned the road in front of my house in every direction, but there was no sign of him anywhere. Unease settled in my chest as I backed into the house and shut the door behind me.

I wanted to tear into the letter right there, but my parents bombarded me, demanding to read the letter before I even got a chance to. They said they *deserved* to see what was in it because they're my parents and they wanted to keep me safe. I refused, and we argued over it, causing me to run out of the house, much to my siblings' protests. But it's the reason I ended up here at the lake by myself. I just need space to figure this out.

They're all well aware of where I am, and I'm grateful that they haven't followed me. This lake has always been my happy place, and I'm the only one who ever comes here, mostly because of where the lake resides. It sits right on the small portion of land on the other side of River Vesta, the body of water that divides the human realm and the Fae realm.

Though Lake Carsin is technically on fae territory, it belongs to the human realm. We were taught in school that the fae gifted this small piece of their continent to the humans right after the realm Gate was constructed in order to keep the peace between them. Since a small part of the lake runs under the gate and into the Fae realm, the fae hoped the humans would take advantage of the small bit of magic that seeped from their lands and into the lake water. But, due to the humans sheer pettiness, the area was never used and eventually feared, yet the fae let them keep it.

The lake and surrounding forest now sits abandoned and overgrown from the human's severe neglect of the land. Long ago, the waters of Lake Carsin used to be crystal-clear, and the lake floor was covered in gems of every color and glass-like rocks. Now, you can't even see the bottom through the murky waters and the bottom is lined with algae covered stones.

It's not much to look at anymore, but I always feel so much peace and familiarity when I come here. Maybe it's because I'm fae, but it really feels like the once magic waters can sense who I really am. Sometimes it feels like it's calling to me.

Crunching leaves sound to my left and I turn my head slowly towards the dense patch of trees next to the gate. I quickly scan the area but there's nothing there. Just full trees and blooming flower bushes against the wall. But I swear I can feel eyes on me and I *know* I'm not hearing things. As I start to move to stand and investigate more, heavy footsteps come up behind me, stopping me from doing something really stupid. The familiar scent of eucalyptus and citrus fill my nose as he sits down on the shore next to me, and I don't even need to look to know it's Wes. We sit in silence for a few moments before he reaches for the dangling letter. I don't even bother to fight him as he takes it from me. He reads the letter in its entirety, then two more times after that.

When he finishes, he gently folds it back up and replaces it between my fingers. He lets out a sigh and leans back on his hands. "Are you okay?"

I can't help but scoff. I don't even know how to respond to that. I pick up a small pebble and toss it into the lake a little harder than I intend to. "Yes. No," I run my hands over my face. "I don't know, Wes. What the fuck is this?"

"It's bullshit and you don't have to pretend you're alright, Li. You're allowed to be angry. Anybody in your situation would be."

"I know and I am. Very much so. I don't want to leave here and go somewhere I've never known. How the hell is that fair?" I spit out harshly, anger boiling inside me.

"It's not fair at all. He may be your birth father, but *we* are your family. Me, Marlene, mom, and dad. Us. Not them. He can't take you from us."

"He's going to try, Wes. He's going to send someone here to take me if I don't show up in five years."

"Well, then, we won't let you go without a fight, right?" he says with a smirk.

"What the hell are you getting at, Wes?"

"You learn to fight, to defend yourself. And you stay here." I can't help but roll my eyes. He makes it sound so easy.

"And who do you think is going to teach me to fight, Wes? Don't you think that'll raise some suspicion?"

"I can teach you. I know it's nothing like a trained professional, but I know some moves." I turn towards him with furrowed brows, confusion blanketing my face. His cheeks begin to redden slightly as he rubs the back of his neck. "The crew got ambushed a few months ago and, after that, I started taking some classes on self-defense from a guy I work with. I just want to be prepared in case it happens again."

"I'm going to pretend I'm not upset that you didn't tell us that your crew got ambushed. Instead, I'm going to take you up on your offer to teach me what you know," I say, staring off across the lake. The stones underneath Wes shift as he stands, wiping the dirt from his pants. He holds out a hand to me and when I don't immediately take it, he comes up behind me and hauls me up by my armpits. His fingers pinch the sensitive skin and my resulting groan of irritation just makes him laugh, which only irritates me more.

"Come on, Li. I know this shit sucks, but I know something that'll take your mind off it." I glare at his still outstretched hand and tentatively take it, as I follow him away from the lake and back towards town.

***

We walk in silence for almost twenty minutes until we're right in the middle of town square. It's bustling with people today, which doesn't surprise me in the least. Today's definitely the warmest spring day of the year so far, so I don't blame everyone for wanting to be out and about now that winter is finally leaving us.

I follow Wes as we pass by the old buildings that are severely falling apart, but still house restaurants and shops of all kinds. Right now, every restaurant has their outdoor tables on the street, and each one is filled with patrons eating light plates for lunch and sipping on bubbly drinks that look far too refreshing. My steps slow briefly, my body begging to sit down at ones of the tables and join in on the spring time activities, but Wes drags me along with him down the street.

We pass by a small cart on the corner of the street, and my eyes instantly find the familiar merchant who is nothing but kind and upbeat. His graying red hair matches the full beard that nearly reaches his bellybutton, and his tattered clothes are extra dirty today. It took me a few years to learn that his name is Nicolas, and seeing his cart in town is one of my favorite times of the year. He's only ever in Peham once a year, always the week of my birthday, and stays for the entirety of the week.

I can never stop myself from buying something from him every since to add to my collection as a birthday present to myself.

"I'll be back for that butterfly later!" I yell, pointing at the small trinket I can see on the top row as we pass. He winks and gives me a small smile before going back to haggle with an elderly woman, gently tucking the dainty butterfly away for me for later.

Wes and I don't stop walking until we reach Café Kawa, the small café-bakery hybrid Marlene works at. The breads and pastries are baked daily, but the coffee the owner uses is unlike anything I've ever had before. I find myself drooling over it just by thinking about it. I used to walk to the café daily to get a cup of coffee and a croissant, but when I lost my job a few months ago after my beloved bookstore shut down, my favorite coffee became a luxury. With my current lack of funds and no jobs available, it's been at least three weeks since I've had the coffee.

"I have been dreaming of this for weeks, now." Wes laughs as we stop in front of the stone storefront and pushes the door open, releasing the intoxicating smells of fresh bread and brewing coffee. Now, I'm genuinely drooling.

I follow him into the café and, the second I'm through the doors, an earsplitting roar of voices sounds from the large crowd gathered inside. My hand flies to my mouth as Marlene and Sierra skip over to me, holding a plate of chocolate croissants between the two of them. The very top one is drizzled in honey and has a candle sticking out of it. My eyes widen as I take in my surroundings, and see all of my friends and loved ones gathered around me singing "Happy Birthday".

"Surprise, Li!" Marlene squeals over the applause as I blow out my candle, and a genuine smile spreads across my face.

"How did you have time to do all of this?" I ask, still clutching Wes' hand. I can feel tears welling in my eyes, and the immense love that's radiating from everyone in the room is overwhelming. My gaze wanders over every face around me and my smile falters briefly when the one person that *should* be here isn't anywhere in the crowd.

Luke.

I wish I could say it doesn't surprise me that he didn't come and, honestly, I don't know if it's because he doesn't *want* to be here or if Marlene and Sierra just didn't invite him. But, that wouldn't surprise me either. They've both made it crystal clear that they don't like him.

A huge part of me is glad he's not here, because I know he'd find something to fight with me about. But, there's another very broken part of me that's hurt that he isn't here. On the outside, Luke seems like the perfect boyfriend. He's always doing everything right around others but, when it's just the two of us, the only time he does something right is when it's beneficial to him. One day he loves me more than anything and the next, I don't know if he even *likes* me. He should be here, though. If not for me, then at the very least to maintain his image.

My shoulders are grabbed and I'm spun around, pulling me from my self-pity and bringing me face to face with Marlene. "Knock it off. Who cares if he didn't show. Everyone that actually matters is here," she says, and I smile softly at her. "Sierra and I have been planning this for weeks now. Put a real smile on that beautiful face and come stuff it with croissants and cake. And..." She reaches behind her and brings around a steaming mug of coffee, not even getting it fully in front of her before I snatch it out of her hands.

"Holy shit, thank you," I say, inhaling the rich smell of the coffee before taking a sip. The hot liquid burns the roof of my mouth momentarily before it soothes my entire body. A far more genuine smile crosses my face now and I shake off the disappointment, letting myself be happy for the first time today. Marlene's right. Everyone that truly matters is here and that's all I need.

Chapter 2

I feel on top of the world when I finally leave the café a few hours later.

Sierra and Marlene truly thought of everything for my birthday, right down to everyone getting a box of four mini croissants as "party favors". There's currently an entire bag of those croissants in my hand and it's taking everything in me not to eat every single one of them before I get to Luke's house.

Sierra strongly advised me not to go to his house when I left the party. I believe her exact words were, "Luke's an idiot for choosing anything else over a party celebrating you. He's a fucking dickhead and I hope he rots." She went on in much more colorful words just how she feels about him, but I snuck away before she realized.

I know I shouldn't go see him, but I need a damn good reason for not showing up for me. Last time he didn't show up for me, I found him drunk out of his mind at the edge of town with his buddies. I ignored him for a few days after that but, of course, he made it up to me by taking me to Halor for a few days, just the two of us. Who knows what shit he got himself into this time but I want to give him the benefit of the doubt before I assume the worst.

The walk to Luke's house isn't too far from the café, but the road he lives down is filled with people today. Something else that doesn't surprise me. Luke lives on the road right next to town and once a month, the residents set up a stall at the end of their driveway and sell their wares. It's like a miniature flea market for Peham filled with handmade goods. Though, I did forget it was today so maybe Luke *does* have a good excuse for not being at my party.

I make my way down the street to the his house at the end, forcing myself not to stop at each stall and browse. It takes all of my willpower not to buy the crocheted sweater from Luke's neighbor and before I can cave, Luke's mom calls my name. I thank the woman for showing me her wares and head to Mrs. Bunt, now standing in front of their stall to greet me.

"Happy birthday, my darling!" she says, pulling me into a hug. She has always been one of my favorite people here, right after my family and Sierra. From the moment Luke and I became friends, she treated me like a daughter and then even more so when we started dating. She insisted I call her Mama B, and anything else would be an insult. "We're so sorry we couldn't make it to your party this afternoon but, as you can see, duty calls." She gives me a slight eye roll, doing her best to keep it from her husband.

"Thank you, Mama B," I say as a smile replaces my worried frown. "I almost forgot today was Market Day until I turned down your street. Is Luke inside? I wanted to see if he had a little time to take a little break and grab a bite to eat."

Mama B's brows come together in confusion and my heart drops. *He's not here.* She looks back at her husband for a moment and he shakes his head in disappointment, before giving me an apologetic look. He lied to them, too. "Honey, I'm so sorry. He said he couldn't work the market today because it was your birthday. He even set up the entire stall for us this morning so that we would let him go to your party instead."

My lip starts to tremble and tears rim my eyes. That fucking *bastard*. "He's...he's not here." I want it to be a question, I don't want to believe that he lied to his parents to do something, or someone, else. But it's not a question. I should've stayed away from here, I should've listened to Sierra. But my dumb heart wanted to believe that he wouldn't do this to me, especially on my birthday. I start to stagger backwards, needing to get away before I completely lose it, but Mama B is in front of me before I can take another step. "I should go, Ma-"

"Why don't we go inside and have some tea, hmm? Ray can handle the stall for a few minutes while we chat, figure out this whole mess," she says, cradling my face in her hands and wiping the tears away. And, *Goddesses*, do I want to go with her and sit on the plush blue couch that sits right in the middle of the living room, sipping on my favorite blueberry mint tea, and wrapped in a blanket while we talk. But I know that if I follow her and do just that, I'll fall apart. And I need to be strong to face Luke, I can't break.

"I can't, I'm so sorry. I need to find Luke. Another time?" I say, backing away from her. Her hands drop to her sides and I can see the hurt splayed all over her face. Not hurt that I denied her, but hurt that she can tell I'm breaking at the seams. She plasters on a smile and nods at me, reaching behind her to grab onto Ray's hand.

"I'll hold you to that, honey. You know you're always welcome here." I swallow the lump in my throat and blink away new tears as I turn on my heels and walk back towards town. If Luke wasn't here, then there are only two other places I can think he could be.

***

There are only two bars in Peham. The Oak Bar and Restaurant is where everyone tends to gravitate towards and is definitely a little more upscale than its competition. The other is Bar Root and it's one of the most disgusting places I've ever stepped foot into. It's an underground bar on the outskirts of the town, right in a dense patch of trees. From the outside, it looks like a small little cottage that couldn't possibly fit an entire bar. But, sure enough, right after passing through the door, there's a staircase that leads down into the dirty, underground bar.

I wish I was at the Oak Bar right now. Unfortunately for me, Bar Root tends to be where Luke likes to hang around the most. He loves it so much that we've spent almost every anniversary getting drinks here before I was given the "real surprise" once he was too drunk to remember. Walking through the front door brings on a whole new bout of anxiety and I can't pinpoint the main cause.

I take the stairs slowly, making sure to step over spilled drinks and something that looks like vomit at the very bottom. *So fucking gross.* I push open the door into the dimly lit room and the smell of cheap liquor and beer fills my nose. No wonder there's vomit out there, this shit would make me throw it back up, too.

I scan the room for Luke, making sure to look in every corner I can see, but there's no sign of him. Not sitting at the bar, not at the pool table, not at the barely hanging dart board. Of course this wasn't going to be easy.

Luckily at this time of day, there aren't too many people here, so I don't have to push my way through a bunch of people to get to the bar itself. I pull one of the barstools out and go to sit, when someone calls over to me from a few seats down. I turn to see an older man looking over at me, with a few missing teeth and a gray beard that reaches his knees.

"You Luke's girl?" His words are slurred and raspy, but he looks more coherent than he sounds.

I wipe the hair away from my face and nod. "Have you seen him?"

"Little bit ago. He was here for a few hours. Played some pool, drank a lot of beer, took shots with some lady. Overheard him saying he was avoiding a birthday party for his girlfriend. Something about none of the people liking him?" he says, tossing back the rest of his beer before signaling for another. "Anyway, he went on to tell his lady friend all about his "woman". Described you perfectly, if I do say so myself."

"Uh, thank you. This lady friend of his...what did she look like? Do you know who she is?"

"Tall, very long blue hair. Looked like the sky. Was wearing a really long jacket, too. Didn't catch her name, though. He left about twenty minutes ago. But his lady friend is over there if you want to fight her for some answers on your man," he says under his breath. I roll my eyes and look to where he pointed. Leaning against the end of the bar is a tall female with light blue hair with bright blonde roots peeking through. It's just as the man described it; long and like the sky. I've never seen her around here before and, with hair like that, she stands out greatly. She must be from the city.

"Fuck," I mumble and let out a breath before taking the few steps over to her. The closer I get, the more her features come into focus. Her eyes are icy blue and almost the same shade as her hair, and are framed by dark brown lashes that seem completely out of place on her body. She is strikingly beautiful and, as I come to a halt next to her, I can see a long scar running from the base of her nose down her face, disappearing down her neck and into the safety of her shirt.

"You're Lianna?" she asks me, barely even glancing my way. She slides a glass filled with something brown and on the rocks to me, sipping the same liquid from her own glass before she turns to face me. "Listen, I don't know what he said to you, but there's nothing going on here. I was just told to meet him here and give him something, that's it."

"I didn't think anything." The lie rolls off my tongue way too easily. I tap my fingers on the glass between my hands, debating on trusting a drink from a complete stranger. "I'm actually looking for him. He was supposed to be at a party for my birthday and he never showed and-" I stop myself mid sentence. She definitely does not give a fuck about any of this. I sigh, "Do you know where he went?"

"He was pretty drunk the entire time I was here with him and most of what he said didn't make any sense whatsoever. But he did say something about going down to breaking? Brecket?"

"Brecken?" I ask and she snaps her finger at me.

"That was it. Something about going down to Brecken and setting up something "really special". His words, not mine." She shrugs and downs the rest of her drink, grabbing a small bag from the stool behind her. She slings it over her shoulder and turns back to face me. "Listen. Not that I really care, but your man seems like an ass and shady as hell. Watch your back."

"Yeah, thanks." I say with a huff. If only she knew the half of it. She narrows her icy eyes at me and looks me up and down, almost like she's assessing every part of me.

"You're not what I expected." She exhales a breath and walks around me, making her way to the stairs. Her long coat flows behind her as she moves and just before she opens the door to leave, she looks back at me and her mouth moves quickly as she says something under her breath. Does she think I can hear a word she's saying? I open my mouth to say something back to her, but she's already gone.

With a defeated sigh, I lift the glass still sitting on the bar to my lips and down its contents in one gulp. It burns all the way down, but settles in my stomach with a comfortable warmth. Whatever this shit is, it's clearly not something they served her here. I go to set the glass back down on the small napkin it was sitting on and notice there's something scribbled in the corner in blue ink.

I drag it to me more and read the sloppy words written on the white napkin, and my heart drops. I shove the napkin into my jacket pocket and beeline for the door, hoping to catch the female who knows too much before she disappears.

***

The darkness will find the ones you love before you realize it.

I see those words over and over in my head the entire walk to Lake Brecken. The female was gone before I was able to catch up to her and I've had the entire twenty minute walk to obsess over the words on the napkin. I can't be a coincidence that she knows about this darkness that Drake's letter said was out to get me. She has to be fae, right? There's no other explanation on how she knows about the darkness other than that. But then that brings up a whole other problem. What the fuck was Luke buying from a fae and how did she get here undetected?

The faint sound of the lake water hitting the shore starts to sound as I get closer and I can hear music playing softly. I pass through the tree line onto the shore of Lake Brecken and see Luke standing down the hill by the edge of the water, right next to a picnic blanket and a somewhat pitiful spread of food. From here, all I can see is a plate of cheese and crackers, a box of strawberries, and a case of beer.

My heart sinks.

Goddesses, I put too much hope into thinking he'd have something far more grand set up, especially since he couldn't be bothered to come to my party this morning. I blink back the tears and debate putting on a fake smile for him, but I decide against it. I *want* him to know I'm angry with him, consequences be damned. I stop a few feet away from him, crossing my arms so he can't grab hold of me and pull me to him.

"Happy birthday, darling," he says with a smirk and starts moving closer to me. I take a noticeable step away from him and his whole attitude falters. I caught him off guard. *Good.* "Are you alright? I thought you'd be in a bit of a better mood and-"

"Where were you?" I blurt, cutting him off. He hates being interrupted and, usually, I sympathize with that. But not today. Not now.

"I was at my house, market day, remember? Sorry I couldn't make it to your party," he explains pathetically.

"Try again, Luke. I know you weren't at your house." His brows come together in confusion. "I stopped there after my party and your mom ratted you out. Then, I went to Bar Root and met your lovely lady friend. What did you buy from her? And don't bother lying again. She already told me." Another lie and this one flows far easier than earlier.

His eyes narrow on me and my heart starts to race. He's always been able to see through my bullshit and now won't be any different. But maybe he'll truly think I have the upper hand here. I mean, clearly he knows I know he was lying about market day so maybe this will work? Damn, I hope this works.

He steps towards me again and, this time, I stand my ground as he runs his hands up and down my biceps. "Here's the thing, Lianna. I know she didn't tell you what I bought because, if she did, you wouldn't be this upset with me."

He goes back over to the picnic basket and pulls out a small yellow box. A *jewelry* box. Oh, no. Fuck, no. This can't be happening right now. The smile on his face reaches from ear to ear as he comes to stand back in front of me, taking my hands in his. "Lianna, darling, *this* is what I bought from that woman in the bar. Custom made for you."

He places the box in my hand and looks at me expectantly, and I swallow the bile that's rising in my throat. I look down at it and slowly open the lid, bracing myself for what's going to come next. And then I freeze.

Sitting on the velvet interior is a pair of silver earrings, with small diamonds at the ends. My eyebrows fly up and, for once, I'm at a loss for words in a surprisingly good way. "Luke, they're beautiful. Thank you."

"I hope you weren't expecting a ring because you know I can't afford that yet," he starts. I shake my head at him and a genuine smile blossoms.

"No, no. These are perfect, I love them." I pin the earrings through the holes in my earlobes and step into Luke's outstretched arms. "I'm so sorry I questioned you. I'm pretty sure Marlene and Sierra would've kicked you out anyway if you showed up."

"Yeah, well, at least we have time together now," he says, and pulls me down to the soft blanket on the ground, nearly crushing the crackers as we go.

Chapter 3

May 19th
Age 21

I'm floating in air. Absolutely weightless.

No, wait, I'm being carried. Carried down a cold, dark, damp tunnel. There's no light, and mists are creeping up behind me and this blurred figure. Nothing about the female holding me is visible, except for her deep, garnet red eyes.

Every step we take gets colder and darker. Small flashes of red light protrude from us and keep the shadows at bay, but not by much. Before I know it, a soft stream of light appears above us and, suddenly, we're climbing.

Cold becomes warm as we ascend into the moonlight. Leaves crunch under her blurry feet as she breaks into a run from the hole we emerged from before crawling into another, more cramped tunnel under a massive wall. We emerge and the running starts again. The darkness begins to slowly leak out of the tunnel we just came from as the looming wall behind us starts to look smaller with each step.

Faster, we have to be quicker.

Just when I think we won't outrun it, the darkness suddenly stops, as if an invisible barrier is keeping it trapped.

We stop right at the edge of a forest and I can see a small home in the distance. The blurred woman tilts her head down to me and she rips an amulet from around her own neck to links it around me, but it's too big. A flash of light and warmth trickles through my veins and flows through me, quickly disappearing.

In the next second, I'm placed on a hard surface. So cold and hard. I long to be in those warm arms and look at those mesmerizing eyes.

Where is she? The one with those eyes? The blurry woman runs away from me towards that massive wall. A small gasp sounds from above me and then I'm in warm arms again. The smell of cinnamon and smoke washing over me.

The darkness behind the invisible barrier consumes the woman as she runs back into it.

Now, it wants me.

I wake up in a panic, drenched in sweat.

It's been a year since the first letter came.

Every night, my dreams are plagued with nightmares. Horrors of what my birth father is like, having to leave my true family behind, defying the *King* and having to suffer the consequences. But, the past few weeks, my dreams have been different. A memory of my birth mother leaving me at my family's home in Peham playing over and over again, engraining itself in my mind. A memory I didn't even know existed until now. No matter how many times I have the dream, or how hard I try to recall any of her features, she's always blurry and I can't see any part of her. Just her eyes.

I don't think I'll ever forget them.

I haven't told anyone about this dream of my mother. I know the minute I mention her, I'll get shut down immediately. No one ever talks to me about her because it always leads to questions about my heritage. All I've ever been told is exactly what my memory keeps showing me. I was left on the doorstep of my home with an amulet, along with a note that I read a few times a year:

"The amulet will guide and protect her. She should wear it at all times. Her name is Lianna. Please keep her safe and her heritage a secret. You are my only hope."

It's that reason alone that I never take off the small, garnet gemstone, and I've pretended to be a human for the last twenty-one years without getting caught. If anyone found out about me being fae, it wouldn't just be me suffering the consequences.

My entire life, we've been taught to despise and fear the fae that live on the other side of the realm Gate that divides Aphria, that none of them are good. 400 years ago, there had been a war between the fae and the humans and, ever since then, the realms have been completely separated. It's the sole reason that Lake Carsin sits in the state that it's in now. Humans don't dare to cross into the Fae realm or get anywhere near it due to their own fear, and the fae don't bother with the humans.

And, in my opinion, it's completely absurd to continue this hatred 400 years later. But what do I know.

When I was younger, disguising myself as a human was fairly easy for a while. For a long time, I was able to keep myself hidden but, as I aged, it became increasingly more difficult. It wasn't until my ears started to point that I got nervous about being discovered. In the beginning stages, I was able to hide them under my hair pretty well but, when I turned ten, the point became extremely exaggerated overnight. The first time I left the house after thinking they were hidden well, I was discovered by an older member of the village, and he threatened to expose my secret and my family. It would have landed us in exile or, worse, executed.

But, the next day, he was found dead at the edge of the forest. To everyone else, it looked like he jumped from the trees, so it was ruled a suicide and never investigated any further. But I saw the truth. I saw the scrapes on the man's knuckles before they took his mangled body away and knew he put up a fight. With who, I have no idea.

Even with the threat died with the old man, my dad still decided to take things into his own hands to keep my heritage a secret once and for all. So, that night after dinner, he made me drink a tonic that tasted like blackberries, potent herbs, and had a distinct medicinal aftertaste. He reassured me it would keep me pain free and comfortable.

It didn't.

I remember begging mom to stay with me when he pulled the knife out, but she refused. The panic consumed me and, with no one else in the room to keep me calm, my father had no choice but to restrain me on my bed as he carved off the tips of my ears, shaping them into rounded, human-like ones. When he was satisfied with the shape, he covered them in a sludge-like concoction that stung when it was lathered on my open wounds. It smelled strongly of sulfur and made me throw up immediately. He explained it would prevent my fae blood from allowing the points to grow back, keeping them human-like for good.

So, now, rough scars adorn the tops of my unnaturally curved ears, and I religiously tuck them into the thickness of my hair to keep them from being noticed by anyone in town. Even from me.

Especially me.

After my ears were "fixed", I didn't think I'd ever have to worry about being discovered again. But, of course, I was wrong. The morning of my sixteenth birthday, I woke up at dawn in such aggravating pain, like I was being stabbed in the back over and over. When I ran to the mirror to look for the source of the pain, I couldn't believe what I saw. Small, feathered wings were sprouting from my back, each one less than a foot long, ripping right through my shirt. They were soft to the touch and a deep blue color that bordered on being black.

They were breathtaking.

And confused the hell out of me.

In every history book I've read about the fae, I've never come across any mention of wings. But they were there, clear as day, sprouting out of my back and there was no way to hide them.

I remember the intense grief that consumed me when I realized what was going to happen to those beautiful wings. How dad would cut them off of me and mold me into something ordinary, just like everyone else.

And I sobbed until my throat was raw and my eyes burned.

I was able to keep the wings a secret until mom came into my room with my birthday breakfast a few hours later. When she saw me curled in a ball on the floor, sobbing, with those precious wings protruding from my back, she froze. She dropped the plate of food on the ground upon seeing me, and took massive steps backwards, horrified of the creature I am.

Before I knew it, my dad was in the room, carrying the tonic, the sludge, and a small saw.

And then he got to work.

It broke me deeply when my parents burned my small wings in the fireplace, but dad kept repeating that we couldn't take any chances. But watching them go up in flames haunts me to this day and now, two scars about a foot long each, run down the middle of my back where the wings once grew. A constant reminder of what could have been in a different life.

A small part of me will never forgive dad for the things he's done and what I've had to endure because of it. But the sensible part of me knows it was all necessary to keep myself and my family safe. Yet, it never makes anything easier.

With a groan, I drag myself out of bed and make my way to the mirror that hangs above my dresser. I tilt my head to the side as I stare at the reflection looking back at me. *Goddesses.* I'm nothing like anyone in Peham, that much is clear. Though, I don't exactly try to blend in anymore, and my heavily tattooed body is always the first giveaway I'm different. But, even without them, my physical features don't resemble anyone here.

Everyone that has ever lived in Peham has always been so ordinary. Our village sits deep in the woods, where the thick tree cover creates a pretty consistent umbrella from all the elements. The town hasn't been renovated in decades, and all of the buildings are simple stone and falling apart as the days go on. Everything is light brown stone and pale earth tones, keeping us blended into our surroundings.

Most of the residents tend to stay in within the forest and rarely come in contact with the sun, leaving them with milky white skin. Though, the ones that work for the lumber company spend far more time out of the trees, resulting in skin a shade or two darker than everyone else. And, along with the lighter skin tones, almost everyone sports light hair colors. Varying hues of blonde and light brown are all that exist here.

Peham dulls in comparison to the other territories in the human realm. Halor is the only other low-class town outside of the city wall, nestled right on the edge of our tree line. Due to the lack of trees surrounding them, the residents of Halor don't bear the same milky white skin, but a tan, freckled complexion.

Because Halor sits right against the wall, it has always been a little more up to date than Peham. Sure, there are some areas there that look almost identical to us, with their old, crumbling buildings and plain colors. But, anything remotely close to the city is far more modern and has definitely been renovated within the past decade.

Landis and Naver are completely different stories.

Landis sits inside the city wall, right on the coast, and it's full of life. The town is home to the higher class residents that chose a quieter life than being directly in the city. The slight tree line divides the busy city from the suburb neighborhoods, and the massive homes are copied and pasted. Every single house is a stark white, with varying roof colors, but they're incredible. I've never been inside of one, but one of the women in Peham has a sister that married a man from Naver and they live in Landis. She told us it's too difficult to explain, but they have absolutely everything they could ever want, yet they take it for granted.

Naver is the capitol of the human territories. It's a massive, sprawling city, filled with the tallest buildings I've ever seen made entirely of glass and metal, far different than the stone buildings here. The streets are paved a dark black and the sidewalks aren't falling apart every few inches. There are luxury stores down every street and the restaurants are far too fancy for my liking.

I visited Naver once with Marlene after the bakery she works at won an all expense paid trip, and I was shocked by what I saw. I always heard rumors about the people that lived there, but I never thought too much about it. It's not just plain, light colors like here, but instead, every shade of *every* color imaginable.

There's nothing ordinary about Naver.

Each person I saw on our trip filled my heart with intense dread when I realized I would've fit in far better here. Not only because of my olive skin and long, wavy dark brown hair. But because my garnet red eyes that are speckled with silver are not so strange compared to the extraordinary eye colors I saw in each person that stared at us. I felt so normal that day.

Not like here in Peham.

Here, I'm the outcast.

I sigh and rub my hands over my face, forcing that memory from my mind, studying the dark freckles that pepper the bridge of my nose. My full, deep pink lips part as I run my tongue along my teeth, feeling where my slightly pointed canines once grew. Ever since the points became elongated, mom makes me file them down once a month to keep them straight. But the rough edges of them don't feel right and I always find myself scraping them along my lower lip which tends to rub them raw at times.

Mom always likes to remind me that the women in her book club frequently comment on how "perfect" I am. That they often tell her how lucky she is that one of her children shares her complexion. Unlike the rest of my family, mom also has smooth, olive skin peppered with freckles, just like I do. The first time I asked why she isn't pale like everyone else, she told me it's because she didn't grow up in Peham. And that was the end of the conversation. But, because of her skin, no one has ever questioned my heritage and, really, no one knows I'm actually adopted.

But, that never stops the book club ladies from leering and making comments about my "perfect" features every time I walk through my house. No matter how many times they say it, I'll never see myself that way. Especially when there's such a stark difference between the rest of my family and me.

Though mom and I have the same skin tone, that's where our similarities end. She has curly, shoulder length blonde hair, the same shade as my sister, Marlene. Her eyes are a striking yellow-orange that glisten when the light hits them, surrounded by light blonde lashes that seem almost invisible.

Marlene, on the other hand, looks just like mom. Though her skin is much more pale, there is the slightest hint of olive, thanks to mom, but she resembles dad a bit more when it comes to that. Her bright green eyes compliment her waist length blonde hair beautifully.

My dad, Grant, and my brother, Weston, both have the same warm, hazel eyes. Wes has short, light brown hair that slightly curls in the front, while dad's hair is beginning to gray, taking over almost all of the light brown that once grew there.

Both males have slightly tanned skin because of their jobs with the lumber company, but no where near the shade of me and moms skin. After the years Wes has worked there, he now has scars all over his forearms, while dads skin stays smooth and pristine, since he doesn't deal with the physical part of the job. Instead, his job deals with transporting the lumber everywhere across the human realm.

He's gone a lot, but always manages to come home to us quickly.

I let out a small sigh and finish brushing the knots out of my hair, throwing it up in a messy bun, and making sure to carefully tuck my scarred ears into the thickness of the up do.

I turn my body ever so slightly, and the small amulet around my neck catches the stream of sunlight coming through my window. It's the only part of my true heritage that I ever show, and I wear it proudly. It's become a permanent part of me, at this point. I rarely, if ever, take it off.

Though, as much as I love and cherish the amulet, I can't help the creeping anxiety that comes to the surface now when I look at it. I always knew it was left by my birth mother but now that the memory replays night after night, how can I not have this anxiety? Knowing it had been *her* amulet. One that she ripped straight from her own chest and left with me.

Chapter 4

May 19th
Age 22

Three more years to go.

It's been two years now since the letters started showing up. Since the first one, a few more have arrived, but none that contain anything I don't know already. Each one contains the same warning as the first one; evil is coming, I have until I'm 25, I have to leave my family, come willingly, or my "father" will send someone to bring me to his kingdom without choice. Blah, blah, blah.

The day Wes found me on the shore of Lake Carsin, I agreed that I'd spend the next few years preparing myself for whatever's waiting for me in the Fae realm. But, that first year was unbearably hard. I let the King's ultimatum break me and, subsequently, I shut everyone out. I stayed in my room for days on end and sank deep into a dark depression.

It took a while for me to dig myself out of the hole I fell into but, eventually, I did thanks to Wes and Marlene. If it hadn't been for their constant checking in and sitting outside my door talking to me when I locked myself away, I might still be in the state I was in then. But, after I stopped feeling sorry for myself, I took Wes up on his offer to help train me and, since then, we've been doing everything we can to get me strong and in shape.

Now, at twenty-two, I feel better than ever. Not only is my body toned and in shape, but my overall physical and mental health has never been better. Most days, we spend our training sessions over the bridge at Lake Carsin, where we know we won't be interrupted, instead of around Peham where too many people will be a distraction.

I roll out of bed and step into the golden rays the spring sun is pushing through my blinds and onto the wooden floor. Each spot the rays touch is warm under my feet and I relish in the feel of it. Every day is warmer than the last as the days inch closer and closer to summer.

I slide open my dresser drawer and pull on a pair of black leggings and a white t-shirt. I plant myself in front of the mirror, debating on pulling my hair back or letting it stay down, when a knock on my door pulls my attention from the tangled mess of waves. I groan and let my unruly hair fall back down my back as I open the door, finding my mom standing there with a small smile on her face. "Happy birthday, honey," she whispers as I open the door wider for her.

"Thanks, mom." I pull her into a tight embrace and withdraw moments later when I feel her tense under my touch. "What's wrong?"

"There's another letter," she says quietly, and the tone of her voice has me on edge. Though the letters don't come as frequently, it's not an odd thing that another one arrived. But this feels different.

"I don't understand," I struggle to say. My body is trembling and it's taking all of my energy to keep it from morphing into full body shakes.

"It didn't come for you," she admits and my brows furrow, confusion lining every inch of my face. I'm suddenly all too aware of the rising panic inside me as she places a pale blue envelope in my hand. I take a moment to stare at her in disbelief before turning my attention to the letter. Along the edges of the envelope are small flowers stamped in each corner and, unlike Drake's letters, this one is not typed out. It's handwritten in a dainty, feminine font, the letters swirling and connecting elegantly.

I scan the words on the front, finally comprehending that it really isn't for me. It's addressed to my mother. I slowly flip the already open envelope, and slip out a small square of paper with the same cursive written in the middle:

"Amara-
I fear I've put you all in danger.

By now, I'm sure Drake knows where Lianna is. When I left her with you all those years ago, I knew the amulet would keep her hidden and protected. What I didn't count on is that he has spies in the human realm, searching for her nonstop. I wish I could give you more information on who the spies are, but I can't.

The darkness is consuming Aphria and, if he hasn't already, he'll send for her soon. You need to make a plan, and keep her safe. You know how much danger she'll be in if they get her.

I placed a spell on her as a baby that pushed her magic away. I figured it would keep her hidden among the humans and keep you and your family safe. But, she's going to need it. When the tether inside of her is broken, her magic will no longer be contained. She will need all the help she can get when her powers manifest.

Amara, you need Shay and Tate for this. Let them help her, please. I've already sent word to them, and they'll find you soon after this letter gets to you.

I can't tell you where I am. I'm in as much danger as she is and even sending out this letter is risky but I needed to warn you. She has the ability to stop all of this. She's the only one that can stop it.

You know who to trust.

-Flora"

Tears sting my eyes as I slide the note back into the blue envelope. There are so many thoughts buzzing through my head and I can't sort through them fast enough. Am I allowed to be mad that there's magic buried inside me that was pushed away? How the hell does my mom know my birth mom?

Feelings of anger and betrayal and sadness rush over me quickly. I force myself to take a deep breath and steady myself before looking back to my mom. Her arms are folded in front of her chest as she walks past me and goes straight to my bed. She sits gingerly and pats the space next to her for me to join her. I slowly make my way to her side, sitting on top of my bed with my legs folded together, keeping a bit of distance between us.

"What is all of this, mom?" I ask through the sting of tears. I force them not to fall and it only burns my eyes more the longer they stay trapped.

"There's a lot I should have told you a long time ago, but I was too afraid," she says after a beat of silence. Her breath quivers as she inhales and lets her head drop back. "I'm sure you're wondering how I know Flora, your birth mom."

"That, among other things. But, yeah, let's start with that, please."

"We can spend time talking about all of this at length another time, but the most important part you need to know is who I really am."

"You're not about to tell me your name really isn't Amara, is it?" I ask, pulling a slight chuckle from her.

"No, no. My name is Amara, that much is true," she pauses and tucks her hair behind her ears. It's such an insignificant act but, a sudden realization hits me as her hands drop back to her lap. In twenty-two years, I've never seen my mother's ears. And, looking at her now, I understand why. With her thick, curly hair moved out of the way, thin scars are visible on the tips of her ears, plain as day. Twins to my own scars, proof of when dad cut the pointed tips off.

That means...

"When your dad was nineteen, his friends dared him to sneak through the realm Gate into the Fae realm, which he did. But he decided to take it a step further and try to get all the way to the castle. It was such a stupid idea for a human to try that, but he was trying to show off to his friends. He traveled through the forest that's on the other side of the gate, the Forest of Truth, in hopes he could keep himself hidden." She stands abruptly and paces on the floor in front of me. "That's when he found me."

"You're fae?" Shock coats my words as she nods her head, and I work to swallow the lump that's rising in my throat. She stops her pacing in front of the window and stares out in the direction of the Fae realm. Her old home.

"The Forest of Truth was the one place I could go and find some peace. He was the first human that ever dared to venture into it after the war. But the minute we locked eyes, I knew. Being fae, I could feel the pull of the universe telling me he was my soulbond. I knew he couldn't feel it since he's human, but I knew he felt *something*. We spent a lot of time together after that, which usually meant sneaking him into the forest just to see each other. We kept that up for a few months, until I realized I couldn't spend another minute apart from him. We had to make a decision."

"I mean, you obviously chose him."

"Of course I did. But before I made my choice, my sister gave me an ultimatum. Go with my soulbond and lose my immortality and magic, or stay in the Fae realm without him and continue to live forever. The choice was obvious to me, but she didn't support my decision at all. Don't get me wrong. She was fond of Grant and loved all the happiness he brought me, but the thought of me giving up my fae life destroyed her. She didn't want to lose me. But I love your dad. I couldn't ignore the soulbond connection. So, I left. We married shortly after in January and by December, Weston was born. Five months later, you were dropped off."

"So, it wasn't a coincidence that I was left with you then. I mean, you're fae. You learned to survive among the humans without being caught. Who better to raise a fae infant in the human world than you?"

"Your mother knew there was one place in the human realm that you would be safe. But, honey, I wasn't just some random fae that she left you with," she pauses and I swear it's like the entire room trembles in time with her body. "You were left with me because your real mom, Flora, is my sister. Making you my true niece, my blood."

***

I don't leave my bed for the rest of the day.

I tuck myself tightly under the sheets and watch as the rain comes down heavier than it has in a while. Usually, the overhead trees act as a sturdy cover from the elements, but today, they don't stand a chance.

It's late, now, and it's been some time since I heard my parents bedroom door shut and the quiet of night fill the house.

I sit up in bed and slide back against the headboard, still trying to grasp what mom admitted earlier. After she dropped the bomb that she's my aunt, and that the family I was adopted into is my blood related family, I shut down, not wanting to hear anything else. Though, in the grand scheme of things, it truly changes nothing, but it still feels like my entire life has been flipped upside down.

I stare at the rain until my breathing calms, when a sudden shift in the air pulls me completely out of bed, forcing the hairs on my arms and neck to raise. I take careful steps over to the window and use the sleeve of my sweatshirt to wipe away the condensation gathering on the glass. I peer out and instantly lock onto two of the most attractive males I've ever seen walking up our barely lit driveway.

The taller of the two has warm, chestnut skin and a very nicely toned body, from what I can see in the dark and through his rain soaked long sleeve shirt. His shoulder-length hair is jet black and hangs unbound, causing the strands to drip water down his back with every movement.

The other male seems a bit shorter, but only by an inch or two. His short brown hair is slicked back from the rain, and there are faint streaks of auburn running through it. He's more covered up than the other male is, wearing a tan jacket over a black shirt, but it's not hard to find the muscle hidden underneath.

There's something about him that feels familiar to me and I can't determine why.

I shamelessly stare at the males for far too long, letting myself get lost in my mind and, when I snap back to reality, they're mere inches from the front door. "Shit." I'm still dressed from this morning, thank the Goddesses, but it's obvious I've been in bed all day.

Heat creeps over my cheeks and the sudden urge to make myself look presentable for these males becomes overwhelming. I don't even know these strangers so why the hell do I feel embarrassed for looking like a mess?

I quickly run a brush through my hair as I speed walk through the hallway to the stairs, just as faint knocking starts on the front door. I start to panic, needing to get to the door before they wake up the rest of my family.

But I'm too late.

As I clear the last few steps, I see the two males standing just inside the doorway, right next to my mom. There are small puddles under their feet where

they stand and, as I stop just a few feet from them, the sudden scent of vanilla
and oak surround me as I stumble back.

Mom turns to me and smiles, before turning to the taller male, leading him
into the kitchen and leaving me alone with the other male.

His hair is no longer plastered to his head, instead it's now messy and spiked,
like he shook all of the water out the minute he was out of the rain. Goddesses,
he is absolutely breathtaking. I can't help but bite my lip at the attraction I feel
for him. I need to get it together.

He looks down at me with a genuine grin plastered on his face that stretches
from ear to ear. Two *pointed* ears. And peeking out from his lips are pointed
canines right where mine would be if I stopped filing them down. He's just like
me.

When he finally speaks, his voice is deep and raspy. "Holy shit, you look just
like your mother," he says in awe as he extends a tattooed hand to me. "I'm
Shay."

Chapter 5

May 19th
Age 23

Only two more years.

The sound of birds chirping outside my window wakes me way earlier than I'm used to. The sun is barely shining through my window and is struggling to get past the rain clouds above, and the dew of the early morning is still visible on the glass panes. Though I'm not a fan of being up this early, I can't help but admire the beauty of how quiet and still everything tends to be.

"Morning, sleepyhead." I startle at the rough voice that comes from the end of my bed, pulling me from my thoughts. I sit up in my bed and see Shay leaning against the wall, staring at me with those piercing blue-green eyes. *Damn those eyes. I could stare at them forever.*

"Why are you here so damn early?" I say, pushing the intrusive thoughts from my mind.

"You're always so cheerful in the morning. And very beautiful, might I add," he says, stepping closer. I feel my breathing start to quicken and a part of me wants him to come even closer. It's almost like my body is gravitating towards him. *Get a fucking grip, Lianna.* "Come on, it's time to get up. There's something I want to show you."

"I'd rather stay in bed," I tell him, laying back down and pulling the covers to my chin. I hear a small growl come from deep within him and I know instantly that he doesn't like my response. But, Goddesses, that growl is something else.

Before I know it, he rips the blankets from my body all too quickly, giving me no time to cover up my half naked body.

I bolt upright once more, and the sudden loss of my warm blankets brings goosebumps up and down my bare legs. The thin t-shirt I put on to sleep in does nothing to conceal my breasts, either. I immediately cross my arms around myself, trying to maintain some of my dignity, but he's already noticed every inch of me.

His gaze hungrily roams up my body slowly and his breathing starts to get heavier with each inch. "That's much more ink than I expected you to have."

I'm completely exposed without the blankets over me, and the majority of my tattoos are now on full display. Even though we've been training together for a year now, I always wear long pants and a t-shirt to keep warm during our early morning training sessions. And, now, it's all exposed to him. *Wonderful.*

While my right leg is filled from hip to ankle with a series of florals and insects, my left leg is completely bare, making it a stark difference to the right one.

My arms are another story. Similar to my leg, my *left* arm has a plethora of leaves, vines, and berries flowing along it. My right arm is filled with various designs I've liked over the years and they make no sense what so ever. But they mean a lot to me, so that's all that really matters.

My upper half, thankfully still covered, is filled with art, too. A few years ago, I chose to cover up my scars from my missing wings. Going down my spine is a garnet red dagger with two massive snakes coiling around it. I dreamt about that particular dagger so many times growing up, it just seemed fitting. It's my "badass" tattoo, according to Marlene. And, though he certainly will never see it, framing my breasts hides a tattoo of a pair of dark blue wings. Identical to the ones taken from me.

I stare at Shay as he continues to blatantly admire my body. I yank the blanket out of his grasp and snap in his face, pulling his gaze back to mine. His eyes are full of fire. My breath catches in my chest at how he looks at me, fueling something deep inside. I pull my lip in between my teeth as his eyes trail back down my body, smirking as he goes.

I shake my head and clear my throat, bringing myself back to reality. "You get a good enough look?"

"I wasn't quite done, actually," he purrs, arching a brow. He begins to close the distance between us but, at the last minute, he hesitates and steps back a few inches.

Why am I so disappointed?

"You're such an ass, Quint," I tease, using his last name just to annoy him. Rolling my eyes, I let go of my hold on the blanket and get out of bed, making my way to my dresser. I can feel his stare on me with each step I take away from him. He doesn't let too much space come between us, though, and he's by my side a moment later, holding out a pale pink disposable coffee cup that I'd know anywhere. A smile creeps over my face as I snatch it from his outstretched hand.

"I may be an ass, but at least I'm an ass that brings your favorite coffee in the morning." A small smile inches onto my face and I look down at the cup, toying with the lid. I don't want to admit it, but he's right. It's been a year since I met Shay and Tate, and in that time, my training has switched from normal exercising with Wes to full on combat training. The first few weeks, I always made them wait for me until I was able to go to my favorite café in town to get my coffee. Since then, Shay has taken a liking to getting it for me himself and has never once gotten my order wrong. He even brings my favorite chocolate croissant whenever they put out a fresh batch.

"Thank you," I say reluctantly, sipping from the cup. And, like always, it's perfect. I hold back a moan of happiness as a slight blush creeps over my face. This small gesture shouldn't mean anything, but it means more and more each time he does it. I can't help but compare him and Luke from time to time which, I know isn't fair, but it's hard not to. Something as simple as getting coffee for me shouldn't be an annoying task, but it's something I know Luke would find a reason to bitch about. And here Shay is, bringing me one plus other treats without me even asking.

I keep finding my thoughts heading down a slippery slope when it comes to Shay, even though I've been adamant that the relationship between him and I has to remain platonic and nothing more.

End of story.

Not only is he my trainer, but he's well aware of my relationship with Luke. No matter how much I want out of my one-sided relationship with him, pining after Shay isn't the way to do it. Even if it's hard to deny the deep attraction I feel for him. And he doesn't make it easy on me, that's for sure. He's constantly flirting and I catch him staring at me far more often than he should be. It's like my own personal torture.

"Can I try fighting with a sword today?" I ask over the brim of my coffee cup. I know the answer before he says it, but it never stops me from asking every day we train.

"You're not ready yet, you know that," he says. I roll my eyes at his back as he turns and walks towards the door. "And, as much as I want to keep admiring all of your beautiful art and the body it belongs to, you should probably put some clothes on."

The hot blush returns once again, and this time it's far more intense than before. I spin around, trying my best to hide it from him, but the smirk on his face tells me I failed at keeping it concealed. I quickly pull on my workout clothes and follow him into the hallway. We walk downstairs in silence and, as soon as we step foot in the kitchen, we're bombarded by my family and their extremely off-key rendition of "Happy Birthday".

Damn it.

Shay lowers his face next to mine and whispers in my ear, "Whose birthday?"

"Mine, dumbass. Which reminds me, your present to me could be letting me try using a sword. It's really the *perfect* gift," I say over my shoulder to him. He leans in close to my ear and I freeze at the closeness. My heart feels like it's about to beat out of my chest as his lips graze my ear, wondering what it'd be like to kiss his full lips.

"It's not your birthday," he says flatly, moving a strand of hair behind my ear. "And when it *is*, your gift will be far more meaningful than sword training." He pulls away from me and I gasp at the absence of his warmth, which annoyingly makes me want to pull him back to me.

Get it together.

"Well, fine, we don't know my real one so this is what I've got," I say, averting my eyes from him and trying to focus on my family as they finish singing. "And anyway, how would you know?"

"In case you've forgotten in the year we've known each other, I was close with your birth-mom. I was there when you were born, *dumbass*," he snaps, just as the song ends. Everyone goes silent at his sharp confession.

"You...you were there when I was born?" I ask, stumbling backwards slightly, all too aware of everyone listening. Tears prick my eyes, but not because I'm angry that he was there when I was born, or that he's kept this information from me. None of that matters. What *does* matter is that he knows my *real* birthday. Not the one that was made up to make me feel normal. But the actual day.

A wave of emotions flood over me all at once, all because of this one, tiny detail about me. My entire life has been spent hiding every true part of who I am. I've been pretending for so long that it's gotten to the point where my whole life feels like a lie, like I don't even know who the real me is. But knowing my actual birthday means I can finally have something that's real. Real and *mine*.

Shay lets his gaze roam over my face, stopping for entirely too long to see the tears spill down my flushed cheeks. We lock eyes for a moment before he lifts his hand to my cheek to gently wipe them away.

"I was," he says softly. "I was your mother's personal guard and I needed to be there to make sure you were both safe." More tears betray me and he doesn't stop trying to wipe them as they come. There are so many questions I want to ask him and they're all far more important than the one I can't hold back.

"When is it?" I spit out. I bite my lower lip to try to keep it from trembling over something so stupid, but it's no use.

"February 9th," he finally says. "It snowed the morning of your birth and completely blanketed the kingdom. There wasn't a single inch uncovered. It hadn't snowed like that in decades. It was so beautiful." The corner of his mouth lifts momentarily only to fall seconds later. His eyes dart around to my family intently watching our interaction and I see the moment he remembers it's not just the two of us. He stands taller and clears his throat. "So, yeah. February, not May."

"February?" That means my twenty-fifth birthday is three months sooner than we thought. That I have *less time* than I originally thought.

The thoughts slamming through my head are so overpowering that my mind starts to shut everything out. I can tell there's a conversation happening around me, or maybe *at* me, but it's all too muddled to make out any words. I don't feel in control of anything, body or mind, and I start to dissociate from everything around me.

I feel a slight squeeze on my hand and slowly look to see Shay's hand slipping from mine as he leaves my house. Then my surroundings are moving, so painfully slow I could scream. But nothing comes out. I feel hands on my shoulders and someone is pushing me down into what I can only assume is a chair or the couch, maybe? I don't know but I *do* know that it doesn't feel like I'm walking on jello legs anymore.

I could stay here in this reality forever, if I really want too. It's calmer here and I don't feel any pain. Nothing but...cold?

I suck in a huge breath and come back to my reality, realizing the cold I was feeling is a bag of ice on the back of my neck. I look over to see Wes standing next to me with the bag in his hand. "Thank you," I whisper. He smiles at me and pulls the ice away, replacing it with a small dishtowel to wipe away the wetness.

Guilt starts to build up in my body. Guilt and fear. I've worked so hard to keep these episodes hidden from my family. Wes is the only one who knows about them after I was forced to explain it to him when he walked in during one. And, since that time five years ago, he has been the only one to know and help me.

Mom pushes her way past the rest of my family and gets in my face a minute later. "Lianna, honey. Are you ok?" she asks frantically. Her hands hover over my face and body, like she's afraid touching me will trigger something else or hurt me somehow.

"Mom, I'm alright. This just happens sometimes. I'll be fine." I take her hand in mine and find her eyes, making her look at me. She has tears lining her eyes and I can see the fear behind them. Maybe keeping this part of me from them was a mistake, but I can't dwell on that now. There's too much going on to think that way.

"You're ok, though?" she says, sniffling. I nod slowly and her own head mirrors mine, coming to terms with this.

"Physically, I'm alright. It's just...I have less time than I thought." *Goddesses. This can't be happening.* I push myself to stand, and though I still feel a little weak, my legs feel a lot less shaky than they did a few moments ago.

I look around at everyone surrounding me, remembering that Shay left during my episode. "I remember Shay leaving. Did he say where he was going? He told me he had something to show me."

"He said he wants you to meet him at Lake Carsin. But he made me promise not to let you go until you were one hundred percent back to normal," Marlene states from behind mom. I huff out a small laugh and nod, sitting back down in my seat to clear my head for whatever Shay wants to show me.

***

Once Marlene is convinced I'm back to myself and normal, I make my way to Lake Carsin...alone.

The walk from my house to the lake is only a short ten-minute trip, but today, it feels like I'm walking for hours. I know that it has everything to do with me just having a bad dissociative episode, but a part deep inside me is so incredibly nervous for whatever Shay wants to show me.

It must've rained a bit in the time I took to compose myself, because I'm avoiding puddles every few feet. Suddenly, I'm more than happy that mom made me throw on my hooded sweatshirt before I left because the damp breeze is much colder than I realized.

When I finally reach the lake and spot Shay sitting on a bench near the water, the dozens of questions I came up with on my walk immediately empty from my head at the sight of him. He's lounging with one leg crossed over the other and both arms are hanging over the back of the bench. The sleeves of his jacket ride up slightly, and I'm able to see hints of the tattoos that start on his hands and work their way all the way to his shoulder.

The light of the morning shines on him and the auburn streaks in his hair almost glow in the light. He is beyond stunning and it just fuels the attraction I feel for him. And I feel myself sliding further down the slope of him.

His head turns slightly as I approach and he scoots over on the bench a few inches to open a space for me. Just before I sit down, he puts a hand up to stop me, and he takes off his jacket and places it on the damp wood, giving me a dry place to sit. I smile, the corners of my mouth barely moving, but I'm able to whisper my thanks to him as I sit.

"I'm sorry if I ruined your birthday celebration. I really didn't mean to," he says after a few moments of us sitting side by side in silence.

I sigh. "Don't be. Even if it was shitty timing, I'm glad you told me," I admit. I turn my head to look at him, finding that he's already staring at me. He reaches out a hand and cups my cheek, still red and blotchy from the crying I did after he left. He drags his thumb along my jaw briefly and then lets his arm fall. He stands and holds out a hand for me to help me to my feet. I pick up his jacket from the bench as I stand, shaking the water off of it gently before handing it back to him.

"Come on, I want to show you something." He pulls me with him as we walk away from the lake towards the other bridge that connects this part of land to a small, abandoned island sitting between the human and Fae realms. There isn't much on the island other than trees and wildlife, but there is a small, crumbling cottage that sits in the middle.

Right after the war, the cottage was constructed for a fae soldier to live in to keep the peace between the humans and the fae. He spent a few years observing and attempting to help the humans, but ultimately went back to the Fae realm when he realized helping them was a lost cause. The humans hated him too much and refused any help he offered. Now, the entire island sits abandoned, just like Lake Carsin.

But, as we approach the cottage, I notice smoke billowing out of the chimney. I look over at Shay when I realize why. "Is this where you've been staying?"

"Where else would we stay?" he asks with an amused smile on his face. I don't really know where I thought him and Tate stayed while they helped me here, but for some reason the abandoned cottage meant for fae never crossed my mind. "Let's go inside before it starts to rain any harder."

I nod and follow Shay up the small set of stairs to the cottage. The front door looks like it was once a vibrant, deep violet, but now there's paint chipping off in various places. As Shay pushes the door open, the joining scents of cinnamon and eucalyptus hit me hard as confusion ripples through me. I know those smells anywhere.

The door creaks open fully to reveal both Wes and Marlene sitting in the dimly lit living room with Tate, talking and laughing as if they've known each other for years. I can't help but do a double take when I realize that Marlene isn't just sitting next to Tate, but his arm is wrapped around her waist, his thumb stroking her hip.

"What the fuck is going on here?" I say more sharply than I mean to, but I can't help it. I feel so caught off guard by everything happening in front of me. I was led in here blindly. I can feel Shay's presence behind me as the anger rises within me. And it's Marlene that stands first, keeping her distance from me and staying in Tate's vicinity.

"Lianna, I can explain."

Chapter 6

"Marlene, you better start explaining fast because I'm still deciding whether to be pissed or not," I seethe, my anger growing quickly inside me. Tate's now standing behind her, and his grip on her waist only tightens, like I'm a danger to her, which only makes me seethe more.

"Lianna, come sit, please," she says gently, lowering herself back onto the couch and patting the empty space next to her. I look behind me to Shay, now protectively at my back, and I ease slightly when his hand brushes mine, urging me to Marlene.

I take a seat with my sister and cross my arms in front of my chest, impatiently waiting for her explanation to come. Both Marlene and Tate noticeably relax when I sit with them, and her gaze darts between him and I before she starts to speak to me.

"I met Tate four years ago, then Shay later that same day. After that first letter arrived on your twentieth birthday, and you ran off to the lake, I noticed Tate in the tree line near the house. When he realized I saw him, he slipped into the forest and disappeared. But I went after him."

"You chased after a fae male...alone?" I ask in shock. A part of me can't help but be angry with her for putting herself in danger at only seventeen, but I'm also insanely impressed with her bravery.

"Well, I didn't know he was fae at the time, ok? But, Weston went after you and I couldn't shake the feeling that Tate might be connected to that letter in some way. I found him waiting for me at the edge of Lake Brecken and he explained everything to me. The next day while you were at Luke's, I brought

Weston with me here to meet them and hear the story himself. We wanted to tell you but..."

"But what, Mar? Wes? I can't believe you guys kept me in the dark on this." I stand abruptly and Shay's attention locks onto me in a second.

"You were spiraling, Lianna! Fuck, we all thought we were going to lose you! Every damn day we wondered if you would decide you couldn't take it anymore!" Marlene cries, tears streaming down her face violently. I suck in a ragged breath. I never stopped to think about what I put my family through. I never once thought about how scared they must have been during it. How could I do that to them?

"I'm so sorry," I say quietly. I sit back on the couch and hug Marlene around the neck as best as I can with Tate still keeping her tightly in his grasp.

"You don't have to be sorry, Li. You were going through a lot and we were just worried." She pauses, taking another shaky breath before the rest spills out rapidly. "But you're better now and you know so much more and got so much stronger. And your time is almost up so, you need to know it all. Everything."

"Can we start with how the hell you and Tate got to this point?" I ask, motioning to his hold on her. Marlene huffs out a laugh as Tate leans in even closer to press a kiss to her temple.

"After I confronted Tate about seeing him in the tree line, I made it a point to see him once a week to get updates and see if he had any news about your situation. It was always a short interaction between us, but every time I saw him, I felt this strong connection to him and I couldn't shake the feeling. A year later, my visits became more frequent and we spent more time together. By your twenty-second birthday, I confessed my feelings for him and he confessed his."

"So, you two are a couple, then?"

"Better, actually," Marlene says, her cheeks turning pink. "We're soulbonds, Lianna. Tate and I are tied together by some connection inside of us. It explains why every romantic relationship I ever tried to have didn't feel right. It was because they *weren't* right. The minute we confessed the love we had for each other, these showed up on each of us." Marlene slips off the intricate silver ring she always wears on her right ring finger and holds up her bare hand to us, while

Tate does the same. On each of their fingers is a thick gold band on their skin, almost like they're tattooed on them.

"Those just showed up?" I question, looking between them.

"In fae culture, the bands magically appear when you accept the connection with your soulbond," Tate explains.

"But Marlene's human. It still works for her?"

"I'm not though, Lianna," Marlene interrupts. "Mom's fae. Which means Weston and I are half-fae." I almost choke at the realization. With all that has happened with me, I've never once come to that conclusion. Of course they are. But they've never shown any physical traits so I never put two and two together.

"It's a lot to process. Trust me, it took both of us some time to really come to terms with it," Wes says, setting up a stool in front of me and taking my hands in his. "But, you have all of us by your side to help with anything."

I give him a small smile and hug him tightly. When I pull away, I realize all eyes are on me once again. "I have questions."

"Ask away," Shay encourages.

"Even though I've known the two of you for a few years now, I spend the majority of my time with Shay training. I feel like I barely know anything about either of you," I say, my attention shifting back and forth from Shay to Tate.

"Anything you ask, we will answer, princess," Shay promises, Tate nodding in agreement. I groan at the incredibly annoying nickname Shay calls me from time to time, pulling a wide grin from his gorgeous mouth. As much as I try to deny it, the attraction I feel for him grows constantly, to the point where my head empties of every rational thought I have, replacing it with thoughts of his mouth consuming mine.

I shake the intrusive thought from my head and look between the two males. "Well then, I'll start with something easy. How old are you?"

"367," Tate answers first with no hesitation. My jaw drops slightly at the information, but Marlene and Wes seem completely unfazed, as if this is prior knowledge. I scoff. *Of course it is.* "But, if that shocks you, just wait till you hear how old gramps over there is." Tate nods towards Shay, who just rolls his eyes in response.

"Out with it, Shay. How old are you?" I laugh slightly. Something about Tate calling this highly skilled in combat male "gramps" is far too amusing to hold back any laughter.

"I'm really not as old as he's letting on," he says. I tilt my head to the side and raise an eyebrow, patiently waiting for the actual answer. "I'm 426, you happy?"

"Damn, you really are old. No wonder you can't have any fun," I say, just as Shay rises from where he sits. My body starts to tingle as he inches towards me, and Wes has the right idea and takes himself and his stool somewhere else. Sheer annoyance radiates from his eyes, but I can't help myself. "Would you like some help over, old man?"

A deep growl rumbles in his throat.

The noise sends chills down my entire body. He makes it to my seat in three massive strides, bending down so he's right above me, not caring that Marlene and Tate are still right next to me. He positions his hands on either side of me, his face mere inches from mine. But his scent is all I can focus on. It's intoxicating and I want to drown in it.

My head tilts back completely, allowing me to meet his gaze once more. Goddesses, he's so damn tall. In the few years I've known Shay, I've tried my best not to focus too much on how stunning he is. His eyes are blue-green, almost like the sea, but being so close, I can see that there's a ring of dark blue surrounding the outer rim.

Like the sea on a stormy night.

I shut my eyes and take a deep breath, convincing myself to snap out of it. We both know there's a strict line drawn when it comes to the two of us. Friends, and that's it. But damn it, sometimes it's too hard to think straight, especially when I can feel the warmth of his body so close to mine. It almost makes me forget that we're in a small living room with others and it's not just Shay and I.

But the whole room seems to disappear the moment he drags his lips along my cheek, making his way to my ear. The damp exhale of his breath brings a warm sensation to my stomach, just as he begins speaking to me. "If you're going to keep talking to me like that, *princess*, then you'll find out I've learned quite a bit in the many years I've been alive," he whispers, biting down softly on my earlobe as he pulls away. I gasp lightly and a warm flush spreads across my cheeks. I can feel it deepen knowing that everyone in the room witnessed what just occurred.

I shouldn't want him this badly. I *can't* want him like this. But I do.

Wes clears his throat, pulling me from my trance, and Shay backs away from me to return to his seat. "Alright, I've had enough of whatever the fuck that was. I'm heading home and I suggest you two come soon before mom sends me back to get you."

Marlene and I nod, and say our goodbyes to Wes. Once we're alone with Tate and Shay, I attempt to bring us back to my original line of questioning. I clear my throat and silence fills the room. "Don't think this means you two are off the hook. I still have a very long list of questions for the both of you, so let's get it going."

***

By the time I get to the last question, the sun is starting to set. Wes has already shown up once to warn us that mom is getting antsy, and I promised I was almost done. But, honestly, I don't even know if I'll even get an answer to the question I want to ask.

For a while after I officially met Tate, he made me incredibly nervous. He still does, if I'm being honest. He always keeps more to himself and stays quiet, and I know less about him than I do Shay. But one thing I do know is that he's covered from head to toe in scars. Even though his fae blood should have healed them, there they stay, lining almost every inch of his skin. I've always been too afraid to ask him about it. Never had the courage.

Until now.

I look right at Tate, now holding Marlene's feet in his lap and talking quietly with her, small giggles coming from both of them. But, when he finally notices I'm staring at him, he goes rigid. "My turn again?"

"Last one, I promise. I'll understand if you don't want to answer it, but it's been something I've wondered since I met you. And I know it might be crossing a line or too personal, but I-"

"Lianna. You can ask the question," Tate interrupts. The look on his face makes me wonder if he knows what I want to ask. And, sure, it might have something to do with that fact that I can't stop staring at his scarred forearms. But, did he really expect me not to ask eventually?

I jerk my chin to his exposed skin, eyeing the scars that are clearly visible with his sleeves pushed up. Seeing them and thinking about my own scars has my ears and back starting to itch. I try to discreetly rub the tip of my right ear to relieve some of the sensation, but I'm all too aware Shay is watching my every move. I drop my hand to my lap quickly and whip my head back towards Tate, straightening in my seat as I turn to face him. "The scars. What..." Shay cuts me off before I can say another word.

"You might not want to go down this road," Shay warns. Even Marlene nods in agreement. But I want to know. *Need* to know. I look over at Tate again, his face now sullen and dark, but staring directly at me.

I clear my throat and force my voice to sound more gentle than it has been all day. "Tate, what happened to you?"

"So much."

Chapter 7

Tate – 260 years ago

The sun is high in the sky, but the winter air still burns deep into my bones. The thin tent doesn't provide much insulation from the snowstorm whipping outside. After three days of this hellhole and scouting the city, I'll make my move tonight. Or else I might freeze out here.

Luckily for me, the walls around the Forbidden City of Fahal have a hidden entrance that can only be opened by magic. Magic I possess. It'll be the rest of the city that's going to be a problem for me. Every inch is crawling with dangerous, Magicless fae all seeking revenge on the soldiers that keep them locked in the city.

Unluckily for me, I happen to be one of those soldiers. And not just any soldier, but the fucking General.

Aris gave me the orders herself, with very specific instructions to act alone and to report solely to her.

Shay hated that. He always says we're a better team together, and he's not wrong. He's always been my right hand, and that's why I put him in charge of the armies while I'm on this mission. He eventually agreed, but is not happy about it. I'm sure he's back in the Sacred City bitching to anyone that will listen that he was "left behind".

But Aris made it clear. Just me. And what she says goes, everyone knows that.

She doesn't want anyone knowing what was stolen from her and it's my job to make sure it stays a secret. A few nights ago, an amulet was stolen from the Temple, one that once belonged to Odessa, one of the original Goddesses. It's just a small emerald, but it's imbued with Odessa's magic, making it one of the most powerful amulets in existence. When used properly, it acts as a protectant to whoever wears it and, when combined with the other gems...it's nearly unstoppable. When it was stolen, the Queen's sources told her a group of Magicless fae from Fahal broke into the Temple to take it, killing four of her priestesses in the process.

I've never seen four females bleed so much.

Strapping my knives into my belt, I pull my hat on and shrug on the thick jacket Shay made me bring. After double-checking my weapons, I open the flaps of my tent and find myself face to face with a group of males, all with arrows pointed at me.

Nothing can ever be fucking easy.

The two on either side of the tent bring me down to my knees in one swift move. Another male shoots an arrow into both of my thighs, keeping me on the ground and unable to rise to fight. I choke back a scream as the ones holding me down twist the arrows with their other hands, sending more blood pouring to the snow.

A dark, feminine laugh drifts from behind the males, and they part to let a tall, cloaked female through. She strides toward me, and I immediately catch the sight of Odessa's amulet clasped around her neck.

"Did you really think that we didn't know you were camping out up here?" She lifts her head, and her eyes glow a deep emerald green, the same shade as the gem. A memory surfaces in my mind, and I thrash, trying to escape the grip of these males, desperate to escape her. She pulls down her hood and dark, midnight black curls pop free. She is definitely the hellish version of her sisters, through and through. "Good luck with that, handsome. What they lack in magic, they make up for in strength."

Standing in front of me is someone everyone has assumed dead for the past three years, killed off by the Magicless simply for who she is. Clearly, we don't know shit. "Izara," I growl.

She circles around me, eyes roaming every inch as she comes up right behind my back. She runs her fingers through my hair, the tips of them stained a deep crimson. From what, I don't even want to know. I strain as best as I can away from her touch. "You've always been such a prize, Tate. I think I'd like to keep you around, *maybe infuriate my sisters a bit," she says, huffing out a laugh as she circles back around to my front. "Not like you have much of a choice."*

"I won't serve you." I spit on the ground, barely missing her boots. She looks down at where it landed and clicks her tongue at me.

"Now, didn't I say you didn't have a choice?" She looks up at the males by my sides. "Take him to my room. Make sure he's ready for me."

***

Every day is the same.

I'm kept in the dungeon under Izara's headquarters. There's a small cot, clearly made for someone half my size, and there's a massive hole right in the middle. Most nights, the floor is the better option. I'm left with the clothes I came in with and, thank the Goddesses, my jacket, but that's it. My weapons were taken upon my capture and stored in Izara's room.

Every week, she sends for me to be brought to her personal chambers. She has her way with me, makes me bathe her intimately, and then sends me back to the dungeon. That itself has been its own kind of torture, but it allows me to keep track of my weapons and where they're kept, just in case I'm ever able to escape.

I don't even know how long I've been here.

Being kept underground, my sense of time is gone. I'm only allowed outside when Izara needs me for target practice for her army, which only happens three times a month, and she looks forward to those days the most. She makes a point to be the one to retrieve me from my cell and drag me to the training ring, my wrists and ankles shackled together with quartz bands.

During the training sessions I'm involved in, there are three different levels the Magicless participate in.

Level one has me tied to a pole in the middle of the field, allowing them to fire their arrows at me, seeing who can get in the best shot. Being tied to a pole and unable to move, it's far too easy, and they almost never miss.

Level two is when I run around a makeshift arena to create a little difficulty for the archers to find their mark. Half of them hit me, while the others struggle to keep up. Some days, I barely get hit at all. I've come to look forward to this level of training the most.

Level three is by far the worst. It's saved for her more experienced soldiers. Her guards shackle me by my wrists only and give me a head start in a contained forest. Then, they hunt me down. In the beginning, it was easier for me to evade their attacks. But the longer I've stayed captive, the weaker I've become.

And any weapon is fair game.

At the end of each day, I'm forced to eat a large meal with Izara in her personal dining room, and then swiftly brought back to the dungeon after I've cleared my plate. I then get chained to the wall of my cell with my bare back exposed, while Izara lets her higher ups take turns whipping me and branding me with hot iron rods.

They keep telling me that it's a game for them to see who can inflict enough pain to get me to throw up the meal I ate prior to the torture. Whoever wins, male or female, is allowed to have their way with me and I can't refuse. Not like I have the strength to, anyway.

Before being allowed to sleep for the night, Izara has me "treated" by the city doctor for the injuries I sustain throughout the day. The wounds that my fae blood can easily heal on its own are coated in a sludge-like tonic that prevents them from properly healing, leaving hundreds of scars along every inch of my body.

And every night when I go to sleep in pain, cold and alone, I pray to the Goddesses that I don't wake up.

***

The room is silent. The only sounds are of the dying fire behind us and our low breathing. I don't know what to feel for Tate, but every emotion is running wild through my body. Hearing what he went through has my stomach in a knot, and it's a struggle to keep my composure in check. Maybe they were right. Maybe I didn't want to go down this road.

The few minutes we sit in silence feels like an eternity but, when I look up at Tate, his gaze is locked on mine.

"How long were you her prisoner?" I finally ask. If I didn't say something soon, we would've sat in silence until Marlene and I had to leave.

Tate shifts in his seat, jostling Marlene slightly, and the light reveals two twin streaks of tears running down her cheeks. Tate wipes them away gently before answering me. "A hundred years." And, this time, it's not my gasp that cuts through the silence. It's Marlenes.

She didn't know.

Her hand flies to cover her mouth, trying to trap the sobs inside, as Tate tucks her head into his neck. Her hand drops from her mouth and they wrap around his neck desperately in a tight embrace. I can tell he's trying his best to keep himself from falling apart as he rubs her back in small circles. His hands are shaking but it's not stopping him from trying to calm the body-shaking sobs that are now coming from her.

"How did you manage to escape her after all that time?" I say quietly. His gaze drops from mine after a moment and drifts slowly behind me to where Shay is sitting. I turn and see Shay's head buried in his hands, not daring to make eye contact with anyone as Tate starts to speak. Not even me.

"He got me out. Said they had been told I was dead for all that time. Apparently they even received proof of my death. But, he was never convinced," Tate explains.

Shay rises from his seat so abruptly that the chair he was sitting in topples over. He keeps his back to us as he stands in front of the fire, and his voice comes out small and broken. "After he was captured, Aris had the walls around Fahal raised and charmed with a much stronger protection spell, so trying to get in became near impossible. I didn't want to risk any of our soldiers, so I went alone. It took fucking forever to figure out when to make my move."

He snatches another log from the pile and throws it on the dying fire with a little more force than needed. Embers fly out and he sidesteps away from the small flames, narrowly missing them landing on his foot and, instead, burning small holes in the carpet. His head falls with a sigh and he turns to face us, the wetness in his eyes glistening.

"Even my damn spies inside the city stopped reporting back to me. I had no other choice but to go in blind. It was dumb luck that I got through undetected and happened upon Tate when he was being transported from the training arena back to his cell one night. I barely had any time to come up with a real plan before I ambushed the guards and he was able to escape." Shay rubs the palms of his hands on his eyes, deepening the redness around them. "We were ten feet from the fucking exit when they shot an arrow into my stomach. Tate tried to help me up but the arrows kept coming. I made him leave me and I let them take me in his place."

"I wouldn't be alive without him," Tate whispers. But I barely register what Tate says. I can't hear anyone talking anymore. Not really. I can't pull my tear-filled eyes from Shay, especially as I watch his own tears fall to the floor.

He saved Tate just to become a prisoner himself.

Chapter 8

"Let's take a walk," Shay says to me quietly, holding his hand out to me. It's so hard to form words with the lump in my throat and, honestly, I'm afraid that if I open my mouth, only sobs will come out. I nod and take his hand, his fingers instantly intertwining with mine, pulling me towards the front door.

A sudden wave of nausea washes over me the second we're alone together. *Oh, Goddesses.* This is absurd I've been alone with him before and I've never felt any of this before. Though, never before has it been right after I learned a massive part of his life or seen him express more emotion than I ever have before. No, this *feels* different.

Besides, Marlene and Tate need some time together, especially after everything he confessed, surprising not just me, but the love of his life, too. I'll gladly deal with these overwhelming emotions for her.

Shay takes me East, away from the cottage and away from the way back to Peham. This way, we're heading right for the cliffs that overlook the a small portion of Derst Sea beside the realm Gate. I've never been to the actual cliffs before, but I've admired them from Lake Brecken before and, damn, are they stunning. Gray rock exposes itself to the splashes of ocean water below and foliage climbs up and down the entire side of the cliff in every shade of green imaginable. At the top, the forest gives way to a small clearing of glass and flowers and, this time of year, it's like a dream.

I stagger forward and out of Shay's grasp as we leave the cover of the trees and step into the blooming clearing. Even though the sun is setting behind us, the entire sky is filled with pastel shades of red, pink, and orange. The sound of the waves hitting the rocks at the bottom of the cliff are muted but put such a sense of calm into me that I can almost feel the anxiety and sadness leave my body.

Fireflies emerge from the grass with each step I take closer to the cliffs edge. "I've never felt so at peace," I say quietly, more so to myself than anything. But I can feel his presence right behind me, so close that his breath warms my neck.

"When Tate and I first came here to keep an eye on you, this was my favorite spot to come to. Being two large fae, we didn't really get to go anywhere where someone might see us, so the cabin and the surrounding areas were all we had," he says, walking to stand at my side. "Though, from what I've heard about your town, I think I would've chosen to spend my time here, anyway."

"There's nothing wrong with Peham," I say defensively. He chuckles and lowers himself to the ground, motioning for me to join him by a nod of his head. I let a groan escape me, but sit down with him anyway.

"I wasn't saying there was something wrong with Peham. But I've heard stories of the people there and I'd rather keep my distance," he says, bringing his hand to my cheek and stroking it with his thumb. I feel like I'm melting into his touch and, Goddesses, I want to kiss this male more than anything. And I know he knows that, because his gaze lowers from mine down to my lips that I can't help but bite. He leans in towards me and my heart starts to race. *This is happening.* My breathing starts to quicken and my traitorous tongue wets my lips. *No, this can't happen. I'm with Luke.*

"Shay," I start, dropping my head so our foreheads touch. He pulls away and stares out at the sea in front of us.

"I know you have questions," he says, and I know he means about his and Tate's past, but I *wish* he meant about what just happened.

"I don't want to pry." Fucking liar. I want to know all of it. He doesn't owe me any sort of explanation but I can't help but wanting to know what happened to him. Hearing what Tate went through was horrendous and a part of me knows for certain that what Shay went through was far worse.

"You're a terrible liar," he comments. I whip my head towards him, expecting him to be giving me a look or smirking from ear to ear, but I'm wrong. He's staring to his left, through the few trees lining the cliffs edge and directly at the realm Gate that I didn't even notice was this close to us. He's staring at home.

My heart cracks for him.

"I do want to know, but I don't want you to have to relive it if it's going to bring you pain," I admit. He takes in a deep breath and turns his head back towards me with tears glistening in trails down his cheeks. *Oh, Shay.*

"I wasn't a prisoner for nearly as long as Tate was. But I endured what he did, plus more. I was told I was being punished for taking his place. There's still a lot I'm not ready to talk about but, one day, you'll know all of it."

I huff out a laugh. "Yeah, until I'm reunited with my father and you'll get paid or whatever and then you'll go back to your life and forget about me." I try to hide the disappointment in my tone but it's no use. And I know he heard every drop of it in my words. I shouldn't even be upset about it and yet, even though I've been reminding myself of that fact since we met, it's still hard to wrap my head around. Because, now, I want him in my life in some form or another, and the thought of him walking away when we get to Aphria to see my father is too much to bear.

"No," he says simply.

"No?" A glimmer of hope starts to grow and I shove it right back down before it hurts me too much.

"There's no life for me without you in it and, trust me, you would be too hard to forget even if I did go back to my life," he says, locking his eyes on mine. I open and close my mouth a few times, not really sure what to say to that. So, I say nothing. I turn back towards the sea and breathe. Breathe through the anxiety sitting low in my stomach. Breathe through the feeling of his eyes still staring at me. Breathe through this feeling of wanting him because I just can't want that, not while I'm with Luke. And breathe through the overwhelming feeling that our lives will be intertwined for far longer than I originally thought.

***

By the time Shay and I get back to the cottage, Marlene is sitting on the front step with Tate waiting for me.

"We have to go," she says when I'm close enough to hear her soft voice. I nod and wait at the small fence for her while she says goodbye to Tate.

"I'm sorry if I overstepped with what I said," Shay says in a whisper as he walks to my side.

"You didn't." Did he? My heart and mind are battling one another for the truth and neither is coming up with a reasonable answer. "I'm assuming I'll see you soon? To train, that is."

"You will," he promises and walks back to the cottage, glancing over his shoulder once to flash a smile towards me. Marlene makes her way over to me once the two males disappear inside, grabbing my hand and sticking close to my side.

The walk back home is eerily quiet. The only sounds are from the crunching gravel under our feet and the occasional sound of the night animals. The sun is long gone and it took the painted crimson red sky with it, leaving us with an onyx sky speckled with bright stars as we follow the moonlit path home.

The dim lights of town start to come into view as we cross over the old bridge into the outskirts of Peham. It all looks so peaceful from here. No one is out and about at this hour, the street lamps are shining a muted gold color every few feet in town, and the homes are barely lit. With the trees encasing the town, the lights remind me of fireflies twinkling in the trees.

"Can we stop for a second, Li?" Marlene says in a hushed tone, grabbing onto my wrist. My eyes go to her hold on me first, but my heart sinks when I drag my gaze up to her face.

There's no hiding the sadness overwhelming her. It's rooted in her so deep, like it's her own pain to carry. My brows knit together in sadness as I wrap her in a tight hug. The second she's in my arms, she falls apart completely, letting out everything she kept inside to spare Tate. By the time we get home, she won't be able to feel all of this without being hounded with a million questions. But right here, right now, I can be her safe space.

I feel every tremor that goes through her petite body and, *Goddesses*, they're vicious enough that I'm afraid she's going to break in half. I squeeze her closer to my chest and breathe through my own sadness, masking my pain to help her. Right now, I can't think about how much I want to fall apart, too. After learning about Shay's history, my heart physically hurt, so I can't imagine what she's feeling inside. The love of her life, her soulbond, her everything. She needs this comfort more than I do.

I guide her down to the forest floor and cradle her in my lap, just like I did when we were kids and she was sad. Back then, it was a hell of a lot easier to calm her when the causes were scrapes to the knees or a broken toy, but this? This is much more to bear.

I stroke her straight blonde hair as she cries and fists her hands in my sweatshirt. I know she'll calm soon, just as soon as she controls her erratic breathing. She stays cradled in my lap for a few more minutes before her grip on my shirt eases and she finally takes a deep, calming breath. "Thank you," she whispers, and I help her into a sitting position next to me, giving her some space to compose herself as best as she can.

"Did you know?" I ask gently.

"Kind of," she says, sniffling. "I knew he was kept prisoner and that Shay saved him, but that's it. I never pushed for more information because I could tell it was something he didn't like to talk about. I wish I had known sooner. He went through all of that suffering for a hundred years and I didn't even know. I swear, Lianna, I swear on every Goddess, I will rip out Izara's throat if I ever get the chance. She will pay for what she did to Tate *and* Shay. Mark my words," she swears and I nod. She wipes her eyes on her sleeve and stands, holding her hand out to me to rise with her.

She links her arm through mine as we continue to walk back to our house, and both of us are shivering as the night chills even more. Even with my sweatshirt on, I can feel the goosebumps rising on my arms under the sleeves. "You know mom is going to have a million questions about why we took so long," I say quietly. "Don't think you have to tell her anything you're not comfortable with, you hear me?"

"I know. I'll tell her about Tate and I, she probably deserves to know that. But, as for how long Wes and I have been involved in all of this? Well, that'll be harder to maneuver."

"She won't be happy you two are involved, you know that," I say as we enter town. Our house starts to come into view, the glow of the lights inside like a lighthouse beckoning us home.

"I don't really care and, quite honestly, it doesn't even matter. Everything we've done has all been for *you*, Lianna. She can be as mad as she wants and she can try her hardest to stop us, but she doesn't get to have an opinion about it. She doesn't get to tell us who we're allowed to protect."

A new batch of tears fills my eyes and I let them fall. I've never felt more proud or less deserving of my sister in this moment. I bring my lips to her temple and kiss her gently, continuing to the house with a new found confidence that she gave me.

Chapter 9

February 9th

Age 24

My last year at home.

Waking up this morning knowing it's my *real* birthday, and not the one that was made up for me, is such a surreal feeling. I've gone my entire life celebrating a day that was chosen for me and, now that I know the truth, I can't even tell anyone or celebrate it properly. At least my family, Shay, and Tate know. Everyone else still thinks it's in May, and that's how it has to stay for now.

My *original* plan was to spend the morning in bed enjoying the day off from training with Shay, until Luke showed up at the crack of dawn. I really tried to ignore his insistent yelling from outside my window, but he only got louder and louder, and I didn't need him waking up my entire family. When I finally met him outside a few minutes later, still half asleep, he pulled me along with him and told me there was a "special surprise" for me.

Now, Luke and I walk side by side through the snowed in town. It's far too early for anyone else to be awake, so the roads are completely snowed over and have yet to be shoveled. I'd be in better mood if I could've stopped for a cup of coffee on our way, but apparently this surprise is too important and he isn't "allowing" me to make any stops. So different from Shay who definitely would've brought me a coffee and a whole box of croissants this morning if we had training. So, now, I'm fuming.

I have absolutely no idea where he's taking me, but I've been angrily trying to build a speech in my head to *finally* break up with him for good this time. I'm sick and tired of him controlling everything I do and, sure, I might not be feeling this way if I hadn't been so rudely waken up this morning, but maybe this is a sign. And no matter how much he tries to make up for all the shitty things he does to me, it'll never be enough to erase all his wrongdoings.

And he has eight years of wrongdoings he needs to make up for. But he never will.

I don't even know how we got to this point.

We've been best friends our entire lives and were basically inseparable. And it was perfect, when that's all it was. We spent every day after school exploring the village and worked early morning shifts together at the breakfast shop in town. We never went anywhere without the other. We told each other everything and he he was always there for me when I was bullied in school. People always joked about us getting married and we *always* laughed it off.

I wanted to keep my best friend, but that's not what he had in mind.

The dynamic between us changed completely the Halloween we were eighteen. After all the kids went trick-or-treating and everyone was busy enjoying the Halloween fair in town square, Marlene and I decided to go to Luke's house to hangout instead while Wes made his way to Sierra's house. We watched movies until Marlene fell asleep on the couch, and Luke came out with a bottle filled with a dark, amber liquid.

His dad's special liquor stash, he told me.

My gut told me to refuse and I tried to, but he kept pushing the bottle my way, not taking no for an answer. Five large glasses later, and my head was spinning. He "helped" me by putting me in his own bed and crawling in beside me. I was so intoxicated that I wasn't able to protest it.

The last thing I remember before the blackness swept over me is Luke undressing me as my consciousness wavered. He positioned himself over me with his long blonde hair concealing his face as he had his way with me. And, through his choppy breaths, he confessed something as he pushed into me. *"I know what you are, Lianna. fae. Hidden in plain sight among us. I should have known. You're a fucking traitor."*

When I woke the next morning and tried to confront him about it, he told me that he'd keep my secret, for a price. He wouldn't tell anyone if I agreed to be with him romantically. Turns out, he'd been in love with me for years and, after he had his way with me, he said he knew we belonged together. I had no choice but to agree to his terms, because him exposing *me* would put my entire family in danger.

That day, I went home and scrubbed my body raw in the shower, trying as best as I could to get his unwarranted touch off of my skin.

The first year of the relationship was surprisingly normal. He treated me just as he always had and it was like nothing changed. I tried my best every day to feel something for him just to make the relationship work for the sake of my family. But once that first year passed and I was locked into the relationship, he changed. Gone was the man that I grew up with and, in his place was someone evil and manipulative.

I couldn't handle it anymore. I made so many plans to leave him but he always had some excuse that he would change and be better. And I clung onto that hope for another year until he just got worse. The first time I tried to end things with him, his response was to hit me. Multiple times. And he didn't stop.

So I stayed. At first, out of fear for my family and, then, out of fear for myself. I hoped that the abuse would stop once I agreed to stay with him, but it only got worse. Even if I wanted to tell someone about it, I never had any proof. My fae heritage heals any mark he leaves on me so quickly, and he knows that. It's probably one of the reasons he feels like he can get away with hurting me.

And its continued for the past eight years.

I'm dissociating so aggressively that I don't realize how far we've walked until we stop in front of a large apartment building in a vaguely familiar town. "Are we in Halor?"

"Welcome to our new home, Lianna," Luke says, grabbing my hands and pulling me into him. I know I'm stiff as a board in his embrace, but I'm in too much shock to pretend to enjoy hugging him.

"Wait, what?" My words come out so silently that I know he didn't hear me. I can feel my heart starting to race and the breathing quickens to the point where I know I'm going to spiral into a panic attack.

"I've been scoping out places for months now and this was just too perfect to pass up. And this is the perfect stepping stone for us to finally move to the city in a few years, just like I've always wanted," he says proudly. Like this whole idea of his is for the both of us when, in reality, this is *his* dream alone.

"You got an apartment?" I say a bit louder this time. I need him to hear me, to understand this is not my dream.

"It's about damn time we leave the shithole of Peham and start our lives together, away from everyone there," he says with a hint of confusion and anger in his tone. "This is what we wanted, isn't it?"

"What about my family, Luke? I'm not ready to leave them just yet," I argue. I know I have limited time with them, but I'll be damned if I spend the last few years in the human realm with Luke in Halor. "I love Peham and you know that. *That's* my home. Not this place."

The City of Halor is settled right between Peham and Naver and, although it isn't the size of the capital, it's still a decently large city. And the thought of living here with Luke is sending a hot panic throughout my entire body and speeding up the panic, while simultaneously breaking me to pieces.

"Fuck them, Lianna, and fuck Peham. I'm the only one that matters. I thought we had an understanding," he seethes, his grip tightening on my arm.

"Let go of me. Please, we're in public."

"It's about time you let go of that perfect little life you think you have in Peham and start getting on board with this. Or else it won't go well for you," he spits out, gripping my arm hard enough to bruise, now. He grins as I wince, knowing he's going to make marks that no one else will know he left on me.

I open my mouth to say something, anything, to him. But before I can even take a breath, the wind brings a familiar scent towards me; vanilla and oak. I feel his presence well before he even steps into view. How the hell did he find me?

"Threatening a female? In broad daylight?" Shay says, clicking his tongue against his teeth. "Pretty pathetic, if you ask me."

"Yeah, thanks for the advice, man but don't tell me how to handle my woman," Luke half-growls out, turning his back to Shay. His nails are now digging into me, causing small dots of blood to well up underneath his fingers. I flinch slightly at the sudden increase of pain and Shay notices instantly.

"Get your hands off her, now," he says calmly, but I can see the anger rising in him.

"Dude, I don't even know you so how about you mind your own business and leave us alone. There are plenty of other women in town you can have, but this one's mine," Luke snarls. The possessiveness he uses towards me makes my stomach turn and I'm fighting to keep the nausea down. The only thing that remotely helps is seeing the grin spreading across Shay's face. It's completely devilish and I know Luke has mere seconds before Shay does something awful. I can't help the twitch of my lips at the thought.

As Shay moves towards us a few steps, his jacket shifts slightly to reveal two daggers strapped to his sides. I almost think Luke doesn't see them but, sure enough, his eyes are bulging out of his head and his gaze is locked onto the blades.

Shay slowly starts to bring his hands to his sides but Luke acts quicker. He lets go of his grip on me and pushes me away from him, causing me to stumble slightly. Shay's quick to catch me and steadies me by his side, keeping his arm secured on my waist until I'm stable. "Are you alright?" he asks in a whisper.

"I'm fine. Let's go." I'm nearly dragging him away from the situation out of pure embarrassment. I've been so good about hiding this part of my life from everyone and him seeing a small portion of it is humiliating.

"Lianna, stop. How long has he been doing this shit to you?" His face darkens with anger but his hold on me never tightens. If anything, he's holding onto me less and more gentle. I sigh and drop my shoulders.

"Eight years," I admit, shame washing over me. This secret that has been locked away for so many years is finally out in the open. Someone *finally* knows. And it hurts.

There's a slight glisten of tears in Shay's eyes as he takes in just what that means. That in the two years he's been here with me, Luke has been hurting me without him having the slightest clue. I can see the guilt and sadness on his face, and he starts to say something to me but I stop him before he can say anymore. Because I *will* fall apart if I talk about it anymore.

"Can we just go, please?" I plead and turn my gaze to my feet. My face is burning red with embarrassment, shame, fear, all of the above. I can feel his eyes on me for a few moments and then he tucks me back into his side, making sure to keep me secure in his grasp. My breathing starts to even out but, I swear, we only make it six feet when Luke starts yelling after us.

"Don't get any fucking ideas, man. That's still my girl, I just don't have the energy to fight you for her." I stop in my tracks. His words cut deep and shatter the last bit of hope I have for him, for *us*. I shouldn't be surprised that he doesn't want to fight for me. He always says how much he loves me but he has proven time after time that he really only loves the *idea* of me and holding my secret over me.

Shay glances down at me and I can tell I'm not hiding the hurt as well as I hope. He pushes me behind him before stalking over to Luke. "Let's get one thing straight. You don't deserve an ounce of the kindness she has shown you. You should want to fight for her no matter what. She's not even mine, but I would still find the *energy* to crawl on my hands and knees to fight for her, even if I was close to death. She deserves that and much more. And, if you won't give that to her," Shay pauses and takes one large step to Luke, getting right in his face, towering over him by at least a foot. "I will."

Luke's jaw drops as Shay comes back to me and wraps an arm around my shoulder, steering me back towards Peham. I should just walk away, figure this all out later. But this is my chance. And I might not ever get the courage again to *finally* be free of him. I stop walking and lightly grasp Shay's hand that's resting comfortably on my shoulder.

"I need to end this, Shay. I've tried before but I've never gotten out. I have to get out," I plead. He looks me up and down, nodding his head after a moment. I take a deep breath and turn to face Luke, who's angrily pacing back and forth in front of the apartment building.

"I'm right here if you need me," Shay whispers from behind me, relocating his hand from my shoulder to the small of my back. I suppress a shiver at the intimate touch, but I instantly feel more grounded and confident than ever.

I stand straighter and lift my head, letting the newfound confidence surge through me. "Luke." At the sound of my voice, his head turns to me. At first, his eyes are filled with hope but, when he sees Shay's slight hold on me, they fill with fire and rage, instead.

"Why is he touching you?" he spits across the few feet of distance I put between us. "I swear, I'll-"

"No." My voice is firm and confident. Strong. "This is done. I'm done with you hurting me and not treating me how I deserve and for hiding under your threat of exposing me for all these years. I won't let you do this to me anymore."

"You know what I'll do Lianna. It will ruin you and you know it." A cruel smile grows over his face with his words. "Are you sure you want to do this?"

The panic is back and my chest begins to tighten as my body begins to tremble. This fear that he'll put my family in harm's way is what has kept me in this relationship for so long. "He knows about me," I say quietly to Shay out of the corner of my mouth, not even looking at him as I speak.

"I'll keep you safe," he promises. I blink away the tears and swallow the lump in my throat, then nod, knowing in my heart that I can trust Shay with my life. My chest starts to loosen with the realization and the panic melts away as my confidence flows back to me. I take a deep breath and lean into Shay's touch, the feel of his hand still on my back continuing to keep the panic at bay.

"I'm done being afraid of you. I've spent too many years as your personal punching bag. I'm done." Luke opens his mouth to argue more but, before he has a chance to say anything else, I spin on my heels and walk away. The tremble is now a full on violent shake, but I'm trying my best to breathe through it and keep in control. The trembling starts to subside with each step closer to home, and it feels like an entire mountain has been lifted off of my shoulders. I can finally breathe again.

"I'm so proud of you, sweetheart," Shay says, his thumb stroking my back gently. I should tell him not to call me that, but the use of this new nickname sends a warm feeling rushing through my core. Something inside pulls at me, wanting me much closer to Shay. It's the same feeling I felt the first time I met him, but this time, it's far fiercer. And, this time, I'm not pushing it away.

"What about my family? If they believe him, they'll come for all of them. They'll *kill* me." The hot panic starts to surface again at the thought of my choice putting them at risk.

"Is this why you stayed all these years, suffered through all of his abuse the entire time?" Anger fills his every word, and his thumb pauses its stroking along my back. But, it's not anger towards me for staying or letting it get this bad. It's anger that he knows I've suffered in this alone without anyone to help me. Anger that Luke has treated me this way for years when he's supposed to love me and care for me, yet chose to hurt me instead. I nod. "I could kill him, Lianna, I really could."

"I know," I whisper. "It's over now. He won't lay another finger on me again, thanks to you."

"I was just there to be your backup, Lianna. You did that all by yourself. You just needed a little push." A small smile grows on both of our faces. I really did it. I found the courage to leave him, but I can't help but wonder how differently that would've gone without Shay there.

"I stopped by your house earlier. I know we don't have any training today but I wanted to give you this," he says, pulling a small box out from his jacket pocket. I gape at him.

"For me?" Holy shit, I sound ridiculous. Of course it's for me or else he wouldn't be handing it directly to me. I feel my cheeks warm slightly and I take the box from his outstretched hand.

"Happy birthday, Lianna." I tear off the shiny gold wrapping paper and lift the top from the box, revealing a gold bracelet with a tiny golden croissant charm hanging from it. I can't help the laugh that comes from me.

"A croissant?" I ask through happy tears.

"Well, yeah. I know how much you love them and I wanted you to remember home when we have to leave. This charm seemed like the most appropriate way to remember Peham when you're missing it," Shay says nervously, rubbing the back of his neck. He seems embarrassed, like this is the absolute worst choice he's made. But, he cannot be more wrong.

"I love it, it's perfect. This is, by far, the best gift I've ever gotten," I say, taking it from the box. I hold my arm out to him and he helps me clasp the bracelet around my wrist. It's a perfect fit. "Thank you so much."

"I told you I'd get you something meaningful for your real birthday, and I meant it. I-" he stops abruptly and shakes his head, dropping his gaze from mine. "I should've come to your house sooner. Maybe if I had been there, none of this would've happened. I could've been there for you."

"Shay, stop. You don't need to place the blame on yourself. If anything, I'm to blame for not leaving sooner," I say, bending down to look him in the eyes. "And if you had shown up, I wouldn't have had the courage to leave him and I would've been stuck that much longer. There's nothing you could've done."

But then I remember what he said to Luke.

"Why'd you say what you did about fighting for me?" I question. "Friends don't say that about friends. It felt...deeper."

"Is it so crazy that I don't want to see you harmed by someone who is supposed to love you?" he asks, but I just stare at him. Because there's more to it than that, and he just won't tell me. He sighs and pulls away from me all together. The absence of his warmth freezes my very core, and I'm suddenly craving his touch more than ever. And the realization hits me like a damn train.

He's what I've been waiting for my entire life, whether I knew it or not. The other half of my heart and soul, connected by some invisible string that is starting to *finally* untangle. And it's destroying me inside knowing that I've been stuck with someone who wanted to hurt me for all these years. But, as much as I would love to see where this could go, there's some fucked up part of me that knows this isn't something I can handle right now.

I need to know, though.

"Shay?" He looks down at me, frozen in place. "Are we...soulbonded?"

"Would it be so terrible if we were?" he asks, something like hurt lacing his tone. I don't know what to say. And as I open my mouth to answer him, we're bombarded by Tate and Marlene bounding out of the forest that separates Halor and Peham.

"We've been looking everywhere for you guys. Something happened." Panic settles in as Marlene bends over panting, fear and urgency lacing her words.

"What happened?"

"Peham," Marlene takes a shaky breath before standing back up and continuing. "A group of fae ambushed the town, it's so bad."

"Marlene, what happened?" I say, grabbing her shoulders and forcing her to look at me.

"It's all burning down."

Chapter 10

We run in a full out sprint towards town and the smell of smoke increases drastically the closer we get. The sound was trapped within the trees along the border of Halor and Peham but now, the sounds of screaming and crackling fires overwhelm the four of us.

"Why isn't Wes with you?" I yell through rapid breaths as I run.

"He stayed behind to help evacuate everyone. The town was crowded with people today and they did the majority of damage there. Some of the homes were hit pretty bad, but a good amount were completely spared. It was all because mom and dad wanted to stay behind and help. Wes and I tried to talk them out of it but, when they wouldn't budge, he chose to stay behind to make sure they stayed safe," Marlene explains.

We break through the last of the trees into the edge town and I skid to a stop when I see the scene playing out in front of me. It's absolutely horrific and I can feel my heart shattering inside my chest. Everywhere I look, homes are crumbling to the ground in a blaze of fire. The town square is nothing but ash and debris, and the smoke is being trapped in town from the heavy tree cover above. The only light around us is the blazing fires and they're casting ominous shadows on every surface. The sound of thick, rough coughing is coming from people scrambling in every direction all around us, not sure where to even go.

"Holy shit," Shay whispers as he stops next to me. I take a step ahead of him but he grabs my arm before I make it too far, pulling me back to him. I turn to him, ready to argue, but he just shakes his head. The pure terror in his eyes is the only reason I'm not arguing back and stay put at his side. Looking at Tate, he speaks loudly over the bloodcurdling screams. "How many were there?"

"Five. They came from the North, directly for Peham," Tate responds, still keeping a tight grip on Marlene.

"Recognize any of them?"

"Just one." He gives Shay a look I can't place and they don't say another word about it. But, Shay nods his head as if he knows exactly who Tate is talking about without even having to say it.

"Are they still here?"

"No. They set the fires and left immediately. It didn't seem like they wanted to fight or do anything other than burn everything," Tate says. "How do you want to go about this?"

"I think we should-" Shay starts, but everything starts to fade out as the racing thoughts in my mind take over. I can't stand around and listen to any of this anymore.

I need to find my family.

I bolt from them and head further into town, searching the faces of each person I pass for any familiarity. Shay shouts my name as I run further from him but the smoke acts as a sound barrier as I pass through it, muffling his voice more with each step. The dense smoke quickly engulfs me and soon, I'm invisible to them.

I make my way towards what used to be the center of town square first. What was once filled with old brick buildings is now littered with crumbled structures, some still burning wildly out of control. The thick, dark smoke that billows out of each ruined building fills the air and scorches my throat. I can barely see a few feet in front of me as I try desperately to blink back the tears the smoke is pulling from me.

The smoke thins slightly as I travel deeper in town and it's obvious it's far from evacuated. All around me, people are trying to run to safety, or offering as much help as they can to those who are injured. I have to turn away when I see people with burns peppering their skin pulling completely charred bodies from burning buildings, just before they collapse.

My fear grows when there's still no sign of my family.

As I make my way further into town, the devastation only gets worse. There are no longer people running for safety, but charred remains of ones littering the streets. Tears flow freely from my eyes as the amount increases the more I walk. These people I've known my entire life are now dead in the streets of their home. All because a group of fae came here, most likely looking for *me*.

My pace slows down drastically as I follow the horrific trail of corpses leading further into town. I force myself to look at each of them but I don't see anyone here that can be saved. I'm the only one alive here.

The fires seem to be dying down for the most part this way. The majority of the buildings are completely burnt to the ground with small embers dimly burning. From what I can see, there are more remains of people that must have gotten trapped in the buildings as they burned, the rubble now their tombs. I stop momentarily to scan the debris around me and to catch my breath, when I hear faint coughing and muffled voices coming from up ahead.

My head jerks up at the sound and I use all the strength I can muster to sprint towards it. Towards someone alive that can be saved from all of this horror.

I round the corner and fall to my knees almost instantly at who I see before me. Covered from head to toe in sweat, blood, and soot are my parents and Wes, trying to lift a large beam off of someone trapped in the rubble. The sobs that escape me are rough and raw from the smoke, but there's nothing I can do to keep it inside.

At the sound of my sobs, all three of their heads turn to me as they pause lifting the beam up momentarily. But, the second my mom sees me, she abandons Wes and my dad, leaving them to carry the weight alone, as she stumbles over the destruction to me. "Oh, my baby. Thank the Goddesses, I was so afraid. We couldn't find you, no one knew where you went. Are you alright? Are you hurt?" she sobs, pulling me into a crushing hug. It's almost too tight, especially with how raw my lungs feel, but I welcome it nonetheless.

"Mom," I breathe out. "I was so worried. When Marlene told me that you all stayed behind to help, I started to panic. And all I saw as I ran through town were charred bodies and I got so scared." Tears streak down both of our faces, cleaning the ash off our cheeks. "I'm so relieved you're ok."

"We couldn't leave without trying to help. Wes insisted on staying to make sure we didn't meet the same fate so many of the others did."

"Speaking of helping," Wes calls out from where he stands with my dad, the two of them starting to struggle, now.

Mom and I run to their sides and crouch underneath the beam, hoisting it onto our shoulders and standing slowly. With my added help, we're able to lift it fully off of the person trapped below. Wes jumps into the rubble the second the beam is moved out of the way, pulling out a woman so dirty and bloody that I can't even tell who it is.

It's not until Wes has her out in the street and begins wiping her face with the inside of his shirt that I recognize her. The deep blue sapphire eyes that I know so well are now a dull gray from pain and exhaustion, and her long, dirty blonde hair is stained blood red from a massive injury to her head. But, the way Wes pulls her to his chest and shakes violently with sobs is a dead giveaway to who it is.

Sierra.

Tears pour out of my eyes with no chance of stopping. Sierra is family. She's been with Wes for ten years and has filled the role of older sister to me for almost half my life. She's the one that helped me get ready for my first date with Luke. All of my clothes came from her. She taught me how to properly do my hair and makeup when I wanted to look put together. She means the absolute world to me and just the thought of her being trapped under the rubble alone starts to break me.

But, looking over at them and then at my parents, my heart begins to race ever faster.

This can't be fixed.

I stumble towards where she's laying on the ground and drop to my knees beside her and Wes. He has a hand placed on the back of her head and deep red blood seeps through his fingers. No, this isn't right. It's too much blood. How is there this much blood, she's so petite.

He has his head buried in her hair and he's whispering something to her as her eyelids flutter, struggling to stay open. I reposition myself in front of her face, trying to compose myself as best as I can. She slowly drags her gaze from him to me, the simple task taking too much of her energy, and weakly smiles, exposing her blood stained teeth. This can't be how it ends for her.

"Hi, Ana." I crack a smile at her nickname for me, from when she misheard my name when Wes introduced us and called me Ana for a good year before I corrected her.

"Hi, sis," I manage to choke out.

"It's pretty bad, isn't it?" she asks, her voice straining. *Goddesses, yes. She won't make it.* I shake my head.

"You're fine, you're going to be fine." I look up at Wes as he sobs into her, nudging him slightly. Tears are flowing freely from his eyes and I can see how close he is to falling apart completely. But he needs to get it together for her, no matter how hard. "Tell her, Wes. Tell her she's going to be fine."

Wes gapes at me, his words failing him, as he shakes his head at me. He drags his gaze down to the love of his life as her eyes begin to shut more, and smiles extra wide for her with trembling lips. "Sierra, I love you so much. You're going to be just fine. I'll be by your side the whole time, you'll see."

"I love you, Wes. Always," Sierra whispers, her once blue eyes dimming more with each second.

"I'll find you again. Nothing will keep me from you. I will love you in every lifetime." The sobs that are coming from him will haunt me for the rest of my life.

"I know you will," she says as she takes a shallow breath, her *final* breath. Her eyes flutter shut as the last of her air leaves her lungs, still cradled in Wes' arms. And the scream that comes from him is ear shattering. I can practically feel his heart breaking the longer it goes on.

"Wes," I say, searching for his eyes through my own tear filled eyes. My vision is nothing but a blurry mess, but I know he's crushing her to his chest, rocking back and forth in the remains of what I now recognize as the small art studio she worked at. "Wes, we have to get out of this smoke." I stand on wobbly legs and try to pull him up with me, but he's so planted in his spot on the ground, it's almost impossible to move him.

I look over to my parents, still standing a few feet away, staring in pure shock and despair at the shell of the woman that would've been their daughter-in-law one day. My eyes dart back and forth between them, so in need of their help, but they don't move an inch. I look back down at Wes cradling Sierra, blood still pooling beneath her from the wound on her head, and try again to lift him to his feet. I know he'll never leave without her, but the smoke in the air is getting thicker by the minute. Soon, we'll lose all ability to breathe properly.

We have to get out of here.

"Wes, come on. I'll help you lift her. We won't leave her here, I promise," I plead, crouching down in front of him, trying to get him to fucking look at me. But he just stares blankly at his love, completely void of any emotion. "Fuck, I can't do this alone!"

Not even a second later, Shay comes racing through the smoke at the sound of my voice. The minute he's by my side, I collapse into him and sob loudly.

"I have you. You're not alone, don't worry." He pulls me away from him and cups my face with his hands, wiping tears and ash from my face. He kisses my forehead and leans over to Wes, whispering something to him so quietly not even I can hear it. But, when he finishes, Wes nods his head and lets Shay take Sierra away from him.

I crawl to Wes' side and grab his arm to help him stand and suddenly Marlene is on his other side lifting him up with me. I look around at her and notice the fresh tears brimming her lids. Some threaten to fall, but she holds them back, trying to stay as strong as she can for Wes in this moment. We walk him forward, using all of our strength to keep his shaking legs from crumbling. His body is such deadweight, and I don't even know if he realizes that we've started to move. We follow behind Shay slowly, down a side street out of town, and make our way closer to the homes that are fully untouched by fire. I still don't know if our home has been spared, but there hasn't been a good time to ask.

I don't know how, but Tate was able to coax my parents out of their shocked state and now they follow behind us closely. We're all slow moving as exhaustion settles over us, but we don't stop. We can't.

As we finally break through the thickest part of the smoke and into somewhat cleaner air, I can finally see what section of town has been spared. I let out a shaky breath of relief seeing our home sitting fully intact, our little corner of the neighborhood free of fire and destruction.

It almost feels unfair that we get to keep our home while so many lost everything.

I know the moment my parents realize it, too, because mom starts to sob behind me and I can hear dad thank the Goddesses under his breath. It's the first sound I've heard from either one of them since Sierra.

In no time, we're just a few steps from home, but instead of going inside, Shay starts to lead us towards the bridge that goes to Lake Carsin. I look around Wes to Marlene. "Do you have him?"

She nods. "Yeah, he's pretty much walking himself now, go see what's going on." I slowly untangle myself from Wes, making sure he won't fall without my side of support, and speed up to Shay. He's still cradling Sierra's body in his blood covered arms, and I can't bring myself to look at her. Not like this.

"Why are we going this way?" I ask once I'm by his side, staying close to Sierra's feet.

"I figured this would be a better place to bury her than in a town that will have to be completely rebuilt. This way, she won't be disturbed," he explains. Every bit of air I have in my scorched lungs leaves my body in a heartbeat with his words. That he would do something so incredibly thoughtful for Wes and our family speaks volumes. How the hell is this male real?

"Really?" I ask, his kindness mending a piece of my shattered heart.

"Really," he says with a sad upturn of his mouth. I nod and look forward, keeping close to his side as we cross over the bridge to the lake where Sierra will rest forever.

PART TWO

Out of Time

Chapter 11

February 9th
Age 25

Out of time.

Waking up this morning is harder than I thought it would be. I've been preparing myself for today for a while now, but knowing I have to leave my home and my family behind in the next few days is terrifying to me. I still don't love the plan Shay and Tate came up with but, it's clear I don't have much say in it.

I have six months from today to make it to Drake, or so it says in his letters, so we have some time to go through with their plan. The only part of it that I do like is that my family is staying here in Peham out of harms way of whatever this darkness is. It makes me feel better knowing they'll be here together, especially with how Wes has been since Sierra died. On the outside, it looks like he's coping. He's smiling and doing the things he enjoys again. But I know him better than that and he's struggling.

I know they only agreed to stay because the town needs their help here. Rebuilding is pretty much complete but, with the loss of so many, it's been all hands on deck. As glad as I am that they're staying here, there's so much fear in the back of my mind about Luke coming after them once me, Shay, and Tate gone. I haven't even seen him since the morning Shay intercepted his abuse and I officially ended things with him. I've assumed that he's been staying at his apartment in Halor all this time, especially with Peham in ruins for a good chunk of the year.

I've felt safer this past year than I have in a long time with him away.

My stomach is in knots as I drag myself out of bed and head over to my dresser.

I dress in thick black leggings and a white long sleeve, pulling on a pair of black boots over my thick, winter socks. My bag has been packed since last night with essentials and small things I can't bear to leave behind. There's a change of clothes, a few backup pairs of underwear and socks, a sweatshirt, the stack of letters I've received over the years, and a small photo album with my favorite family memories.

No matter what happens, I can't afford to forget anything about this life.

I pull my hair into a low ponytail and go to pick up the bag, when slight noises from the other side of my closed door distract me. It takes me a second, but when I figure out what the noises are, hot tears brim my eyes. I furiously wipe them away and compose myself for what waits for me.

On the other side, I hear my parents and siblings hushing each other and shuffling impatiently for me to come out of my room. I leave the bag where it is and take a deep breath before pulling the door open.

"HAPPY BIRTHDAY, LIANNA!" they all yell in unison, while simultaneously throwing confetti everywhere. It's been a while since this extent of celebration was done, the last time being Marlene's fifteenth birthday. We all agreed we were a little too old for it, but today is different.

I won't spend another birthday here with them.

Marlene steps forward, holding a massive version of my favorite chocolate croissant. It's cut in half and the middle is filled with a deliciously fluffy whipped cream, while the edges are lined with strawberry pieces. Twenty five miniature candles are stuck in the top and burning brightly in a row. I bite my lip to keep it from trembling as the four of them sing to me. When they finish, I make a completely selfish wish and blow out the candles.

A wish to not have to be separated.

Marlene and Wes lead the way down the stairs and into the kitchen where the best birthday tradition waits for me. Covering every inch of the table is a massive breakfast with all of my favorites; bacon, eggs, cheeses, berries, French toast, Marlene's homemade blackberry jam. It's all here.

Mom squeezes my arm and pulls me into an embrace before setting me down in my chair to enjoy my last birthday breakfast in this home. I savor every little bite because I don't know when I'll be able to eat food like this again. Everyone is silent as we eat as the reality of today settles over us like a heavy fog.

An hour later, after breakfast is done and it's all cleaned up, I reluctantly make my way back to my room to get my stuff together to leave. The second I close my door behind me, my mind races. Like I was trapping it in a cage all morning and now it can finally run free. I'm not ready for this. Of course, Shay and Tate have prepared me for this so, *technically*, I am ready. But I don't want to leave. This is the home I grew up in and lived my whole life in. No amount of preparing can get me ready to abandon it. A small knock on my door pulls me from my racing thoughts and my pacing ceases for a moment.

"Come in," I call lightly. The door opens and my parents walk in, shutting the door quietly behind them. I give them a genuine smile and clear my throat. "Thank you for this morning. It meant so much to me."

"You know we would do anything for you, baby," mom says, tears filling her eyes. Dad walks up behind her and places a hand on her shoulder, rubbing gently and calming her slightly. I notice his other hand is held behind his back and I peer slightly around him, trying to see what he's holding.

He notices instantly, of course, and brings his hand out from behind him, revealing three boxes; one small, one medium, and one large. The corners of my lips turn up in a grin when I realize these are birthday presents for me.

"You didn't have to get me anything, I tell you this every year."

"And every year we tell you that's ridiculous, you're our baby, and we're getting you birthday gifts," mom counters. I roll my eyes at her and thank them both for the gifts. I sit on the edge of my bed, mom on one side, dad on the other, and tear the wrapping paper off the small box, first, as per their instructions.

I take the lid off, revealing an intricately carved wooden box inside. I lift it out of the gift box and place it on my lap, running my hands along the beautiful floral carvings that run along each side. There's a large phoenix with its wings spread out completely on top, the bird taking up the entirety of the lid. "This is stunning, thank you."

Mom chuckles. "Open it, sweetie." I do as she says and let out a gasp when the lid is separated from the bottom. Placed on the red velvet interior are two twin daggers placed side by side. My eyes shoot between my mother and father, both beaming at me with pride filling their faces.

I look back down at the blades, a little afraid to remove them from the safety of their box. They're almost as long as my forearm and both are made from a dark steel material that makes them look as dark as night. They seem to completely embody darkness, all except for the hilts, where small red garnets adorn each handle. My hand flies to my neck where my amulet sits and run my fingers on the gem. The ones in the blades are near replicas of it. And, engraved along each blade are leaves and butterflies in varying shades of red and silver.

I'm at a loss for words.

"Where did these come from?" I ask no one in particular. "They're incredible."

"When you're ready, pick them up," mom says shakily. I can hear the caution and nervousness in her voice and, if I'm honest, it's putting me on edge a bit. I look up at her, expecting to see that cautiousness all over her face, but all I see is pride. She nods her hand at the blades and grabs onto dad's hand tightly. I take a deep breath and prepare myself for whatever is about to happen.

Then, once I'm as ready as I can be, I pick up my blades.

The second I touch the cool metal, my body instantly warms, starting in the middle and working its way outwards. It feels like an internal fuse is lit in my core and, now, a fire is growing within me. The daggers start to hum in my palms, like they're calling out to me, begging me to follow them.

It feels all too familiar.

Panic fills me when I realize what's happening, and I see those words from her letter over and over in my head. *"...pushed her magic down. Once she finds a way to break that tether inside of her..."*

Bits and pieces of my birth mother's letter to my mom comes rushing back to me and I know this is it. This feeling, this *fuse*, is the tether to my magic and the blades are meant to break it apart.

It just needs my help.

I squeeze my eyes shut and blindly follow the fuse and search until the very core of it is right in front of me, thrumming with magic, begging to be released after too many years locked away. I urge my mind to touch it and, when it does, a massive wave of power surges through me faster than I can process.

My skin begins to tingle with the sudden rush of power and my eyes fly open. I look down and stagger back into wall at the sight of myself. Every inch of my skin is glowing iridescent, as if this glow is replacing my very skin.

"Holy shit," I exhale. I run my fingers along my glowing forearm, expecting it to feel...different. Each touch of my finger on my skin leaves a ripple, like I'm touching a puddle of water. But, other than the rippling and it feeling slightly warmer, it just feels like my skin. I keep turning my arms in front of my face, examining every inch, when the power surge suddenly halts.

But, it doesn't stop. It almost feels like the power itself is taking a deep breath. And, as it exhales, my entire body floods with my trapped magic, and a white fog erupts out from me, blanketing the room fully.

"Grant, the door!" my mom orders as she runs over to me and grab onto me, trying to ground me, as my dad shuts the door in an attempt to conceal the thick fog. My mind is foggy, and I'm vaguely aware of mom lowering my head into her lap, while my sweat drenched skin sticks to her cotton pants. I can feel myself spiraling out of control and I'm trying to hold onto reality as best as I can, but it's no use. There's no stopping the flare up of this power.

Mom keeps a good hold on me as she rubs her thumb along my temple. "You're okay, baby, mom has you." My whole body strains as the power keeps coming and coming, and I'm the one that broke the hold on it. What if I'm not ready for this? What if this destroys me?

Almost as suddenly as it started, the heat of the fire inside calms to a comfortable warmth and my panic settles. The power is starting to level out.

Thank the Goddesses that's over.

"Mom," I try to say, but the words won't come. I try to reach out to her, but I can't. My limbs are heavy and unmoving, and I'm not sure if it's because of the power surging through me or because of my far too high levels of anxiety.

"It has only just begun," a strange, ethereal voice echoes through my head. Chills run down my warm, glowing skin and my breathing quickens alongside my tightening chest. *What the hell is going on?*

Moms voice starts to become garbled, almost like I'm underwater trying to decipher what she's trying to say to me, but it's impossible to understand her. I will my mind to swim to the surface and get control of something, *anything*, but I'm enveloped by a never ending darkness. My vision is going in and out, and my mind starts to fog, but something inside me grants me a brief moment of clarity.

When the fog thins briefly, I see the sheer panic on dad's face. He's sitting on the ground right next to me and mom, now, and I can't remember when he got here, but he's scanning me up and down. And that is terror on his face. Raw, unbridled terror. It takes far too much effort to follow his scanning eyes and see what's filling him with panic.

But, when I do, I don't blame him. Because, now, it's filling *me* with panic.

My entire body is beginning to evaporate in a wisp of smoke. Still glowing, but fading away into nothing. I use all the strength I have to look up at mom for help, but she only smiles at me, tears lining her eyes, and says, "Don't be afraid, this is where you need to be."

I swallow the lump in my throat and let the darkness consume me, as my body completely evaporates away.

***

The smell of lavender and honeysuckle surrounds me, and my body begins to materialize from the smoke it left home in. The grass around me is slick with dew and a heavy morning fog still hovers in the field before me. I look around, trying to find some familiar landmarks to clue me into where the hell I am, but nothing around me is recognizable.

My head throbs as I stagger to my feet, my newfound powers doing absolutely nothing to ease the pain. What a letdown.

The warmth of power is still running through my body at full speed with no sign of slowing, but at least now it's not an inferno. I bring my hands to my face with the intention of rubbing at my eyes, but pause when I realize my skin is still glowing iridescent, bordering on translucent. Whatever this state is, I can *see* the power running through me, like blood in my veins.

I can't help but be in awe of myself.

I roll my eyes at how ridiculous that is, and continue to look around the field I'm standing in.

Above me, the morning sun is just starting to rise. Even this early in the day, the air is sticky and hot, a telltale sign that it's summer wherever I am. The fog is slowly evaporating, revealing a field filled with tall grass and flowers. I look down and realize I'm standing right in the middle of a trampled path. When I look straight ahead to the North, the path leads to blurry nothingness. But, directly behind me to the South, the path leads to a dense forest.

There's something inside me that's pulling me towards that forest, even knowing nothing about my surroundings. But, it makes sense, seeing as it's the only area that's not blurry. I start down the pathway and brush the waist-high grass around me with my hand. As my fingers skim the grass, hundreds of gold winged butterflies emerge from the blooms. They're incredible. Their wings gleam in the sunlight and shimmer with each beat as they fly in place, just hovering above the blooms. It feels so magical and serene.

What *is* this place?

The only sounds come from my own steps on the damp ground and the faint fluttering of butterfly wings as they start to follow me as I head for the forest. Other than that, the quiet seems to surround me. As I get closer to the tree line, the calming floral smells from before are replaced by the smell of moss and wood, and it reminds me so much of home.

I cautiously venture into the forest, taking care of where I step to keep myself as concealed as possible. I have no idea what's lurking in these trees and I don't particularly want to find out. I make it maybe fifty feet into the trees when I spot two cloaked figures by a small stream just ahead of me. I duck behind a large tree stump to my left, praying they haven't seen me already.

I peer around the stump and watch the two strangers interact with each other. Both are draped in floor length black cloaks with large hoods that completely conceal their faces, making their identities a complete mystery to me. But I can't help but notice a particular feature on one of the figures that has my heart aching. Sprouting from the ones back is beautiful dark red wings, tucked closely to their body.

It's another fae like me.

It makes me wonder if that's what my own wings could have become if I had been allowed to keep them. Mine had only been a foot when they were sawed off of my body, but this fae's wings have to be almost three feet. A wave of emotions washes over me and just thinking about my own wings makes the scars on my back throb incessantly as if in recognition of what could've been.

Blinking away tears, I notice a satchel hanging by the winged fae's side, and I watch as the two converse about whatever's inside it. Even with my enhanced hearing, I can't make out a single word they're saying.

I have to get closer.

From my current hiding spot, I can see a boulder a few feet away from them. Close enough that I should be able to hear them much better. I slowly start to crawl over to it, trying my best to keep my head and body close to the ground. A small twig snaps under my knee, freezing me in place. *Shit.* I stay as still as I possibly can and hold my breath until I'm sure I'm not exposed.

I slowly peek at the strangers and hold back a sigh of relief. They're both still talking and it doesn't seem like they heard a thing. *Thank the Goddesses.* I resume my crawling, making sure to watch out for anymore damn twigs. I crouch behind the boulder once I make it undetected and sit on my knees. From here, I can hear them almost perfectly. Just as I thought.

"You're sure she'll need these?" A warm, feminine voice comes from the stranger without wings. That voice. I'm sure I know *that voice* from somewhere. Why the hell does it sound so damn familiar?

I peer around the boulder ever so slightly, just enough to try and catch a glimpse of the two figures without being caught. I look just in time to see the winged fae pull a wooden box from the satchel and place it into the other ones hands.

I stare closely at that box, confusion rippling through me. There's no way, right?

The winged fae drops their hands from the sides of the box once it's secure in the wingless females palms, and I catch a glimpse of the intricate floral carvings along the side. And I know that if I was able to see the top, I'd see a gorgeous phoenix spread out on the lid.

She's holding *my* box.

"They were forged by Aris herself when she first came into power. The gems hold an essence of her magic and it flows throughout the blade. When the time comes, *these* will be what she needs to break the enchantment and grant her access to the full potential of her magic," says the winged fae, another female with brown curls peeking out from her hood. She opens the lid and pulls out the twin blades my parents gifted me moments ago.

"Will you come back for her when that time comes?" the unwinged female asks, nervously shuffling the box in her outstretched hands.

"No. I fear that if I return for her, they'll find her too quickly. I brought her to you for a reason. I will not lead her into danger until she's ready to defeat it." The winged fae turns away from her companion. "I trust in you to keep my sweet Lianna safe."

My stomach drops straight to the ground at her words and, suddenly, it all clicks. When I disappeared, I didn't come to some random place. I'm not even in the same time. No, this has to be the past and this...this is a memory I've stepped into. And this winged fae standing a few feet away from me is my birth mother.

Which means...

My birth mother's companion, the figure without wings and the all too familiar voice, is the woman who raised me my entire life. My mother. A younger version of her, but still my mom. This is all so surreal. There's so much I want to ask her, ask them both.

Faint shouting in the distance jolts me from my racing thoughts, and both females tense at the sound. My birth mother grabs hold of my mom's face and brings their heads together so their foreheads gently touch. I watch as they both close their eyes and despair washes over their features. And that's when I remember. When mom left her home in the Fae realm when she married my dad, she never went back. This memory is most likely the first time they've seen each other since mom left her home.

And it was only to keep me protected.

"I didn't want to leave her, Amara. Either of them. Please protect her. For me," my birth mother whispers, grief consuming her every word.

"I swear, I'll keep her safe."

"You are forever in my debt, sister," my birth mother says as she backs away slowly, just as the shouts get closer. "Not a day goes by that I don't miss you." Before my mom can say anything else, my birth mother is gone quicker than should be possible. And I know I would've missed it completely if my eyes haven't been glued to her every move. My gaze turns back to my mom as she holds the box containing my blades close to her chest before running in the opposite direction.

I track her movements as she runs straight into the fog surrounding the small area the memory was in. The moment she disappears, I can feel the magic start to surge inside me again. I close my eyes as my body heats and the smoke starts to envelop me, taking me away from this place. This moment in time.

Chapter 12

I don't know how I did it, but when I open my eyes again, I'm back in my bedroom. The warmth flowing through my body goes back to normal, but there's now a permanent smolder that lingers deep inside me. Just a small ember of magic, longing to burn brightly again. The white fog still conceals me as my body fully materializes, and the iridescent glow dims to nothing.

When it finally clears, mom comes into focus, staring down at me and brushing a stray hair from my face. My dad sits exhausted at the other end of me, holding my feet in his lap, and letting his head rest against my bed.

"Grant, she's back," mom says in relief. Dad whips his head up and tightens his hold on my feet, like his grasp will keep me from disappearing again. He smiles as tears stream down his face, relief also settling over him now that the fog is completely gone and I'm back with them. I can't even imagine what they went through after I vanished. As stressed as I was, at least my mind was distracted from being away from them by the memory. They just sat here, waiting for me to reappear.

I reach out my hand to dad, interlocking our fingers and looking back up at mom, seeing a look of peace settling over her face. She knew this was going to happen. And I'm guessing she's known since the night I was left with them all those years ago. This is all getting to be too much to handle, and this is just the beginning of it. *Great.*

My body feels more drained and exhausted than it ever has, but I manage to pull myself into a sitting position, rubbing my hands down my face. Mom still has a hold on me, now at arms length, and is looking me over to make sure everything is where it should be.

"Where did you go when you disappeared?" she asks me, and I'm not sure if she knows and just wants to hear it from me, or if she's genuinely out of the loop. I chew on my lip, eyes darting between her and my dad, and then I explain everything about what just happened. Though it seems to shock dad, she doesn't seem phased at all and, honestly, it doesn't surprise me. I figured she knew where I was.

"I watched the day you got my knives. It was so realistic. It felt like I was right there when it happened," I say, mind still reeling over the whole thing.

"You *were* there, honey, just in the shadows. No one involved in the memory would've been able to see you, or even sense your presence. You're something called a Memory Walker," she says, shaking her head. "When Flora left you with us as a baby, I received a letter a few days later asking if I could meet with her in the Fae realm. That's where you disappeared to just now. That forest you mentioned is right on the other side of the realm Gate. It's called the Forest of Truth."

"That's where you met dad, isn't it?"

Mom nods. "She explained that when you turned twenty-five, we were to give you the daggers, but not anytime before then. She was very adamant about that. Neither of us knew what kind of powers you'd end up having, but Flora was certain you'd be far different than anyone expected."

"Is this the extent of my powers, then? Or should I expect something else?" I question and push away the anxiety. I could barely handle this power, how will I handle any more? "I need to know what else to expect."

"Honestly, I don't know. The full knowledge of your powers is completely unknown until they manifest. And, being repressed for so many years, it might take some time for them to appear. But Flora said she was sure you'd have many." Mom looks at me, her eyes searching my face. "She never went into much detail about what she believed you to be but, after watching what you just accomplished? I mean, it was amazing."

"What I am? What do you mean? I'm fae, we've always known that."

Mom takes a deep breath. "There are different types of fae in the world, Lianna, types that have been completely erased from history for the most absurd reasons. And, you, me, your mom...we're part of a bloodline that many believed was eradicated centuries ago."

Different types of fae? An eradicated bloodline? Okay, now this is getting to be *way* too much. And mom beating around the bush about it needs to stop. I need answers.

"Are you going to tell me about it or am I going to sit here guessing?" I ask with a snarky tone. I feel bad for snapping but, at the same time, I don't. I've been asking for years to be told more about my heritage and I have always been told no, or that they don't know more than what I was already told. Mom opens her mouth and then looks to my dad for help. But he shakes his head at her before she can get out a word.

"In time, Shay will tell you all you need to know. But, right now, you need to focus on other things, like getting a hold on the magic you've set free. Now," mom says, pulling the other two gifts across the floor and wiping the tears from her face, "let's finish your gifts, shall we?"

What? Just like that and the conversation is over, once again. But I know that, no matter how hard I try, I won't get anymore information out of her or dad. I huff out a breath and smile at her, taking the medium sized box from her outstretched hands and tear the paper off. I lift the lid to find two simple pieces of black leather placed on the tissue paper inside. They look like belts, with leaves carved into the leather and golden buckles on the ends.

"Your father made them for your daggers." She pulls what I'm now realizing are thigh holsters from the box and pulls me to my feet to help me step into them, clasping each gold buckle behind my thighs. Then, she grabs both daggers from where I dropped them on the floor, situating them into a slot on either leg.

"I never imagined I'd get a gift like this to hold knives," I say, chuckling. "Dad, you did such a great job, they're so beautiful."

"I wish we could give you normal birthday gifts but, unfortunately, these will be the most useful ones we can offer," he says, coming over to where mom and I stand. "The knives get tucked into the pockets on the sides. There are some extra slots if you find you need them, kid." He points to each holster and I notice there are four slots on each one. "I wanted to make you a harness to wear over your ribcage, but I don't know what kind of clothes you'll be wearing and I wanted them to be easily accessible."

"They're perfect, dad. Thank you," I say, smiling up at him.

"One more and then I promise that's it," mom says, handing me the largest box. I take it and look between them both.

"You've given me plenty already," I say as I gently open the final gift, so grateful for what I've already been given. As I'm about to take the lid off of the box, mom places her hand on top of mine, halting me in my tracks.

"Honey, before you open this one, I need to tell you something." She takes a deep, steadying breath and then continues. "I never, ever wanted to destroy your wings. And I am so sorry I couldn't bring myself to be there when you needed me. But, knowing what you were going through brought up too many bad memories of when I had to lose mine and I spiraled. I needed to distance myself to distract myself from my own trauma."

Oh, shit. *Of course* she had wings. My birth mother is her sister and, if she has wings, my mom must have at some point, too.

I can't believe it didn't even cross my mind. I always thought my wings were out of the ordinary for fae, so even knowing that she's my blood relative, I thought it was just me that had them. But it makes so much sense now, especially after seeing the memory of her with my birth mother. "When did you lose yours?" I ask, treading very carefully in case it stirs up her old trauma.

"When I came here to be with your father. It was my choice. I made him do it so I wouldn't be discovered. If we were normal fae, I would've been safe," she says, and there it is again. *Normal fae.* What does that even mean?

"I never blamed either one of you for it. I know you only did it to protect me," I admit.

"I knew how much it would destroy you more than anyone and, for that, I am so sorry." Mom glances down at the box underneath our hands. "I started this project two years ago, and I know it will never compare, but it's something." She moves her hand and allows me to finally pull off the lid.

Folded neatly inside the box is a black denim jacket with sapphire buttons going down the front. I pull it out and let it unfold in the air in front of me, when I feel something soft grazing my fingers. I turn it over and embroidered on the back of the jacket are beautiful wings. I run my fingers over the small, deep blue design, astounded at how identical they look to the ones taken from me. They're even the same size and color as they were when I lost them, and the softness of the material is luxuriously soft and velvety.

I can't slide the jacket on quick enough. It comes to my hips, and fits me perfectly. The minute it's wrapped around my body, I feel deeply complete. Since that night, I've always yearned for my wings to reappear. I knew it would never happen, but it was hard not to desire them when I go day by day feeling like something's missing. But, now, it feels like I'm one step closer to being whole again, and it's all thanks to this simple jacket.

As I readjust it slightly, something catches my eye on the inside of the jacket. I pull open the left side and see a small, blue-black feather sewn inside, right over my heart. I nearly stop breathing and my heart almost pounds out of my chest at the familiarity of it. I run my finger over the length of it and a sudden rush of emotions flood over me. Tears stream down my face, because I know what this is, but I just can't believe it. I don't want to hope too hard.

"I saved one," mom says, placing her hand on my cheek and pulling my gaze to hers. "I couldn't let them be completely destroyed. And, now it lives with you, where it belongs." I gape at her as she confirms exactly what I'm thinking, and that hope soars through my chest, cracking it wide open. This small feather is all that's left of my precious wings. The only piece of them that remains.

I try to find the words to properly thank my parents, because I don't think they truly realize what their love and care has done for me. Knowing I have to leave them soon kills me.

Of course, I fail at finding the right words, and all I can manage to do is let my tears run free and hug them closely and tightly. Because, honestly, no words will ever be enough.

***

After we finish eating the birthday dinner mom spent the majority of the afternoon making for me, I head back to my room to check my backpack for the fifth time today, making sure I have everything I need. Today went by too quickly and, now, I have no time left. I *have* to leave my home and my family.

I strap on one of the leg holsters and tuck the other one safely in my bag, making sure the daggers are secure in their pockets. Then, I button my new jacket over the hooded sweatshirt I pulled on to keep myself as warm as possible for our journey. Since this morning, the snowfall has increased and a few inches fully cover the ground. It's going to be such a pain in the ass to have to travel through this.

I sigh and take one last look around the room I grew up in, dread sitting deep in my stomach. Part of me wants to throw up.

As I take it all in, goosebumps come to the surface of my skin as I feel Shay's presence behind me, and I tense slightly. Things between us have felt different ever since he interrupted Luke's abuse and I figured out that Shay and I are soulbonds. After everything that happened, I'm afraid to let myself fall for him just yet. In the year since I left Luke, I've been solely focused on getting ready for this moment, and even more time to come to terms with Sierra's death and the destruction of Peham.

I can't let myself be with him...yet.

"You ready, Lianna?" he asks. *Lianna*. No nickname, no hint of any flirting. I know this is my choice, but it doesn't mean it doesn't hurt. I nod without turning to face him and walk out of the room, gently shutting the door behind me. The click of the lock brings tears to my eyes almost instantly, but I wipe them away quickly before Shay can see.

I follow him down the stairs and, as we descend, I can hear my mom sniffling softly. As we get closer to the bottom, Wes and Marlene come into view and I see them standing at the front door with packed bags of their own. My brows furrow and I nearly fall down the last few steps, but Shay is right there to catch me. I steady myself quickly and don't even thank him as I rush over to my siblings.

"What the hell is this?" I say harshly, panic rising in me as my breathing becoming quick and shallow. Shay comes up behind me and places his hand on the small of my back, rubbing light circles right in the middle. Even though we've been in this weird limbo, he knows just how to keep me grounded. I close my eyes and take a deep breath, focusing my attention between Wes and Marlene.

"We're coming with you," Wes says calmly when I open my eyes.

"No the hell you're not. You're staying here with mom and dad and *staying safe*," I spit out, turning to look at Shay. "Tell them, Shay. They're not coming with us." He looks down at me and his eyes are full of shame and an apology slips from his lips. I stumble back. *He knew.* I whip my head back to my siblings and frantically shake my head. "And when was I going to be filled in on this change of plans?"

"We knew you would say no, Li," Marlene says simply, as if it's such an obvious answer. No shit I would've said no. This change puts both of my siblings in extreme danger and I'm not okay with that. I will *never* be okay with that.

I look over at my parents. "Did you know?"

"No. We just found out," dad says as he consoles mom. And I believe him. They both look just as shocked as I feel.

"We aren't letting you do this yourself, Lianna. We know the risks and we're willing to take them, for you." Wes is in front of me now, gripping my shoulders tightly. I can't say it surprises me that they're pulling shit like this. They've always been my fiercest protectors, so why did I expect any of my situation to change that?

Brutal understanding flows through me and I nod, reluctantly accepting this. They both say their final goodbyes to our parents, who are now losing all of their kids instead of just one. Shay holds the door open for them, thick flakes of snow blowing in with the sudden rush of air, and they both file out of the home we all grew up in. Once they're outside waiting, Shay turns to look at me and then drags his gaze to my parents, standing with teary eyes looking at me.

"I'll be right out here when you're ready," he says and closes the door silently behind him, giving me a moment alone with my parents.

"I promise I'll bring them back to you," I say, closing the distance between my parents and I so I can give them one last hug each. My chest tightens as I hold them, not knowing if I'll ever get a chance to feel their embrace again. I am so desperate to commit their feel and smells to memory.

One day, Marlene and Wes will get to come back here to them, but I might not get that chance. The odds I'll have to stay in the Fae realm are far too high.

Mom pulls away from me slightly and looks down at the amulet around my neck, running her finger along the edge of the garnet. "This has been in my family for centuries, you know. The gem. The minute I saw it on you, I knew who you were without even needing to read the note. Did you know that you've been protecting all of us your entire life without even knowing it?" She taps the gem. "I wish I could thank your mother for that. For everything she's given me."

No, of course I didn't know that I've been a source of protection to my family for all these years and, now, I'm taking that away from them. "When I find her, I *will* bring her to you," I say quietly, not even sure if that'll ever be a real possibility. She gives me a small appreciative grin, but the look in her eyes tells me she knows it's not a strong possibility, either.

"You have grown to be the most beautiful, selfless female I have ever known. I feel so lucky to have been able to be your mom. I love you, baby."

"I love you too, mom," I say, wiping tears from her cheeks. I look around her to find dads gaze, his eyes glistening with tears. "And I love you, dad. Nothing will ever change the fact that you two are my parents. Nothing," I promise. And then, I turn and leave the place I've called home for twenty-five years, just to save a home I've never known.

Chapter 13

My siblings, Shay, and I walk along the outskirts of Peham by the ocean in an attempt to remain undetected on our way to the cottage. The last thing we need is for others in town to see us sneaking away from town with packed bags. It would raise too many questions.

Marlene is ahead of us by a long shot, nearly twenty feet further than we are. We all know it's because she wants to get back to Tate as soon as possible, but the snow is definitely hindering how fast she can move. If the ground was clear, I have no doubt that she would be going in a full out sprint to him. Shay had been by my side for a few minutes, but fell back to Wes behind me not long ago to talk about a training schedule for him, which leaves me alone in the middle of the group.

And, quite frankly, I'm over it.

I stop walking and wait for Shay and Wes as they slowly make their way to where I'm waiting. I can tell the moment they're in earshot that whatever fight Wes put up about training did not go his way. "Want some company?" Shay blurts out, the corner of his mouth turning up slightly.

I roll my eyes at him but, inside, my heart clenches at the familiar joking that has been absent for some time, now. "Maybe, but," I walk around Shay to Wes' side. "not from you." I turn to look at my brother. "Can I talk to you for a minute?"

"Of course you can," he says, running his thumb along something enclosed in his hand. My brows furrow as he continues to turn the object around, taking care to keep it hidden in his palm. I wonder what it even is. I can feel Shay staring into the back of my head, no doubt a little angry I shut him down. I look up at him and arch an eyebrow. He huffs out a sigh.

"I'll be up here, by myself," he groans and quickens his pace just enough to give us a bit of privacy.

"How're you doing? You sure you're up for this?" I ask.

"No less sure than the last time you asked me," Wes says on laugh. "Li, I can't stay in that town anymore. People keep telling me how sorry they are and everywhere I look reminds me of what I lost. This is better for me."

"What's that?" I ask, nodding to his hand. He stops playing with it and holds his fist out in front of me, gesturing to my hand. I hold it out underneath his and he drops a small ring into my palm. And the more I look at it, the more I realize it's not just any old ring.

It's an engagement ring.

Holy shit.

Sitting on top of a thin silver band is a beautiful square sapphire that glistens in the dim moonlight. A far too loud gasp escapes my mouth, and Shay looks back at me in confusion. "Sorry," I yell up before turning back to Wes. "Is this...?"

"Yeah. It was for Sierra." He glances at the ring in my palm and breathes shakily. "I saved all my earnings from the lumber yard for something perfect for her. I had every intention of getting her a diamond, but I couldn't afford one. I almost left without anything, planned on saving a few more months earnings, but then I saw the stack of sapphires on the shelf. The jeweler tried to talk me out of it. Said that it was untraditional to propose with anything other than a diamond." He plucks the ring from my palm and looks at it longingly, and a sad smile grows on his face. "But it reminded me of her eyes."

"She would have loved it, Wes." Tears well in my own eyes. We always knew Wes and Sierra would get married one day, even Sierra knew. She often talked to Marlene and I about what she wanted it to be like and her dream wedding dress. And now, she won't ever get to have that. And neither will Wes. My heart breaks for him.

"I miss her every day," he says quietly. "For a while after the fires, I wanted to blame someone for her death. Sure, I know who was responsible for the fires, but I needed to blame someone for *her* death. I wanted to blame you for them being there. I wanted to hate you for it, just to feel something again."

"You should hate me for it."

"No, because it wasn't your fault, Lianna. You had no idea any of that was going to happen. You're my sister, I could never hate you for what *they* did," he says to me, stopping mid stride and pulling me into a hug.

I can't stop replaying everything that happened that day. I've been blaming myself for it all every day since she died. That she'd still be alive if it wasn't for my heritage. Deep down, I think I wanted Wes to hate me for her death, just so he could feel some sort of closure. But I know he's right. That it's not my fault and I can't blame myself for what happened. If he can believe that, then shouldn't I?

I stay by Wes' side as we start walking again and, before we know it, the small, abandoned island comes into view. Surprisingly enough, Marlene's waiting for us at the foot of the bridge and, once the four of us are together again, we cross over the ice covered bridge.

Thick swirls of smoke pour from the chimney of the small cottage, and Marlene starts to break away from us once again as we get closer. The minute she opens the gate to the fence surrounding the cottage, Tate comes bounding out of the cottage and runs directly at her, taking her down into the soft snow bank behind her. The impact leaves Wes and I with a light layer of snow covering us, but Shay is halfway to the cottage already, not even sparing a look back. *Goddesses, I really need to fix this.*

"Oh, wow, that's our cue to be anywhere but here," Wes says awkwardly and heads for the cottage. My brows knit together and I look at where Tate and Marlene are, finding exactly why Wes left so uncomfortably. The two of them are intertwined in the snow with their lips locked, fully immersed in a passionate kiss.

"We'll be in soon, don't wait up," Tate yells to me as he picks Marlene up from the ground and takes her towards the small patch of trees.

"Animals," I mumble under my breath, turning to the cottage. I climb the few steps to the door, grabbing it before it can shut on me, and the smell of fresh bread wafts from inside.

My stomach growls loudly at the smell. I didn't think I'd be so hungry after moms massive dinner but, watching as Wes puts together a sandwich for himself, the fresh loaf just barely cut into, I can't help but salivate at the sight.

"That looks good," I say, inching closer. He looks at me in defeat and drops his head, pushing his sandwich towards me without a second thought. "I can make my own, you don't have to give me yours."

"Oh, shut up and take it. I can make another," he says as he starts to slice more pieces of bread. "I guess I'll make one for Marlene, too, while I'm at it."

"Probably a good idea, she's working up an appetite out there," I say through bites.

"And just like that, *my* appetite is gone." He drops the knife on the counter and stalks towards the small staircase in the corner. "I'm going to bed. And I'm going to be so pissed at you if that visual keeps me up all night."

"Love you, too," I call after him. He climbs the creaky stairs and, shortly after, I hear a door shut from somewhere upstairs. The second I'm alone, heavy boots sound from behind me and Shay's scent fills my nose.

The hairs all over my body stand straight up. His left hand comes from behind me and grips the edge of the counter, while the other one snakes around to my face, his fingers lightly grazing my jawline. "You could be having just as much fun as Marlene, you know," he growls in my ear, his lips dangerously close to my neck.

I can feel the warmth of his body on my backside, even without any physical touch. It's taking everything in me to hold back the urge to lean into him, to let him do to me what he wants.

What *I* want.

I turn myself around between his arms to face him head on. He's staring down at me, a dark look glossing over his eyes. My chest is mere inches away from his, and I feel his gaze lower to the sweatshirt I put on under my denim jacket.

"There's some unnecessary space between us, sweetheart," he says roughly.

My whole body tingles at the way his voice sounds, especially now that he's back to calling me sweetheart, again. I didn't realize how much I missed it until he stopped. And, fuck, it's taking a considerable amount of willpower to not move right up against him. Why the hell am I still denying the connection between us? My reasoning before was so I could concentrate on training and get ready for this moment but, we're here, now. I'm not with Luke anymore, there's an obvious attraction between us. What is stopping me?

I lightly pull my bottom lip between my teeth as I weigh my options, and his gaze drops down to my mouth at the slight movement. The tip of his tongue leaves his mouth slightly, licking his lips as a quiet growl sounds in his chest.

I'm being stupid, right? I place my hand in the middle of his chest and trace the defined muscles underneath the sweatshirt he has on. I push him away from me the smallest bit and meet his gaze.

"I don't want to deny this anymore, Shay. Honestly, I don't think I *can* keep denying it." He arches a brow at me, clearly not thinking this is what his teasing was going to lead to. "I can admit that I've felt something for you the minute I met you. And I know I've needed some time but, the moment I was finally free from Luke and took my life back, all I've wanted is to do this with *you*."

He brings his hand to my face and gently caresses my cheek, and I lean into it. This small, intimate touch feels so good and so right, and I can't believe I've gone my entire life not knowing his touch.

"Are you sure you're ready, Lianna?" he says, stroking my cheek with his thumb. "Because you would've been mine the minute that asshole was out of your life if I had it my way, but I wanted to give you the time you needed."

I nod. "I'm sure, Shay. I want you." And before I can get another word out, he's on me. But he's gentle. He doesn't force his tongue into my mouth, or nip at my lips at all. He doesn't go too fast, and it's not aggressive. Instead, he's soft and gentle, and he takes his time with our kiss, almost like he doesn't want to miss a single second of it. Like he's memorizing the way my lips feel on his. It's deep and intimate, and I'm all too aware that this is what I'm meant to do for the rest of my long life.

It's intoxicating.

And I want more. He must sense my thoughts, because suddenly I'm being lifted off the ground and placed on the counter behind me, all while our lips are still fused together.

I can feel a wicked grin spread across his face as we kiss, and just as his tongue parts my lips, we're interrupted by Tate and Marlene coming back in from their own rendezvous. "Of fucking course," he mumbles into my mouth, pulling away and dropping his head against my shoulder, arm still around my waist.

"Oh, wow, sorry to interrupt," Marlene says with a grin, peering around Shay to look at me. My face is flushed from our moment and I can feel it get hotter by the second with embarrassment. "We can leave again, if you want."

"No!" I say harshly. "I mean, no, it's ok. We were just talking." Shay huffs out a laugh at the blatant lie and I glare at him.

"I'm sure that's all that was happening here," Tate says sarcastically. "Anyway, I'm thinking Shay and I will make a plan while the rest of you get some sleep. We'll leave sometime tomorrow afternoon once we're all fully charged. Because, once we cross into the Fae realm, there's really no telling what's waiting for us."

"We don't have to rush?" I ask curiously.

"No, we have some time. Your father can be a dick, but he did give you six months after your birthday to make it to him," Shay says calmly and I nod.

"In that case, can you show me to a bed?"

"Of course. Come on, the rooms are all upstairs." Shay lifts me up by my waist and helps me off the counter. He grabs my discarded backpack and leads me up the stairs to a long hallway with four doors lining it. "The brown door at the very end of the hallway is the bathroom. All the other doors are the bedrooms. I'm assuming Wes is in the one with the closed door so, choose a different one and get some rest."

I pace down the hall and stop in front of a room that has a large bay window covering almost the entire wall. The curtains are drawn and I walk over to the window, peering out into the night sky. The snow is still falling rapidly and, with how much is blanketing the ground, the moonlight reflecting off of it makes it look almost like daytime. It's so beautiful.

The room backs up the the realm Gate, and seeing it this close at night is almost magical. The entire wall is made of a gray rock called gneiss, and there's a blue mineral called kyanite that lattices throughout it. The moonlight shines off of the intricate blue stones, casting blue hues onto the snow below. The entire span of the snowy ground looks like it's been splashed with blue paint.

It's breathtaking.

"My room, huh? Good choice, princess." I roll my eyes at him and snatch my bag from his hands.

"You know, I would prefer if you didn't call me that."

"It bothers you that much?" he asks with concern in his voice.

"It does," I admit. I'm a little thrown off that he's genuinely asking instead of getting defensive and telling me I'm overreacting. Holy shit, I put up with far too much with Luke. "I know I'm *technically* a princess or whatever, but it doesn't feel right. And it sounds like you're mocking me, which I know you aren't but, still."

"Noted. I promise I won't call you that again," he says, walking a few steps closer to me. "How about sweetheart? You've seemed to enjoy that one."

I nod as my cheeks grow hot. "I like sweetheart. Sweetheart is okay."

"Sweetheart it is, then." He stands in front of me and slips my jacket off of me, laying it neatly over the footboard of the bed. "Now, let's get you into bed." He pulls me towards the messy, unmade bed and pushes me down to sit on the edge. He kneels in front of me and the sight of it makes my heart pound damn near out of my chest. When he picks up one of my feet, shock courses through me. "May I?"

"Go ahead," I say softly. He starts to unlace the strings of my boots and pulls each one off gently, placing them side by side next to the door. Then, he unbuckles my leg holster and places it on the bedside table before lifting my legs into the bed and lays me back, pulling the soft blanket up to my chin. I blink away my shock and let myself be taken care of. I'm so not used to being treated with such respect. Is this what it's supposed to be like?

"I'll wake you in the morning when it's time to leave." He leans down and kisses my forehead, just before placing another deep kiss on my lips. "Sweet dreams, beautiful."

How the hell am I supposed to sleep when my mind is alive and buzzing from him and those kisses. Even after he's long gone from the room, all I can think about is him.

Chapter 14

The deafening creaking of the bedroom door wakes me the next morning. I cover my head with the pillow and groan, more than a little annoyed I'm being woken up already. But, I have to say, I feel so incredibly well-rested, that it can't be as early as I think it is. I don't even have to wonder who's in the room with me, because I can smell Shay before I even open my eyes and it calms me instantly. I don't know why that irritates me, but it does. I toss the pillow to the side and rub the sleep from my eyes to see him leaning against the doorframe staring at me.

"What?"

"Nothing, you just look really beautiful when you wake up," he says, like he hasn't seen me first thing in the morning before.

"Thanks," I say, already missing my morning coffee and it's only been a few days. "Where are the others? It seems so quiet in here."

"They're all at Lake Carsin waiting for us. I wanted to let you sleep for as long as I could, so I told them we'd meet them there," he says. I nod and sit up in the bed, swinging my feet over the side. A second later, Shay is, once again, on his knees in front of me with my boots in hand, ready to put them on for me.

"You know I can put boots on, right?"

"Yeah, but it's far more enjoyable when I get to do it for you," he says with a smirk. I can't even complain. Having things done for me is such a drastic change from having to do *everything* on my own. I'm going to take advantage of this while I can.

"What time is it?" I ask, trying to quiet my rumbling stomach. I'm so hungry and just by looking at the curtained windows, I'm sure I missed breakfast.

"A little after noon," he says, starting to lace up my second boot. "And don't worry, I packed something for you to eat on the road." He pulls my holster from the table and buckles it around my thigh, taking extra time as he goes. He stands and holds out his hand for me. "Ready?"

I reach for his hand but hesitate just before making contact. And, in that small moment of hesitation, everything truly sinks in for the first time. And I'm fucking terrified.

I'm really leaving my home.

I might never see my parents again. I could die, my siblings could die, Shay or Tate could die. They might come for my parents. I will never be normal again after today. Every terrible scenario comes rushing into my head, and it all starts to build up inside of me, to the point where I feel like I'm about to explode. No, that's a real feeling I'm having right now. Something's building up inside of me and it's begging to come out.

I stumble backwards, and my breathing starts to become more erratic as the panic grows. My skin begins to tingle as it slowly transforms from its normal, olive tone to the iridescent glow. Just like when I held my daggers for the first time. *Oh, fuck.*

"What's going on? Are you ok?" Shay's distorted voice is filled with fear and sounds so far away from me. I crumble to the ground, crashing to the floor in an explosion of sobs and mist. Varying shades of red shimmer around me and fill the room, far different than the white fog memory walking brought on. The air around me feels damp and destroyed, like my emotions are being projected into the beautiful mist that surrounds us.

Shay stands unmoving, mesmerized by everything I am in this moment and, I have to admit, it is beautiful. But the sounds of my deepening sobs seem to snap him back to reality, pulling him to the ground with me. He grabs my face to make me look at him and I'm vaguely aware of him speaking to me. His lips move, but I can't hear any of the words that are coming from them.

All of the fear and grief coursing through me makes me feel so frail, so unlike I usually feel. Shay lets go of my face as my tears flow harder pulling my entire self into his lap. His massive body completely engulfs me and, as soon as I'm cocooned in his embrace, something inside of me erupts. My body starts to warm to extreme temperatures as he holds me, far hotter than my powers felt the first time.

I try desperately to reign in the magic that's surfacing, but it's useless. It just keeps coming and I keep getting hotter. My blood feels like it's boiling inside of me, which only intensifies my panic. Sweat and tears try to fall down my face, but they turn to steam the moment they drop. I try to speak to Shay, but my throat is completely charred, like I swallowed hot ash. It feels just like it did the day Peham went up in flames and a jolt of sadness runs through me, fueling my internal fires even more.

"Shay, I'm burning," I finally cough out. I look up at him in severe pain and agony. He looks down at me and wipes a damp piece of hair from my forehead, tucking it behind my ear. His eyes are darting up and down my body before he closes them, his hand going still on my burning forehead.

I shut my eyes tightly to block out the pain that's building when, out of nowhere, my mind is flooded with thoughts of anything and everything cold. My insides go from feeling like a blazing inferno to a snowy wonderland. Slowly, the fire inside dies down, and the burning becomes more tolerable as each second passes. Relief sweeps over me as the pain subsides and I'm so grateful for whatever the hell just happened.

I open one eye and gasp at the scene in front of me. Shay's body covered in a thin layer of frost. Even the room around us is coated in snow. The red shimmer that erupted from me is now intertwining in the air around us with a muted gray fog that's seeping out of Shay.

The tears that leak from my eyes now instantly freeze in streaks down my cheeks, and my damp eyelashes are snowy and white. I look up at Shay, and our frosty gazes lock onto each other.

I reach up a hand to caress his face. The warmth of my skin makes the ice coating on his face feel slick, but it's comforting as it continues to cool me down. He pulls me in closer to extinguish the rest of the fire inside me until the frost creeps along my body and stays put instead of melting away.

And then, it all comes to a halt. The intertwining fogs evaporate, and the ice that coats us both thaws and melts away as we return to normal body temperatures. He holds me at arm's length for a few moments, looking me over to make sure I'm not hurt. Maybe a little cold, but I feel fine.

"What the hell was that?" I say, partially in awe but more so in confusion.

He chuckles. "What, me or you?"

"How about explaining both?" I demand. He wraps his arms around me and picks me up as he stands, setting me on my feet and making sure I'm stable before he lets go. He picks up my backpack from the floor with one hand and takes my hand with the other, pulling me from the defrosting room.

"It's a lot. I'll explain on the way."

***

We walk side by side to the lake, hands intertwined, and our boots crunching on the tightly packed snow. It's no longer falling from the sky, but it had enough overnight that we woke up to at least four inches covering the ground. It's not freezing outside, but it's cold enough that I can see our breath as Shay tries to get away with explaining what I am in minimal detail. I cut him off mid-sentence and basically demand more of an explanation.

"From the beginning, then?" he sighs.

"Everything. I deserve the truth."

He rakes his fingers through his hair and begins a history lesson. "When the continent first formed centuries ago, there were three groups; the Omni, the fae, and the humans. Each group claimed their own territories in the realm, but there were no borders separating them like there is today. The Omni weren't fae, but the Goddesses that everyone worships today, human and fae alike; Kaleen, Odessa, Lucienne, and Aislinn. They bore beautiful, feathered wings and possessed every power imaginable. Over time, they mastered these powers and truly became the most powerful beings in the realm. Meanwhile, the fae were lucky to possess just one power, while the humans had none."

"Wait, Aislinn? There was no Goddess Aislinn, Shay. There's always just been the three of them." Hadn't there?

"There was and she was killed. Some say it was her sisters that killed her because she became more powerful than the three of them. Others say it was the humans that ambushed her out of fear and murdered her. Few say that she had a secret human lover and they killed themselves together. No one knows the truth of her death, only that she was found at the bottom of a trench with her head severed and her wings cut from her back and placed around her," he explains.

"Why isn't she in any of the texts about the Goddesses?" I ask.

"Probably because she died so young and didn't go on to do what her sisters had." He shrugs and continues. "As time went on, the three remaining Omni sisters started to mate with the neighboring fae. The children that were born from these bonds were half Omni and half fae. They didn't possess as many powers as their Omni mothers, yet still had three, at most, which was still more than a typical fae had. These offspring also bore the same stunning wings as the Omni's. The Goddesses chose to call them the Angel Fae and, once they established just how powerful they were, the Omni Goddess sisters vanished without a trace. Then, it was just the Angel Fae, fae, and the humans in existence."

"They just disappeared? Where the hell are they? Why would they abandon the realm like that?" I question, unable to understand how they could just leave like that. Not just the realm, but their children and mates as well.

"No one knows why they disappeared, but there are many that think they're still here and just secluded somewhere," he says. "Anyway, many years after they disappeared, Aris was crowned as the Queen of the Angel Fae. Both Tate and I served her when she was in power. She and her soulbond, Dennin, were the sole rulers of the Angel Fae and they worshipped her endlessly. It wasn't long before the former King of fae, King Ashton, made it his goal to get rid of the Angel Fae completely."

I pause, my heart in my throat, hoping I misheard Shay. "He wanted to get rid of them? Why?"

"He felt threatened by them because he knew they overpowered him greatly. For years, he spread rumors so wildly untrue just so the fae would fear them."

I scoff. "Fear based on lies."

"Yeah, but they believed him. And why wouldn't they? He was their King, how could they question him? But, turns out there were some fae that refused to believe his lies and wanted to help and protect the Angel Fae in need. When he learned some of his subjects supported the Angel Fae, he snapped. 300 years ago, he began hunting the Angel Fae himself, executing any that he could get his hands on. It went on for a few weeks and would've continued if it hadn't been for his council urging him to step back due to their fear that the fae would rebel against him. He agreed but built a massive wall of pure quartz around the entirety of the Angel Fae territories, keeping them completely separate from the fae kingdom."

"It sounds like the King was a little jealous he wasn't as powerful," I say, rolling my eyes and stomping over fallen leaves.

Shay laughs. "I guess you could say that. It was no surprise that he didn't like that they were more powerful than he was. Didn't matter that the Angel Fae and fae lived in peace for centuries. But, even before the wall, the Angel Fae typically stayed in the four cities that had originally belonged to the Omni; Shal, Eldolon, Fahal, and the Sacred City of the Goddesses."

"Wait, Fahal? Isn't that where Tate was captured all those years ago?"

"Mhm. It used to be such a beautiful city filled with Magicless fae," Shay states.

"Magicless fae? That's what Tate was talking about earlier." I vaguely recall that when Tate mentioned the Magicless, it confused me but, there was so much going on that it slipped my mind. I've never heard of them, though. In the limited texts in Peham about the fae, none of them mention Magicless fae. None mention the Angel Fae, either. What are they hiding from us?

"Throughout history, there have been fae that mated with humans. Their offspring were fae that bore none of the characteristics of the fae, making them look just like their human parent. But, the majority were born without any powers, while a rare few were born with one lesser power so minuscule that they could barely do anything with it. King Ashton wanted any Magicless that was born eliminated. He was repulsed at the thought of fae and humans mating and called it a "crime of nature". But Aris protected them. She turned Fahal into a safe haven for them within the safety of the Quartz Wall in the Angel Fae territories. The King despised her for it."

"I'm sure he did. She protected these innocent fae and gave them an entire city to feel safe in instead of fearing death everyday. She was in control, he wasn't."

"Yeah, until one day the Magicless rebelled. Every single one of them, completely out of the blue, and no one knows why. Aris had done nothing but protect them, and she tried her best to reason with them and control the rebellion but, they became too dangerous. She had no choice but to put an enchanted wall around the once peaceful city and keep them inside. She hated herself for doing exactly what the King had done to the Angel Fae."

"Going from a realm with no boundaries, to one with three separate walls. I can't even imagine how hard that must've been for her," I say quietly, my brows furrowed. There's a sudden shift in the air as Shay stays quiet. I can tell there's more he wants to say, but something's stopping him from saying it.

"If you don't feel comfortable telling me everything, I understand," I say, trying to hide the disappointment in my tone.

"It's not that, Lianna. It's just...I'm about to tell you things that very few know. And it has nothing to do with trust because I trust you with my life. It's just a little strange voicing it after having to keep it to myself all these years."

"You can take your time. I promise, I understand," I say, looking ahead of us. We're getting close to the bridge, which means our time alone is dwindling. I squeeze Shay's hand and feel his body relax at the movement.

"Aris and Dennin had three daughters. Triplets. They had to banish one of them, Izara, to Fahal when they discovered that she was offering up the Magicless to Ashton. Their thought was that she would be kept prisoner by the Magicless for all she's done to them, but she rose to power instead. When Izara became leader of the Magicless, her sisters tried to do everything they could to stop her, but she refused to listen. She started a three-year war with the Angel Fae as a ploy to show the realm how powerful the Magicless could be, even without magic."

"So, Izara's Angel Fae and she's leading the Magicless fae? What the hell changed when she was banished that she went from serving them up to be killed to leading them?" None of this makes any sense.

He shakes his head. "No one expected any of it to happen. And it's not common knowledge that she's alive and leading them. Aris and her sisters found out, but kept it to themselves. Izara tends to keep herself hidden away in her fortress in Fahal."

"And what about her two sisters? What happened to them?"

"They're still alive," he says quickly, his jaw clenching. There's still something he's keeping from me.

"Shay, what's going on? What aren't you telling me?" I ask. He keeps his eyes straight ahead as I stare at him, refusing to make eye contact with me as he speaks.

"One of her sisters married a human and left the Fae realm. The other married a fae royal and left the Angel Fae territories," he says cryptically. But, it all sounds too familiar.

"What are their names?"

"You know their names," he says, dropping his head low. I stop walking the second the words come out of his mouth. Not in anger, but in pure shock. Shay comes to a halt a moment later and finally turns to me, locking eyes with my damp ones.

"Amara and Flora," I say softly, and he nods. "Let me get this straight, because this seems just a little insane. My adoptive mother and my real mother are Izara's sisters?"

"Correct."

"And they're the daughters of Aris, Queen of the Angel Fae?"

"Again, yes. Making her your maternal grandmother." He steps closer to me and takes my hands in his, dragging his thumb along my knuckles. "I know this is a lot to process, and if you have more questions, I'm happy-"

The realization sinks in, then. "I'm Angel Fae?" I breathe out. The scars on my back where my wings once grew start to throb as the understanding why they had grown in the first place courses through me.

"Not exactly," Shay begins, his words trailing off as he drops his gaze to my hand, now tightly squeezing his.

"What do you mean by not exactly?"

"You're more than that. I didn't realize it until what just happened in the cottage." I'm starting to get really fed up with him skating around the truth, trying to protect me. I can take the truth, it's all I've ever wanted.

"Spit it out, Shay. What the hell did you realize? What am I?" It feels like a lifetime goes by before he finally gets out the words he's been holding back.

"You're not Angel Fae," he says, and my eyes widen. "You're an Omni. The first one since the original three, the one that will fulfill the centuries old prophecy. You will be the last to ever exist."

Chapter 15

A thin layer of ice crackles under Shay and I's feet as we cross over the bridge.

My mind is racing with everything Shay revealed to me about my lineage. All the fear I have about the magic inside of me is far worse knowing what I truly am. Not even fae like I always thought, but a *Goddess*. And, even though this new information gives me such anxiety, it's the most I've ever known about myself, and I don't think he realizes how much it means to me.

I link my arm around his waist as we walk and I take a moment to really study his gorgeous profile. "What made you realize I'm Omni?"

Shay looks down at me, and how completely cozied up to him I am, and puts his own arm around my shoulders, tucking me into him. "Have you noticed that your skin glows iridescent when your powers surge?"

I nod, rolling my eyes. "It's a little hard to miss my entire body glowing."

He huffs out a quiet laugh. "That's how. The Omni are the only ones that have the ability to do that."

"None of their Angel Fae offspring can?"

"No, just the Goddesses."

"And my powers? Didn't the Omni have all of them?" I ask anxiously.

"They did," he confirms. "You'll have three that'll be more powerful than the rest. It's called the Triad. What you did in the cottage just then is something called Feeler Magic, so I'm going to assume that's probably one of your Triad."

"I'm a Memory Walker, too." Shay whips his head to mine. I exhale, "The day we left Peham, and my parents gifted me my daggers, I touched the blades and I memory walked to the day they were given to Amara from Flora. Touching them initially is what broke the spell that was put on my magic and, once the tether was cut, all of my magic surged at once."

"Shit."

"Yeah. But I haven't done it since then so I don't know if it's something I have to *will* to happen, but that has to be one of the Triad, right?"

"Without a doubt. Memory walking is a very rare power to have. I've only ever known five throughout my life," Shay says. We walk in silence for a few moments when another question surfaces.

"When did you figure out we're soulbonded?"

"I knew the minute I saw you on your twentieth birthday. The connection made itself well known to me, but I refused to pull at it. You were with Luke, and you didn't know me. I didn't want to act on it until you could decide if you wanted it or not."

"Hasn't that been torture? Knowing for that long and not being able to act on it?" Though, now that I think about it, he's been shamelessly flirting with me since we met. He was doing everything he could without crossing any lines.

"It's been agonizing. Why do you think I flirted so damn hard? I needed to release the pent up need for you somehow," he says, laughing. It's full and deep, and I don't think that's something I'll ever get tired of. But, then, it stops suddenly and he catches his breath, then inhales shakily. "Are you sure you want this?"

I jerk my head so quickly towards him that a sharp pain radiates through my neck as I stare at him. "I can't tell if you're being serious or not," I say. And when he doesn't answer immediately, I feel my defenses start to rise. "I told you I want you, Shay."

"I know you want me, trust me, I can feel it."

"Then why don't you believe me?"

"You haven't accepted the bond, yet," he says, his eyes narrowing on my right hand. I look down at my own hand, and then at his. I can't deny that fact, as harsh as it seems. Unlike Marlene and Tate, neither Shay nor I have the gold band around our right ring fingers, proof of our soulbond tie to each other.

"I'm scared," I admit, stopping in my tracks at my confession.

"Of me?"

"No, not of you. Never of you," I reassure him. "I've never been with anyone other than Luke. He's all I've ever known and we both know it wasn't a positive experience. And you show me day after day that you'd never treat me that way, but I think it's that fear of being treated that way again that's stopping myself from accepting the bond completely." The truth rolls out of my mouth with ease and it feels like a weight has been lifted off my shoulders. I didn't realize how much that was burdening me until now.

"I know it can't be easy to open your heart up after someone else has mistreated it for so long. But I hope you know that I will do damn near anything I can to fix what he broke, no matter how long it takes. It sounds cliché, but I'm nothing like him."

"Thank you," I say, placing my hand on his chest. "I want to accept it, and I will, I promise. I just need some time. But nothing is going to change my mind on the way I feel about you. I want this with you, badly." I stand on my toes and aim to kiss him on the cheek, but he moves much faster than me. He kisses me hard on the lips, biting the bottom one as he pulls away. My lips are parted as he draws away from my face, cupping my jaw with his hands as he keeps his gaze locked on mine.

"I'll be here matter what, sweetheart. I'm not going anywhere," he whispers as we resume walking, coming up on the final stretch to the lake. As we get closer, I can see Marlene and Tate standing side by side at the edge of the frozen lake sliding rocks over the slippery surface, seeing who can get theirs the farthest. I look around for Wes and find him just where I thought he'd be. He's standing right in front of the gravestone we erected for Sierra. He must have brushed all the snow off of the white stone because I can see the dark sapphire lettering of her name clear as day on the face of the grave.

I walk over to Wes and stand next to him quietly, leaning my head on his shoulder. His body is shaking slightly as he cries silently for his lost love, but I keep quiet and remember the female we both loved dearly.

A few minutes of silence pass when I hear footsteps come up behind us. I lift my head from Wes' shoulder at the sound of someone clearing their throat to see the the others waiting a few feet away. I nudge Wes and he brings his tear-filled gaze to mine. I gesture behind me to the group. "Time to go." He nods and holds out his arm for me, letting me link my own through his as we trek out of the deep snow around her grave.

As soon as Wes and I rejoin the group, Tate starts to speak. "Getting through the realm Gate will be fairly easy. As for what's waiting for us on the other side, I don't know. Shay and I haven't been in the Fae realm in years and have no idea what new dangers have appeared past the wall. When we left, the darkness just started to reappear in the kingdom. But, if what the King said in his letters is true, then the darkness may very well have consumed more than just the kingdom."

"The gate doors were sealed centuries ago, so we can't go straight through. But, there are a few secret openings we can use instead. There's one right on the other side of the lake that'll bring us to the outskirts of the Forest of Truth. We should be able to make it undetected along the forests edge and then make our way to Shal. We'll stay there for a while," Shay says.

"What happens if Shal isn't safe?" Marlene questions and I notice her body is starting to tremble. Her nerves are starting to get the best of her and there's nothing any of us can say to make it better for her. We all look at Shay and Tate for an answer, and when they look to each other with uncertainty, my stomach flips. They don't know if it'll be safe. But it's our only option.

After a moment of tense silence, Tate answers Marlene's question. "As far as we know, the magic Aris enchanted the Quartz Wall with is still in place around Shal. It might not be much at this point, but it'll be enough to keep the darkness from getting in." Marlene nods and exhales shakily. Tate instinctually moves closer to her and wraps her into his chest, kissing the top of her head once she's folded into him. The sight of my little sister being cared for so deeply makes my heart so full.

The sweet moment is cut short by Shay as he throws his bag over his shoulder. "Let's get a move on. I'd like to get the hell out of this place and do so while it's still light out."

We all grab our bags and follow Tate and Shay as we make our way around the bottom of Lake Carsin. This part of the walk is a little nerve-wracking, because the small strip of land we're currently walking on is very open to the edge of Peham. Granted, there's a thick lines of trees on the shore of Peham, and it's close to the fae territories so we *shouldn't* see anyone from town here, but I can't shake the feeling that someone is going to venture a little farther than usual and see my siblings and I traveling with two fae.

The only thing that makes me more nervous right now is how close we're getting to the realm Gate. The wall itself doesn't scare me. I've been close to it a few times now but, heading straight for it and knowing we're going *through* it is a far more intimidating thought.

Intimidating, yet so damn beautiful.

The gneiss and kyanite wall stands about twenty feet tall and stretches the full length between the Fae realm and the human realm. There are massive towers at each end of the wall that are built on small, minimally populated islands. As far as I know, the only beings that live there are the Keepers of the Gate, and a small village on each that has less than twenty residents per town.

The walk around the lake doesn't take too long, maybe thirty minutes, but it gives us enough time to go over the plan again. As the gate comes into view more, my steps falter and I hang back a bit as the rest of them continue on. The spike in my anxiety started to overpower me a few minutes ago and I hoped it would've been gone by now. Instead, it has only gotten worse and I just need to create some space between me and the gate.

Shay notices my absence right away, of course, and he slows his pace to match mine, until we're walking side by side. "Everything alright?"

"Just overwhelmed," I say, hoping my tone is believable enough. I nod up at the wall ahead of us. "What kind of entrance is this going to be?"

Shay looks at me, not very convinced that I'm alright, but answers my question anyway. "All of the hidden entrances were made by humans to sneak into our territories. The one we're using is actually the one Grant used to sneak into the forest when he met Amara. It's just a hole in the ground that tunnels under the wall, and it's a tight fit but, if Tate and I are able to get through it, the three of you will have no problem." Immediately after the words leave his mouth, he looks down at my backside. "Although, you might have some issues with that ass of yours."

My jaw almost hits the ground. No way did he just say that. His gaze roams hungrily over every inch of me, and I snap my fingers in front of his face. "My eyes are up here, thank you very much." I smack his arm with a good amount of force as I stride by him and continue to walk towards the others. I don't make it very far before he pulls me back to him by my hair. "Hey, what the-"

"Let me make this very clear, sweetheart." His voice is a low, quiet growl in my ear. "Even though the soulbond mark hasn't appeared yet, you're still mine and I will look at whatever gorgeous piece of you I wish, whenever I want to. Understood?"

"Crystal clear." I swallow, biting my lip. I can't help the thoughts barreling through my head, just wishing I was able to act on the thoughts that are on repeat in my head. Fuck, I want him. That much is clear enough. And I want this soulbond connection between us. I've been trying so hard to push my fear down because I know he'll never treat me the way Luke did. I've come to terms with the fact that Luke was terrible and Shay is incredible, so why won't my heart let me accept the bond?

Are we really soulbonds?

Tate's booming voice pulls me from my thoughts. They're pretty far ahead of us and are now making their way underneath a small cluster of trees right up against the gate. "Come on you two! Let's get a move on!"

Shay holds his hand out to me, and I grab it without any hesitation this time. I intertwine our fingers together and he gives me a light squeeze before he leads us towards the others. I expect him to drop my hand when we reach them, but he doesn't. He just keeps me close to his side.

As we get to Tate's side, I can see that he and Wes have already cleared away a good bit of snow and are pulling a large bush apart, revealing a tunnel just big enough for a fae male to get through. And it's pitch black through there. How thick is this wall and how long will I be underneath it? Tate turns towards us again once the tunnel is completely exposed. "I'll go first. I'll make sure it's safe on the other side and then I'll give you the all clear to make your way through. *Do not* leave here until you hear my signal, but get through quickly."

"Be careful, brother. See you in a minute," Shay says to Tate, clasping him on the shoulder. He gives a quick nod and shimmies himself into the hole, pulling his bag down after him. The four of us huddle around the opening, intently listening for Tate's signal. After a few anxious minutes, his voice floats through from the other side.

"All clear for now. Get through quickly, something feels off over here," he calls. His voice sounds tense and hurried. I really don't like what that insinuates. Marlene steps towards the hole first with no hesitation, and Wes follows closely behind her. They both slide through with ease, their half-human bodies giving them plenty of room to get through unscathed.

Pretty soon, it's my turn and I feel rooted in the ground where I stand. Not only does crawling in a dark tunnel under a heavy stone wall terrify me, but crawling through there means I'm leaving my home. This is the first real step and I don't want to take it. Shay notices my hesitation and stands in front of me, grasping my shoulders in both hands. "You're going to be fine, I'll be right behind you. And the others will be right there on the other side waiting."

"I know. It's just...this is it. I'm really leaving." I swallow the lump in my throat and take a deep breath, leaning my head against Shay's chest. If Wes and Marlene can leave it behind for me, I need to be able to do the same. I look up at Shay and give him a small smile. "Help me in?"

He holds my hands as I step down and before I crouch to crawl under, he plants a kiss on the top of my head. "Once I make it through, get ready to start running. I didn't like the tone of Tate's voice," he says, his voice laced with fear. I knew I heard something off when Tate called to us, I just didn't want to be right.

I nod and crawl through the rocky tunnel and, when I emerge on the other side, Tate and Wes help pull me from the deep hole. I brush the dirt from my pants and, when I look around me, a massive wave of recognition hits me as I stare at the forest in front of me. It just looks all wrong, now. When I saw the Forest of Truth in the memory, it had been lively and vibrant and magical.

The trees that loom over me now look like they're decaying and leeched of all magic. Each tree trunk has a gray rot that starts from its roots and climbs towards the top. The leaves are falling to the ground and disintegrate before they have a chance to hit the cobweb filled forest floor.

The entire forest is dark and uninviting. Any trace of the once lively forest is gone.

And it puts me on edge.

I turn to look at the others, immediately noticing how on guard Tate is. His knives are unsheathed from wherever they were hidden and firmly in front of him, with Marlene tucked behind him safely. I follow his line of sight to something deep in the forest, but there's nothing there that I can see or even hear. But I can *feel* the presence of whatever it is over the entire forest, waiting.

I reach down to my thigh and unsheathe my own daggers, keeping them by my side just in case I have to use them. Marlene gives me a sideways glance, clearly not loving the idea of me wielding knives and not knowing how to properly use them.

I really don't blame her. Even I'm not loving the idea of having to use them yet.

I keep my eyes fixed in front of me as Shay climbs out of the hole, his own blades already in hand. He looks where Tate and I have our gazes fixed and sends out a burst of magic. Gray fog exudes from his fingers and sweeps through the trees, and within seconds, small shrieks rise from deep within.

"Run," Shay whispers.

I throw my backpack on and slide my daggers back into their slots as quickly as I can before turning on my heels and running. My feet carry me as fast as they can on the slippery snow as we all sprint West, each step closer to Shal. Tate leads us down the coastline as we run parallel to the tree line of the dark forest.

I glance back at Shay to make sure he's still right behind me and gasp at what I see, almost tripping over a rock in the process.

Behind us, Shay's magic is projecting a gray fog screen that's keeping shadowed figures from latching onto us. The creatures seem to glide over the ground, at a speed that seems unreal for just how decaying and horrifying they are. And they're getting far too close for comfort.

I turn back around and speed up to my siblings. "Don't you dare look behind us." I grab onto Marlene's hand and run on her left side, while Wes stays to her right, keeping the two of us safely between himself and the coastline at our left.

The distance between the tunnel and Shal seems to go on for miles, and I can sense everyone's energy levels dropping the further we go. Shay's magic is still holding strong and keeping the creatures at bay, but every few feet, I can see the fog dwindle slightly.

He's starting to run out of steam.

I open my mouth to yell up to Tate when I hear the sound of rushing water up ahead. As we get closer to the sound, an extremely tattered bridge appears, but what I can't keep my eyes off of is the massive Quartz Wall beyond the river. I can't help but stare as we run towards it, admiring how the sunlight bounces off the exterior, the rays creating tiny rainbows all along the surface. I tip my head back as far as it can go in hopes to find the top but it seems to disappear into the clouds.

I can't believe I'm saying this, but it's even more beautiful than the realm Gate.

Tate turns his head slightly to shout at us as we close the distance to the bridge. "Run fast and don't stop, we're almost there." A new fear joins the other ones looking at this bridge we have to cross. It's an old wooden bridge and the ropes holding it up are fraying terribly. There are boards missing from the middle and one of the posts is halfway out of the ground. It looks like it's going to collapse any minute, but Tate makes it over with ease, proving it's more sturdy than it looks.

When my feet are safely on the other side of the bridge and I'm a few feet away by the Quartz Wall, I whip around and wait for Shay to catch up. I nervously watch as Shay plants his feet at the edge of the bridge and forces more magic from his hands, using more energy than he has. Out of one hand, the gray fog continues to shield us, while he uses the other hand to reach out towards the bridge and send a stream of magic to destroy the bridge. The ruined wood falls piece by piece into the river and the creatures come to a stop at the other side, contemplating how to cross.

"I can only hold them for so much longer, Tate. Get fucking moving, please!" he yells over his shoulder. I spin back around to see Tate place his hands flat on the gleaming stone. The area around them starts to glow a deep red and then, a small entrance appears out of nowhere, as if the stone simply melted away from whatever magic Tate is using.

"Don't just stand there, get through now!" Tate yells frantically with his hands still firmly planted on the wall, the three of us frozen in place with exhaustion and fear. I snap out of it and push Marlene and Wes in before running through the entrance myself. The second I'm through the doorway, I turn to make sure Shay makes it to us, to me. I keep my eyes on him as he drops his hands to his sides, the gray fog screen dropping simultaneously, leaving him and Tate vulnerable outside the wall. He runs in a full out sprint towards us, and I watch in horror as the shadowed figures begin to find a way across the river now that his shield is gone.

As soon as Shay passes through the doorway, he places his hands on our side of the wall, allowing his magic to flow through him to keep the entrance open just long enough for Tate to drop his hands and slip in safely. Shay's hands drop the moment we're all together and we watch as the entrance slowly mends itself shut.

"Let's hope her magic is as strong as it once was," Shay mutters as the shadowed figures approach the still closing entrance. The five of us stand together in silence as the creatures that make it over the river try to slip through the thin sliver in the wall. Thankfully, each one that makes contact instantly disintegrates and the others halt their movements to hiss at us, just as the hole closes completely.

Only when the wall fully fuses back together do we all let out a breath of relief.

Chapter 16

"Holy shit," Wes says, trying to catch his breath as he stumbles back onto a rock behind him. Marlene is already in Tate's arms, her body shaking from fear and exhaustion. I find Shay sitting on the ground, his back against the wall and his breathing heavy. I sit down next to him and speak quietly.

"What the hell were those things?"

"They're called the Caviax. Pure darkness in physical form, shrouded from head to toe in shadows. Those are some of the creatures that the darkness brought to the Kingdom. It's gotten so much worse," he says quietly, his head dropping between his knees. He brings his hand to his shoulder blade and starts to absentmindedly rub it, letting out small winces with each touch.

"Did you get hurt?" I reach for him, but he grabs my wrist, stopping me right as I graze his shirt.

"I'm fine, it's nothing," he pants. He's trying, and failing, to be convincing but I don't believe him for a second. I move my trapped arm in a way that makes his entire shoulder contort. He lets out a loud, but brief, roar of pain and Tate's immediately on his feet, concern written all over his face.

"He's fine, I got him." I wave him off and turn back to Shay. "You are not fine. If you were, that wouldn't have hurt so bad. What the hell happened?" I demand. I give him a pointed look and, when he looks away from me, I go to twist my arm again. He drops his hold on me and lets out a defeated sigh, taking off his shirt and showing me his back.

I heart sinks at the sight.

"Right before my magic created the shield, one of the Caviax sent out a whip of darkness and it clipped my shoulder. It just needs some time to heal and then I'll be fine," he assures me. I see the wound from the Caviax plain as day, and he's right, it'll heal quickly. But my eyes are locked on something else entirely.

It's what's in the middle of his back near his spine that brings hot tears to my eyes. Two long scars run along either side of his spine, each a foot long, just like mine. I lightly touch them, running my fingers along their length.

He winces.

Not in pain, but in shame. The shame that it happened to him, or the shame that he hasn't yet told me his full truth, I'm not quite sure. But it's almost like he forgot they were even there in the first place, and now he's exposing himself to me fully, whether he's ready or not.

"Shay," I whisper, continuing to touch the raised scars. "I know these scars. I know how these are made, what used to grow here."

"Lianna, I can explain. I-" I grab his hands and push them up under my shirt, so his palms are flat against my own two scars. His eyes momentarily widen in shock and I would've missed it if I wasn't intently staring at him. They quickly soften with sadness before filling with fiery rage. "Who cut them off?" he asks, his expression turning murderous.

"My dad. They sprouted when I turned sixteen. He didn't want anyone to discover me." The memory slowing starts to creep up but I quickly push it back down. Not now. I can't feel all of that right now.

"When I first realized what your true lineage was, I figured the wings skipped a generation since your father is fae and not Angel Fae. I *hoped* they skipped you. Because the other conclusion was that someone *took* them from you and it's hard to imagine that someone who loves you would have been so cruel to take away a part of you."

"It was for my family's protection," I argue, not sure why I'm even defending my dad for what he did. Even though I don't blame him, Shay's right, he still took them from me. This is besides the point though, we're talking about him. "Why didn't you tell me the truth about *you*?"

Shay runs his thumbs along the lines of my scars before pulling out from underneath my shirt and cupping my face with both hands. The tears that fill my eyes now have nothing to do with me, but are solely for Shay and what he's been through. I know it all too well. He wipes the tears from my cheeks and puts his forehead to mine, and I breathe in his scent with each inhale.

"My history is...complicated. And something I tend not to dwell in. I was always going to tell you the truth. I just needed some time to figure out where to start. And the harder I fell for you, the more I realized I needed to tell you about me soon."

"Shay, the moment I knew we were soulbonds, I told myself I needed time and space because of everything that happened with Luke. But that never stopped me from falling for you as each day passed. After all the time I spent being someone's punching bag, it was scary to open my heart up to someone else. But you make me feel safe. I finally feel free and that I deserve something good, and I know that good is you. You are everything. And I want to know it all. The good and the bad." I reach up and grab his face with my own hands, sitting knee to knee with our heads still pressed together.

"I have waited so long for you. You are the reason for everything I have ever done, so I could get to this moment with you." He pulls back and lightly kisses my forehead. "I promise, once we get into Shal and find shelter, I will tell you everything about me. As long as you promise to tell me everything, too."

He tucks a loose piece of hair behind my ear, revealing my scarred ears that always get tucked away from view. Just another part of my past that I've yet to tell him and my stomach turns thinking about what he must think looking at them. And, instead of balking away from them, he lowers my head slightly and kisses the tips of my disfigured ears gently and lovingly.

"I will not leave out a single detail, my soulbond," I say gently.

My soulbond. Mine.

My heart starts to pound wildly and it feels like I'm being physically pulled towards him, even though we're nearly chest to chest. Before I realize what I'm doing, I give into the pull and gently press my lips to his. And, though I've kissed him before, this one feels different.

Sparks dance through my entire body, intensifying with each second our lips stay locked together. When I start to pull away, he tightens his grip on me and brings me closer, returning the kiss with a deep passion and intensity I've never felt before. His fingers tangle in my hair to keep me close, and the feeling that this is where I belong is all I can think about.

As we kiss, I feel a sharp tingling move through my right arm and down to my hand, pinching harder as it reaches my finger. I jerk away from him and look down to where the pain was just a second ago. The tingling has stopped and in its place is something I've been waiting to see. I search Shay and quickly spot the same mark on him, and I can't help the grin that spreads across my face.

A thin, gold band now wraps around each of our ring fingers on our right hands. The permanent sign of the acceptance of our soulbond connection. What I've looked for every day since I chose him, and what Shay has been waiting for since he first set eyes on me. And it's finally here. I look up at him with fresh tears brimming my eyes, beaming at me with a smile wider than I've ever seen on him, putting his pointed canines on full display.

"*Thank you* for accepting me, soulbond," he chokes out, and kisses me over and over.

***

We take a few minutes to rest and catch our breath before we're up again and walking along the inside of the Quartz Wall. Like when we entered the Fae realm, there's the wall on one side and a dense forest on the other. After Marlene spotted our soulbond bands, she made sure that they all went ahead of us so we could have some privacy, which is how we ended up at the back of our group.

"So, Queen Aris' magic really runs through the wall?" I ask Shay, watching the reflection of my fingers as I run them along the cool stone.

I can feel Shay's stare at the back of my head as he watches me intently. "That's why the Caviax couldn't come through."

"Lucky for us that the magic held up after all these years." I pull my attention from the wall and look ahead to where the others are stopped in front of a small gate, waiting for us to catch up.

"Just through those gates is Shal. When the Angel Fae were executed, the city was abandoned and fell to ruins. There's no telling what it looks like now," Shay informs me as we reach our friends.

"No one resides here anymore, so it should be the safest place for us to stay," Tate states as he pushes the rusted gates open, almost tripping over a hidden hole in the ground as he steps forward. "Just watch your step."

We follow behind Tate carefully as we walk down the overgrown path, the snow not as deep here thanks to the trees overhead. After walking for a few minutes in silence, the trees begin to part ahead of us, letting in more light than the trees allow in. And, when we step out of the forest and into a small clearing, a beautiful town is revealed ahead of us.

"Welcome to Shal," Tate announces. We definitely didn't come through the main entrance of the city, but even the backs of the buildings are beautiful. Tate and Shay lead us between two buildings and, suddenly, we're on a cobblestone street covered in a thin layer of snow and ice. The buildings lining the street are a beautiful dark gray stone and creeping up the sides and going into the buildings themselves are vines and flowers of all colors. They disappear into the light blue rooftops that have thin icicles hanging from the gutters.

The further we walk down the streets, we come across abandoned carriages and overturned market stalls, proof that life existed here at one point. Some of the smaller buildings have started to crumble but the larger ones seem so intact, looking like they just need to be restored. But, other than that, it doesn't look like a city in ruins. Just an abandoned one.

"This place is considered in ruins?" Marlene questions, reading my mind and looking equally as mesmerized as I am.

"Compared to what it used to look like, yes, this is in ruins," Tate mournfully says.

"Are we just wandering through this city or is there somewhere in particular we're going?" Wes yells, right as Tate turns down a side street just before a large fountain in what I'm assuming is town square. As we all make the turn behind him, a village of beautiful cottages appears up ahead, the homes all in near perfect condition. My eyes widen in awe at the simple beauty of each of them.

"This is the lower village, Redhelm. This is where the majority of the Angel Fae lived," Shay tells us as we walk through the streets of the village. The cottages are all average sized homes, enough to house a family of four with room to spare. The majority of them look identical, with their light gray exterior and green rooftops, while others are painted and decorated differently, reflecting the families that once inhabited them. Some of the small yards still have small toys and outdoor tools in them, and it makes me wonder what these families were like once upon a time.

We come to the exit of the village and continue to walk along a stone road until we make it to a small set of stairs, eight steps to be exact, carved into a hill. Before we even make the climb, I can see that there are larger manors built at the top of the hill overlooking Redhelm.

"Woah," I let out as we reach the top. It's such a stark difference from the homes we just saw below. Equally as beautiful, but in such a different way.

"Welcome to Oldbrook, Lianna," Shay says, coming to a halt next to me and grasping my hand in his. He starts to walk again, but this time his steps are less confident and falter slightly. I stick by his side as we follow behind Tate and Marlene, also sticking by his side. We pass by an entire row of homes before Tate stops in front of a brick manor with a black roof and a dark wooden fence surrounding it. A large raised garden sits in the front yard, the overgrown plants dead and sticking out from the snow layered on top of the dirt. There's a large brick mailbox at the edge of the property, but there's snow covering the last name.

Shay lightly squeezes my hand as Tate turns to him with tears in his eyes. He immediately drops my hand and pushes past Wes on his way up to Tate, pulling him into a tight embrace. With both my hands free, I step over to the mailbox and wipe away the snow covering the last name. Q-U-I-

"Welcome home, brother," Tate whispers, both males silently sobbing.

"This is your home." I say quietly, staring at the fully revealed last name on the mailbox. *Quint.* Shay pulls away and answers me, but keeps his glistening eyes locked on Tate.

"This is where we grew up. We moved here after mom brought Tate into the family and it became home." Shay's hand clasps Tate's shoulder, and the two of them let out small laughs, grinning from ear to ear. It hits me that neither of them expected to ever get to come back here, or that it would still be standing after all these years. What a surreal feeling.

"It looks the same. Even Darcy's garden is still here. It doesn't even look like the village was touched after the city fell," Tate says, his tone a mix of shock and happiness. "Are you ready for this?"

Shay takes a moment to look around at the manor before nodding slowly. "Let's do this."

The two of them take the lead, striding up the front walk towards the massive front door. It stands taller than both Tate and Shay by a good foot or two, and the dark wood of it matches the surrounding fence. They both pause momentarily and compose themselves before pushing open the heavy door together. It swings wide and we're greeted with a rush of cold air and a cloud of dust that sends all of us into a coughing fit. We're all waving our hands around us to try to clear the dust and, when it does, I find that I'm standing in the most beautiful home I've ever seen.

The brick that covers the exterior disappears going inside, revealing beige painted walls with hand painted floral accents. There's a massive bay window along the front wall with a cushioned bench underneath, letting in large rays of light and warmth. The furniture, in what I assume is the living room, is made from beautifully carved wood with an olive-green fabric covering the cushions and pillows. Across from the couches is a massive fireplace so large that I imagine I could stand in it straight and there'd still be room.

Across from the living room is a dining room with a large wooden table set with two long benches on either side and a chair at each end. There are six place settings still at each spot, not disturbed in the slightest, but covered with grime and cobwebs. There's a runner going down the middle of the table that's made of the same olive-green fabric as the couch cushions, and a vase still sits in the center of the table. The flowers inside are dead and dried, and I know that just one touch will have them falling apart.

I walk through the curved archway and wander into the large kitchen attached to the dining room. The walls are light sage green and the counter tops are some sort of polished white stone, now coated in a thick layer of dirt. The pots and pans that hang from a rack on the ceiling are in great condition as long as they get a good wash, as long as Tate succeeds in getting the electricity and water running again. He says it's just a matter of getting the main generators going in the basement, so I hope he actually knows what he's doing and doesn't make it worse for us.

I continue walking through the lower level of the house when a heart wrenching realization slams into me that almost brings me to my knees. Everywhere I look, the home is lived in. Dirty dishes still sit in the sink. Blankets are strewn off the couch, like they've been casually tossed off of someone. Laundry is half folded on the living room floor. And, the more I look, the more I realize that Shay's family left their home one day, expecting to come back.

But they never did.

I walk room to room looking for Shay and finally see him through the bay window sitting in the snow out front, right next to the overgrown garden. *For fuck's sake.* I grab a thick blanket and walk out the front door, shutting it quietly behind me. "You're going to have a frozen ass if you keep this up," I reprimand, handing him the thick blanket. He smiles up at me and takes it from my outstretched hands, lifting up slightly to put it underneath himself. I lower myself to the ground next to him, making sure to keep myself fully on the blanket. I stare ahead at the village in front of us and admire the shadows that the setting sun casts from behind the other manors.

"What happened here?" I breathe. Shay wipes at his eyes and falls back on the blanket, pulling me down with him by my waist. I rest my head on his chest, and I feel the quickened beating of his heart as he wraps his arms around me.

"The day started out like any other day. Tate and I were out back training like we usually were. We weren't even serving Aris yet, but it was our goal to get there one day. So, we were pushing ourselves through boot camp to train as soldiers for her. Most days we would be outside from the moment we woke up until dinner. Mom and dad were in the kitchen baking, and my sister, Darcy, was working in this very garden. Tate and I were in the middle of sparring when we heard Darcy scream. We dropped everything and started running to the front to check on her when we heard mom scream next, followed by my dad yelling her name. So, we split up. Tate went to Darcy, and I went to my parents. By the time we got there, they were all gone," he trails off.

"What happened to them?"

"King Ashton happened. He raided the village and took them to be executed. It was during the time when he lost his mind and went on a killing spree. They were held as prisoners for a few days and then, they were all publicly executed on the steps of his castle for everyone to see. I still don't know how I managed not to get captured, but the guilt eats me alive constantly."

"Shay, I'm so sorry. I don't even know what to say." I burrow my face into his neck, hugging him a little harder than before. I feel his chest rise as he takes a deep breath and shake slightly as he exhales. I wonder how long its been since he has talked about that day, or even his family.

"I hid in the square that day and saw them force my mom to watch as they murdered my dad first before killing her, too."

"And Darcy?" He goes unnaturally still and I can feel the moment his jaw tightens on top of my head.

"I-I don't know. She should have been up there with them. But she just...wasn't. I don't know if it means she escaped, or that they killed her beforehand, but she wasn't up there with our parents. I searched for her for years but never found any trace of her. Eventually, I realized I was looking for someone who was already dead." A warm tear lands on my cheek, but it's not mine. It's Shay's. "I had to give up."

"How soon after all that did you leave here?" I motion to the area surrounding us.

"Right after the executions. We planned on staying as long as we could, just in case Darcy showed up, but Aris personally summoned us to the Sacred City.

Tate and I took what we could carry and left our home. When we got to the city, the Queen requested to speak to us about my family. Turns out, she knew my mother well and, when she got the news that she was one of the executed, we were immediately sent for."

"Your mother must have been very important to her."

"She was. It wasn't just her power that Aris was interested in, but the friendship Aris said they shared sounded almost too good to be true. But, it was because of that friendship that Aris insisted that Tate and I become her personal guards, no questions asked. By anybody."

Chapter 17

I can hear Marlene' squealing from the backyard clear as day, even with the massive manor separating us. If I can hear her this clearly, I can only imagine what Shay must've gone through when Darcy was taken. I take a breath and turn my attention back to Shay.

"Once the triplets were born, me, Tate, and another male were reassigned to guard each one of them as their personal guards. Tate was Amara's, I was Flora's, and the other male, Caz, was Izara's. As they got older, they didn't need us as much and, when they turned sixteen, Aris sent us to Eldolon to keep an eye on the rebelling Magicless. She felt it was a more pressing issue than being a glorified babysitter."

"I didn't realize that's how you knew them so well. I guess I just expected you to have been their friend," I admit.

He huffs out a laugh. "It started out as just being a guard, but it definitely turned into a friendship after time." He moves one of his arms from around me and folds it underneath his head, propping himself up slightly. "When Ashton died and Drake became King, Flora insisted I come with them to the castle in the Fae realm. At that point, Aris was dead, so it just made sense to stay by Flora's side. Tate and Amara came shortly after I did."

I shoot up to a sitting position, as a weird sense of betrayal run through me that I can't explain. "So, there was no one left to rule the Angel Fae territories anymore? You all just abandoned it, just like that?"

"The Sacred City was *already* abandoned. When I escaped Izara, I came back to an abandoned territory. Every city was barren. And then I learned why. King Ashton had done what he always wanted to while I was kept prisoner;

execute all the Angel Fae. Besides the ones that were lucky enough to make it into hiding, he killed them all. The day after he held his executions, he was found murdered and somehow Drake came into power. Flora was spared from it because Drake protected her, and Amara had been hidden by Tate. But, once Drake was officially the King, Flora basically forced Amara to come live in the castle so that she knew she'd be safe. So, we all lived there together up until Amara left for the human realm when she married Grant. Flora made Tate discreetly follow her and live in the cottage to keep an eye on her, giving him free reign to move between the realms as he pleased."

"And you?"

"I stayed in the castle for another year after Tate left. Then, Flora disappeared with you. No one knew where she took you until Tate sent a letter for me to come meet him at the cottage. He brought me to your house and that's when I discovered you were left with Amara."

"Were you always there watching me?"

"No, sweetheart," he says, pulling me back down into his arms and chuckling into my hair. "I wasn't watching you your entire life. Tate and I stayed for the first year just to make sure the darkness couldn't reach you, and then we returned to Odrera to help the King and keep the Fae realm intact. We only came back to the cottage when the darkness started to creep back into the kingdom looking for you and Drake sent a messenger to give you the first letter."

"And I know the rest of that story," I mumble, suddenly remembering something about the day the first letter arrived. "Shay. When the messenger came to my house, he said something weird before he left. I remember seeing his hands and feet shackled together by quartz, but he was so nervous to say what he did, like he thought he'd get in trouble for it."

Shay fully turns his head to face me. "And you're just telling me this now?"

"I'm sorry, I honestly forgot. A lot happened that day and it just slipped my mind."

"What did he say?"

"'She lives'. And that's it. I had no idea what he meant at the time, but now I think he was talking about my mother, Flora. Do you think it's possible she's alive somewhere?" I ask, hope building in my chest.

Shay pushes himself into a sitting position and pulls his knees to his chest, leaning on them with his forearms. I prop myself up on my elbow and look up at him as he rubs his jaw in contemplation. "It's possible she found somewhere to hide that no one knows about. And not just from the darkness, but from Drake, too."

I think about all the places in the Fae realm that I'm completely unaware of. I don't even know where to begin looking for her. I turn back to Shay, his wet eyelashes clumping together and streaks of dry tears staining his cheeks. I reach my hand out and touch his thigh gently. "Thank you for telling me about your family. I know it must've been hard, but it means a lot."

"Thank you for listening. It's been a long time since I've talked about them. It's just so easy to talk to you and-"

"Well, I'll be damned," a deep voice booms from the road. Shay's head snaps up and he's on his feet in an instant, tucking me protectively behind his back. I peer around Shay to get a look at whoever's here. The male smirks at Shay and pulls back his hood, letting a mess of dark brown hair free. When he pushes it out of the way, I notice a giant scar that goes straight down his right eye socket, where the eye underneath is missing. I continue blatantly scanning the male and realize that, not only is he missing his right eye, but his left arm is severed at the elbow.

Movement behind him catches my attention and I see something behind him twitching. My eyes widen when I realize that what I initially thought was a cape dragging along the ground behind him is not that at all.

They're wings.

They're tattered and drooping and dirty, but they're fully attached to his body. They're about the same size as my mothers were in the memory I saw of her and, beneath the dirt, they look to be a light gray color. It's the first time I've ever seen wings on a fae outside of the memory walking and it's taking everything in me to contain the happiness at seeing a fae like him.

No, not just a fae. An Angel Fae.

"Holy shit, Desmond?" Shay says on a gasp, releasing me as he races over to the male, almost tackling him to the ground. I watch as Shay tries to fight the shake in his legs, knowing his knees are seconds from buckling. But this male, Desmond, only holds him tighter with his one arm, keeping him steady.

"Hey, man. Long time, no see," Desmond says with a shaky tone before looking over at me, standing just behind the fence watching the two of them. His face drops the moment he meets my gaze. His breathing becomes uneven the longer our gazes lock, and tears start to line his lids. "Shay. Tell me that's who I think it is."

"It is, Des. It's Lianna," Shay confirms. Desmond stumbles backwards, shock exploding over his face. I can't quite place the expression that comes next but, as he wipes the tears from his eye with the back of his hand, my heart starts to ache deeply.

He huffs out a sad, yet relieved laugh. "I thought you were fucking dead."

***

While Shay and Tate have a small reunion with Desmond, Marlene and I are preparing dinner from the scraps of food we have. Desmond was nice enough to offer up some of the food he has, and ran back to wherever he's been staying and brought back some meat and a bowl of vegetables.

"So, remind me again who this is, Li?" Marlene asks once we're alone.

"From the brief introduction I got before Tate ambushed us, he used to be a guard in the castle and was friends with Shay and Tate. He said he was close with Flora, too. But, other than that, I don't know much."

"He seems really nice. Do you think he's going to join us?"

"I'm not sure," I say. Shay and Tate seem so happy that he's here, but there's something about him that I can't explain. And it's not necessarily a bad thing, but I can't shake it. I peer into the dining room where Wes has now joined the three males at the dining table. Shay catches me staring and excuses himself from the table, making his way to the kitchen. To *me*.

"I'm going to take this food out to them so you can have some privacy," Marlene says as he walks under the archway. He gives her a smile as she passes him, then turns his attention to me.

"Want to tell me what you're thinking?" he says, eyes narrowing.

"I don't know, Shay. I keep feeling like I know him somehow, which I know sounds crazy. But it's just putting me on edge a bit. I don't want to separate you from your friend, and I would never ask that of you. If you trust him, I have to trust in you that this is a good decision," I say, biting my lip anxiously. He walks over to me and lifts me by my waist, placing me on the counter so we're looking at each other eye to eye.

"I watched him grow up. He was Flora's best friend their entire lives. I promise, we can trust him." He tucks a stray hair behind my ear and gently kisses my nose. Goddesses, this male makes me melt.

"Ok, then whatever you decide, I'll back you up." I place my hand on his chest and lightly kiss him on the lips before jumping off the counter. "Come on, you need to eat. And I very much want to hear any stories he has about you."

"You're in for a wild ride, then," he says as we walk back into the dining room. I come to a stop just under the archway, and my heart nearly leaps out of my chest at the scene in front of me. Sure, seeing everyone together around the table makes me happy, but it's the sight of Marlene and Wes that makes my heart overflow with joy.

Marlene and Tate are sitting side by side, as closely as possible, and her hand is resting tenderly on his thigh. The smile that lights up her face is so bright, and I know without a doubt that it rivals the sun. For years, she has given up hope for so much, but always finds a way to push through it. But I've watched the light inside her dim. And, after everything that happened with me, I've been so afraid that light would go out for good and I'd never see that beautiful smile again.

But Tate has made the light in her brighter than it has ever been. And I don't know if I'll ever be able to repay him for it.

Wes is sitting at the head of the table, directly across from Desmond, and he's bent forward laughing at whatever was said right before we walked in. Seeing him get out a real, genuine laugh is something I thought died when Sierra died.

There was a period of time where we all thought we were going to lose Wes after her death. I never blamed him for how he felt and completely understood the feelings but, eventually, he pulled himself out of the hole. But, his laugh is something I thought I lost and to hear it now, though it's most likely over a vulgar joke, is everything.

I wipe the wetness from my eyes and follow Shay to the empty side of the table, right across from where Tate and Marlene are. Even as I sit, I can't stop admiring my siblings and the life that's coming back into them.

But my happiness quickly turns to sorrow as I think more about what's in front of me. How much longer will we get to enjoy these small, happy moments before everything changes? All because of me. This happiness and life that my siblings have found can so easily be taken away all because they want to protect me.

Shay glances at me and frowns. I must not be concealing my fear as well as I think I am. Yet, even if I was able keep the fear from my face, I have a feeling that he'd know my thoughts anyway. He reaches out his hand to stop me as I mindlessly fill my plate with bits of every food on the table. The fear that's building inside me is causing my mind to dissociate from reality and I allow it far too easily.

"Come back to me, love," Shay whispers in my ear after a few moments. I blink rapidly, clearing the fog that washed over me and give him a small smile before picking up my fork and turning my attention to the food on my plate.

After taking a few small bites, I feel eyes on me and I look up to see Desmond trying to hide the fact that he was staring. Everything seems to fade away as I make direct eye contact with his deep silver eyes. I straighten in my seat and swallow the food in my mouth before speaking. "I want you to tell me everything." *Oh, Goddesses, I can't do this.*

One side of his mouth turns up in a small grin. "Everything, huh? Fire away, then." I feel a massive wave of anxiety building inside me and I really wish I had kept my mouth shut. But, I know that if I don't just got for it, I won't have the courage to do it yet and I'm not sure how long we have him with us.

"Would you rather me ease into them? Or I could just rip the band-aid off and go for the unfiltered questions," I say, pushing down the nerves.

"I've never been one to take the easy way," Desmond answers without a second thought, laughing slightly.

"Unfiltered it is," I retort, taking a deep breath. I nod at Desmond's missing arm. "What happened to your arm? Or even your eye?"

"For fuck's sake, Lianna. You can't say shit like that." Wes pushes out of his chair and races to my side, putting himself between me and Desmond, almost like he thinks he'll hurt me over a dumb question. And, as ridiculous as it seems to me, Tate's also on his feet with Marlene tucked behind him, and his knives unsheathed in front of him.

Shay remains seated, thank the Goddesses, but his body is moved slightly so that he's another barrier between me and Desmond. His right hand grips my thigh almost hard enough to bruise, but the moment I place my own hand over his, his grip loosens and steadies.

"You have quite the protective detail, Lianna," Desmond says, his laughter almost knocking him out of his seat. When he sits upright again and sees that the three males are still on high alert around me, he sighs. "For fuck's sake, Shay, I'm not going to hurt her for asking what I *know* everyone wants to know. Plus, I fucking gave her the go ahead to ask them."

"Never did know with you, Des," Shay says as he relaxes slightly and leans back in his chair, his hand twitching on my leg. "And as happy as I am to see you, after everything that went down with Landon the last time I saw you, I'm not quite sure where your head is anymore. No offense."

"Low blow, Shay," Tate mumbles as he sits back down in his seat, placing his knives in front of him on the table. Though he keeps his eyes on Desmond, he pulls Marlene back to his side and goes right back to eating.

I push Wes out from in front of me and narrow my eyes at him, trying to silently communicate that he needs to go back to his seat. He rolls his eyes and sulks back to his chair, his eyes darting between Desmond and I. "Now that that's all cleared up, are you going to answer my question?" I keep my face unreadable and take a sip of what seems to be really old wine, patiently waiting for his answer, even though I am fucking shaking inside.

"You've got a lot of fire in you, I admire that." He smiles. "You want the long or the short version?"

I let myself look like I'm thinking hard about my choices, when in reality, I'm trying to work up the courage to use my memory walking power on him. I'm still not sure how it all works, but from what I do understand, touching him should be enough. I close my eyes and take a deep breath, squeezing Shay's hand as I feel the magic start to warm inside me. When I open my eyes, there's a confused look on Shay's face. I see the moment he realizes what I want to do, because I know my skin is warming slightly from my magic surging and he can feel it. He shakes his head at me but I look away from him, letting my gaze fall on Desmond as I stand and walk over to him.

"I want the real version." I desperately will my hands to stop shaking as I stop next to him, even though the trembling in my voice is hard to ignore. Before I can chicken out, I reach for his hand as my skin begins to glow iridescent, pulling a genuine smile from me. I pause right before I touch his hand and look in his all too familiar eyes. "And I want to see it myself."

"I don't understand..." Desmond starts, but before he has a chance to say another word, my body is drenched in iridescence as I grab hold of him, the manor exploding in a white fog around us.

And I'm gone.

Chapter 18

The ground where I land is cold and hard. My eyes blink rapidly and try to adjust to this intense darkness I've stumbled into. Though I can't see much of my surroundings, I can tell that I'm sitting in a stone stairwell. Behind me, there's a large wooden door with the smallest stream of moonlight coming in through the gap underneath it.

A faint fluttering sounds next to my ear and, when I glance to my right, there are three gold winged butterflies hovering next to me. I stare at them in awe as they continue to flap their wings at me, and realize they're identical to the ones I saw in the first memory I went into.

I reach out a finger towards them but as I get close, they flutter away towards the large door at the top of the steps and then disappear.

Curious.

I push myself to my feet and climb the few steps to the door, heaving it open with all the strength I can muster. I'm greeted by a warm, calming breeze and a full moon overhead, illuminating the stone landing that the stairwell led out to.

More specifically, the landing at the top of a tower. And, if I have to guess, it's a tower on the castle in Odrera. I look around me for the butterflies, but they're long gone now.

Boots shuffle along the stone behind me and I turn to see a familiar face walking towards the edge of the tower wall. His brown hair is much shorter and a hell of a lot neater, and this younger version still has both arms and two deep silver-gray eyes, instead of just one. Even his wings are free of rips and tears, held high and tucked tightly into his back.

Desmond.

He starts pacing, but keeps his focus on the lands beyond the castle grounds. I step up beside him and, when I look over the wall, I'm not prepared for the view. From here, I can see almost every inch of the Fae realm. And it's nothing like the books I've read depicted it as. It's so much better. And, no matter what direction I turn, there's beauty everywhere. Every inch of the realm is bathed in moonlight, making it appear more magical than it already is.

Looking to the North, I can vaguely see stretches of deserts and mountain ranges. The desert sparkles in the moonlight, almost like tiny diamonds have replaced the sand granules.

I turn to the right a bit to the East, and there's ocean as far as I can see. It reminds me so much of the small beaches on the outskirts of the forest in Peham. There's a small section of docks below, where I can see large boats coming and going. Off of the docks is a run-down looking town, most likely filled with fisherman, and the entire area is at the base of a crescent shaped cliff, keeping the area concealed from the rest of the kingdom.

To the West, there's a strange stretch of water inhabited by small islands, but they seem empty and desolate. I can't see a single structure built there, just flat land. The massive Quartz Wall is far in the distance beyond the stretch of water, but it's plain as day, sectioning off the Angel Fae territories from the rest of the Fae realm.

When I look South, I'm greeted by that all too familiar stone wall climbing high into the air. The blue kyanite glitters as the moon hits it, making it seem more vibrant than ever. And, acting as a barrier between the length of the wall and the Fae realm, all the way to the river, is that breathtaking forest my heart recognizes way before my mind does.

The Forest of Truth.

There's an expansive stretch of field between the forest and the kingdom's village and, even in the moonlight, I can see hundreds of flowers and sections of tall grass scattered around. And then it clicks. That open area is where I was transported to the first time I memory-walked. I just didn't know it because my surroundings were all a blur.

My gaze travels to the village surrounding the castle walls. They're most likely homes to the fae that are privileged enough to live in the Kingdom, or families of some sort of nobility. As I stare at the fae walking through the streets, Desmond sucks in a sharp breath and breaks me from my trance. Something clatters to the ground, and I whip around completely to find his sword abandoned on the ground, still vibrating from the impact of being dropped. All color is completely drained from his face and he's gripping the edge of the wall far too tightly, making his tanned knuckles turn milky white.

I come up next to him and follow his gaze Northwest, quickly realizing the cause of his panic. Slowly creeping over the mountains far in the distance behind the Quartz Wall is a thick, black mist headed directly for the castle grounds.

Desmond turns on his heels and races for the door I originally came from, and I'm quick to follow him. I can feel his panic increase as he descends the stairs, stopping at a door halfway down. When he swings it open, he runs right into a hooded woman with dark red wings folded against her back, holding a small bundle in her arms. When she looks up at him, tears are already spilling from her vibrant, garnet red eyes, and it takes all of my strength to keep myself upright.

The eyes that haunt my dreams. And clasped around her neck is the amulet I wear daily. Just seeing those eyes makes my dream flood into my mind. The female carrying my infant self through the tunnel and to the human realm is always blurry and never in focus. But now when I picture the dream, she's no longer blurry. It's her. And here, in her arms...

She adjusts her hold on the bundle, revealing a cherubic face wrapped in blankets and staring up at her with deep red eyes that are speckled with silver.

"Mom," I whisper as she drops her hood. I know she can't hear me but something inside of me clicks, like puzzle pieces are finally starting to fit into place.

Desmond covers my infant self back up with the blankets and takes my mother's face in his hands, tears flowing down both of their faces. They look at each other for a moment and then he drops his hands from her face, speaking quietly as he pulls her hood back over her head.

"Run, Flora. Take her and run far from here." I can see the fear flash over her face as her eyebrows furrow together, and for a moment I think she might try to fight him on it. Her eyes dart frantically and he gives her a look, like he's pleading her to listen to him. She gives him a shallow nod and shocks me by kissing him deeply before disappearing down the stairwell to the very bottom. Desmond doesn't move a muscle as he watches her leave, just to be certain she does what he asks.

Only when he hears the door slam shut at the bottom does he burst through the door in front of him and races down the hallway it opens into. I try to keep up with him as we run a few feet into a large courtyard where a few other guards stand around waiting for direction.

"Open those fucking gates! Let anyone seeking refuge in and take them down to the shelter rooms below!" Desmond commands. Two of the guards haul the gates open to let in those who're trapped on the other side but, as the gates part, my heart sinks. The mists came too quickly. They now surround the entire castle, and the village beyond is completely swallowed up by it. The crowd in front of the gate isn't as large as it should be and, with the size of the village, I know too many have fallen.

I glance at Desmond and, by the look on his face, he knows it too. I can see the guilt growing on his face by the second, and I'm sure he's been carrying it around ever since.

Gasps sound from around me and I turn back towards the gate to see that the mists are parting slightly, letting out a heart sinking sound. Screams escape from the heart of the village very briefly before the mists come back together, cutting off the sounds once more. It almost seems like it's mocking Desmond and all the others who escaped its clutches.

A young-looking fae male comes up beside Desmond, trembling hard and trying to catch his breath. And, on second glance, I can see that he's Angel Fae, too. His small gray wings look to be slightly larger than mine were when I lost them, which means he's much younger than I thought. Recognition floods my mind because he looks so damn familiar, but I can't place where I ever would've seen him.

"What the hell do we do, dad?" he yells. *Dad?* This has to be Landon, then. No wonder he looks so familiar, he looks just like a teenage version of Desmond.

Desmond puts his hand on his shoulder, turning him to face him fully. "Go down below with the villagers, be their protector. I'll make sure we get them all down there to you."

"And you? You too, right?"

"Yeah, me too." He brings his son in for a tight embrace and then pushes him towards the screaming crowd of villagers running to the castle. Then, he turns to his other guards, not sparing a moment to keep an eye on Landon. But I do. He veers from the group of villagers and towards the other gate. Alone. And, Goddesses, I want to follow him so badly just to see what the hell he's doing. But, it's a memory. And I know the minute I try to stray from the memory I'm in, especially one Desmond doesn't *have* a memory of, I'll be thrown right back to where I am now.

Desmond's booming voice pulls my attention away from a fleeing Landon and back to him. "Those of you who want to head down, go now. Go with Landon. Protect the royal family. Those who want to stay with me, I would be honored."

Two of the younger males leave to go to the castle, leaving Desmond with four older males to defend the front. I stand back, helpless, as I watch the five of them usher in as many of the remaining villagers as they can. There are maybe two dozen left to cross through when everything goes completely silent. *Eerily* silent.

Not a single sound comes from inside the mists or from any of the fae scrambling through the castle courtyard behind me, almost like whatever this force is took the ability to make sound right from us. I watch as the mists slowly begins to crawl up to the front gate as the five males ready themselves for whatever's to come. But right before it crosses the threshold, it stops and stills right in front of them, hovering in place. A small crackling noise sounds from within, and Desmond's head tilts to the side.

A second later, two dark green lights begin to glow from the mist.

He staggers backwards, the other guards completely unaware of the presence within the mists. Desmond opens his mouth to shout a warning to them but no sound comes out. Tendrils of black mist snake out and aim for each one of Desmond's guards, and none of them stand a chance. The tendrils latch onto their ankles and yank them down to the ground, and all I can do is watch in horror at what's unfolding in front of my eyes.

One by one, the males are dragged into the mist, their screams lasting only a few seconds before they're swallowed up by the mists. I look up as a tendril snatches Desmond, coiling around his left forearm and suspends him in the air.

The crackling noise sounds again, this time even louder, as the mists part again and a tall female steps out, cloaked head to toe in a dark green cloak with black curls peeking out of the sides of her hood. As she gets closer, I notice that a small band of mist is wrapped around the upper half of her face, allowing the glow of her eyes to shine through but no other features from the mouth up. She has plump lips that are painted a glossy black color and she has a hint of freckles peppering her cheeks.

"What the hell do you want?" Desmond yells, using his free arm to unsheathe the remaining sword from his back.

"What do I want? I *want* what is mine. What *she* stole from me! It's my birthright, it belongs to me!" she barks out, pointing angrily at the castle. She tilts her head at Desmond, clenching her fist to tighten the mist snaking its way along Desmond's arm.

"It belongs to *her*, not you. You lost that right a long time ago," Desmond hisses, clenching his teeth in pain. He...knows her? He better not be connected to the mists somehow and I just agreed to let him join us.

She looks at him curiously, her lips parting slightly to expose pointed canines that are black and rotting around the gums. She slinks closer to where he hangs midair and circles him as she speaks. "You know, I heard the *Queen* gave birth to a beautiful baby girl." The green glow of her eyes narrows as she talks to him. "I sensed her unique magic the minute she was born. Strange that she was born with such power when he father is just a Fae, isn't it?"

Desmond groans in pain and small trails of blood start to run down his arm. "Here I was, hoping I could pay a little visit to them, but..." she trails off and the corners of her lips turn up in a sinister smile.

The scream that erupts from Desmond brings me to my knees with my hands covering my ears as he hits ground with a hard thump. The female pulls her bottom lip between her rotting teeth as a dark laugh comes from her. I swallow the lump in my throat when I realize what just played out. She manipulated the mists to coil so tightly around his arm that it severed it cleanly, right at the elbow. He's doing all that he can to put pressure on what's left, but there's too much blood pouring from him and he can't stop it.

"I can sense neither the Queen *nor* the new Princess are here, but I know where they are now," she practically sings those last words to Desmond. He tries so hard to get to his feet but the female just clicks her tongue at him and sulks back into the mists. The moment she's back in the darkness, they close around her immediately and, in the blink of an eye, every inch of black mist evaporates, leaving a trail of bodies in its wake.

Desmond lays back on the ground, bleeding and moaning with tears streaming down his face. I try to run over to him to do something, *anything*, besides just standing and watching. But, with the first step I take, the memory swirls in front of me and vanishes before my eyes, and I feel the warmth of my magic roil inside me.

***

I hold my head between my legs as my vision clears and the wave of nausea subsides. I try my best to calm my breathing and hold back the sobs forming in my throat, but it's proving to be more difficult with each second. I'm back in the manor, thank the Goddesses, and I'm sitting on the floor with my back against the table leg. Shay must have sensed me the moment I materialized because he's already by my side and fussing over me.

He pulls me into his arms and starts to rub my back in circular motions, easing the nausea quickly. He pushes away strands of hair that are stuck to my damp forehead and kisses me a few times on the head. "I can't say I love this power of yours, sweetheart." I pull my head out from between my legs to smirk at him just to have Marlene right in my face.

"What the FUCK was that?" she yells, her voice a roaring in my ears.

"Goddesses, Marlene, not so loud." I press my hands over my ears to ease the ringing her booming voice created.

"Lianna, where- I don't- what?" She's struggling to get her words out, and her face is paler than normal. I don't blame her. She looks how I feel.

"Just one of my lovely, *rare* powers. You'll get used to it. Maybe. I still haven't."

"But...where did you go? One minute you were here, and then white smoke swirled around you. When it cleared you were just, gone!"

"Mom said it's called memory walking," I say, realizing all eyes are fixated on me. But, when my gaze lands on Desmond, he doesn't look afraid or worried in the slightest. Instead, his face is beaming with pride with a huge grin spanning the width of his face.

"An Omni?" Desmond whispers, turning his attention to Shay. "Are you telling me that she's a fucking Omni?"

"A what?" Marlene questions, but Desmond's attention is still on Shay, waiting for the confirmation of Shay's nod. Desmond shakes his head and stands as his eye fills with tears. He makes his way to me and crouches on the floor in front of me.

"You saw how I lost my arm, didn't you?"

I nod at him, the image of the mist severing it replaying over and over. I feel like I'm going to be sick all over again. Tears well in my own eyes as I look at him, now knowing the horror he endured. "I'm so sorry."

"Eh, I've learned to adapt. The eye was a bigger disappointment, but that's another story," he says, meeting my gaze and backing out of reach before adding, "for another day."

I throw up my hands in defeat, the corner of my mouth turning up. "Understood."

"I'm sorry, but for those of us without these super rare powers, can someone please give us a shortened version of how the arm was lost?" I look down at the floor, hiding my grin as Marlene stares down Desmond with an expectant gaze. For a moment, I think he might get offended by her bold question, but he only chuckles and begins to explain what happened that night.

As he begins his story, I quietly stand and leave the room, not wanting to relive it a second time.

I walk out the back door and stand at the edge of the stone patio overlooking the vast grassy area behind the house. The sun has completely set now, and the moon is illuminating everything around me, just like in Desmond's memory.

I hear the door slide open and close and I know it's Shay before he even says anything. He drapes a heavy blanket over my shoulders and stands behind me, wrapping his arms around my chest. We stand in silence for a few moments while the cool air calms me until I feel ready to talk about...anything.

"Where were you that night?" I ask, shifting slightly.

"Not where I should have been," he says flatly.

My eyebrows furrow together, and I turn my head to look at him. "What do you mean?"

"I was supposed to be on the tower with Des that night for lookout duty. But, at the last minute, I was pulled to a different station by the King. It left Des completely alone. I could've helped him if I had been there."

I turn back towards the yard, leaning into his chest more, and his chin comes down to rest on top of my head. "Or you would've been killed. There was nothing you would've been able to do to stop it. I saw what happened to the other guards. Chances are, you would've suffered the same fate as they did. She only spared Desmond because she sensed my mom escaping with me."

"Deep down I know that's true. But that night, when the chaos let up and Des was brought to the infirmary, he was on the brink of death. His Angel Fae blood wasn't healing him fast enough. The guilt was eating me up and watching him fight for his life on that bed was too much. So, I left his side. Again," he says, and his grip on me tightens every so slightly. I can feel his heart pounding against my back and it makes me so sad for him knowing he has carried this around for over twenty years now.

I shake my head. "I'm sure he didn't expect you to wait by his side the entire time he tried to heal, Shay."

"I know but, with Landon missing, he just had me."

I twist completely in his grasp, pressing our chests together, and tilting my head back significantly to see his eyes. "What happened to him? I saw him in Desmond's memory, and he just wandered off."

"He was *supposed* to escort villagers to safety. But, when the other guards made it down there, he was nowhere to be found. Each villager that was questioned told the same exact story. Landon stopped abruptly as a haze cast over him, his eyes fogged over, and he just walked off into the woods behind the castle."

"Was he ever found?"

Shay shakes his head. "The King sent me and a few other soldiers out to look for him. We found his sword and clothes in a puddle of blood on the edge of the Meobith desert, but that's it. We had to assume the worst. Then few days later, I got the letter from Tate to come to the cottage. I commanded another guard to inform Des about what we found out about Landon and left without saying a word to him. I couldn't face him."

"I doubt he ever blamed you for any of it. You're not the one who cut off his arm. You went looking for his son. You did everything you could for him."

"She's right, you know." We both turn to see Desmond leaning against the doorframe. "And I looked for you everywhere. Both you and Tate were gone, Landon was missing. Everything was spiraling in the Kingdom."

"I'm so sorry, Des, I should've stayed," Shay mutters, but Desmond holds up his hand and shakes his head at him.

"I don't even want to hear the rest of that because you have nothing to apologize for." He walks over to us and claps Shay on the back. "Come on, Tate and Weston want to do some nighttime exploring. We can give the ladies come peace and quiet to themselves. Tate says everything should be up and running, again, so that means water."

"I could use a hot bath, if we're being totally honest here," I say, planting a kiss on Shay's cheek. "Go. We'll be fine here, I promise."

"Wonderful!" Desmond sticks his head inside the manor and yells far too loudly. "WESTON, TATE, LET'S GO!" Within a second, the two males come bounding out the door and set off running down the snowy hill. Marlene strolls out behind them carrying a dishtowel in her hands.

"This group sure is something," she says, her eyes never leaving Tate. "I think Desmond will be a good addition, especially for Tate and Shay."

I smile as I watch them run away from the manor and then turn to my sister, pulling her back inside. "We are both in dire need of a hot bath."

"I second that. And we have first dibs on bedrooms," she says, grabbing my hand and pulling me behind her to the stairs, both of us laughing so hard that tears cloud my vision.

This is the happiness I need to keep close to me. I refuse to lose it.

Chapter 19

I need to remember to thoroughly thank Tate for getting the power and water working again. I just know I would've been completely miserable if I wasn't able to take a bath or a shower or even brush my teeth while we stay here.

Steam fills the large bathroom and fogs up the floor to ceiling mirror residing behind two deep sinks along the wall. I'm grateful the steam is making my reflection practically invisible to me because I'm not used to seeing the entirety of my body all at once. At home, there's never been a large enough mirror to see anything other than my upper half.

I turn to face the porcelain, clawfoot tub sitting underneath the only window in the room, directly opposite the sinks. The water is definitely scalding now, and bubbles are threatening to spill over the lip of the tub. I know the moment I plunge into the water, the floor under me will become a soapy puddle that I'll have to clean up. But I don't care. It looks all too inviting, especially now that it's snowing once again.

I head over to the closet next to the door and open it in search of any type of soap to use. *Oh, thank the Goddesses.* The shelves are filled with various scents of shampoos, conditioners, and body washes, along with a variety of perfumes and colognes. The highest shelves are lined with soft towels and washcloths, as well as a few exfoliating pumice stones. I will definitely be using one of those.

I spend a few minutes deciding on which scent I want to use, and eventually chose a trio of lavender scented soaps. The smell is so close to the one I usually use and just the scent reminds me of my family. It smells like home.

Carefully, I climb into the bath and sink down slowly, trying to contain the high rising water, all while letting the warmth of it calm my aching muscles. The feel is damn near intoxicating. I grab the bottle labeled shampoo and begin to wash my hair with the sweet-smelling soap. The aroma fills the air and intermingles with the steam, making my bath that much more relaxing. I really needed this. Though I showered at home before we left for the last time, the small journey we've already had and having to run from the Caviax made me feel gross and sore.

After conditioning my hair and scrubbing my body clean with the washcloth and the exfoliating stone, I begrudgingly lift myself out of the, now, lukewarm bath water. Almost immediately, thousands of goosebumps pepper my skin from the chilled air hitting my wet body. I dry myself off as best as I can before slipping into a fluffy white robe I found, and then pad into the connecting master suite. Marlene was the first to discover this room, but immediately handed it over to me when she realized it was once Shay's parents' room.

The air in the bedroom is no longer musty, thanks to Marlene helping me open all of the windows to air the room out. She also helped me dust every visible surface and strip the bed of the dirt covered quilt. The plan was to strip the sheets, too, but when I saw that they've been perfectly protected by the quilt for all these years, I wouldn't let her touch them. They seem clean enough and are completely intact, so on they stay.

Just the thought of removing the one thing in this house that still has traces of Shay's parents on them is something I can't bear to do. So, instead, I washed the quilt and hung it to dry, but left their old bed looking like they just rolled out of it this morning.

I pull my extra set of clothes out of my backpack and get dressed in the cotton pants and gray sweater before heading back into the bathroom to brush my teeth and hair, leaving it to hang down my back to dry. The bathroom is now cleared of all steam and I wipe away a small circle of fog on the mirror, just enough to see my face in. Satisfied with how I look, I leave the bathroom and head for the double doors of the room that lead into the hallway. I peer into each room in the hall until I find Marlene in what I'm assuming must've been Tate's room growing up. She's snooping in every nook and cranny as I come to a stop outside the door.

"Find anything embarrassing?" I ask from the doorway. She doesn't even flinch, just continues to search in the desk drawer she's moved onto.

"Mmm, unless you count old underwear and a teddy bear embarrassing, then no. I found countless training schedules and weapons everywhere in here, though. And this," she says as she walks to me and hands me a small photograph. "I think these are his birth parents."

I take the photo from her and look at the happy little family. His parents are grinning widely as they hold a small toddler between them, his ears not even pointed yet. Even as a toddler, it's easy to recognize the small child as Tate. But, looking at his dad, I would think this is a current photo of Tate today. The two of them are damn near identical.

"Has he ever told you about them?" I ask, still admiring the family photo.

"No. I don't think he remembers them much. I always knew that Shay's mom took him in, but it never felt right to pry about his real parents," she says as she gingerly takes the photo back from me, replacing it on the desk where she found it. "Shay's room is down the hall if you want to snoop, too."

I huff out a laugh. "Did you already snoop through it if you know which is his room?"

"No, it's just pretty obvious which one is his," she says, glancing at me. "Look for the door with a chunk missing from the top." I shake my head and turn out of Tate's room into the carpeted hallway. I make it a few steps when a white door adorned with floral drawings catches my attention. I know it isn't Shay's, but I feel so drawn to it. And then I realize whose room this has to be.

It's Darcy's.

I freeze in place, at war with myself on what to do. On one hand, I really want to go and see what she was like. But, on the other hand, it's probably not appropriate to do that without asking. I reach for the doorknob and then drop my hand away, getting ready to walk away, when two toned arms hug me from behind.

"You can go in, if you want," Shay's voice is low and shaky, and I know he just watched me wage war against myself.

"We don't have to open this door ever if you don't want to," I say, leaning my head against his trembling chest.

"I haven't been in her room since they were taken." He nudges me forward slightly. "It's time."

I nod and grasp the crystal door handle firmly, twisting it open. I feel around the dust covered wall directly inside the door looking for the light switch and, when I do, I illuminate the space in front of us. Shay drops his arms from my waist and pushes around me, taking small steps to the middle of the room. I keep my gaze on him as he stands in silence for a few moments, glancing around at everything that's entombed in dust, before falling to his knees.

Sadness fills my chest and I make my way to him, silently sitting down beside him while he feels everything he needs to. Thinking about how long it's been since he's been here and seen everything that was *theirs* is heartbreaking. My hand makes circles along his back as silent sobs shake his body. I wish I could take all of this pain away from him.

I look around the room myself and instantly figure out the type of female Darcy had been.

Along the longest wall of the room is a massive bookshelf filled with books of every genre. Opposite that, there's a large, canopied bed pushed against the wall, the pale pink sheets unmade and strewn halfway on the floor.

There are plants of all kinds lining the window sills and hanging in the window frames themselves, all dried and dead from years of neglect. I wish I could've seen them when they were lively and blooming. This room must've been incredible.

Shay stands suddenly and walks over to the desk that's built into the book-shelf wall. He slowly scans the tidy surface and picks up a framed photo. I walk up behind him and look at the photo of Tate, Darcy, and himself all covered in dirt standing in the garden out front. Even under all the dirt, I can tell that Darcy was breathtaking. The first thing I notice are her icy blue eyes framed by dark, long lashes. Her white-blonde hair is cut short, and ends just below her chin, and the color is such a beautiful contrast against her tan skin.

"She's beautiful," I say quietly, but I can't tear my eyes from the photo. Something about her seems so familiar, and I swear I know her. I rack my brain for any hint but I come up empty. But, fuck, does she look familiar.

"She was. She looked just like my mother," he says solemnly, his thumb brushing over the glass of the picture frame, clearing the dust. "She tried so hard to get Tate and I interested in gardening. She wanted there to be something that all three of us could do together. But our seeds never grew more than a sprout. And the ones that did get bigger, died after a few days. She thought it was hilarious." He huffs out a small laugh and puts the photo back down.

"I wish I could've met her," I say quietly. The corner of his mouth twitches and he drops his head.

"I don't know if I can come back in this room again."

I intertwine my fingers with his. "You don't have to. We can keep it off limits." He nods and walks towards the door, pulling me with him. "I claimed your parents' old room for us if that's alright with you. Figured it was better for us to be in there rather than Wes or Desmond."

"Good idea, love." He takes one more look around before switching off the lights and leaving Darcy's room, locking the door behind us. "Did you want to see my old room? I assume that's what you were initially looking for."

"Yes, please," I say, following him to the end of the hall. I point to the huge hole in the top of his door, just as Marlene said. "I need to know the backstory to this first."

"I took a sword to it the night they killed my parents," he says with a laugh. But I can feel the pain behind it and know all too well that being here again is stirring up a lot of old memories, and not necessarily good ones. He turns my face to him and kisses my lips lightly. "Go ahead and take a look around, I'm going to get a shower."

"Anything you'd like to warn me about before I go in?" I give him a mischievous grin, biting my lower lip.

"I'm surprised you haven't realized yet that I am a very simple male." He starts to walk towards our room, but stops, turning back to me with a grin plastered on his face. "Although, I will be very impressed if you can find my old journal." He winks at me before closing the double doors, leaving me to explore his old room.

Challenge accepted.

I open the broken door and step into the dark room, palming the wall for the light switch. When I finally find it, a warm glow fills the room, and I'm a little shocked when I look around.

He's not kidding about being a simple male. I don't know what I expected but, for some reason, this wasn't it. His room barely has anything in it, save for a few pieces of furniture. The walls are painted a deep green, with dark hardwood floors, and a small white rug in the center. There's a large, four poster bed that's fully made with black silk sheets and black pillows. Opposite the bed is a bookcase with a few books lining the shelves, but it pales in comparison to Darcy's. Right next to the shelves is a small leather couch with a single bookmarked book thrown on the cushion.

I pick up the discarded book titled, *The History of the Sacred City*, and thumb to the page marked. It's labeled, simply, *Aris*. Not much of a surprise considering it was him and Tate's goal to serve her. I put the book back down and walk to the balcony door. I switch on the outdoor light and peer out to find a chair, a trashcan filled with empty beer bottles, and an overflowing ashtray.

To say I'm disappointed so far is an understatement.

I switch the outdoor light off and continue to snoop around, not finding anything interesting. Instead, I find exactly what I thought I would; dressers filled with folded clothes, notebooks and writing tools in the desk, and miscellaneous items in the nightstands.

"If I were a journal, where the hell would I be?" I stand in the middle of the bare room with my hands on my hips. He said he'd be impressed with me if I could find it, so it's not going to be somewhere easy. But there aren't many places for it to be hidden in here.

I look back to the bookcase and sit on the floor in front of it. I scan the titles, all seemingly normal, until one in particular catches my eye. One I *know* doesn't belong on Shay's shelves. "*Advanced Gardening Tips and Tricks*? Yeah right, Shay. Advanced, my ass." I pull the book out and, sure enough, something is rattling around inside. I lay it on the floor and open the cover, finding that the entire book is hollowed out just enough for a leather-bound journal to be hidden inside.

I bite my lip and try to control the massive grin that's spreading across my face as I lift it out of the fake book. I hop up from the floor and waltz out of his room with a cocky grin on my face, heading back to the master suite to show him my victory. As I get closer to Tate's room, I can hear muffled groans and thumping coming from behind the partially closed door.

I shutter at the realization and pull the door shut fully as I pass, hearing Marlene and Tate giggle in response. I roll my eyes and enter mine and Shay's room, shutting the door behind me and staring down at the journal in my hands. I push away from the doors and bring my gaze up to see Shay standing in front of me, dripping wet with only a towel wrapped around his hips.

"Holy shit," I blurt out, the words escaping my mouth before I have a chance to stop them. I slowly drag my gaze up his tattooed chest, a mural of flowers and snakes roaming from side to side, making my way to his face. His own gaze is completely locked on my every move, with the dark haze settling over his eyes.

I lift the journal in front of me, raising an eyebrow. "Found it."

"So, you did," he growls. He takes one step towards me, and backs me into the closed doors. He wets his lips slightly, his eyes roaming up and down my own body, just as I did to him. "Would you like your reward?"

Chills travel down the entirety of my body as I nod. I let the journal drop to the floor next to me as he closes the distance between us, until there isn't much more than a few centimeters of space. He braces his left hand on the door beside me, and locks the door with the other. As he drags his right hand up to mirror the other, he grazes my backside gently and grabs hold of the bottom of my shirt as he passes. I lift my arms up subconsciously as he pulls it off of me, exposing the lacy black bra I have on underneath.

Shay glances down at my barely covered chest and lets out a small groan, his breathing beginning to get heavier as he glances down. I follow his gaze down and immediately see the proof of his desire underneath the towel he barely has on.

I bite my lower lip and let out a shaky breath, my voice barely a whisper, but there is fire in my eyes and I know he sees it. "What're you waiting for?"

The desire in his eyes darkens and, with my invitation, he wraps his arm around my waist and pulls me right up against him, his arousal settling right between my thighs. His hand travels to the top of my leggings, his thumb teasing the band of them, and I'm internally screaming for him to just take them off.

I open my mouth to tell him exactly that but, before I can even get a word out, Shay has his lips on mine, kissing me greedily. I wrap my arms around his neck so I'm even closer to him and return the kiss with even more greed.

He lifts me off the ground and carries me to the small couch in the corner of the room, leaving a trail of clothing on the floor behind us.

***

Twenty minutes later, we're still undressed and far too lazy to get up to retrieve our clothes. But I'm more than happy to stay exactly like this for the rest of the day if I could have it my way. He has me tucked into his side, his thumb stroking lazily on my shoulder, and our legs are intertwined towards the bottom of the couch. We're both so at peace and comfortable, and this type of intimacy is so unfamiliar to me. It feels so natural but, at the same time, so scary that I can be so at ease with someone like this.

I close my eyes, trying to soak up every bit of this that I can, when a brief zap of pain hits my finger. An all too familiar pain. I bring my right hand up in front of me and notice something above my soulbond band. Sitting right above it is a thinner, silver band, now.

"What does this one mean?" I ask, turning my hand around as I examine it.

Shay lifts his head and opens his eyes to look at my hand, holding his own up next to mine. The same thin silver band is on his hand, too, right above his gold band. "It's another part of fae culture. The gold one shows up when there's a mutual acceptance of the bond. But the silver one appears when an accepted bond is...solidified."

"Solidified? Like having sex?"

"Exactly," he says roughly, intertwining our fingers and kissing me on the forehead, placing our joined hands on his chest. He lets his head fall back down on the pillow and closes his eyes again.

"Can I tell you something?"

"Of course you can, love. Absolutely anything," he says, eyes still closed.

I sit up and bring my knees to my chest. I take a deep, shuddering breath and I can feel my anxiety start to spike inside me. I want to tell him this truth I'm so ashamed of, but it's something I've never told anyone. And even though he's my soulbond, it doesn't make admitting my secret any easier.

Shay sits up next to me when I start to tremble. He wraps me up in his arms and holds me tightly, trying to ease the rising panic. "Hey, what's going on? Talk to me."

I glance up at the ceiling, trying to blink away the tears that are threatening to drip out of my eyes and take another shaky breath. "You know how I told you about how Luke blackmailed me into the relationship we had?" His brows come together slightly and I can see the moment the confusion settles over his features.

"Yeah. He knew you were fae and was going to tell everyone if you didn't agree to be with him, I remember."

"Well, that's not all that happened. The night that he confessed he knew my secret, he took advantage of me." I feel more hot tears forming and, when I close my eyes, they spill down my cheeks and don't stop. "I was drunk and could barely move or speak, and he used that to have his way with me. To finally get what he wanted."

"Lianna..." Shay starts. I hold up my hand to stop him because I know that if he tries to console me in any way right now, I will completely lose it and have a breakdown. And I can't do that. I need to get this out.

"He told me that after we were together, he knew we were meant to be. And, every time he wanted sex after that, I would secretly get so drunk so I wouldn't feel it or remember any of it." I can't stop the tears now. They're coming full force, like me finally telling my secret was what I needed to break the dam holding back the hot, angry tears. Shay tightens his grip on me and pulls me fully in his lap, and tucks my head underneath his chin. I can feel his jaw grinding with anger and I know it's not because I kept it from him but, instead, because he can't get revenge on Luke for what he did to me.

"I will kill him one day. Mark my words," he growls. And I fully believe he will, and that I'll do nothing to stop him. I'll even help him.

"I just needed you to know that. After leaving him, I know I took a while to admit my feelings for you. I was so afraid that he ruined me. But you make me feel like everything in the world is good and I...I just needed you to know." My vision is completely blurred, so I can't tell what Shay is doing or feeling, but I get nervous when he doesn't respond right away. He just continues to hold me, idly rubbing my back and pressing kisses to my temple.

"Are you alright?" he finally gets out, genuine concern in his tone.

"I wasn't, but it's getting easier."

"Thank you for telling me." He cups my chin and kisses me lightly on the lips. It's not a needy kiss filled with desire or lust, but a kiss filled with understanding and love.

He lifts me from his lap and stands, pulling me up with him before leaving my side momentarily to head over to his bag next to the dresser. He pulls out two large shirts and a pair of boxers. He dresses himself first, pulling the shirt over his head and stepping into the boxers, and then comes back over to me. He helps me put the other large shirt over my head and it hangs loosely on me, fitting me like a nightgown. He holds out my underwear next and watches me like a hawk as I pull them up my legs.

I go to move towards him but he shakes his head and gently pushes me down to sit on the couch. Then, he kneels in front of me and rolls on a pair of knitted socks that I don't recognize. But I've never been more comfortable in my entire life, so I'm not complaining. Plus, I love being tended to like this by him. It makes me feel so safe and wanted.

He grabs my hand once more and walks us over to the bed that's now made with brand new sheets. The ones that had been his parents are now gone.

"What happened to the other sheets?"

"I figured we shouldn't sleep on dirty, old sheets that have been sitting under dust for almost three centuries," he says. He notes the distress on my face and holds my cheeks in his hands. "Don't worry, love. I folded them and put them away in a safe spot. Thank you for preserving that bit of them for me."

"Anything for you," I say gently as a huge yawn escapes me. I rub at my eyes and, suddenly, it feels like the entire day is weighing me down. It all feels too much to bear and I impatiently watch as Shay pulls down the sheets just enough for us to get in.

"Ready to sleep?" he asks sarcastically as another yawn comes out of me. I nod my head lazily and Shay scoops me up in his arms and tucks me into the bed, covering me with the fluffy comforter he put on top. He makes his way to the other side of the bed and crawls in beside me. After kissing me a few times and making sure the tears are no longer falling, he pulls me into his body with my back against his chest, holding me tightly and nuzzling himself into my neck.

And it all feels so fucking *right*.

It feels like this is what I've been waiting for my entire life. I've only ever laid next to Luke and it was always in fear or sadness or drunk off my ass. But, now? Getting to share this bed with Shay, my soulbond, and feeling this peace and serenity and happiness is something I know will take me some time to get used to. Not just sleeping beside him, but also feeling this overwhelming sense that he genuinely cares for me and will do anything to protect me.

I let his heavy breathing relax me as he holds me close, and the rise and fall of his chest lulls me to sleep. I hold out my hand to admire the bands that now adorn my right ring finger. The gold and silver bands look like they're a part of my skin, almost like tattoos but more...magical.

I can't help the smile that spreads across my face as I intertwine my fingers with Shay's. The movement makes him pull me in tighter, his breath warming the back of my neck as he sleeps peacefully.

With one final kiss to his hand, I let my eyes flutter shut and sleep more soundly than I ever have in my entire life.

Chapter 20

A frozen breeze washes over me in the morning, bringing chills down my entire body and ruining a very peaceful sleep. I probably should've closed that damn window before we fell asleep last night. I pull the blankets over me more as I violently shiver and move closer to Shay's side in hopes of stealing some of his body heat. But the bed next to me is cold and empty. I jolt upright and look around the room, finding I'm all alone. I sleepily throw the blankets off me with a huff and slip on the robe that's hanging on the bedpost and a pair of cotton pants. I rub the sleep from my eyes, already annoyed that I woke up to an empty bed, and hear faint grunting coming from outside.

I stride to the open window that overlooks the front yard and stick my head out to delicate snow flurries that are falling from the gray sky. I roll my eyes, already sick and tired of the damn snow that doesn't want to stop. But when I look around, the fenced in yard is empty. I shut the window and turn on my heels, making my way to the balcony doors towards the back of the bedroom.

When I make it to the doors, I slip on a pair of fur lined slippers Shay said once belonged to Darcy, savoring the way the fur feels against my toes. Before I even open the doors, I can clearly hear the sound of clanging iron and more male grunting. I step out onto the balcony and peer over the railing into the backyard to see Shay and Desmond sparring, while Tate and Wes sit in chairs on the patio cheering them on.

"Keep your head up, Shay! He's going to knock you on your ass if you don't pay attention!" Tate's laughing from the side as Shay throws up his middle finger at him, while simultaneously trying to hold back Desmond from, quite literally, knocking him on his ass.

I lean on the railing, watching as sweat glistens on his forehead and his gray shirt sticks to his drenched torso. Something about him being hot and sweaty makes me shiver and I can't tear my gaze from him.

"I don't know why Tate's laughing. Desmond had him on the ground after three minutes." I turn around to see Marlene standing in the doorway sipping on a cup of coffee, holding another out for me. "Quite a few times, actually."

"I'm impressed, nonetheless."

"I'd like to see Tate and Shay go up against Desmond as a team. I have a feeling he could take them both down easily." She nods down towards Wes, now leaning back in his chair laughing. "It's nice to hear him laughing again. Do you think he'll finally agree to start training with them? I know he and Shay talked about a training schedule, but from what Tate says, they don't think he'll actually commit to it."

"I think being away from Peham and everyone there has helped him cope a little. And I think he will, eventually. Plus, if he knows it'll give him a chance to protect you and I, there's a bigger chance he'll agree. He won't enjoy it but, he'll do it."

"If he knows it'll help *you*, then he'll do it," she mumbles. I sense the slightest bit of resentment in her tone, and I know she thinks she's hiding it from me well. But, she's never been that good at hiding her true feelings from me.

"What's that supposed to mean?" I don't even try to disguise my own disbelief that she would even say something so insane, but she just rolls her eyes at me.

"Oh, come on, Li. You're like two peas in a pod. I'm not saying he doesn't love me or wouldn't protect me, but you've always been his top priority. And, if it comes down to it, he'll save you over me," she says, and when I open my mouth to object, she cuts me off. "Don't even try to argue it. You know it's the truth and that's fine. I've come to live with it because I would do the same thing for you."

I hate admitting that she's right, but I know she is and it's not fair. Every bit of trouble I've ever gotten into, Wes has always been there to help without question. I know he'll agree to learn how to fight for me, and that bit of knowledge warms my heart. But it also tears it apart a little knowing that he won't do it to help himself or Marlene, but just for me.

"I never thanked you." I nudge her slightly with my elbow to keep my hands wrapped around the warm coffee mug, grabbing her attention from Tate, who's back in the ring with Desmond.

"You don't have to thank me, it's just coffee. I figured making a whole pot made more sense than just one cup for me."

"I didn't mean the coffee." She turns her entire body towards me as I try to get the words out. But it's harder than I thought it'd be. "For all of...this." I gesture to everything around me. "I know how hard it was to leave mom and dad behind and, as mad as I was at first, I'm so thankful that both of you are by my side. You could've stayed home and stayed safe, but you both chose me. I don't know how I would've done this without you."

She puts her mug down on the small table behind her and gently pries my own mug from my hands, placing it next to hers. "You're my big sister. Where you go, I go. Always and forever." She pulls me into a tight embrace and, since I have a good eight inches on her, her head tucks into my chest as I wrap my arms around her neck.

When I pull away, Tate and Desmond are still sparring, but Shay's eyes are locked on mine, beaming up at me. Wes notices his gaze soon after and turns his whole body towards the two of us. When he sees Marlene and I, he grins from ear to ear, aggressively waving at us and nearly falling off the edge of his chair. His smile is infectious and, as glad as I am that he seems happier, it also makes me so damn nervous. It's the sudden rush of happiness in him that makes me worry slightly. Like we're all just waiting for the other shoe to drop and see him get pulled down with it.

"Come on down! We were just talking about coming in for breakfast!" he calls up to us. Marlene takes my hand and pulls my head down to her level, leaning her forehead against mine. The way we're standing reminds me so much of the first memory I walked into, seeing Flora and Amara do this exact thing. And a calming warmth spreads throughout my body at the familiarity of it.

"They're going to be highly disappointed when they realize all we have is dry cereal and fruit." I follow her into my room and shake my head at her when she walks from the room belly-laughing. She nearly bumps into a very sweaty Shay on her way out, making her laugh even harder.

"Should I even ask what that was about?" Shay asks, closing the door behind him.

"She thinks our lack of food is comedic," I explain, patting the side of his face and planting a small kiss on his lips. He palms my hips and tries to pull me closer, but I gently push him away from me before he gets too in the moment. "I'm sorry, but you smell so bad. I'm begging you to take a long shower before leaving this room again."

Shay lifts his arm and smells himself, disgust washing over him. "Can't argue with you on that." He raises an eyebrow and locks eyes with me, the darkness consuming his own. "Would you care to join me?"

"As long as I get to pick the soap we use," I tease, a smile blossoming over my face as I bite my lower lip. Shay tugs at the tie of my robe and lets it fall to the ground. He makes quick work of tugging off my sleep shirt and the cotton pants I slipped on, before nearly ripping my underwear off so I'm standing in front of him completely naked.

"I suppose that's fine if it means you'll be in the shower with me, wet and soapy." The smile on my face grows even bigger when he throws me over his shoulder and strolls into the bathroom. He turns the nozzles with one hand, keeping his other firmly planted on my ass, and brings us both into the oversized shower.

***

When Shay and I finally finish our shower and get dressed for the day, we make our way downstairs where everyone else is already finished eating their breakfast. Marlene is washing dishes and peering out the window above the sink at the males out back sparring again when Shay and I walk in.

Her head barely turns at the sound of our steps. "You'll be lucky if they left behind any food at all for you two."

"Thank you, Marlene. It all looks delicious," Shay says to my sister. She dries her hands off and waves him away.

"It's cereal and fruit, Shay. There's not much to it. Now, when I get some real ingredients? Then you'll be impressed." She replaces the dish towel on the edge of the sink and walks to the back door. "I'll be out back watching Tate get all hot and sweaty if you need me."

"Lovely," Shay says between bites. I start laughing to myself at the thought of this morning. "What's so funny?"

"Nothing. It's just...I was doing the same exact thing this morning when you were training. I was practically drooling over your sweaty body," I say, keeping my attention on peeling the orange I plucked from the fruit bowl. I shrug. "Just reliving it, I suppose."

"I like when you drool over me," he says leaning over to kiss me and stealing the slice of orange I just peeled. "So, what would you like to do today? Any requests?"

My jaw practically drops, and I feel so stupid. But in all the years I was with Luke, it was never up to me to decide what we got to do. He always chose everything and, for the most part, it was always something only he wanted to do. It's nice being considered, now. "I know it's cold, but I'd love to see the rest of the village. We might be able to find some useful stuff lying around."

"If that's what you want to do, then of course we can explore, my love." My heart warms at the pet name and I smile into my coffee mug as Shay continues to talk, so unaware of what his words do to me. "I would love to show you where I grew up. It's been a while since I've been here and I'm curious to see what has become of it."

I finish my breakfast and hop off the kitchen stool. "I'm ready whenever you are. I just need to grab my backpack, and we can go."

"I've got a few more bites left. By the time you get back down here, I'll be ready."

"You're wonderful, I'll be right down." I stand on my toes and kiss him again as I pass, taking the stairs two at a time as I bolt to our room, beaming with excitement on getting to see the lands I've only ever read about.

I dump out the contents of my backpack onto the bed, wanting it empty for anything we might come across. I'm about to head back downstairs when I stop myself and grab one of my holsters, buckling it around my thigh.

Better safe than sorry.

I stroll down the stairs and find Shay waiting for me at the bottom, holding my jacket, a hat, and a pair of gloves. His eyes roam over me, his eyes landing on the daggers strapped to my thigh, and he arches a brow at me.

"What?" I demand.

"Are the daggers really necessary? It's just a walk through the village."

"Yeah. A village you haven't been to in how many years? You have no idea what we might come across and I am *not* taking any chances." I let him help me put my jacket on before slipping the fur lined gloves on and tugging the wool hat onto my braided hair. I stroll to the front door and swing it open, pausing before I step into the cold February morning. "And, if you were smart, you'd follow my lead and bring your own weapons."

I walk out and hear Shay grunt behind me. A moment later I hear the sound of iron on leather, and I know that his own short swords are sheathed in his hip holsters. He catches up to me and stares straight ahead as we walk side by side, trying his best to avoid my stare. "I don't want to hear it, love."

I throw up my hands. "Hear what? I wasn't going to say *anything*." I stay silent, staring straight ahead just like him. "But, if I *was* going to say something, I would say that I was glad you came to your senses and listened to me."

I know I hit a nerve when he pushes me into a pile of snow right outside the fence. Shay stops and bends forward with his hands on his knees and laughing hard as I lay sprawled on my back. I give him the middle finger behind his back and force myself to stand, wiping melting snow off my pants. Great, now I'm going to be cold *and* damp.

"You think you're so funny, don't you?" I sneer at him as I stomp by. He wipes a tear from his eye and comes to my side, clasping his hand in mine as we walk.

"Won't happen again, I am *very* sorry." Sarcasm laces his every word, and I can tell he's holding back a laugh that really wants to be set free. I roll my eyes at him and look around Oldbrook. Now that we've had a chance to breathe and settle in, it's nice being able to take in this place fully.

"So, give me the run-down of this place," I say, keeping my eyes ahead of me. He exhales and tightens his grip on my hand.

"Shal used to be an extremely vibrant and lively city. After the Sacred City, it was the largest city in the Angel Fae territories. There are the two villages, Redhelm and Oldbrook, and then the main city. The cottages in Redhelm were for the majority of the Angel Fae, while the manors here were for the wealthy and those that held important jobs in Shal, or even in the Sacred City."

"Was your family wealthy or of high importance? Or both?" I ask. Shay kicks a loose stone on the ground as we head towards the town square. There's a beautiful fountain in the middle, with a statue of a winged female spewing water. We stop just underneath one of the massive wings and sit for a moment on the benches surrounding the fountain. My gaze travels to the face of the statue, taking in every detail. She looks so familiar. Why the hell does everyone look so fucking familiar?

I push away my racing thoughts and focus my attention back on Shay. "My parents didn't start out wealthy. Before I was born, they lived in Eldolon. There's not much left of it today but it was basically the slums of the Angel Fae territories. The entire city is tucked away in the mountains on the edge of the Quartz Wall. Its land is connected to fae territory, so there was a lot of violence that went on. Most that lived there never got the chance to leave."

"How did your parents get out?"

"Mom was extremely gifted. She possessed magic that Aris had great need for and so she pulled them out of Eldolon herself and moved them here. Aris took care of everything for awhile but, once mom started to gain her wealth, they could afford everything they ever wanted."

"What sort of powers did she have, exactly?" It must've been something insanely useful for the Queen to personally bring them to one of the wealthiest places in the Angel Fae territories.

"She was a Resurrector," he says nonchalantly.

"A what? You're making it sound like she could bring someone back to life and that's something no one should be able to do."

"She could," he goes on. Why is he being so relaxed about this? She had a power that shouldn't be allowed. I know I don't know much about magic, but that seems like the type of power that could be extremely dangerous. Shay rubs his hands down his face and continues."There were only two Resurrector's in her time and the other was imprisoned by King Ashton. My mother was extremely valuable, and Aris kept her power hidden from everyone."

"That was probably a really smart idea," I start. "Have there been any other Resurrector's since your mom?"

"Not that I'm aware of, just her and the other one that was imprisoned." He pulls his hood up over his head and brings me closer to him. "Shortly after they moved here, they had me. Mom was terrified to have more, though. She had a hard birth, and it almost killed her. It took 25 years before they tried again and had Darcy."

"I think I would've really admired your mom."

"You remind me of her a little." He gives me a small smile. "She had a heart of gold but was extremely bold and headstrong, just like you."

My heart clenches at his words. Everything I've heard him say about his mother makes me see just how much he admired her, and being compared to her feels like such a huge honor. He stands up next to me and drags me with him. I follow his pace as he starts to walk away from the town square. I quick glance back at the fountain, my eyes locking on the female's face again. I just can't stop looking at her.

"Who is that statue made after?" I question.

"That would be Kaleen, one of the original Omni Goddesses. There are statues of her sisters, too. Odessa is in Redhelm and Lucienne is in the main city."

"And Aislinn...?"

"There isn't one of her. Her sisters refused to acknowledge her existence after she was killed, too stuck in their own grief, essentially erasing her from history," he says. I trail behind him as we enter into Redhelm, observing the smaller cottages as we pass by them. Each one is made up of gray stone and the significantly smaller yards are fenced in with short, light brown wooden fences. Compared to the manor Shay grew up in, it feels like a completely different world here.

I stop in front of a cottage that looks to be a little less destroyed than the others. The yard seems maintained and there's no sense of abandonment here. I cock my head to the side and furrow my brows at the neatness of it all.

"You have a very keen sense, sweetheart." Shay nods to the pristine house. "That was Desmond's house when I lived here and, I'm assuming, where he's been holed up all these years."

I walk past him up the small walkway to the front door and grab onto the doorknob tightly, but I don't turn it. It's not like me to want to intrude on someone's home, but there's something in there that's calling me. I felt it the minute we stepped foot into Redhelm the other day and it won't stop. The pulling sensation is just getting stronger.

I scan the door with my eyes, the structure humming viciously under my hand, and I let go of the doorknob. *Another day*, I tell myself.

I *will* come back. Something in there wants me to find it.

And I will.

Chapter 21

We make our way down the row of homes, searching each one for any-thing that'll be useful to us. So far, we have some clothes and a lot of spices, but other than that, we've found nothing salvageable.

We get to the last house in the village, a small cottage painted light yellow with garden boxes filling the front yard. The front gate is attached by only one hinge, so Shay gently opens it as wide as he can without it falling off completely. Though all of these homes are abandoned, Shay has treated each one with the respect that their occupants will return to them one day.

Even though they never will.

As we approach the door, my core tightens and it feels like my stomach is filled with rocks. Unlike Desmond's house that urged me to come in, something here is drenching me in despair. I suddenly have no desire whatsoever to go in. I stand frozen in place on the front step, unable to bring myself to open the door.

Behind me, Shay puts his hand around my waist and stands at my side. "Are you okay?"

"Something about this place is giving me a bad feeling." And it's only getting worse. I swallow down the nausea that starts to creep up my throat and my head is swimming with far too much anxiety.

"We can skip this one, love. We've found all that we can, I think," he urges, starting to turn me from the house. But, as much as I want to leave, there's another feeling battling my urge to leave, and begging me to go inside.

"No, no I-I want to go in," I insist. He looks at me for a moment and sighs, walking ahead of me to open the door for us. The stagnant, dusty air hits us instantly, just like in all the other homes. But this feels different. It feels haunted, almost. The conflicting emotions rage at each other the longer I stand unmoving in the doorway, so I make a decision and walk into the front hall, seeing nothing but a once beautiful home.

After Shay is barely convinced that I'm fine, we break off and complete our tasks. Just like in every other home, he searches the living room and cellar, while I explore the kitchen and the bedrooms. I start to feel a little better as I rummage through the kitchen, finding an entire drawer of unopened seed packets for all sorts of fruits and vegetables.

The other drawers don't have much, but once my bag is filled with their contents, I head for the next room. Just on the other side of the kitchen wall is a short staircase that leads to the top floor. I start the short climb while being mindful of any loose boards that might give way to my weight. I do a quick search of the bathroom and come up completely empty. Not even a lousy bar of soap.

At the other homes, at least I had more than just seed packers, and I'm starting to feel defeated. Hopefully Shay is finding a bit more.

I sigh and start walking to what I deem to be the master bedroom. The white wooden door is massive and there are beautiful carvings across the frame. I push it open and step into the large room, the sun casting beautiful, dusty shadows on the floor.

There's not much in here other than a canopied bed, two dressers, a large mirror, and a small bench settled at the end of the bed. I rummage through the dressers and find some male and female clothes that are in great condition, so I shove them into my bag. Now we're getting somewhere.

I turn to leave, certain I've found all I can in here, when a faint tinkling noise stops me in my tracks, and the sinking feeling in my gut returns with a vengeance. I look around, unsure where the sound could've even come from in the barely furnished room, when I notice the mirror again. There's something off about that mirror.

I cautiously walk over to the wall it's leaned up against and peer behind it, gasping audibly to myself. I grab the edge of it and try my hardest to move it over, cursing how heavy it is as I struggle with it. I walk around to the other side and push it the rest of the way to reveal a dark brown, wooden door with a silver handle hidden behind it. I step back in disbelief and stare.

What the hell is going on here?

The door is a little under six feet tall, and the silver handle is almost fully tarnished. I doesn't look like there's a lock on it, but after years of neglect, who knows how easily it'll open for me.

"Please, please don't be stuck," I whisper to myself.

I grasp the handle and turn it carefully and, thank the Goddesses, the door opens with ease. I duck inside a small room with pink wallpaper peeling off the walls. The design on it is almost completely faded off, but I can see hints of bunnies and ducks. There's a single oval window on the back wall with one long crack running through it from top to bottom. Sheer white curtains hang in front of it, letting in the faintest bit of sunlight that makes a rainbow through the broken glass.

As I look around at all that inhabits the room, it dawns on me what this family used it for. In the furthest corner, there's a beautiful wooden rocking chair sitting next to a small bookshelf that's filled with children's books. A wicker basket is sitting on the ground beside it overflowing with stuffed animals and blankets.

The white cradle against the back wall is so tiny and there's a pink blanket filled with holes draped over the edge. A small wind chime hangs from the ceiling above the cradle, and the slight breeze from the broken window moves the pieces together, creating a little tune.

The source of the tinkling.

Someone's precious, baby girl once slept in this sweet room, and I can only imagine the amount of love there was here. But why was it hidden behind the oversized mirror? It makes no sense.

I step over to the cradle and gently rub the edge of the blanket between my fingers. Even with all the holes, it's still the softest cotton blanket I've ever touched. I smile at the thought of a small fae baby being swaddled in this soft material and, when I let it drop from my grasp, it falls to the floor. I bend down to pick it up and, when I go to replace it in the cradle, I freeze at what the fallen blanket has revealed. I clutch the blanket in my fist and a devastating scream erupts from deep in my chest. So many emotions fly through me; fear, grief, horror, shock.

Oh, Goddesses, I'm going to throw up.

Shay finds me in a matter of seconds sitting against the wall on the opposite side of the room with my head between my knees. He drops to the floor next to me and tries to pry my head up so I'll look at him.

"What is it, sweetheart?" he asks, his voice shaking. I drag my gaze up to his and try to get words out. But I can't. "Lianna, what happened?" I shake my head and point to the cradle I crawled away from. He rises from where we're sitting and walks over to it cautiously, stumbling back as he gets a look at what I saw.

Bones.

The smallest bones I've ever laid eyes on. A small, dirty bonnet is still tied around her head, and she's swaddled tightly in a darker pink blanket.

I'm not naive. I'm well aware of how high the death toll is for those who lived here. But I didn't expect to actually *see* this. It's the most heart wrenching thing I've ever stumbled across and the sight of her will be branded in my memory forever. A part of me wants to just walk away from her, to try not to pry about who she was so I don't have to feel more grief for her too short life. But the other part of me needs to know more about this poor soul; who she was, why she was hidden, who her parents were, why she was left behind. I want to know it all.

"I wish I knew who she was," I say quietly from my spot on the floor. I lay my cheek on my knees and stare at the wall but, when Shay doesn't respond to me, I prop my chin up and look over at him. He's frozen in place, his entire body shaking, with tears streaming down his face. My heart rate quickens and I jump to my feet, getting to his side in an instant. "Shay?"

"I didn't know," he mumbles. The sadness in his voice is heart-breaking and it feels deep and dark, but I can't place why.

"Didn't know what? Do you know who she was?" I pry. He turns to me slightly and holds out a picture frame to me. I didn't even notice him carrying it when he came in to console me. I take it from him and look at the family in the photo.

The dark-skinned male is very plain looking. He has brown hair and haunting forest green eyes that almost get lost in the darkness of his skin. The female, on the other hand, is stunning. Unlike the male, she's clearly Angel Fae. She has dusky blue eyes that match the wings draped behind them and long brown hair that's pin straight hanging in front of her chest. Her skin isn't dark like the male, but more olive toned, like mine.

But it's the infant they're holding that pulls at my heartstrings. She's the sweetest thing. Her skin reminds me of caramel and her eyes are a stunning gray blue, so wide and full of sparkle. She has a mop of dark brown hair on top of her head that curls right at the nape of her neck. She's squeezing tightly onto her mother's finger, and both parents are beaming with smiles from ear to ear.

"Calum," Shay says, pointing to the male and then to the female. "And Vanessa."

"You...you knew them?"

Shay nods and takes the photo back from me. "They were my best friends growing up. Before Darcy, before Tate. They were always there." He glances back at the cradle. "I never knew they had a daughter."

"We shouldn't have come in here. Why didn't you stop me?" Guilt courses through me. We're only in here because I wanted to explore. We should've listened to my initial feeling and left this place alone.

"I didn't know this was their house," he starts, shaking his head. "When King Ashton first came into power, they got scared because Vanessa was Angel Fae. We all knew how threatened he was of the race, and they knew they wouldn't stand a chance. So, they left to seek shelter in Perpet and, last I heard, they were welcomed in the safe haven. They never should've come back here."

"Where's Perpet?" I ask, feeling stupid for even having to ask that question, proving the limited knowledge I have of the Fae realm.

"It's an island off the coast of the Angel Fae territories. Technically, it's part of the Angel Fae territories but, being an isolated island, the Quartz Wall was never erected around it. It was abandoned for a while and then some fae rebels that didn't agree with Ashton took up residence there. There's a hidden shelter that the fae created to keep Angel Fae safe but it was destroyed by King Ashton.

The shelter, the town, and everyone that resided there, no matter if they were Angel Fae or not."

"That's awful. *He* was awful."

"Yeah..." Shay says solemnly, holding out something else to me.

"What's this?" I ask, taking a sealed envelope from him. Shock fills my body when I see that it's addressed to him at the manor, but looks as if it has been returned to the sender multiple times.

"I found it in the living room, in a pile of their old mail. After I realized who wrote it, I just couldn't bring myself to open it. I don't think I'm ready."

"I can hold onto it for you, if you want. And, whenever you're ready, you'll know it's safe." He nods, so I tuck the envelope into my bag gently, careful not to bend the delicate paper. I plant a kiss on his cheek and wipe away the tears staining his cheeks. There's so much old pain surfacing and I can see the toll it's taking on him. I wish I could take it all away.

"Thank you," he says flatly, unable to tear his gaze from the cradle. I place my hand on his cheek and pull his stare from the bones to me. When his gaze locks with mine, I give him a small smile and continue to brush my thumb along his cheek. He clears his throat and turns to face me. "Are you ready to go?"

"More than ever. Lead the way, handsome." He walks by me and kisses the top of my head, and I follow as we head for the door. Standing in the doorway, I take once last look around the room and that feeling churns in my gut again, pulling me to the cradle. I walk slowly over to it and look at the infants bones once more. She never had a fucking chance.

"Are you coming, love?" Shay calls from the stairwell.

"Be right there," I yell. And, without thinking, I gently wrap the bones in the blanket and tightly tie a knot at the top, keeping them secure within the material. I slowly lift her from the cradle, making sure my knot and the tattered blanket hold. I lay her in my arms like I'm cradling a newborn, and glance around the room for something to keep her safe in.

My eyes land on a satchel that's hanging on the back of the door the perfect size for her. I grab it from the hook and tuck her in slowly, making sure not to disturb the bones too much. I secure it across my chest and leave the room, leaving the door open behind me and leaving the mirror where I pulled it away. That room has been hidden and closed for too long.

And, now, it's no longer a tomb.

Chapter 22

By late afternoon, Shay and I are on our way back to the manor. My backpack is filled with spice jars, clothing, some stationary, and seed packets. We were able to salvage far more than I thought we would when we started this morning.

The satchel with the infants bones is still strapped across my chest, much to Shay's discomfort. At first he argued that I was disrupting her soul by taking her. But when I told him my plans to give her a proper burial, he couldn't find any reason to argue any longer.

"I don't know why I expected everything to seem more disheveled. But every house looked like the family just disappeared into thin air." My shoulders get heavier as I speak. I can't stop thinking about the small yellow home that's been a tomb for Goddesses know how long.

"They basically did. After the first round of executions where my parents died, everyone thought it was over. No one was prepared for the day the King came for the rest of them."

My heart sinks even more imagining the turn of events these families went through. They went lived their lives like usual, going about their day like normal, until it wasn't.

"Shay, I have questions." He looks down at me for a second before dragging his eyes back to the road. He nods slightly, his cue that I can start with the questions that are brewing in my mind. "How long was Calum and Vanessa's baby in that cradle before she died?"

Though I have limited knowledge of the fae, and even less about the Angel Fae, what I do know is that they're not immortal. From what I've read, fae can live to be 2,000 years old, and I think Shay told me the Angel Fae live to be double, maybe? But, even with the long lifespan, being so young and starved, she couldn't have lasted long.

"Not long. She was small enough to be a few months old, so I would say, at most, a week," he says, grief lacing his every word.

"I thought knowing that would make me feel better." I kick a rock in my path. "It didn't."

"Can you do me a favor?" He stops as the words leave his mouth and walks behind me. I pause as he takes the letter from its safe spot in my backpack and makes his way back to my side. He gently removes the other bag from around my chest, handing me the letter in return.

"You want me to read it?" I ask, watching him secure the bag of bones across his own chest. He nods and I carefully unseal the old letter, making sure to open it with care so I don't rip it. The parchment is now a yellow-brown color after years of sitting around and decaying, while the lines where it has been folded blur some of the words written there.

I start to scan the dainty cursive writing, when Shay stops me a few words in. "Out loud, if you don't mind." I clear my throat and start to read:

Shay,

I debated for days about writing you. With how we left things before, I didn't know if you'd want to hear from me. I wasn't sure where to send this, so I prayed to the Goddesses that sending it to your parents house was the best choice. I don't even know if you still live there or if any of you are still in Shal. I just pray you're still alive.

I'm sure you thought we were dead. You knew the last place we went was Perpet, but we left just before Ashton destroyed it and everyone there. We went to Meobith for a while but, Calum and I decided to come back to Shal when we heard that Aris was killed. We felt like we had no choice, no matter how dangerous it might be. We should've written you the minute we came back, but we didn't and I'm sorry.

I had a baby, Shay. I'm a mom and you were the first one I wanted to tell. No matter how far we've drifted over the years, you're my best friend. We should've been there with you.

Her name is Aminta, it means savior. She saved Calum and I, gave us hope that we will make it through King Ashton's reign.

There weren't many Angel Fae in Perpet. A lot less than we expected. And here, in Shal, there are even less. Maybe ten families, at most. But they've been whispering, Shay. They think the King is going to finish what he started with the Angel Fae. We have a plan to escape, though. Someone here says there's a secret island in the Northwest and we're going to try to find it.

I know this letter is all over the place, and trust me, there's so much more I want to tell you. But, for now, I just need you to know the important stuff. One day we will see each other again and we'll catch up on everything that has happened since we've been apart.

I want you to know that Aminta's nursery is hidden in our bedroom, just behind the mirror. If the King does what they're all talking about, she will be hidden away there until you can get to her, just in case we don't make it.

But I'm hopeful. We'll be fine.

We love you, Shay. We can't wait for you to meet your goddaughter.

Vanessa

I carefully tuck the letter back in the envelope and hold it out to Shay. He takes it with shaking hands and, when I look at him, I expect to see tears running down his face, just like my own. Instead, his face is like stone. Emotionless and blank. I can't read him for once and it's incredibly unsettling.

"Are you alright?" I whisper. He doesn't answer me, just continues to stare blankly ahead, his eyes dark and dull. I arch my head in front of him more, trying to pull him from his stupor. And maybe he didn't hear me. I clear my throat and try again, projecting my voice to more than a whisper this time. "Shay, talk to me. Are you alright?"

Though he doesn't look at me, I can see the anger, grief, and guilt completely take over his face in an expression I've never seen on him. I've watched him experience all of these emotions before, but this is different. And it scares me. "Yeah, fine," he bites out. His tone is rough and sharp, like it's being dragged through glass shards.

"They could've gotten out, Shay," I say, trying to comfort him and change the course of his thoughts. Because I know what he's thinking. That they're gone, just like Aminta. Just like his parents. Just like Darcy. I reach out and touch his arm, and he flinches under my touch.

"Just leave it," he mutters.

"We should try to find this island she talked about. What if there are more Angel Fae there? What if *they're* there?" I say, trying not to let myself hope too much. But Shay skids to a stop and yanks his arm from under my light grasp. He whips around to face me and I watch as his jaw tightens just looking at me.

"They're fucking dead, Lianna. There's no *secret island*. Vanessa always believed others for the dumbest shit and this was just another dumb thing she believed. They were here and Ashton raided it AGAIN. They're *fucking* dead. Get that through your thick skull. I've lost everyone that matters, except for Tate," he grits out through his teeth. Hurt sears through me at his words and I flinch, not expecting to be shoved aside or spoken to this way. I should've kept my fucking mouth shut.

I swallow the lump in my throat as Shay storms off towards the house, leaving me behind. I let out a shuddering breath and sit down on the bench facing the statue of Kaleen, noticing how close to home we are.

I look up at Kaleen, silently praying to her to keep Shay safe from his own mind. I don't even know if that's something she can do. But what I saw on Shay's face was unkind and unforgiving. I can't ignore that.

A strong wind sweeps through the town square and settles at the base of the statue, pushing aside debris and snow in its wake. When it subsides, there's a group of markings on the ground in front of me that definitely weren't there before.

Right?

I study the symbols etched into the stone and pull out a small notebook and pen I found in one of the homes we searched. I write down the symbols exactly as I see them, in the exact same pattern as they are on the ground.

I shut the notebook and replace it in my bag, rising from the bench to head back to the house. But when I turn in the direction of the manor, I come face to face with a cloaked figure in the road, blocking my path. There's a mess of tangled auburn hair peeking from beneath the hood, hanging in knots down to her waist. Her hollow eye sockets glow a muted sapphire blue and, when she opens her mouth in a wide grin, her teeth are yellowed and rotting, but the canines are elongated and pointed.

I open my mouth to call for Shay, but he's too far away now. The figure brings a withered finger to her lips to quiet me, then points to the ground around me.

The markings.

"Do you know these?" I ask. She tilts her head to the side and stares right at me.

"I know *you*, Omni," she whispers into the air, barely loud enough for me to hear. But the wind carries it to my ear and I hear it clear as day. I take a small step towards her but, as I do, she takes an equally small step backwards and shakes her head side to side. "We will meet one day. Not today."

"What are these markings?" I ask again, her cryptic answers confusing me more than I already am.

"Runes of the Goddesses, from another world," she hisses. I want to ask her more, like what they mean exactly or what they do. But as the words leave her mouth, she vanishes into thin air, leaving a black feather on the ground where she once stood.

The runes around me float away in a swirl of black dust, and the wind removes all traces of what was etched on the ground around me. I scoop up the feather the wind missed and tuck it into my backpack, my pace quickening as I head to the house. This has all been too much for one day and I'm ready for some food and sleep.

And hopefully Shay to let me in.

***

The first thing I notice when I get back to the house is the bag of Aminta's bones leaning against the fence with a small shovel laid beside them. I almost forgot that Shay still had the bag when he walked away from me.

Inside, I can hear everyone talking and utensils scraping on plates as they all devour dinner. My stomach growls but, looking down at the bag carrying Aminta, all I want to do is focus solely on her.

I pick up the bag and shovel and make my way around to the backyard. The setting sun is casting hues of red and orange across the snowy yard, illuminating the large willow tree at the edge of the property.

When I reach the shadows of the willow, I drop my backpack to the ground and gently place the other one down on the cold, damp grass. The branches of the tree have kept this part of the yard snow-free, but it's frozen solid. I immediately get to work digging, hoping to make the hole deep enough so that her remains won't ever be disturbed by anyone.

It's taking all of my energy to get my shovel more than a few inches into the frozen ground and I'm struggling to make any hole at all. I curse loudly to myself and drop the shovel, leaving against the trunk of the tree. I hear faint footsteps coming from the direction of the house, but I don't even bother to look up because I already know who it is, and no one needs my attention more than Aminta right now.

I go back to digging, bringing the smallest pile of dirt with me, when Shay's voice sounds from behind me. "Want some help?" I pause my pathetic digging and stand with my back to him.

"As long as you don't push me away again," I say as my chest tightens once more.

He puts something at the base of the tree and comes to stand in front of me, just on the other side of the small hole. "I won't, I'm so sorry for earlier. I know you were just trying to help and I thought I needed space to make the pain about them subside, but I was wrong. I feel so much guilt over Aminta. If I had just gotten that damn letter, she would still be alive."

I let my shovel drop to the ground and step over the hole so I'm right in front of him. "You are not to blame for her death. There was nothing you could've done. You had no idea she was there or that Calum and Vanessa came back to Shal. I don't blame you for getting overwhelmed about this situation, anyone would have. But your words hurt me, even if they weren't intentional."

"I know. And I was wrong. In so many ways. Because I don't just have Tate anymore. Now, I have you," he says, reaching out to grab my hand. I open my mouth to add on some names, but he beats me to it. "Yes, and Desmond, Marlene, and Wes. But you're the most important to me. I didn't mean to hurt you, love."

"Thank you." I smile softly at him and look to the tree, finally noticing what he brought with him. Leaning against the roots is a small wooden box, not even two feet in length. "What's that?"

"I didn't have time to make an actual casket fro her, but I figured it'd be more respectful to put her in this instead of just the blanket." He bends down to pick it up and holds it out to me. It looks like it was once a decorative box from the house, and he used a knife to carve an "A" into the top. In fact, I'm almost certain that's what he did.

"That was really thoughtful of you," I say, giving him an appreciative smile. I pull Aminta's bones from the bag and reposition the blanket around her before settling her into the small makeshift casket. Tears fill my eyes as I close the lid and place it on the ground next to the shallow hole. "I'm always here for you, Shay. Just don't shut me out, please."

Shay drops to the ground next to me and wraps me in an engulfing hug with his chin resting on the top of my head. "I don't know what Goddess I need to thank for giving you to me, but I will thank every single one for the rest of my life."

I pull my head from underneath his chin, and see matching tears gleaming in his eyes. I take his face in my numb hands and bring his head to mine, letting our foreheads rest against each other.

We stay there for a moment until I'm shivering, reminding me why we're out here in the first place. I pull away from him and pass him the shovel. "I hope you were serious about helping me because I truly can't get through this frozen dirt."

He chuckles and takes the shovel from me, making quick work of digging a much deeper hole than the one I attempted. *Show off.* He drops the shovel and, together, we lower Aminta's tiny casket into the hole before covering it back up with dirt. Shay grabs my hands when we finish, rubbing them between his to bring some warmth back into them. "Thank you for doing this, sweetheart."

"For you, anything." I kiss his knuckles in response and stand, wiping the snow from my soaked through pants. "Come on, let's head in. I could use a very hot bath if you'd like to join me."

The smile that blooms on Shay's face is filled with pure lust as he scoops me into his arms, set on carrying me the entire way the house. I can't find a single reason to protest it because his body is a furnace and it's warming my cold limbs instantaneously. "Now, that, is a wonderful idea."

Chapter 23

Everyone is sitting around a small bonfire drinking something out of mugs as we approach the patio. The smell of the smoke is comforting and, even though I know there's no way it is, I'm hoping they have hot chocolate in those mugs.

One minute, they're all smiling at us and, in a split second, I watch as Tate's entire face drops, tossing Marlene off his lap and pushing her towards the house. Shay puts me down in a heartbeat and whirls around to where Tate is looking, pushing me protectively behind him, but not letting me leave his side. In the distance, not far from the willow that Shay and I just left, is a group of four tall figures staring directly at us.

From here, I can't see much detail. But what I can see is that all four of them are carrying a weapon of some sort. A hot panic starts to course through my body at the sight of them. *Where the fuck did they come from?*

It doesn't take long for the fire to start within me and I glance down at myself to see that red mist seeping from my body, just like it did in the cottage. The iridescence of my skin throbs slightly, almost like it's warning me of the impending danger.

"Shay," I whisper from behind him, grabbing his forearm tightly. "You need to tell me how to control this. Quickly."

He looks back at me and the mist surrounding us, his eyes darting up and down my body. "I don't know how to control it," he admits.

My face drops at his confession. What does he mean he doesn't know how? He's Angel Fae, he's supposed to know. My tone shifts to anger immediately.

"What the fuck do you mean, Shay? You're supposed to be able to help me with this! And, right now, I need help. I need it controlled!"

"I know, I fucked up," he says shakily. "I know *of* your powers, not how to wield them. I thought I could understand them over time and help you, but I haven't had enough time. I'm so sorry, I don't know what to do." I slowly back away from him, my eyes darting to the figures slowly stalking towards us.

"Lianna, I know how to control it." A voice comes from the house just behind me. I whip my head around to see Desmond staring at me, his weapon drawn from its sheath.

"Help me," I plead. He moves closer to me, as Shay turns back around to face whoever is coming for us, and talks lowly.

"Concentrate. Concentrate on *where* you feel the mist running through your body and search for the connection. Grab onto it and follow it to the heart of the power. When you find it, will it to your every beck and call. *You* are in control. Once you have full control over it, imagine that the mists are a part of you, like an extension of your limbs," Desmond instructs, but I shake my head quickly, anxiety settling in. He puts his sword back in its sheath and grasps my shoulder. You can do it."

I squeeze my eyes shut and let my mind wander along the mists running through me, like I'm floating along a river. I will my mind to find the heart of it just like he said and, like I summoned it, a small ball of red light appears, calling to me.

I concentrate deeply on that small ball and will the mists to sink into the earth and reappear around the figures stalking towards us. When I open my eyes, they're engulfed by the red mist, surrounding them like a cage, and slowly sucking the air out of the confined space.

The corners of my mouth turn slightly, and my concentration dips momentarily. And that moment is just enough for the mists to disobey me and sink back into the ground, setting them free. The three in the front of the group look up at me with feral, vengeful grins on their faces, and break out in a sprint towards us. The fourth stays behind, though, and stares right at me.

Shay instantly throws up his gray fog shield, slowing them down slightly, giving Tate time to gather knives in his hands and throw them at the sprinting males.

"Let's go!" Wes appears behind me and pulls me towards the house where Marlene is waiting. Desmond leads us to the door and stands next to it with his sword at the ready, making sure we make it in safely.

The door slams shut behind us, and I watch in horror as Shay, Tate, and Desmond begin to fight the males. From where I stand, I can see them a bit clearer than before and almost instantly notice the lack of pointed ears on each one.

They're all human.

Shay, Tate, and Desmond should be able to take them down with ease yet, the human males aren't faltering and are fighting equally as hard. And, as the light hits each of them, I can see a faint shimmer running along their skin.

It almost reminds me of...magic.

I'm so focused on the fight that I almost miss the slight movement coming from the side of the yard. I drag my gaze from the males to the movement and see the fourth figure making their way closer to the house. They're wearing a hooded cloak, but long blonde hair hangs out of each side.

A female?

She's moving slowly, trying not to catch anyone's attention as she inches closer. I quickly open the door and slip outside before my siblings can pull me back in, as I keep my eyes trained on the female creeping along the perimeter.

I will my power to come to the surface but, no matter how much I try, it won't come. I'm too distracted by what's going on to get hold of my powers. I should've stayed inside with my siblings because now I'm heading right towards this female without any magic. She's no more than ten feet from me now and, with her head raised and looking right at me, my stomach flips.

My knees give out under me, and I fall to the ground hard. Tears fall from my eyes rapidly, and I feel my skin start to glow, as huge bouts of fear and magic run through me. I vaguely hear Shay calling out to me but when I open my eyes, I'm surrounded by a wall of rocks. Rocks that somehow my magic pulled from the ground, keeping me protected inside. *Safe*. I let out a breath of relief, but suck it right back in when I hear a scoff from behind me.

I turn slowly and, standing in the middle of my shield with me, is Luke.

***

"Oh, sweet little Lianna. You didn't think you could get rid of me that easily, did you?" Luke prowls towards me and I inch myself closer and closer to the wall of stone. My heart feels like it's going to beat right out of my chest, and my rising anxiety and magic isn't helping whatsoever. I feel so out of control.

"What the hell do you want?" My voice cracks and my eyes burn with tears. I know what he'll do to me if I give him the chance. But I'm frozen in fear and I can't even get up to defend myself.

"What do *I* want?" He's mere inches from me now. "I *want* you. You're mine, Lianna. Not this disgusting fae's plaything. No, no. You belong to me."

I try to command my magic to let the stones fall, but they won't budge. I *feel* the magic coursing through me, but it's my fear that's commanding my magic to keep the walls up to shield me from harm. But what it doesn't realize is that the harm is inside with me.

I feel like the helpless version of me I've worked so hard to erase. All of the training and workouts I've done, useless. I try to scream, but my voice is gone. But, not gone from too much use. Gone, like something has taken it from me. For a split second, I think my mind is playing tricks on me as he stands in front of me, shimmering a dark green. There's no way this is possible.

He sees me eyeing his shimmer and sinister smile spreads across his face. "You know, when I first found out about this power, it disgusted me. But then, I realized it could make me...*better*. It's not much but, I feel a hell of a lot stronger with it."

My stomach drops even further. I really wanted my theory to be wrong. I've never wanted to be wrong more in my entire life. "Where the hell did you get *magic*, Luke?" I need answers. This shouldn't be possible. I know his family, there's no way one of them is secretly fae.

"Well, apparently, my parents have been hiding quite a lot from me," he says, tilting his head to the side when my brows furrow. He clicks his tongue on his teeth and keeps going. "Oh, don't tell me you had no idea my parents, the people you loved more than me, were pretending to be humans just like you?" I must be hallucinating because I swear he just said his parents are fae.

"What the hell are you talking about?" None of this makes sense. I need to get out of this stone shield. I can hear Shay and Desmond on the other side screaming for me, pounding on the stone. But they can't get through. Of course they can't. My magic is too strong right now.

"Not too long ago, someone delivered something to me. A history book from the Fae realm filled with family trees. And wouldn't you know, both of my parents are fae. You know, my dad was actually something called an Angel Fae, and his heritage passed a little bit of magic to me. They told me everything...once their lives were at stake."

"No!" I scream, fear rising at the thought of him killing his own parents, two people that are so dear to me. But, the look on his face gives it all away. There's no way he ever would've let them live.

"Oh, yes. And right after I put a hole in my poor mothers head, dad told me all about how they fled here centuries ago to escape being killed. Changed their appearances every so years and moved around a lot, changed their names, too. I killed him before he could tell me more about his disgusting past." He gets right in front of me now, lowering his voice slightly. "See, this magic is pretty damn useful. With just a simple touch and some concentration, I can give anyone just a drop of magic, fae or human."

My blood begins to boil. I will kill him, if it's the last thing I do. He doesn't *deserve* to live. Not after what he did to his parents, not for what he's done to me for years, and certainly not for what he's *going* to do to me. "You will not survive this, Luke. Mark my words."

"Maybe not. But, I'm going to have a lot of fun with this for a little," he says with a malicious grin. And, with one swift movement, he has his forearm over my neck and restricts me from most of my air. He uses his other hand to yank both of our pants down as he positions himself on top of me. I try to scream, and Goddesses know I fucking scream loud, but it doesn't matter. No one can hear me, and my magic is draining. My fear is forcing it to work overtime and I can't stop it. I can't fight him off.

The only thing I can do position myself differently so that his arm constricts my neck harder, depriving me of the air I need to stay conscious. Because, fuck, I need to be unconscious before he does this to me.

"If I can't have you all to myself, then I will *take* what I can *whenever* I can," he whispers in my ear as he pushes himself into me, just as I drift away into sweet oblivion.

***

I feel my magic slow and retreat back to my core. *Thank the Goddesses.* My body starts to substantially cool from the inferno the magic creates and I feel calmer almost instantly. But the calm doesn't last long when I remember where the hell I am.

I jolt upright way too quickly and my head starts to swim. How long was I out for? My head whips around but Luke is nowhere in sight and my stone walls are slowly settling back into the ground where I pulled them from. But, as the stones disappear, something completely different appears. In a clear circle around where the stones once were, is a blazing ring of fire, burning from the ground.

Everyone is standing around the clear break in the snow, staring at me in a panic. They're all standing a few feet away, keeping a safe distance from the flames, all except for Shay. He's right up against the flames, using his ice powers to cool the base of the fires but it does nothing.

I take a deep breath and push the last bit of remaining magic to the core, willing the flames to subside. They listen and die down quickly, and my nerves settle a little knowing I have control over my magic again.

The second there's enough space between the dying flames, Shay is through to me and wrapping me in his arms. "Oh, fuck, you're okay."

But I'm far from okay. Violated and terrified and destroyed, yes. But definitely not okay. "Yeah, I'm okay. I'll be fine," I lie. "But, where did the three males go?"

"The minute your stone wall went up, they disappeared into thin air," Desmond says behind Shay. "It was creepy, too. One of them muttered something about taking what's theirs and then gave us a crooked smile."

"There was a fourth one," I admit. Fuck, I don't want them to know but they need to. They need to know to look out for him. I search for my siblings behind Shay and Desmond, finding them just at the edge of the patio with Tate. I've never seen them look so worried. And this will just worry them more.

"Where?" Shay asks gently, stroking my face with the back of his hand, his eyes trailing to my neck, which I'm sure is completely bruised. "*Where*, Lianna?"

"Inside my shield. I don't know how he got in before the stones went up, but I couldn't control my magic. I was too afraid and I think that fear was taking over." I don't think I can do this. I should've kept my damn mouth shut. No, they have to be warned. "It was Luke."

PART THREE

The Undoing

Chapter 24

April 21st

"Again."

Shay commands me from where he stands at the edge of the makeshift training rink in the backyard. We've been at this for almost two hours now, and sweat is dripping off every inch of me. Now that winter has passed and spring is here, the mornings just get increasingly warmer and I find myself missing the snow some days.

I bend over with my hands on wobbly knees as I try to take in a deep enough breath to ease the burning in my lungs. I raise my head to look at Shay and roll my eyes as he stands there with his arms crossed, very impatiently waiting for me to go through the routine for the last and hundredth time today.

Not a day goes by that I don't think about Luke since he was trapped with me in my shield of stones.

When I told Shay that it was Luke that got away, him and Desmond went out searching. Tate stayed behind with my siblings and I, just in case he came back. Thankfully, he didn't.

They were gone through the night and didn't come back until early morning. But, they came up with nothing. No Luke, not even the other three that were with him. There's no trace of them anywhere. Desmond is continuing to do early perimeter checks every morning even though there's no sign any form of life is here except for us. But, he says it keeps him busy and keeps his mind of off the terrifying type of magic I told them Luke has.

I haven't told anyone what happened inside the shield. I need to keep that horrifying moment a secret. Just another fucked up thing Luke has done to me. But I don't want to have to tell anyone.

Even Shay.

Since that day, though, they've been adamant about getting my magic in check. It's proven to be too wild and unpredictable, and I need to get it under control before I accidentally hurt someone I don't intend to. Or before my emotions run too wild again and I can't control it.

I stand and get back into my starting stance as Shay hurls magic and punches alike at me in random patterns.

Punch. *Duck.*

Kick. *Block.*

Magic. *Shield, counterattack.*

Holy shit, I'm tired. My muscles have never hurt this badly. He's pushing me, and I know it. But I also know it's because he's scared for me.

"Can we please be done, Shay? I'm fucking exhausted," I whine.

"After you show me your progress with your powers, we can go inside and I'll run you a nice, hot bath." He grins slyly at me, dragging his gaze up and down my body as he drawls out his words. "Maybe you'll earn a massage, too."

"Now that's some motivation," I say, pushing my growing arousal to the side. Not the time to act on that, but definitely once his hands are on me. I dive into my magic and my skin starts to glow iridescent as I touch my power core. We've been focusing on my elemental powers the most, after it proved to be the wildest of my gifts and, of course, the last of my Triad.

Memory-walker, Feeler, Elementalist. All three of my Triad.

I imagine the ground underneath me rising, lifting me a few feet into the air on a stone platform. Next, I conjure water to build a wall around me and to fill the hole in the ground where my stone platform once resided.

When I open my eyes, I look around and see Shay below me beaming with pride. I'm almost ten feet in the air with the elements surrounding me. Everything I pictured in my mind came to life around me.

I grin from ear to ear at my seemingly flawless display of elemental magic. So flawless that I decide to take it a step further. I've been practicing little bits of this magic by myself, sometimes when I'm alone in the shower, and Shay has yet to see it. I squeeze my eyes shut and will the wall of water around me to freeze solid. I only open my eyes when the wind blows a cold breeze in my face. I sigh with relief as it cools my hot face and blows away the sweat droplets.

The wall of water is now a solid sheet of ice.

"Alright, showoff, put the ground back and let's go inside," Shay calls up to me. I giggle and force it all back and I'm safely on the ground in less than a minute.

I stride over to Shay and he pulls me into a tight embrace once I'm in arms reach of him. "How'd I do?" I sigh into him and let him guide us back to the house.

"It's clear you've been practicing. I haven't seen those little tricks yet." His arm is draped over my shoulder lazily, the heat of the day and sparring with me weighing down on him almost as much as it is for me.

"I didn't want to show you until I knew I could do it perfectly." I glance up at him. Beads of sweat start to gather at his hair line and a slight heat rash is creeping up the back of his neck. But that's not what catches my attention. It's the slight mood shift that anyone else would've missed. He looks nervous. His throat bobs and his jaw keeps clenching and unclenching. I tilt my head and nudge his side. "Alright, out with it."

He looks down at me, the minuscule expression disappearing the moment I open my mouth. "Out with what, exactly?" He gives me a playful grin, attempting to distract me from whatever's on his mind. Yeah, not going to work.

"Seriously? Shay, I saw the look on your face. Say what you need to say and get it over with." I jab at him with my pointer finger, and he swats me away quickly. And then he sucks in a long breath and tilts his head back to the sky.

"Something happened to you that day. I know Luke was in there with you, but you won't give us any other details. I've let it go for a while but it's still there, love. You were terrified for days after and, even now, you look over your shoulder so often I'm afraid you're going to break your neck."

I look down at the ground. I didn't realize my fear has become so readable. My stomach twists in knots as I remember the day in excruciating detail, and I'm so scared to admit the truth to him. Not that I think he'll be mad at me or look at me differently. But because I couldn't *stop him*. I keep my eyes fixed straight ahead as we walk, absentmindedly kicking a rock with each step.

"I have no idea how he found me, Shay. When I saw him, I panicked. I threw up my shields and I was so certain I was safe," I pause and take a deep breath. "But I wasn't. And he did the same shit he always does to me, just because he can." I'm choking back tears now, begging them not to fall. I don't want this moment to drag me back down when I've worked so hard to get to where I am now. But when I look at Shay, he's looking at me with unrelenting fury etched on his entire face.

"He fucking touched you?" Shay hisses. I nod and blink back more hot tears, but it's no use once he smothers me with a body consuming hug, crushing me into his heaving chest. His breathing is so erratic, I'm almost certain he's about to have a panic attack. And then I feel his tears hitting my forehead, and my own dam bursts and tears flood from my eyes with no stopping.

"I'll be okay, I will be," I assure him, even though I'm not so sure that's the truth. I keep telling myself I'll be fine, but what if I'm not this time?

"I'm so sorry. I'm so *fucking* sorry. I should've been by your side protecting you from that monster. I promised I would kill him once, and now I will swear it to you. I will hunt him down and give him the death he deserves."

"No one could've guessed that he would find me or that something like this would've happened," I say into his chest, still tightly in his grasp. He pulls away and puts his damp forehead against mine, as thin lines of tears trail down his dirty cheeks. "Shay, I am the luckiest female alive to get to have you by my side."

"*We* are lucky, don't get it twisted. The Goddesses knew we needed each other, and I will be by your side for the rest of our days." He lightly kisses my lips and pulls me back into him, letting his chin rest on the top of my sweaty head. "Come on, I promised you a hot bath and a massage."

***

When I walk out of the bathroom almost forty minutes later, I feel like a whole new version of myself. I still feel incredibly loose from the massage Shay gave me, and all of the knots that ran through my muscles have disappeared. My skin and hair smell like lavender, all thanks to the soap he picked out for me. I tried to go with an orange scent today but wouldn't let me. Apparently, I smell like flowers and that's all I should ever smell like, according to him. I mean, it makes sense. Even back in Peham, I used lavender scented everything.

I find Shay standing at the mirrored dresser, pulling clothes out of it for me to change into. I come up behind him and wrap my arms around his middle, squeezing tightly. One of his hands abandons his search for clothes and wraps around my forearm, stroking the skin gently.

He pulls out a loose pair of cotton pants and a pale pink t-shirt, turning in my grasp once he finds a bra and underwear in the drawer. He holds out the bundle of clothes to me, kissing my brow as he walks behind me to help clasp my bra. The intimate gesture makes me blush, even though he has seen all of it before, most recently before *and* during my massage. But, I've never had someone care for me this deeply and it's a nice feeling to be taken care of for such small things.

"Thanks," I whisper, watching his every move as he takes a seat on the edge of the bed right in front of me, leaning back on his hands. He grins and arches his own brow as I stare. I let out a small chuckle. "What?"

"Just admiring the view. Please, continue," he says smiling. I slowly continue to dress as his eyes roam my entire body, the clothed and unclothed parts alike. When I finish, I turn back to the mirror and look around for my brush. When I find it, I make to start detangling my hair when I catch a glimpse of my reflection, staring a minute too long at myself.

In the time I've spent away from home, I haven't filed my canines down once. Now, they end in delicate points, making my features appear sharper and stronger. When I look up slightly, I blissfully hope that my ears have regained some point to them, too, just like my teeth. But, that's just a dream, and my disfigured ears still poke out from my wet hair, the scars shining in the late afternoon sun.

Shay stands slowly from the bed and walks up behind me, wrapping his arms around my neck and shoulder, showering the scars with kisses. I shudder and wiggle out of his grip, quickly brushing the hair over my ears to conceal them once more with tears welling in my eyes.

"Lianna..." he starts. I throw the brush down on the floor and rub at my eyes with my palms as I turn my back to the stupid, fucking mirror. *Goddesses, I hate mirrors.*

"It's not fair," I say at last, my voice breaking a bit. "It was all taken from me."

"No, it's not fair," he says, grasping my shoulders to spin me back around to face the damn mirror again. I avert my gaze and tilt my head down so I don't have to look at my reflection, but he's not having that. He gently takes my chin in his hand and guides my face back to the mirror. Then, he frees my ears from their hair prison.

"What're you doing?" I blurt out, my eyes going wild with panic. I go to shove them back when he grabs hold of my wrists and puts them at my side.

"You're allowed to mourn the loss of your heritage. You're allowed to be angry for having to hide your true self all these years." He runs a thumb along my cheek. "But you also need to realize that you are more beautiful than you believe, regardless of the scars you bear. *Especially* with the scars you bear."

"But-" I start.

"And you don't have to hide. Not here. *Never* here," he finishes.

With his words, I can't control the wave of emotions that barrel through me. I feel it all course through me, side by side with my Feeler magic. My tears flow freely, and I feel my magic start to overflow. No, shit, not now. Please not now. I try to remember everything Desmond has taught me about keeping my emotions in control.

I just need to breathe.

"Open your eyes, love," Shay whispers in my ear. I have no energy to fight it, so I obey and look at myself in the mirror. I gasp and stumble backwards slightly. I can't believe I've never actually seen how I shine when my magic courses through me.

It's otherworldly.

Every inch of me is glowing iridescent, like a sparkling rainbow took place of my skin. On top of that, a faint red mist is hovering over my body, like a magical second skin, controlled and contained tightly along every curve.

"Wow," I whisper, reaching up to graze my face. The iridescence ripples with each touch, like I'm dipping my finger into a pool of water. I make eye contact with Shay through the mirror. "Was my mom like this? My grandmother?"

"No. You're the first Omni in centuries, so there hasn't been someone like you since the Goddesses. I'm going to assume it's the reason the darkness wants you and why your mom took you out of the Fae realm." He leans his cheek against the side of my head. "And now that you've learned to control your Triad, your lesser magic might start to show."

"Great, more magic."

"Hey, it's a good thing, love." He turns me to face him, bringing my hands to his lips, kissing my glowing palms. "Besides, with it being lesser magic, it won't be as strong as your Triad. Not until you train those powers and make them stronger."

"Great, more *training*," I mock. I earn a light slap to my bicep, which pulls a small laugh from me.

"You've got this. I'll be here every step of the way. So will Weston, and Marlene, and Tate, and Desmond. Anything we can do to help you, we will." He kisses me first on my nose, then my forehead, both cheeks, and finally my lips. Then, he turns be back towards the mirror and, this time, I don't want to turn away.

It's the first time I've ever felt truly beautiful in my own skin.

Chapter 25

My siblings and I sit around the kitchen table in complete silence the next morning. We're all anxious for the conversation that's bound to happen when Shay and Tate get back from Desmond's house. The plan is to get moving from Shal to Odrera but, because it's been some time since Shay and Tate have been here, they decided letting Desmond plan out our route for us is most likely the best idea.

It's a little after eight in the morning and, after a night of tossing and turning, I'm utterly exhausted. My limbs feel so heavy and I know that if I put my head down on this table, I'd fall asleep in an instant. Shay was long gone from our bed when I woke up this morning, and I've been impatient for him to get back the minute I opened my eyes.

At this point, we've been in Shal for almost three months training. Which means that we have less than four months until my father expects me in Odrera with him. Meanwhile, the darkness and all that comes with it continues to rage beyond the Quartz Wall. We still have no idea the extent of it, but we expect that a lot of the Fae realm is shrouded in darkness.

I push the remainder of my food around on my plate, the little bit I've already eaten sitting like a rock in my stomach. I don't have much of an appetite right now, but I know I'll need the energy, so I'm forcing myself.

"We knew this day was going to come sooner or later," Wes says, breaking the silence. "I know we'd all like to stay here, but we've already used up half of our time and we still have a lot to get done."

The knot in my stomach tightens knowing my time is getting closer to an end. Even though I've been consistently training, being here with everyone has felt like a little break from everything. I'm at ease, too, with my siblings here, knowing they're safe. I look up at Wes, glancing between him and my sister. "I still think you both should stay here. You'd be so much safer at the manor."

"And we already told you that's not happening, so you need to stop," Marlene snaps. She closes her eyes and takes a deep breath. "Sorry. But we've made it very clear that we are with you no matter what."

"Fine," I mumble, pushing my food around more. "But just because I'm agreeing doesn't mean I like it."

The front door swings open, bringing in a rush of warm air and the smell of spring in bloom with it. A moment later, Shay and Tate file into the dining room and head directly to their seats, not even bothering to fix themselves plates of food. The plans must be stressing them both out if neither one of them is getting something to eat. *Well, shit.* Desmond, however, follows closely behind and beelines it to the kitchen, filling a plate high with food. Guess stress doesn't affect his appetite.

I immediately feel a rush of relief as soon as Shay is sitting next to me, even with the intense anxiousness radiating from him. He plants a kiss on my head as he sits down and plucks an uneaten sausage off my plate and into his mouth. It may not be a full meal, but at least he's eating *something*.

"So? What plan did you come up with that took three hours?" Marlene asks, impatience lacing her every word.

"We're going to Meobith," Desmond's voice booms from the archway separating the kitchen and the dining room. My head whips to his, and Wes and Marlene do the same. That can't be right.

"What?" I ask, shocked. "We're supposed to be going to Odrera. That's where my father is expecting us."

"Yeah, I know, but-" Desmond starts, but I'm quick to cut him off.

"And what's going to happen when I don't show up there when his timeline comes to an end?"

"The other cities need us more. Odrera is safe for now and they can defend themselves. The other cities can't," Desmond informs us. "As for Drake, he can try all he wants to find you, but we'll keep you safe until *we're* ready to give you up." He holds my gaze for a moment, and something like agony flashes over his face before it disappears completely.

"There might be information about Flora in Meobith, too," Shay says quietly to me. Hope rises in me and I look at him with wide eyes.

"But my father said he hasn't been able to find her. Wouldn't you think he would've searched every city for his wife? His soulbond?"

Desmond scoffs loudly from the archway, still refusing to sit down. I glare at him with my brows furrowed. How dare he fucking *scoff* at the bond my parents have. "*His* soulbond. Fucking bullshit."

"Oh, I'm sorry. Do you not think he's done all he can to find her?" I demand, irritation rising in me. My skin heats but I ignore it, demanding it to go away. Desmond pushes away from the wall and leans on the edge of the wooden table, getting up to my face.

"No. I don't think he would have," Desmond blurts out. He lets out a breath and backs away from me a few inches. His face reddens just slightly and his eye closes, as he curses under his breath.

"Why the hell not?" I spit out the question in defense, but there's something about Desmond's demeanor that has me second guessing my emotions. The regret is clear as day on his face and, now, he's avoiding eye contact with me. And I don't know what to think.

His jaw clenches as his eye flutters open, darting between the five of us staring at him, waiting for an answer. His gaze finally lands on me, and his face softens ever so slightly. And, for the first time since I met him, I really look at him, and notice each feature a little more clearly.

His remaining eye is a gleaming silver, nearly the same shade as the flecks of silver in my own eyes. His skin is a deep olive tone and there are various scars strewn about, including the scar over his missing eye and down his arm.

But, really looking at him, I notice that our features seem to match one another. Same eye shape, same arch in our feathered brows, semi-full lips, and dark freckles pepper our faces.

And, as I scan him, I see it. On his right hand, there's a thin, gold soulbond band with the silver one right on top of it. Now, the way he scoffed at me calling my father Flora's soulbond makes a little more sense. He was disgusted with the thought. My eyes widen at the theory running through my mind and I try to push it away, but it all makes too much sense.

Why Desmond and I share so many physical attributes.

Why he seemed so distraught and broken in the memory I saw when my mother appeared with me in the tower.

Why Landon looks so familiar, like looking in a mirror.

Why Desmond almost cried when he first saw me and discovered who I am.

I look at him, anger and curiosity and *grief* building inside me. I feel my magic surge again and, this time, I let it come barely to the surface instead of pushing it away, hoping it'll keep me grounded.

"Who the hell are you?" I choke out, tears welling and blurring my vision. Confused eyes lock onto me, everyone completely unaware of the conclusion I've come to. But he knows. Goddesses, does he know I've figured it out.

He's staring straight into my eyes, a multitude of emotions flashing over his face. But the one that stands out the most, the one that was on his face the minute he saw me that I couldn't place, is love.

Desmond grinds out the words he's clearly trying to keep inside. "Drake was *never* your mothers soulbond. I was. Am."

Every head whips from me to Desmond at his confession. "Tell me," I plead, ignoring everyone's stares. He's dancing around the truth, telling every other detail instead of what I'm dying to know. But I don't stop him. I need answers and this is more than I've ever known about my mother.

"Flora and I grew up together. We were born just a few months apart and, since my father was one of Dennin's guards at the time, we lived side-by-side in the castle. Our soulbond tether snapped into place when we turned sixteen."

"I always saw how close you two were but, soulbonds? How the hell didn't I know? I was Flora's guard," Shay spits out. He's so tense beside me, like he's angry at himself for never noticing. I lean into his side a little and I feel him ease up the second our bodies touch.

"We didn't start romantically seeing each other until the soulbond connection was made. And by that time, you already left for Eldolon," Desmond explains.

"How did she meet Drake?" my voice quivers as I speak, doing all that I can to keep calm and not spiral into a full blown breakdown. But it's so damn hard. Especially with all of this information being thrown at me.

"Honestly, we don't really know where he came from. He isn't Angel Fae, but we saw him around our territories often. We officially met him when we caught him trying to sneak through the Quartz Wall." Desmond sits down in his chair and leans his elbow on the table, rubbing his face with his hand. "The three of us became friends after some time, and met at the wall almost daily. I didn't realize it at first, but he was doing everything in his power to steal her from me."

"How did you know?" I'm on the edge of my seat now, absorbing every single word that comes from him.

"He only ever wanted to spend time with me when she was there and, once she left, he left, too. I eventually saw through the whole act, but she didn't. My interest in spending time with him lessened and I made it clear to Flora that he was trying to take her from me, which only angered her. We only ever argued over Drake, and he saw it as an opportunity. One day he tricked her into thinking I said something cruel, something that was far from the truth. She believed his lie and he got what he wanted. She left me. She went right to Drake, even knowing the soulbond connection between us would always be there."

"Keep going, please," I urge.

Desmond sighs and stands again, walking to look out the window, but keeping his back to us. "Flora and I were together for 84 years before she left me for him. When we were 24, Flora got pregnant. We were so happy that we could finally start our family and live the life we always dreamed. So, that month, we secretly married in the castle chapel. One step closer."

"She was married to you before Drake? What happened?" Marlene chimes in, breaking her silence. She's just as invested in this as I am, but I don't think the realization has hit her yet. His real truth.

"Halfway through the pregnancy, Flora got sick. Nothing serious, just a minor illness and, because of her Angel Fae blood, it was a breeze to heal." Desmond rubs his eye, clearing the dampness away before tears can fall. "But it's not as easy to save a baby from that kind of sickness, even a full-blooded Angel Fae baby. We lost our child, and it destroyed us."

My heart sinks at his loss, and I realize that if no one here knew about him and Flora, he's probably never told anyone this before. It's been trapped inside for centuries and I can't imagine the emotions he's battling now that he's telling us.

Telling *me*.

"Flora and I healed in time and eventually tried again. The year we met Drake, Flora was pregnant. She was extremely early along and not even showing signs yet, but Drake sensed it somehow and seemed almost disgusted by it. A few days later, Flora got into a small accident in the castle, and it caused us to lose that child, too."

I drop my head, fighting back tears. "I'm so sorry," I whisper.

Desmond nods his chin at me in a silent thanks. "We healed again but, three years later, she left me because of the lie Drake fed her and it killed me inside." He pauses and takes a deep breath, blinking away tears once more.

"What the hell kind of lie could Drake have told her to get her to leave you?" Shay asks, genuinely in shock about everything he's telling us. And I don't blame him. He's been so close with Desmond for a very long time, and he was completely in the dark about this. I'm sure he's feeling a little hurt.

"He told her that I confessed to him I was glad our two children died. That I never wanted them with her." The grief that haunts Desmond as he says those words, destroys me.

Red hot anger flows through me instantly. At the hurt that Drake intentionally brought to Desmond and my mother. I am furious and I feel it building inside me.

"I tried so hard to convince her that he was lying, but wouldn't hear it. She believed him over me. When she left me, my heart shattered. The love of my life, my soulbond, gone. A few weeks later, she announced to her mother that she was leaving with Drake to marry him and live in Odrera."

"I can't imagine what Aris said to that," Tate mutters.

"She wasn't happy, to say the least. Her own daughter chose to go to the land that her enemy ruled. She was so afraid Ashton would use Flora as a way to hurt her, but she convinced her mother if Ashton and the fae saw an Angel Fae marrying a fae, living in Odrera, and living among them normally, it would strengthen the relationship and Ashton would no longer see the Angel Fae as a threat."

Desmond smiles sadly and continues. "On the surface, it *looked* like their marriage did exactly that. But, twenty years later, Aris turned up dead on the steps of the castle in the Sacred City with her wings cut off and positioned next to her. A few years after *that*, Ashton finished his mission and executed the remaining Angel Fae. He saved Flora for last. But, on his way back to Odrera, he was slain, and his decapitated head was posted on a stake outside of the castle walls. The King had no heirs, but for some reason, he left the Kingdom to Drake in his will. After that, he became King, and he put Flora in charge of creating a new court and guards for him. She brought Shay and Tate on immediately, and then sent for me to come to the castle. I hadn't seen her in over twenty years. Yet, the moment I set eyes on her, it was like no time passed at all."

"The two of you didn't have any contact for over twenty years?" I ask, barely able to hide the shakiness in my voice. It's a miracle I've been able to control my shaking hands this entire time.

"She left me, Lianna. She married Drake and he became the King. They had a daughter, Mariah. They had a whole life. I couldn't exactly just barge into the castle and demand her back. I would've been imprisoned or killed." His silver eye looks metallic with the tears that are building up, and the anger behind them is unmistakable. "She believed the lies Drake fed her about me. I had no way of knowing if she would ever want to speak to me again."

"But she brought you to the castle, even after all that time," Marlene blurts out. "I'm sorry, but that's not something someone would do if they still hated you."

"You're right. And when I got there, when we finally saw each other again, she apologized profusely for never believing me and that she spent all those years apart wishing she acted differently. "

"I remember the day you came to the castle. Flora was so happy. It'd been a long time since I saw her like that. Drake made her so damn miserable," Shay states. Tate nods in agreement, lightly squeezing Marlene's shoulder with the movement.

"I figured that out pretty quickly. We started having an affair not long after I arrived," Desmond admits.

Everyone's jaws drop at his confession. It's a secret that can easily get him killed if the wrong ears hear it, even now that she's missing.

But it's not shock that courses through me like everyone else. Instead, fierce anxiety powers through me, and my breathing begins to quicken. I know what secret is coming next.

Shay squeezes my hand as my heart rate spikes and I anxiously pick at my nail beds. "Are you alright, sweetheart?" he asks with concern, but nothing comes out when I try to answer. I can only squeeze his hand back and stare right into Desmond's eye.

He swallows the lump in his throat and finally reaches the part of his story I've been so nervous to hear. "When Flora was pregnant with you, Lianna, Drake never suspected it wasn't his because she was still performing her wifely duties for him," he says with disgust.

Heat creeps up my neck and I'm all too aware that everyone's eyes are on me. Traitorous tears slip from my eyes and slide quickly down my hot cheeks, sizzling as they go. Red mist blankets my skin as I hold firmly onto Shay, the only thing keeping me grounded as I watch Desmond open his mouth to reveal his deepest secret. *Our* deepest secret.

"Lianna, Drake is not your father." His jaw tightens. "I am."

Chapter 26

I burst out of the front door in a panic, my heart threatening to rip free from my chest at Desmond's confession. I already guessed that's what he was going to say, and I thought I was prepared. But, I was so fucking wrong. I thought I had all the information I needed about my birth family and I've come to terms with it all. But now, my life is flipped upside down once again and I can't keep up with it all.

I've been around my real father this whole time without even knowing and something about that is tearing me apart.

By now, I know this city like the back of my hand, and I run until I make it to the familiar run-down store in town that was once a small bakery. I squeeze through the broken door and sink to my knees the moment I step foot on the dusty ground inside.

Hot, angry tears stream down my cheeks and my breathing is quick and rough. I clutch my chest and try like hell to control my breathing so my magic doesn't surge in here. But it's no use. The rising panic in me is too much and it's controlling everything. I don't even bother to fight it. I let my arms fall to my sides and I curl onto the floor.

With my cheek pressed to the cold ground, I watch the red mist escape me, but nothing happens. There's no surge of my Elemental magic, no Feeler magic like in the cottage, nothing. The mist just settles over me like a blanket, it's wispy feel caressing my body like it's embracing me.

I let the tears flow freely in the privacy of the abandoned store. Let the dust fill my lungs with each painful inhale.

I stay there for a while, breathing through the panic and anger as it runs its course, when gentle footsteps sound behind me. I don't have any energy to open my eyes to see who's interrupting my meltdown. The panic and magic surge took everything from me, leaving me feeling like an empty shell.

But I smell him. Eucalyptus and citrus.

The floorboards creak slightly as Wes sits on the ground behind me, his muffled voice calling my name. And, when I don't answer, his hands are suddenly underneath my neck and legs. He doesn't even check to see if my mists will hurt him because it won't matter, not to him. He'll never let me be in agony alone.

But they won't hurt him. I'll never let them.

He cradles me in his arms and wipes the sweaty hair from sticking to my face as he rocks me back and forth, just like he always has whenever he finds me in the middle of a panic attack.

I open my mouth to speak but, when I try, nothing but a thick cough comes out. Wes gives me a sympathetic smile and continues to rock me back and forth, his cheek resting on my damp forehead. "You don't need to say anything until you're ready. Take as much time as you need, I'm not going anywhere."

I've never been more sure of someone's words before. I know he won't leave me and I know he won't force me to walk out of here until I want to. He has always been the one to keep me grounded when the panic creeps in.

As he sits here with me now, holding me tightly against his chest, small memories flood into my mind of all the times he has protected me and did all he could to keep me safe.

When he found out the other girls in town made fun of me because I look differently than everyone else, and he went to all of their parents and got them in trouble.

The few days after Luke took advantage of me for the first time and I isolated myself from everyone, and he sat at the foot of my bed reading while I slept without even knowing why I was being distant.

The days I came home bruised from Luke and he stayed by my side until they were healed, not even knowing what they were from.

How he sat outside my bedroom door when dad took my pointed ears and wings, and how he held my hand each time mom filed my canines down.

And now, he's left the safety of home to do what he can to keep me safe from this new life I'm venturing into.

Every moment in my life that I've needed him, even when I didn't know I did, he dropped everything for me. I don't deserve a brother like him. I've caused countless problems throughout our life that he has rescued me from and, even though he always says he'll do anything for me, I can't stop the guilt from building higher and higher as the years go on.

"I love you, Wes," I say, my tone barely more than a whisper. "And I know I don't say it enough but thank you for always saving me. For everything you do for me."

"I got so insanely lucky to have sisters like you and Marlene. I will stand before you two, always, to keep you from harm. Until my last breath, Lianna, I will protect you."

A lump forms in my throat and I turn my face away from him so he won't see the fresh tears spilling from my eyes. And it's this moment that really hits me that he genuinely will put himself in harms way to save me and Marlene, and I can't let him do that.

He kisses the top of my head and brushes his fingers through my unbound hair in silence until I drift to sleep.

***

I wake up drenched in sweat, and a feeling of deja vu sweeps over me as I remember waking up feeling just like this when the dreams started about my real mother. How has it been five years already since I got that first letter?

Shifting slightly, I realize I'm no longer on the hard floor of the bakery in Wes' lap. Now, I'm tucked under blankets in a soft bed and the open window offers a breeze that cools my sweaty forehead. I open my eyes and look around at the familiarity of the bedroom Shay and I share. *Home.*

My head is throbbing, so I take it slowly as I sit up in the bed, tossing some of the blankets off my overheating body. I rub the sleep from my eyes and scan the room, stopping when I see Shay at the dresser packing our bags. "Hey," is all I manage to get out. He turns, dropping a shirt back into the drawer, and walks over to sit with me in bed.

"How're you feeling, beautiful?" he asks, tucking stray hairs behind my ears, exposing the disfigured tips. But, for once, I don't hide them away. I leave the hair behind them, exposing it completely.

"Better than I was earlier. The nap definitely helped get some energy back." I look to the window where bright rays of sunlight are being cast into the room. "How long did I sleep for?"

"A little over four hours," he says planting a kiss on my forehead. I nod towards the bags on top of the dresser.

"Are we leaving?" I ask.

"Yeah. We decided we should head out as soon as everyone's packed. It's going to be a long and rough trip to Meobith."

"I still don't think Desmond choosing to go Meobith is the right choice," I snap, and it sounds so much harsher than I intend it to be. Shay tilts his head to the side and places his hand on my cheek.

"Look, I understand this is a lot to take in and no one's blaming you for how you feel. But, Meobith is a decision we made together. It makes the most sense. He knows more than we do."

I'm quiet for a moment as guilt settles heavily on me. I'm letting my emotions get the best of me and that's not fair to Desmond. He hasn't done anything wrong. "I'm sorry. I'm not trying to be rude, it's just a lot to process. When I was under the assumption Drake was my dad, I knew I had all this time to mentally prepare myself to meet him. And although I've known Desmond for a few months now, having that bomb dropped that *he's* my dad...I wasn't ready," I admit, blinking back tears.

"Love, I know you're not trying to hurt anyones feelings. And no one if faulting you for what you're going through. Desmond especially. After you left, he broke down. He said he's just as overwhelmed and this isn't how he wanted to tell you. He's had to pretend for your whole life that he wasn't your dad to keep both you and Flora safe. He had to watch as she took you away from him to keep *you* protected from the darkness. I don't think he was ever expecting to see you again, let alone with Tate and I."

My stomach starts to twist. I haven't even stopped to think about Desmond's feelings and how hard this must have been for him. When he saw me for the first time, he said he thought I was dead. He's gone twenty-five years thinking his daughter was dead and I can't even imagine what was going through his head when he saw me alive and back in his life completely by chance.

"I should give him a chance," I say to Shay.

"I would. He's one of the best males I've ever known. I know you've come to see that in the time you've spent with him. I've seen how close you two have gotten." He takes my face in my hands. "Start with that, love. See what becomes of it."

He hops off the bed and returns to the bags, continuing to pack them for the both of us. "Do you want some help?" I offer, walking to his side.

"Why don't you go take a nice relaxing bath and get ready. I've got this covered. We'll head out when you're done," he says. I nod and head for the bathroom. "I'm glad you agreed because you smell like old, stale bread and it's really not pleasant."

I hear him snicker under his breath, so I concentrate and use the energy I have left to send a controlled wave of magic towards him. I visualize the drawer in front of his shins to burst free and it does just that, slamming into his leg full force. He winces and I turn my head slightly, sticking my tongue out at him.

His jaw drops as I try to hide my smile and the laugh that follows. Then, a deep belly laugh bursts from him as he throws a decorative pillow at me. But I'm quicker, and I shut the bathroom door just as it comes crashing into it.

"Even though it was used against me, I'm very impressed with that display of magic, love," he yells from the main room and I faintly hear the bottom drawer slide closed.

I shake my head with a wild grin on my face and go to pick out soap. I stand in front of the various scents, eyeing up the orange scented soap again, but I finally decide to just stick with the lavender. One day I'll try out something new. I grab the bottles from the shelf and set them on the lip of the tub. I turn the hot water on fully and peel off my damp clothes, throwing them in the corner. I lift my leg over the edge, mere inches from soaking down into the water, when I hear a muffled sound through the door. It sounds almost like balcony doors opening and immediately slamming shut.

It's too faint to be the ones in our room, leaving three other rooms with balconies that it could've been. I reluctantly back away from the bath with a disappointed sigh and pull my robe on, the hot steam from the bathroom disappearing as I open the door. I walk into the bedroom, still tying my robe, and call out to Shay. "Hey, did you hear that?" I look up for his answer, but he's already gone, along with our bags.

I huff out a groan and unlock our balcony doors, taking a step into the warm midday air. The hot sun beats down on me deliciously and the breeze keeps it from bringing beads of sweat to the surface. I peer down the back of the house, trying to get a glimpse of which door was opened, but it's near impossible. From this angle I can see that none of the doors are open, but I can't tell if any of the balconies have been disturbed by someone opening the door.

Defeated, I turn to go back inside, deciding it was just this old house making noise, when a movement in the distance catches my eye. I scan the yard and stare with furrowed brows, thinking my mind is playing yet another trick on me, when I see it. Running away from the manor is a tall female with long blue hair flying wildly behind her. She's wearing dark clothing and jutting from her back is light brown wings. She's not too far away, and I can tell that she's carrying what looks like a book under her arm.

I must be seeing things. Right? There's no way that the female Luke met at the bar is here right now, sneaking out of Shay's childhood home with a book.

But, when she turns back to look at the house, we lock eyes, and I know I'm not just seeing things. And then it fucking clicks. Why the photo of Darcy Quint looked so damn familiar. Because, staring right at me smiling, is the female from the bar. It's Darcy.

Chapter 27

I let myself soak in the tub for much longer than I should. My fingers are starting to prune in the lukewarm water and there's no longer a blanket of steam in the bathroom. I spent the first fifteen minutes in a haze, replaying what I saw outside over and over in my head. There's no way the female from the bar in Peham is Darcy, they must just look similar. Because if that was Darcy, and she's alive, surely she would've come to see her brother by now. Wouldn't she?

This will destroy Shay if it's really her.

I'm pulled from my stupor by banging on the bathroom door, accompanied by yelling.

"Lianna, let's go! This is the longest bath ever, even for you! We're all waiting!" Marlene screams through the door. I look at the small clock on the vanity. It reads four o'clock, which means I've been soaking in the tub for well over an hour. *Shit.* This is by far the longest I've ever sat in a bath.

"Be right out!" I yell back, pouring water over my head and scrubbing the nearly dried soap out completely. I step out of the water and dry my hair as best as I can before brushing through it and putting it in two loose braids. I grab a spare toothbrush and toothpaste from the cabinet and brush quickly, before wrapping myself in a towel and heading into our room. Shay left out an outfit on the bed for me, along with my boots and both holsters with my knives secured in the sheathes.

I can't help but smile at the thoughtfulness of it all.

I step into the black leggings and pull an olive-green short sleeved shirt over my head, making sure to strap my thigh holsters on tightly. I lace up my boots and tug my denim jacket on last, untucking my braids from under the collar.

I look around our peaceful room as a bought of sadness washes over me at the realization that I don't know how long it'll be until I see this place again, if ever. I make sure all the doors and windows are shut and locked before I turn the lights off and step into the hallway.

I make my way downstairs and into the living room where everyone is all ready to go. "Sorry, I lost track of time," I say to everyone, noticing Desmond isn't here. My heart drops, praying that I didn't push him away.

"Des ran back to his house. We're going to meet him there. He said he needs to show you something before we leave for Meobith," Tate says when he notices me searching for him. My anxiety slowly starts to creep back as my mind starts to wonder what it is that he needs to show me.

I take a deep breath and remind myself that I need to give him a real, genuine chance. "Should we get going, then?" Everyone nods and they file outside, leaving Shay and I alone in the manor.

"I never thought I'd ever get the chance to come back here. But, now that I have, I don't want to leave," he says to me quietly, drawing me in for a hug. "I hope we can come back here one day."

"We will, I promise." And even with the confidence in my voice, deep down I'm afraid. I really hope I'll be able to keep this promise for him. Because in the short time I've been here, it's become a home to me, too.

I pull away from his embrace and intertwine my hand with his, squeezing lightly as we walk out of the beautiful manor together.

***

The short walk to Desmond's house is muscle memory at this point. After Shay and I explored the village months ago and I felt that strange pull towards his cottage, I've made it a point to add this street to my daily run just for a chance to pass it every day.

When we make it to the house, I see Desmond laying flat on a bench in the front yard under a small orange tree. He opens his eye when he hears us walking up and sits on the edge, watching as we make our way through the front gate. His gaze immediately finds mine and he walks over to us.

"I assume they told you I have something to show you?" he asks me. I nod slowly and push my way to the front of the group to him. He gestures towards his house and turns, walking the short distance to it. I start to follow, but I feel a presence looming behind me. I stop in my tracks and turn to Shay, less than a foot behind me, and reach up to kiss his cheek.

"I'm okay. Just give us a minute," I say, and he gives me a soft, proud smile before returning to the others. I turn back around and take a deep breath, walking up the stone path to the cottage. If only he knew how nervous I am to face whatever is pulling at me.

The closer I get to the door, the stronger the pull becomes. My once confident steps start to falter as the weight of it all hits me. This feeling is so familiar and it really feels like it's calling out to me. I look up at Desmond. "Shall we?"

"After you," he says stepping out from in front of the door. Just as I'm about to grab the door handle, I pause with my hand hovering above it, shifting where I stand. Desmond glances at where my hands tremble over the knob. "Can you feel it?"

I barely turn my head to him and speak quietly. "Feel what, exactly?" Does he feel it too?

"The pull," he says simply, not explaining any further. "Come on, I'll show you why." He gently lowers my hand away from the handle and opens it himself, letting me walk in first. He shuts the door behind him and I let go of the breath I didn't realize I was holding. I wait until he closes the door behind him to start speaking again. This isn't something I really want to announce to the entire group. Inanimate things calling out to me just feels abnormal.

"I felt the pull the minute we stepped foot into Shal. At the time, I figured it was because I was in the Angel Fae realm, and there's so much magic surrounding me. But then, Shay and I passed your house on one of our walks and I felt the pull stronger than ever," I explain as we stand in the front hall of the cottage.

"I expected as much, honestly. I am surprised you didn't bring it up though," he says shrugging. He walks into the room to our left and I venture further into the house, looking around at what Desmond calls home.

The interior of his house is drastically different than the manor. White walls and beige carpeted floors line every inch of the cottage, except for where the kitchen sits. It's pretty open, except for a short half wall that sections it off from the rest of the house, where the floor goes from carpet to white marble floors paired with light brown walls.

Desmond is waiting for me in the living room, which doesn't have much other than a couch, coffee table, and a large bookshelf stuffed with books. "Come sit with me for a minute."

I walk over to the plush couch in the middle of the room and sit down on the soft fabric next to him. There's a small wooden box in his lap with a silver clasp on the front. "What's in there?" I ask, and I know that, whatever it is, is the source of the pull I've been feeling all this time.

"Something from your mother. You were supposed to get it on your sixteenth birthday, but..." he trails off.

"But I was in Peham," I finish for him. He nods and places the box in my lap, encouraging me to open it.

I run my hands along the intricate carvings adorning the box. There's a mix of flowers and vines running along the sides and, on the top, there's a carving of a large phoenix with its wings spread wide. It reminds me so much of the box my daggers came in, which doesn't surprise me since my mother gifted me both.

I unhook the clasp and slowly raise the top to reveal a stunning tiara sitting on black velvet. The base of the crown is bronze, with gold and silver vines weaving upwards to create the look of the crown. Hanging right from the middle of the band, just where it would sit on my forehead, are three gems: a garnet wrapped in bronze, citrine wrapped in silver, and an emerald wrapped in gold.

"This is for me?" I gasp, in awe over the beautiful crown in front of me. "But I'm not the heir. The letters from Drake say Mariah is and I'm not even his child. I'm no princess."

"Well, you may not be Drake's heir, but you *are* Flora's heir. And she is the Queen of the Angel Fae's daughter, and *she* is Aris' heir. You may not be a princess in Odrera, but you certainly are the Princess of the Angel Fae, even if they're nonexistent."

"How do you even have this?"

"Right after she gave birth to you, I secretly escorted you and her to the Sacred City. She was adamant about getting to the Temple where this tiara was hidden away. It's forged from the three crowns of the Omni Goddesses, Kaleen, Odessa, and Lucienne. Kaleen's was made of bronze with garnet jewels, Odessa's was gold with emeralds, and Lucienne's was silver with citrine gemstones," he explains. But no mention of Aislinn. I can't help but wonder if she ever had a crown, or if Desmond even knows about her like Shay does.

"I've never seen something so beautiful." I run my finger along the gems, stopping on the garnet in the middle. It's identical to the one hanging around my neck.

"The garnet you wear is the original gem, and the one imbued with Kaleen's powers. It once adorned her original crown. The gems on this one are all replicas," he explains.

"So, the other Goddesses gems are out there somewhere?"

"They are. But they've been lost to the world for far too long," he says, then arches a brow. "Have you heard the story of the gems before?"

I shake my head. "Amara told me that my gem protected them and that my mother left it with me. And Tate told me that Izara stole Odessa's emerald from the Temple. Other than that, I don't know any of the history, I'm sorry."

"Don't be sorry, the humans never would've taught any of this to you, and Amara was probably too nervous to give you too much information about your heritage," he reassures and inhales deeply. "Aris was the daughter of Kaleen and an unknown fae male. Right before Aris' mother and aunts disappeared, they suspected something might happen to them. So they took apart their crowns and made this one from the melted metals and the gems. When Aris received it, it had the three original gems in it. But, when the triplets were born, she took the gems from the crown and gifted each daughter with one in the form of a necklace, replacing the spots in the crown with replicas of the original gems. Each gem is a protection stone for different things. The garnet gives protection from harm and nightmares, the citrine against venoms and evil thoughts, and the emerald against demons. Separately, the gems are decently powerful. But, when the three are brought together, the wearer has the ultimate protection. There's an old prophecy, legend, whatever you want to call it, that says that only the true Omni Goddess can wield all of them at once. If anyone else tries, it'll result in their death."

"So, my gem really was protecting my family all those years?"

"It was. Flora knew what she was doing when she gave you the gem. It left her vulnerable, but she only ever worried about you," he says, nudging me. A corner of my mouth turns up in a smile at the truth of it. I spent a lot of time being angry at her for leaving me, when she has really been protecting me my entire life. That's a debt I'll never be able to pay.

"How does no one know where the other gems are? I mean, if each daughter got one, aren't their locations pretty obvious?" They should be with each triplet, except for the garnet.

"You would think. But when Amara left for the human realm, and Flora took her immortality away, she also made her leave the gem with her. Flora hid the citrine in the vault of the castle in Odrera, and it went missing shortly after. No one has been able to track it down."

"And does Izara still have the emerald?" I ask.

"I don't know. She had it for a while, but I have no idea if she still does," he admits.

I take a deep breath and tear my gaze from the crown, turning to look right into Desmond's eye. An eye that is identical to mine, and it took me this long to notice. "Have you ever heard of Memory Walkers bringing others with them into a memory?" I question.

"I don't think anyone has ever tried," he says, looking at me curiously until it clicks in his mind. "You want to bring me into a memory with you?"

I nod. "I do. I know you actually lived it but, I..."

"You don't want to be alone," Desmond finishes for me. "I get it. Though I've never done it before, it sounds like it can be a stressful experience. Especially seeing how you came back from the day we met."

Before I knew how to control my magic, simply touching the crown would suck me into the memory without warning. But, after countless training sessions with Desmond, I command every aspect of my magic. Even when I want to memory walk.

I glance down at the crown in my lap and pull it out of the box. I place the surprisingly light tiara on top of my head and suddenly a small surge of magic pulses through it. Within seconds, the slightly too big tiara molds to my head and tightens to fit me perfectly.

I can't help the grin that blossoms on my face at the way it feels on me. Like it truly belongs to me and the magic flowing through it recognizes that. Recognizes *me*. I look up at Desmond, beaming at me with what looks like pride, as I slowly take his hand and hold it tightly in mine.

"There will be a dense fog that completely surrounds us, and then your vision will start to fade. Don't fight it and don't fear it. Just breathe through it and, whatever you do, don't let go of my hand until we're solid again," I instruct. He nods and readjusts his grip on my hand.

I close my eyes and open up my powers to the memories the tiara holds, searching through them for the right moment. When I find it, I will my magic to take us to just that memory, and my body starts to warm. The white fog slowly start to envelop Desmond and I, and the tingle I feel when my powers surge is almost comforting, now.

The edges of my vision begin to darken, and I can feel Desmond's pulse quicken with the sudden loss of his surroundings. I lightly squeeze his hand to comfort him and, within a moment, he calms significantly when he realizes I'm still right here with him.

Just in time for us to be completely whisked away in the fog.

Chapter 28

The fog doesn't take too long to clear and, when it does, I can see that we're in a small field with the Quartz Wall at our backs. To our right, there's an expansive mountain range that barely reaches the top of the wall, while a dense forest takes up the majority of our surroundings.

The sound of fluttering fills my ears and I know the gold winged butterflies are next to me without even looking. I grin, their presence when I memory walk becoming a comforting feeling. After practicing my power with Desmond, it became clear that these beautiful creatures appear every time I memory walk. Apparently they're a sign that I'm inside a memory and not the real world. They'll keep me sane and able to differentiate real from memory.

They never stay for too long. They usually appear as soon as I get into the memory and then fly in the direction I need to head before disappearing. I wish they would stay with me the entire time. The thump of their delicate wings in the breeze is calming and tends to keep my anxiety at bay. My thoughts begin to wander as I contemplate if there's a way I can use my magic to keep them with me.

Desmond drops my hand as soon as we're fully in the memory and leans against the wall. I give him a moment to catch his breath and blink away the vision loss but, for it being his first time memory walking, he's doing pretty well. I'm not going to lie, I was a little nervous bringing him. I've only memory walked a handful of times and it's always been just me. I wasn't entirely sure if bringing someone else would harm them in any way, or even work, but I knew he'd be willing no matter what.

"All good?" I ask. He nods and gives me a thumbs up before pushing off of the wall and looking around us. We can't see much past the forest, but he knows where we are without thinking twice.

"We're in the Sacred City," he says on a gasp, making his way forward. "You brought us to the Sacred City." He turns to me and there are tears streaming down his cheek.

"I wanted to see the day you came here to get the tiara," I say slightly embarrassed, but I'm not sure why. Desmond smiles sadly and opens his mouth, only to immediately close it.

"Thank you for bringing me with you. You know, I didn't think I'd ever get a chance to see either of you again. But now that *you're* here, I can't help but wonder if I'll ever see-" he inhales sharply and falls to his knees, like the air has been completely knocked out of him. "Flora."

I turn to where he's facing and see exactly what stopped him. Coming through a passageway in the wall, almost identical to the one Tate opened for us when we first arrived in the Angel Fae territories, is Desmond and my mother, carrying my infant self in a light purple blanket.

I stand at Desmond's side as the three of them pass by us, close enough to touch. My breath catches in my throat seeing her. She's so beautiful. She looks just like Amara, obviously, but there are differences in her that I recognize as traits I see in myself. I lightly touch Desmond's forearm, and he speaks as he stares at my mother. "I still haven't given up hope that she's out there somewhere." He faces me, then. "We will find her, Lianna. We have to."

I smile at him and clasp his hand in mine as we follow behind the trio ahead of us. "One day, I'd like to hear more stories about you and my mom when you guys were younger. If that's alright with you."

"I'll be happy to share them all with you." He lightly squeezes my hand and nods at his past self. "After your mother disappeared with you, I had nightmares every night. Always the same, where I was stuck watching the two of you walk away from me that day in the tower. But this? This has always been my favorite dream. Being able to be a real family and not have to hide. On this day in particular, I had to stop myself from begging Flora to stay here with me and not go back to Odrera. Find a way to bring Landon to us and start a whole new life."

"Why didn't you?" I feel so stupid asking that the second it leaves my mouth. There are so many reasons he couldn't ask that of her.

"She was the Queen. I couldn't. It wouldn't have ended well for any of us." He glances down at his feet, the grass parting beneath each step.

"Desmond?" I say quietly as nerves course through me.

"Yeah, kid?"

"Is Landon my mother's son, too? Is he my brother?" Images of Landon run through my mind from Desmond's memory. Thinking of him now, I can't stop seeing a male version of myself in him.

"He is. He was born three years after I came to the castle."

"Does Drake know? I mean, I saw your memory. Landon didn't even try to hide the fact you're his father."

"No. Drake doesn't know. When he was born, Flora immediately had him brought to my home in the Sacred City. Her midwives knew everything about the two of us and they kept it all a secret from Drake. Truthfully, I think they preferred me over Drake. But, they concocted this elaborate plan to tell him that the child was stillborn and I raised Landon without her."

"And he believed it?"

"The midwives made it very believable, and Drake believed it to be karma for what he did to break Flora and I apart, especially since I was in the castle with them. After that, he "changed his ways" and made amends with me, while also changing his way of life, so he said. When you were born, Flora kept you in the castle, so he didn't suspect you weren't his. He thought that *you* were his reward for making amends."

The trio's halfway through the dense woods now, their low chattering almost like a soothing background noise as Desmond explains his past, *our* past, to me. "What about Mariah? Is she yours, too?"

"No, and she isn't even your mothers. Mariah's only a year younger than Landon, but she belongs to the mistress Drake had. When he made amends with me, he broke off his relationship with his mistress, only to find out that she was pregnant with his child."

"So, Landon is my full brother, and Mariah isn't even related to me?" I huff out a sigh of irritation and tilt my head back to the sky briefly. Five years ago, I believed I had a King for a father and an older sister waiting for me in Odrera. Now, I have my real father, a brother missing or deceased somewhere, a missing mother, and two aunts, one who raised me as her own. Holy shit, my family tree is insane.

"I know it's confusing and a lot to take in, learning about this part of your family. But you're handling it a lot better than I expected," Desmond praises.

"Did Landon know about me?" I blurt out, not even sure if it even matters, especially if he really is dead like everyone believes.

"He knew. He met you a few times but, because the two of you were separated, it was always brief encounters whenever he was on guard duty. But he wanted to know you more than anything," he explains. He stares at the trio ahead as they step out of the dense forest. I can see sunlight through the trees ahead, so I know we're just as close.

"Things could have been so different for all of us," I say, squeezing his hand lightly.

"Your mother wanted to leave Drake so badly, but it would've been too difficult for her to try to leave the King and admit we have two children together. It wasn't fair for either of us, but I stayed by her side every day just to keep her safe," he says sadly. "And you, too. I watched over you as much as I could without it seeming out of the ordinary."

"I'm sorry for what you had to go through, the both of you. And I want you to know that I don't blame you for any of it. You two were given such an unfair situation," I say, meaning it with everything I have in me.

"I miss her every day. And I sure as hell have never stopped loving her. I don't think I could if I tried," he says with a huff of a laugh. But there's so much pain behind it. Maybe bringing him into the memory with me was a bad idea. Seeing the love of his life again after twenty-five years and then having to go back to the real world where she isn't might be torture.

"We'll find her. And if what you think about Meobith is true, we'll be one step closer to getting her back."

A few feet later, Desmond and I are out of the forest. The mid-afternoon sun blinds us both as we leave the shadowed trees, pulling tears from my eyes. I rub away the wetness and blink rapidly, letting my eyes adjust to the new brightness. When I'm able to see properly again, I gasp at the sight in front of me.

We're standing at the top of a cliff right on the outskirts of the Sacred City, looking down upon the abandoned city. Even abandoned, it's more beautiful than I ever could've imagined.

I gaze around at the landmarks of the city that stand before me. The entirety of the city is located in the basin of the cliffs, while mountains and forests surround it along the top.

I expected the mountain tops to be covered in snow but, instead, dark green grass grows from every inch.

Down below, it looks as if every building is built from white rock and topped with deep red roofs, and the streets look to be a white cobblestone. The homes and the town are directly at the bottom of the cliff and, on an island in the middle of the basin, is what I'm assuming is the Temple.

But, most impressive of all, is the massive castle looming above the entire city. It sits on top of the cliff on the other side of where we stand, with a small forest of fruit trees on one side, and a river and waterfall on the other.

Unlike the homes in the city, the castle is light brown in color. Blooming along the exterior and crawling up the walls are various flowers in every color imaginable, vibrant and full of life. It's almost like there's a floral rainbow permanently growing out of the structure.

There are arched stained glass windows that litter the castle walls, letting in all the natural light the world can offer, filtered through a rainbow of colors. As the sun bounces off of them, they sparkle with a glow that looks eerily similar to the iridescent glow of my skin when my powers are active.

Extending from the castle are a multitude of sky-high towers, almost touching the clouds. One, however, reaches a bit higher than the rest, the singular window on it smashed. In fact, it's the *only* window that's smashed among the whole castle.

Interesting.

I follow Desmond as he veers to the left, following the trio down a ramp built into the cliff that is going to take us right into the village below.

I wish we had time to explore the homes in this memory, but I know that, even if we did, we'd be taken out of the memory as soon as we veer from the course. The insides of the homes aren't part of the core memory, so I'm out of luck. One day I'll see this place.

I observe the Temple as we walk through the main street of the village, really noting its features. It look just like a smaller version of the castle above. It's made from the same light brown stone and there are stained-glass windows covering almost every surface. The only thing missing that makes it slightly different is the lack of rainbow flowers along the walls. Instead, ivy creeps up on all sides, with small white flowers intermixed.

The river that surrounds it isn't too wide, but there are bridges that are made of the same light brown stone for easy access.

When we cross over the bridge and come face to face with the Temple, I'm a little caught off guard, if I'm being honest. From where we started on the cliff, it seemed so small, and I expected it to be a little larger than the manor. But I'm so very wrong. The Temple rises high into the air, surpassing the height of the manor by at least twenty feet. Makes me wonder just how high the castle itself reaches.

A small movement in my peripheral catches my attention as I admire the beauty of the Temple. I glance up and slowly pull Desmond to my side. "Do you see that? Up towards the top," I hiss.

He looks in the direction my eyes are locked and squints, cursing under his breath when he spots it, too. Perched on the highest point of the Temple is a dark, shrouded creature, staring right at the trio as they make their way towards the building.

Desmond steps back a few inches and inhales sharply. "Is that what I think it is?" I ask, praying I'm wrong.

"Yes," he breathes. "Fucking Caviax."

Chapter 29

I can see the panic surfacing in Desmond, just like it does for me. I guess I don't have to wonder where the hell all of my anxiety came from. "I don't even remember feeling its presence that day. How the hell did I miss it?" he says, frozen in place.

"You had much different priorities that day," I assure, trying to channel Wes as I try to calm him. "Look, clearly it never made a move, or else you would've remembered. Let's keep going, we'll keep an eye out for anything else strange."

Desmond takes a deep breath and nods, and we continue towards the Temple doors. The Caviax doesn't move from its spot, but it's obvious that it's tracking the trio as they enter the Temple.

The large doors are made of opal, bronze, gold, and silver, just like the crown that's on my head now. I've never seen a more beautiful building. The main structure of the door is solid opal, while the handles are silver and the intricate designs on them are made of gold and bronze intermingled.

As we close the distance between us and the Temple, I can't help but notice that the building is in near pristine condition. The only flaw I can see are long scratches along the exterior of the doors that carve deep into the opal. *What the hell kind of creature can make marks like that?* Desmond opens the doors for me and we walk into the abandoned Temple, making sure to stick together. And the pristine beauty only continues on the inside, neglected for centuries.

It's a large, open space with chandeliers strewn throughout the vaulted glass ceiling. None of the candles are lit, but the openness of the ceiling allows for every bit of natural light to shine in.

There are a few rows of pews in front of a small alter, where completely melted down candles line the walkway. Looking at it now, I can only imagine how spectacular it was in its prime, filled with Angel Fae.

"Even covered in dust and grime, this place is still magical to me," Desmond says in awe. "Back in the day, before Aris died, the whole city was so lively and constantly full of music and happiness. There was always a festival of some sort going on and no one ever seemed to tire of them. And here? There were always Angel Fae in here paying their respects to the Goddesses. It was never empty, until there wasn't anyone left to fills the seats."

"What happened when Aris died?" I ask timidly as we walk through the main aisle.

"When she was murdered, everything changed. There weren't many Angel Fae left after his first round of executions, but everyone that escaped his grasp was on edge every second of the day, and rightfully so. There was a constant wondering of when Ashton would come for the rest of us. Knowing we had Dennin to keep us safe made things better. But it only lasted for a short while."

"Because he died, too, right?"

"Yeah. He only held on for a month after Aris was killed. He ran things as best he could but, ultimately, being without his soulbond broke him too deeply. He took his own life and left us alone. After that, Amara was the only royal left in the Sacred City. Izara was still banished to Fahal, and Flora lived in Odrera with Drake. Suddenly, all eyes were on her to rule. She never wanted that responsibility in the first place but she had no other choice."

"Wait. Are you saying my mother, I mean, my aunt, ruled the Sacred City? She was the *Queen*?" Leave it to her to keep that massive piece of information from me.

"For a short time, yes. She did her best with the lack of training she had. She was never educated on how to rule or be a Queen, because it was Flora who was the heir. Of course her reign was different, but everyone eventually adjusted and quickly got back to where we were before. She ruled for a little less than three years before Ashton and his men invaded and executed any remaining Angel Fae he could get his hands on."

"How did she escape it?"

"We hid. At the time, Tate and I were Amara's guards and, when we got word that Ashton was invading the village, I took them to the hidden tunnels under the castle and we waited it out. It was cowardly, but she needed to live."

I can tell there's more to it but I don't want to push him. Not when I'm sure reliving all of this is painful for him.

We walk down the aisle in between the pews in silence, and head for the back of the Temple. I can't see the past versions of Desmond and Flora anymore, but I'm not too worried about losing them since I have present day Desmond with me. And he's already done this once before.

I duck under a mess of cobwebs in an iron archway and what's right on the other side is breathtaking.

We step foot into a small indoor grassy area. Nestled in the perfectly trimmed grass are three tombs, each inscribed with the names of the Goddesses: Kaleen, Odessa, and Lucienne. But still, no Aislinn. Shay's right. Her sisters really did erase her from history. But why? They could've immortalized the memory of her in so many ways, but they chose this? It doesn't make any sense.

I run my fingers along the raised lettering of their names, the golden sheen faded after years of others touching them. "I thought the Goddesses just disappeared one day. Why the tombs?"

"No one knows if the Goddesses are dead or just gone, but the tombs were built to let people worship them and the memory of them."

I nod and turn my gaze to the wall behind the tombs. Against the ivy-covered wall are two statues, much newer looking than the tombs in the middle. There are plaques half buried in the grass in front of the bases and I walk over to get a better look.

"Aris Solace, our eternal Queen. Dennin Solace, our broken hearted King," I read aloud. "Are these their graves?"

Desmond stands next to me and sighs, reading the plaques. "In a way. Amara commissioned these statues to be left up here so the Angel Fae could pay their respects. Their actual tombs are in the hidden catacombs so no one could disrespect their remains."

He turns and walks away from the statues, making his way to an arch coming out of the wall on the other side of the grassy area. There's something written on it in a language I don't know but Desmond places his hand in the middle of the arch, directly against the wall, and whispers the foreign words.

The wall instantly melts away, just like our passage through the Quartz Wall did. I suck in a breath and slowly step over to his side. "Tate and Shay did the same thing with the Quartz Wall. Can anyone do that kind of magic?"

"Not exactly. Only those that Aris gifted the ability to are able to do it. Because it's her magic coursing through the wall and in the Temple, she was able to choose who had access to the magic. As far as I know, only Amara, Flora, Tate, Shay and myself can do it," he explains. If that's true, then how the hell did Luke get in a few months back? Even with his parents having magic, he doesn't have Aris' favor. So what the hell is going on? I sigh and turn back to the open archway.

The archway is now completely open, revealing a winding staircase that's lined with lit torches going all the way to the bottom. The flame is so strange to look at and it's shining a deep gold. "Is this fire-"

"Magic?" Desmond interrupts. "Yeah. Cool, isn't it? Aris wanted to make sure there was always light down here so the oil would never have to be refilled." He starts to descend the steps, holding out his hand for me to follow. I hesitate a moment before taking hold of his hand, following closely behind towards the hushed voices of Desmond and Flora already at the bottom.

The temperature drops drastically with each step down the dimly lit staircase. The torches continue every few feet with cobwebs floating between them.

Desmond lets go of my hand suddenly, catching himself on the railing my other hand is running along. My heart starts to pound. Can you get hurt in a memory? If you get hurt here, are you hurt in real life? Fuck, I need to learn more about this power. "Holy shit, Desmond, are you alright?"

He takes a second to catch his breath and nods quickly. "I'm good. There's something slippery on the step and I didn't see it. Come on, let's keep going."

After basically forcing Desmond to hold onto the railing, too, we continue the rest of the descend. It's a decently short staircase, and after a little less than ten minutes of walking, we're at the bottom. The stairs let out into a large, open room that's lit by a massive caged in fire in the middle of the room, roaring with lifelike flames.

Desmond walks towards the fire and I stay planted at the bottom of the stairs, looking around the large space we're in. The earthen floors are littered with riches and treasures, enough to aid an entire city for years.

Positioned in a line right behind the fire are three tombs far more extravagant than the ones upstairs. One bronze adorned with garnets, one golden with emeralds lining the edges, and one silver with citrine along the top. The firelight dances on their surfaces, illuminating the gems and casting long shadows over three portraits hanging behind them, one for each Goddess.

I recognize them from the rough sketches in my textbooks and from their statues in Shal, but those are nothing compared to what I'm seeing now. These portraits show every detail of them. Details I've never seen before.

They're magnificent.

Kaleen's portrait hangs in the middle over the bronze tomb. She has curly brown hair and garnet red eyes, vibrant and full of life. Her skin, however, is milky white, so unlike my olive skin. She's wearing a crown of bronze with small garnets placed throughout, with a sheer red veil extending from it.

Lucienne is to the left of her. She, too, has milky white skin and her curly blonde hair almost blends in with her fair skin. Her eyes are bright citrine, just like the gems that adorn her own silver crown. Like her sister, she has a pale-yellow veil coming from the tip of the crown.

Then there's Odessa, who is placed to the right of Kaleen. Her jet black hair is also curled, and it's such a stark comparison to her pale skin. Her eyes are a mesmerizing emerald green framed by long, dark eyelashes. Her own crown is golden with a sea of emeralds, along with a sheer green veil, just like the other Goddesses.

At first glance, the three of them look like complete opposites. But, looking at them closer, they all share the same physical features and facial structures. They're identical in every way except for their colors.

"They're so beautiful," I whisper, staring between the three portraits. There's no answer from Desmond and, when I look around the cave, I find him standing a few feet from the past version of himself, holding Flora's hand tightly as they walk to another pile of artifacts.

I creep up behind him and watch as past Desmond crouches in front of a pile and rifles through it carefully, while my mother stands closely behind, rocking me back and forth. "Sometimes I can still feel her touch. Like right now, I swear I can feel her hand in mine," Desmond says, looking down at his missing arm. "Even though the hand she once held is no longer there."

I wish there was something I could say to him to reassure him but I don't even know what I *would* say. I doesn't matter, anyway, because I'm interrupted by Desmond speaking to my mother. "Are you sure it's down here, Flora?" he asks.

"I'm sure, Des. No one would have known its whereabouts except for my sisters and I. We know Amara doesn't have it and Izara hasn't been seen around here in centuries," my mother says. "Just keep looking, it has to be here."

We stand back while the two of them continue to search for the crown. This would all be so much easier if Desmond could tell his past self where the hell to look. "How long did you guys spend looking-" I start to say, but I'm cut off by the sound of rejoicing. I whip my head around as Desmond raises the crown above his head in celebration.

My mother smiles widely as he runs to her and pulls her to him by her waist, making sure not to crush the small bundle between them. Then, he kisses my mother deeply with a passion I've never seen before.

I look down between Desmond and I and notice his hand trembling. Seeing it makes my heart physically hurt for him. I can't imagine how hard this is for him. Watching this moment he once shared with the love of his life and not being able to have this in the present.

I reach down and grab his hand to calm the trembling as the two in front of us break apart from each other. Desmond smoothes back my mother's hair and runs a thumb down her cheek gently.

"Thank you," she says, leaning into his touch. "It means so much to me that Lianna will get to have this when she gets older."

"You know I would do anything for you, Flora. Say the word and I'll make it happen. You want to stay here and start a life? I'll do it." Oh, this is the moment. The moment he told me he wished he begged her to stay here with him. But he isn't actually asking her. Instead, he's giving her the choice to choose for herself.

My mother really looks at him and I can see how badly she wants to say yes. It's written all over her face. But, she can't say yes, and they both know it. She plasters a smile on her face and grabs Desmond's hand. "Get us out of here? There's a weird feeling and I really don't like it. Something feels stale," she says, and Desmond nods at her. He sticks the crown into the satchel around his chest and takes my mother by the hand, pulling her up the winding stairs.

We follow closely behind but, as we reach the top, Desmond holds me back by his arm, stopping me in my tracks. I stick my head over his forearm and open my mouth to question him, but he turns to me and shakes his head violently, silencing me.

He lowers his arm and points towards one of the stained glass windows lining the Temple walls, and I bite back a gasp at the sight.

Directly on the other side of the glass is the Caviax, staring directly at us. Not at the *figures* in the memory, but current Desmond and I, the invaders of this memory.

"Is it looking at us?" I ask.

"Yes," Desmond quickly replies.

"But there's no way it can *actually* see us...right?" I say nervously. When he doesn't respond right away, I try again. "Right, Desmond? It can't really see us?"

"I don't know. It sure seems like it can," he finally answers, taking one step closer to the window. But, with his slight movement, the Caviax narrows its dark eyes and smiles at us, revealing jagged gray teeth with a strange black substance coating its gums.

Not even ten seconds later, the Caviax disappears into thin air, leaving behind a dense black smoke where it once stood. Desmond starts to run to the window to see where it went but the warm feeling of my magic surges within me and

I know our time in the memory is done. "Desmond, there's no time!" I yell to him.

He turns his head to me, ready to argue, but I grab his hand just in time as the white fog envelopes us and rips us from the memory.

Chapter 30

esmond and I land in the living room, right back on the couch where we were before we memory walked. I squeeze my eyes shut for a moment to fight off the slight nausea that always comes after using the power and, when I'm sure it's passed, I look over to Desmond.

His head is hanging low and his breaths are rapid and shaky, and I watch as a slight tremble runs through his body. I remember how much of a bitch it was when I memory walked for the first time and how terrible I felt after, and I hate that he's going through this torture just for me.

I scoot closer to him and rub my hand in circles on his back. "It'll pass, just keep breathing," I say standing. I pace around the living room towards the bookshelf, finding similar books on his shelf that were on Darcy's. They're all completely free of dust and look very well used. Seeing Desmond's love of books makes my heart swell, and his collection reminds me so much of the bookstore I loved so dearly back in Peham, now leveled from the fires.

I slide the book I took out back in its place and walk over to the front window, partially shaded by mismatched curtains. Our group is still standing right where we left them, and it looks like no one has moved a muscle. It's almost like no time has passed at all for them.

"How long would you say we were gone?" I ask curiously, feeling Desmond's presence behind me.

"Maybe an hour or two? Closer to two hours, probably."

"Right," I say, trailing off. I turn around and find Desmond staring at me with his brows furrowed. I can almost see the gears in his head turning. "What?"

"Have you ever interacted with beings in a memory before?"

"In the few times I've used this power, no, I haven't," I say, shaking my head and sucking in a sharp breath. I don't like where this is going. My heart rate starts to rise but I take a deep breath and try to ground myself before I start a whole chain of events with my magic.

"That creature shouldn't have known we were there, Lianna. We were invisible bystanders to the memory. We should've been invisible to it if it was part of that memory. But..."

"But, what?" I demand when he trails off. Because I know what he's going to say. Every fear that's racing through my mind is going to come out of his mouth. Because what happened in that memory shouldn't be possible. That *thing* saw us and knew we were there the moment we entered the memory. *It* was the intruder, not Desmond and I.

"But, it didn't seem like it was part of the memory," he spits out. *Oh, fuck. There it is.* "And my gut is telling me that bastard was sent to watch us."

I let my head fall forward as he grabs his belongings from the couch. When he's back at my side, I let out a shuddering breath. "I'm scared," I blurt out, shocking myself that I'm admitting this fact to anyone, let alone Desmond.

"Of the Caviax?" he asks. I sigh and let my head drop into my hands. I drag them down my face and then bring my gaze back to his.

"It just doesn't make any sense how it could've gotten into that memory with us. And knowing that can happen makes me terrified to use that power again. What if it sees something I don't want it to? I don't know how to keep others out," I blurt in a panic.

"Honey, calm down," he says, reaching out to grab my shoulder. And suddenly, the panic rising in me just stops. A warm feeling rushes through my chest at the way he calls me honey. It doesn't feel like the way someone older than me would say it. It feels *fatherly*. And, even though I've grown up with a father, this feels like something more. He doesn't even seem to notice he called me it. It's like it's second nature for him.

And it should be second nature. It should be a normal thing for him to call me. Because this is my real father. We finally found each other and, now, we have all of this time together to build the bond we should have had from the moment I was born.

I start to get lost in my thoughts of this new life, but they're quickly snatched away when Desmond opens the door. I absentmindedly follow him out the door to the warmth of the spring afternoon and start making my way to everyone else. Marlene and Tate are crouched in front of the fence, examining a group of flowers climbing up the side, while Shay and Wes chat quietly under the orange tree.

They all turn as they hear us approach and all of their eyes are directly on me, mouths gaping.

Shay's the first to reach me and, as he stops in front of me, Desmond gives me a small glance and pulls Wes along with him to where Marlene and Tate stand.

Shay arches a brow at me and the corner of his mouth turns up, exposing one of his pointed canines. "New accessory?" he asks, nodding to my head as the smile on his face grows.

Confusion washes over my face as I reach up and feel the tiara still hugging my head. I never took it off when Desmond and I got back from the memory and it feels so weightless on my head, I almost forgot about it.

"That explains why everyone was staring," I say shyly. I lift my hands to it and, as my fingers graze it, the tiara loosens and I gently lift it from my head, putting it back in the box I have tucked under my arm.

"Not in a bad way, love. You looked like a Queen when you walked out. It was hard not to stare."

"I'm no Queen, Shay. I'm not Drake's heir and the kingdom I have a claim over is completely fallen. I'm the Queen of a fallen realm." The admission spills out of my mouth before I can stop it. But it's true. There aren't any Angel Fae for me to rule over and I'm still holding onto the hope that my mother is out there somewhere. The *rightful* queen of the Angel Fae, even if she's technically the Queen of Odrera.

"We don't know what the future holds and, if that's the path you end up choosing, it'll be one I'll walk side by side down with you," he promises. He kisses me gently on the lips before bringing my right hand to his mouth, kissing my ring finger where my soulbond band is tattooed. "I'm assuming that's what Des wanted to show you. You two weren't in there too long."

I narrow my eyes at Shay. "How long were we in there for?"

"Five minutes, maybe even less," he says, tilting his head when he sees the shock cross my face. "Everything ok?"

"I guess. We memory walked," I tell him.

"You brought Desmond into a memory with you?" he asks bewildered.

I nod. "He pulled out the tiara and said my mother dragged him to the Sacred City to get it for *me*. I wanted to see the day they got it. I wanted to see *them* together...my parents," I admit, tears brimming my eyes as I shake my head. "So I took him with me."

After a moment, he lowers his head to mine so we're eye level. "I didn't know you could do that."

I shrug. "Neither did I. But I figured it was worth a try for him to see her again."

"You find a new way to amaze me every single day," he says, pulling me into a tight embrace. It doesn't last long before we're interrupted by Wes.

"Alright *your Highness*, can we get a move on, please?" Wes teases. I roll my eyes, knowing my brother will never get tired of this line of teasing and I'll have to endure it for the foreseeable future. Shay snickers while he picks my bag up from the ground and hands it to me. I swing it onto my back with a huff, but I still take his hand when he holds it out to me when we start to walk away from Desmond's house.

***

"So, how exactly are we going to get into Meobith without being caught by anyone?" I say, leaning against a tree while Shay empties his bladder in a bush a few feet from the road.

"The longer we stay in the Angel Fae territories, the better. And, once we cross into Meobith from Eldolon, it'll be all uninhabited desert for a while," he calls back. I hear rustling and look around the trunk to see Shay pushing through the shrubbery. He smiles when he sees me watching him. "But, in a few hours, we'll reach the Trench of Aislinn. Unfortunately, the only way to Eldolon from here is by crossing the trench. The wall has cut off every other possible path to the other side of our territories so this is what we're stuck with. It'll probably be the most dangerous part of our journey. Even more dangerous than trekking through the Fae realm undetected."

"Other than it being a literal trench, what other dangers are in there?" I ask absentmindedly. But all that's going through my head is why the hell there's a trench named after the fourth Goddess, when basically no one has any knowledge of who she even is. It makes no fucking sense.

"A long time ago, there were magical creatures that lived at the bottom. There may still be some that linger but it's very unlikely," Shay says, shrugging. He grabs my hand and pulls me close to him, keeping our pace quicker to catch up to the others.

"And what if the creatures are still there?"

"If any of them are still alive, they'll be completely feral now. At that point, we'd have a fight on our hands," he says as we enter the forest, this time heading North along the Quartz Wall.

"What kind of creatures are we talking about?" I ask, ducking under a branch Shay lifts up for me. "Thanks."

"Honestly, I only know of a few. There's the Chimera, which was Odessa's favorite of them all. It had the head of a lion, body of a goat, and the tail of a serpent. There weren't many of them, but she was obsessed with them."

"They sound terrifying." I try to picture what that would even look like and all of my visualizations are horrible. Why was she so obsessed with a creature like that?

"I'm sure they were. Apparently, they could breathe fire, too, which makes them sound even worse," he goes on. Breathes fire? Of course it can.

I shudder at the thought. "What else?"

"There used to be large wolves that lived in the caves, along with basilisks and scorpions. There are rumors of a few other creatures, but no one has ever been able to find any proof of them existing. Two male dragons that come out just to hunt, a large phoenix that flies the length of the trench like it's patrolling and lives in a small cave towards the Bay of Souls, and a group of panthers that roam freely, three of them. But, again, no proof of any of those creatures has ever been found."

"Oh, is that it?" I huff out an unamused laugh. "And you're pretty positive that these creatures are gone?"

"Like I said, it's unlikely any of them are alive. But we'll keep our eyes open when we get there," he says, gripping my hand tighter as we slow our walking.

The sun is starting to set and the sky gets darker with each passing minute, so I'm going to assume we've been walking for around two hours or so. Thanks to my extra-long bath, we started our trip much later than any of them wanted, and I'm guessing we'll stop to make camp somewhat soon.

Sometimes I swear they can all read my mind because not even twenty seconds after that thought, Tate and Desmond stop ahead of us and drop their bags on the ground right in a small clearing in the dense woods. "This is as good a place as any to set up for the night," Desmond announces.

We didn't bring a tent for everyone, solely because it would have been too much weight to carry on the week-long trip to Meobith. Well, a week when you factor in all the times we'll need to stop and the types of terrain we have to get across. Shay said if it was all flat land and we traveled nonstop, we'd get there in three days.

So, we ended up bringing two tents in addition to everyone getting their own sleeping bag. They're pretty thin and tattered from years of not being used, but they'll get the job done. Luckily we're making this trip in the Spring when the nights are still somewhat warm.

Everyone unhooks their sleeping bags, while Tate and Wes set up the two tents they carried with them. Tate and Marlene are sharing one, and Wes will get the other. He tried so hard to make Shay and I take the tent, but I've been very adamant that I want him to have it and that I'll be fine sleeping outside. At first, I really just wanted my siblings safely in the tents. But, after thinking about it, getting to sleep under the stars around the fire has been something I've only ever dreamed of.

Once the tents are set up and the fire pit is built, Desmond and Shay set off for firewood, while Tate goes hunting for some food for dinner.

After all of our bellies are full of rabbit and apples, we all get cozied into our tents and sleeping bags around the roaring fire Desmond made. Being completely out in the open, the air is a little chilly, but the fire is letting off a lot of heat, keeping my toes from going numb. Luckily, being squished up next to Shay, I'm getting all of his body heat to keep me warm through the night.

I lie on my back and stare up into the sky, completely mesmerized by the view we have here. Nothing but stars fill the sky and there's nothing to block out the view. Living in Peham and being completely tree covered, I've never had the chance to have star-gazing nights like this unless I went to Lake Carsin, which rarely happened after dark.

But, here, it's like I'm in a different world with a whole new life. And, when I think about it, that's exactly what's happening and it's so crazy. I've found my birth father and he's far more than I ever could've hoped for. I have my siblings with me because they want to be part of this with me. And now I have my soulbond here by my side.

And I know that things will change drastically for all of us soon but, in this moment, I have never been happier.

Chapter 31

I'm awake the minute the sun rises. Just one of the downsides to sleeping outside.

Desmond, Shay, and I are the only ones that slept outside so we all wake up around the same time. I watch Desmond get out of his sleeping bag and head into the forest with a knife as Shay pulls me back into the sleeping bag. "Shay, I really don't think I'll be able to sleep with the sun shining right in my eyes." He groans and rolls over in the bag.

"Suit yourself, love, but I'm getting all the sleep I can," he says, his voice sleepy and muffled by the clothes he threw over his face to block the sun. I chuckle and slip out of the sleeping bag, making my way to the fire. It died a bit over night, so I do what I can to feed it and get it roaring again. It doesn't take long before the flames are happy and it's giving off a nice warm heat, easing the chill from my body.

With everyone else still sleeping, I have a few minutes to myself around the fire, and it's peaceful. I hear Desmond come back into camp not long after and he looks victorious. "Hey," I say nodding to his satchel. "You bring us some goodies?"

"Morning, kiddo," he says, setting down a few small rabbits next to the fire and holding out his bag to me. Berries fill the sack almost to the point of overflowing. My eyes widen at the amount and I look up at him with pure joy on my face. "There was a whole big patch of berry bushes back there. We must've missed them in the dark but, damn, are they tasty."

I pluck a berry from the bag and throw it in my mouth. It instantly melts on my tongue with a mix of sweet and sour. It reminds me of a blackberry, but there's something different about them that I can't place. "These are so good, thank you." I pour some in my hand and pass them back to him, trying not to be too greedy.

"No need to thank me. I want to make sure we all have energy and full stomachs before the next part of our journey," he says nervously, handing me a charred rabbit leg. I take it, knowing exactly why he's nervous. Because the next part is when we get to the Trench of Aislinn. We'll walk all day today and get to the edge of the trench where we'll make camp for the night. Then, tomorrow, we'll do what I'm most nervous about.

Climb into the trench.

"Do you think there are still creatures in the trench?" I ask, biting a piece of meat off the leg.

"I think it's possible."

I don't think my eyes have ever rolled so far into my head. "That's exactly what Shay said."

"Listen, there's no way to know for sure if anything exists there anymore. I know I've been living in this realm for a while, but I haven't dared venture to the trench," he says, cooking another rabbit over the fire. When he feels my eyes on him, he looks up at me. "What? I was scared. It's a scary place."

"I'm not judging you in the slightest. It's just weird to imagine you afraid of anything. You just seem like nothing phases you." I shrug my shoulders. "So, afraid of the trench. Anything else?" He looks sideways at me and then goes back to the rabbit. "There's something else, isn't there?"

"You're going to make fun of me," he says, avoiding my gaze.

"No, I won't," I promise. "How about this? I'll tell you what I'm afraid of if you tell me. Deal?" I give him a big smile, hoping I'll get him to agree. At this point, I'll tell him anything because I can't think of what someone as brave and strong as him could be scared of.

"Fine," he starts, and I almost jump off of the log in happiness. "But, you have to go first." Damn. I should've been prepared for that.

"With the life I've had, my fears aren't things like spiders or the dark or snakes." Desmond watches me intently as I speak. "I was so young when I had my wings and my pointed ears taken from me. I know you must've wondered about them and thank you for not asking, because they're things I try not to think about. But I replay those nights over in my head every day. And one of my biggest fears growing up was that they would grow back and I would have to go through the physical, mental, and emotional pain of losing them all over again." My voice begins to tremble and I realize I've never actually told anyone what I'm afraid of.

"Lianna-" he says, but I cut him off. If I'm going to get this out, I need to do it before I lose my courage.

"On top of those fears, I was always afraid I'd be discovered. My ex-boyfriend, Luke, knew my secret. He was abusive and manipulative, and he threatened to expose me and my family if I ever left him. He's a monster. I'm afraid of him most of all," I say. "And now, I'm afraid I'm going to lose all of you because of some fucking darkness that just wants me. You're all risking your lives for me and I'm afraid I'm not worth the risk and you'll have done of all this for nothing." I wipe at the tears streaming down my face.

He doesn't say anything as he gets up from his seat and sits next to me. We sit side by side in silence for a moment before he starts talking. "Before I met your mom, I wasn't afraid of anything. I was a kid but, still, nothing scared me. It wasn't until I realized I loved her that all of these fears started showing up. Afraid our love wouldn't be allowed, afraid that she wouldn't love me back, afraid she would love someone more. And after we lost our first child, I was so afraid I would lose Flora to her own demons. Then Drake happened and I was afraid I would never see her again. And when I finally did, I was afraid of losing her all over again. And then, the darkness came and Landon disappeared. And I watched your mother leave with you, and suddenly my whole family was gone. And I have never been so afraid in my entire life. And years went by and there was no sign of her and no sign of you and no sign of Landon."

He pauses and looks down at his feet. "Take your time," I tell him.

"Then, you came back. And now, my new biggest fear is losing you again," he finishes. I look at him with tears blurring my vision. This male that used to be so fearless is now filled with fears centered around his little family. And the amount of love I can feel coming from his every declaration is so strong, that my own heart starts to warm.

I don't know what to say to him, or if there are any words that even *should* be said. So I keep my mouth shut and lean my head on his shoulder.

"Anything good for breakfast?" Marlene's voice from behind us makes me jump and almost drop my handful of berries on the ground. I whip my head around to see her standing outside her tent wrapped in a blanket, just looking at us.

"You scared the shit out of me, Mar," I pant. "I'm sorry if we woke you."

She shakes her head. "You didn't wake me, Tate's stomach did. You would think he hasn't eaten in days with how loud it's growling," she complains.

"I *can* hear you, you know," Tate calls out from their tent. A second later, he bursts out of the flaps and walks over to Shay, gently kicking him in the side before heading to Wes' tent and shaking the whole thing lightly. The responding groans from both males is comical.

"That's one way to get them up," I say and they all join us around the fire within a few minutes.

While the males discuss plans for the day, I follow Marlene's lead to freshen up while I have the time. I grab my toothbrush and paste from my bag and make my way into the forest. Once I'm deeply in the trees and bushes, and sure no one can see or hear me, I brush my teeth and then relieve myself behind a large bush a decent way away from our camp.

I tuck my supplies into my jacket pocket and look around at my surroundings, and a feeling of familiarity washes over me. Why does this particular spot seem so familiar? And then it hits me, and my legs start to move in a full out sprint to the edge of the forest away from camp. My heart is pounding damn near out of my chest.

When I clear the trees and see what I knew was going to be here, I stop and bend forward to catch my breath with tears in my eyes. The buildings below me look just like they did in the memory, but seeing them in real life is more magical than I ever could've imagined.

I sink down to the grass a few feet from the cliffs edge and admire the abandoned Sacred City in front of me, doing what I can to take it all in, when footsteps sound behind me. I turn and see Shay walking towards me with a soft smile on his face.

"It's beautiful, isn't it?" he asks.

"It really is. I wish I could've seen it when it was full of life," I say to him as he sits in the grass behind me. He wraps his arms around my front, and I sink back into his chest, wondering what he was like when he lived here. What would he be doing right now?

"I'm certain you will one day," he says, kissing my temple. We admire the city in silence for a few minutes before he stands and pulls me up with him. "We should probably get back. It's about time to go."

I let out a sigh. "Yeah, okay." I take one final look and follow him back towards the trees when a strange feeling stops me in my tracks, causing the hairs on the back of my neck to rise and goosebumps to form. I let loose a shuddering breath and slowly check my surroundings, but there's nothing. But this sensation reminds me of how I felt when the Caviax appeared in the memory and my entire body shudders, but I shake it off as nerves. Someone would've noticed a creature like that if it was here.

I trudge through the forest quicker than usual to catch up to Shay and, when we get back to camp, everything is all packed up and ready to go.

The next few hours are uneventful, to say the least. The majority of the trip is through the forest, which keeps us out of the blazing sun, but it gets fairly boring after time. Once we get to the pass between the mountains leading to the trench, it'll get "fun", as Tate and Shay like to joke.

I'm told that the plan is to make camp at the base of one of the mountains right at the edge of the trench. Close enough to the actual trench that we're hidden but just far enough so any creatures that *do* still lurk below won't be aware of our presence.

Yet.

By the time we reach the start of the mountain pass, it's nearing dinner. Desmond says it'll only take an hour to get to where we want to camp, so we decide to push on and delay eating, much to Tate and Wes' dismay.

Of course, Desmond's right. An hour later and we're here. Along the entire edge of the trench are mountains, except for the small area leading from the pass. It's all flat, barren rock and dirt, and not a single blade of grass is worming its way through.

I set my bag down with everyone else's while Tate and Shay start to set up camp for the night, and cautiously walk to the edge so I can peer into the trench. My breathing quickens as I hastily push my anxiety down, convincing myself that I'm safe here. But this is terrifying. It's a straight drop down to the bottom, covered with jagged rocks and browned vegetation. There's a small stream that runs along the bottom and I can see many cave openings along the walls of the trench but, so far, no creatures that I can see. Thank the Goddesses. Now, if only our luck continues.

"That's got to be two miles deep," Wes says, strolling up next to me.

"Three, but good guess," Desmond corrects from behind us. "There used to be a bridge across to the other side but, clearly, that's long gone." He points to the left where a broken rope bridge is hanging from the edge a few feet over.

"If there's no bridge, then how..." Wes starts, trailing off as the realization sinks in. Something I don't think anyone has told him or my sister. That we aren't traveling safely *above* the trench.

Tomorrow morning, we'll be going *into* the trench.

Chapter 32

None of us wake up when the sun rises in the morning. We all went to bed last night with the same idea. To sleep as late as possible in order to have as much energy as we can to hike down into the trench today. That's why me, Shay, and Desmond all tied shirts around our eyes before we fell asleep so that the sun wouldn't wake us this morning.

I'm still feeling a little irritated after I lost an argument between me and, well, everyone. I wanted to tell Marlene last night about going down into the trench so she could be ready today. But, ultimately, I lost and Tate decided it'd be better if we told her this morning so she could get a good nights sleep and be well rested instead of up all night worrying. Which, yes, definitely seems like a better idea. But I hate not telling her when we all know. I don't want her mad at me for keeping it from her.

I take my spot next to Shay around the fire after rolling up my sleeping bag, and listen as Desmond starts to talk about the plan for the day. "So, the trip down should only take an hour. The trench itself is five miles wide, so it'll take roughly two hours to walk across it, and then another hour to climb back up to the top on the other side. So, all in all, about four hours total until we're on the other ridge."

Marlene starts to panic as soon as he finishes speaking. "We're going down there?" This is exactly why I wanted to tell her last night. We just sprung this terrifying plan on her and that's not fucking fair. I reach over Shay's lap to grab hold of her arm but she rips her arm away from me and shoots me a look of betrayal. A second later, she bolts out of her seat and heads towards one of the mountains behind camp. Tate is on his feet in an instant and follows after her, holding her while she yells and panics. This was the wrong choice.

Wes pulls me to side, away from the commotion, and speaks quietly to me. "What happens if something's down there? You all have strength and powers. Marlene and I have nothing," he says through gritted teeth, his eyes darting between me and Marlene.

"Listen, we don't even know if there's anything down there for sure. And you're right. We have powers and strength. None of us are going to let anything happen to either of you," I promise him. He gives me another skeptical look but lets it go. I really hope he believes me.

Shay walks over to me as Wes walks away. "Tate has Marlene calm, but we need to get going now before she starts panicking again." I look around Shay to my sister who is now tucked into Tate's chest and breathing less erratically.

I nod. It has to be around noon so, if everything goes according to plan, we'll make it to the other side of the trench and making camp by dinner. "Lead the way."

It takes us a while to maneuver the steep ramp to the bottom of the trench but, when we finally do, I'm overwhelmed with the sheer size of it. Even though we were able to see the massive size of the trench from the cliffs up top, being in the bottom of it makes it feel far larger than it actually is.

Everyone keeps fairly quiet as we walk along the bottom slowly and carefully, keeping our eyes open for anything out of the ordinary. Desmond is in the front of the group, while Tate and Marlene trail directly behind him, followed by Wes and me, leaving Shay to bring up the rear. "Did you notice the fresh deer carcass a few feet back?" he whispers into my ear from behind me.

I nod, swallowing the lump in my throat. I noticed it immediately, and I pray Marlene missed it. I can only guess the kind of thoughts that are racing through her head right now. She doesn't need to know there's something alive down here.

We're about halfway through the walk when Marlene starts to panic again. But this time, it's not as manageable. Tate tried so hard to distract her from the large black panther prowling on a small cliff a few feet away, but her gaze found it quickly and she can't handle it. All of this is too much for her and the anxiety I know she always keeps hidden away.

"Tate, you have to keep her quiet," Desmond whispers back to him, his eye never leaving the panther. It notices us, but it isn't doing anything but prowling on the rock. It's just watching. Tate panics and throws his hand over her mouth as he holds her, whispering how sorry he is in her ear the entire time. But her eyes continue to dart back and forth as she claws at his hand, trying to break free of his grasp.

"Remind me again why you couldn't use your cool elemental magic to build a bridge across," Wes whispers to me. I shoot him a look so he'll stop talking, but he knows why. I offered to do it but Desmond was very clear it was too dangerous.

"We can't risk disrupting the earth down there. If there really are creatures still living in the trench, we don't want to disturb their home. It would only anger the Goddesses. They are their pets, after all," he told me, not giving me any room to argue.

Wes' next words are cut off by an ear-piercing scream and we whip our heads around to see Marlene frozen in fear, shielded behind Tate. Desmond is still in front of them but he's now face to face with the massive panther.

Desmond has his hand palm out to the creature, trying to settle it as it stares at him with its teeth bared. Tate stands directly behind him, one hand on his sword and the other holding Marlene away from the danger.

The hairs on the back of my neck rise again, and that strange feeling comes over me again. That, combined with the pure fear that's coursing through me looking at this panther, makes my power hum just beneath my skin, begging to be released.

No, no, no. Not now, this is *definitely* not the place to lose control. I desperately push my magic down so I don't unleash it and destroy the trench around us. Instead, I unsheathe one of my knives and grab behind me for Shay, only to find my hand cutting through empty air.

I spin around expecting to see him already wielding his weapons but, instead, the space where Shay was standing is now empty. My heart starts to pound harder as all of the possibilities run through my head, especially when I see one of his knives abandoned on the ground with a few drops of blood staining the dirt next to it.

I bend down and retrieve it, tucking it into one of my holster slots. "Wes, Shay's gone," I say quietly to him.

As I slowly start to stand back up, I hear him spin on his heels as he puts his back to the large panther in front of Desmond when my words register. "What the hell do you mean Shay's gone?" he hisses, eyes darting everywhere.

"I mean, he was here and now he's not," I spit out angrily. I can't help it, I'm fucking panicking. I take a breath, though it does nothing to calm me, and compose myself as best as I can. "There's some blood on the ground and he dropped one of his knives."

Wes walks up behind me and grabs my forearm, slowly pulling me back towards the others. "Stay fucking quiet, Li, and look up to your left very slowly."

I do what he says, mostly because the tone of his voice is scaring the shit out of me. When I look to my left, my eyes widen at the sight of two more panthers prowling on a raised rock structure next to us, one noticeably larger than the other two. I pray this is the extent of them because now there are three massive female panthers surrounding us. And we're missing Shay.

It takes everything in me to ignore the massive lump that's forming in my throat and the tears welling in my eyes. I don't have the luxury to panic about Shay. Right now, I need to figure out how the hell we're going to get out of this predicament without angering the Goddesses or their pets. A million thoughts start to race through my head, but there's only one that stands out more than the others.

And it's what Desmond just told me in his home back in Shal. That I'm the last Omni Goddess in existence. I'm a *Goddess*.

What I'm thinking about doing is certifiably insane but it's the only thing I can think of that might actually work. It even feels like my magic is urging me to do it. It's flowing right at the surface and it feels like water rippling through me. It's the strangest, most comforting feeling.

I step around Wes, only going a few inches in front of him. "What the hell do you think you're doing, Li. Get back here," Wes seethes, trying to pull me back to him. But I push his arm away and summon only the essence of my power, wanting just my skin to glow iridescent and nothing more. I lock eyes with the largest of the three panthers, trying my best to stand tall and confident in front of her, ensuring that she gets a good look at my glowing skin. I just hope she realizes what it means.

The two panthers on the rock in front of me prowl forward slightly, teeth baring and heads low to the ground. But they don't attack. They just stare at me. And I know if I turn around, the first one we encountered is right behind me in the same position these two are.

But I'm not afraid. I strangely feel drawn to them, and it feels like my very blood is calling out to them now, not just my magic.

I faintly hear Marlene's muffled cries for me through someone's hand, but I don't dare break the eye contact I have with the largest panther. She no longer has her teeth bared to me and her face softens the longer we keep eye contact.

Being this close, I can see that she has dark, garnet eyes the same shade as mine. The panther on her left has deep, emerald eyes. And, without even turning around to look, I know in my heart that the panther right behind me has bright, citrine eyes.

Kaleen. Odessa. Lucienne.

Chapter 33

This can't be possible.

I take another step towards the panthers. All three of them are now standing directly in front of me and not even paying attention to anyone else. "Lianna, stop moving!" Tate hisses from behind me, still guarding Marlene as best as he can. I wave him away without taking my eyes off the garnet eyed panther and I move slowly.

The three large cats watch me as I inch closer, the rainbow iridescence of my skin shimmering brightly and beautifully, thrumming in beat with my heart. There's no way this is real.

I stretch out my hand in front of the biggest one, silently pleading that I'm right and I'm not about to get my arm bitten off by a massive cat. She lowers her head forward a bit, still eyeing me, but nudges my chest, right where my garnet sits. "Kaleen?" I whisper. Her gaze shoots back to mine at the whispered name that comes out of my mouth. A low growl escapes her throat that has the others stumbling back in fear behind me. But I don't move. I stay planted to the ground as the two panthers behind Kaleen, the ones I'm assuming are Odessa and Lucienne, bring their entire bodies down to lie on the ground before me.

"It is you, isn't it?" I say, tears welling in my eyes. She nudges my hand in confirmation and allows me to stroke her nose gently. I move in closer to her, no longer filled with fear but instead with hope and happiness. I hesitate a moment before throwing my arms around Kaleen's neck and burying my face into her silky fur, her own head wrapping around me, hugging me as best as she can in this form. I feel my magic settling in my body, no longer needing to show who I am. I let it dim and lock it back inside me.

My glow fades completely after a few moments and I pull away from Kaleen, wiping away my tears with my sleeve. "How is this even possible?" I ask her. I don't know why I expect her to speak to me. She's a panther, she can't talk. But to say I'm not disappointed would be a lie. She breaks her gaze with me and lowers her head in front of mine. I don't really understand what she wants me to do, but suddenly a warm sensation hits me like a summer breeze. I look at her as understanding washes through me.

I step forward and lean my forehead against the soft fur between her piercing eyes. Almost immediately, the all too familiar feeling of memory walking overpowers me and, in a rush of white fog, Kaleen and I are gone.

***

I open my eyes and immediately recognize the Sacred City surrounding me. Though, this version is different. It's so full of life and peace everywhere I look. The buildings are in pristine condition and the white rock homes are pearly white, with no yellowing to them. Their deep red roofs compliment them beautifully and are free of dirt and grime. Each home has a yard that is filled with vibrant green grass and fenced in by white rock fences, just like they do today but, now, I can see children playing in them and others gardening in the small patches of dirt. In the present, the fields that surround the homes are filled with decayed trees and broken down buildings. Looking at it now, the trees are all abundant fruit trees of all kinds and the buildings are barns with every animal I can imagine roaming around in the fields.

But, what really catches my attention is the lack of the wall around me. Here, there is no Quartz Wall surrounding the Angel Fae realm. It's nothing but open land in every direction I turn. And, when I look to my left in the South where the realm Gate is meant to be, there's nothing there. No walls separating anyone.

And then it hits me. I'm in a memory so far in the past that it's a time before the separation of the species. And, if Kaleen is the one showing me this memory, it must be a time when the Omni Goddesses still exist in the world. Before the Angel Fae became the most powerful species in the realms.

I turn to face Kaleen and a gasp escapes me. Gone is the sleek, black panther I entered the memory with and, in its place, is the Goddess in her true form, with three gold winged butterflies perched on her shoulders. She stands taller than me, and her curly brown hair stops right above her waist. Her skin is as milky white as her portrait in the Temple depicts her, and her garnet adorned bronze crown sits daintily on her head, its sheer red veil trailing down to the ground, right down the center of her massive wings.

I've been impressed by the wings I've seen in Desmond's memory and in the memory of my knives, but seeing Kaleen's, the first wings to exist in the realm, is magical. They look like they're made of the softest velvet imaginable and the deep red color of them matches the garnets that pepper her crown and the color of her eyes perfectly. They're incredible.

"Kaleen," I say breathlessly. A smile widens over my face at the sight of her, and getting to have the privilege to be in the presence of a Goddess everyone thinks is dead is the biggest honor of my life.

"Lianna," she responds. Her voice is raspy and has a slight accent to it that I don't recognize. When she smiles at me, I see her pointed canines peeking out of her deep red lips. I feel a sudden rush of jealousy as I look at her, and all the features that I'm supposed to have, but don't.

She lifts her hand and gently picks up the garnet hanging around my neck with her dark red painted nails, and a sad smile graces her face. "I do love knowing that my gem is with someone who deserves it," she says, placing it back down against my chest and taking my hand in hers.

"How is this happening?" I ask her, with so many other questions forming in my mind.

"That's what you're going to see, child." She leads me towards the middle of town, closer to the Temple. "The world believes that my sisters and I are long gone, but that is far from the truth. We have always been here, watching all of the travesties that my children have had to endure with no way to intervene. When we disappeared this day long ago, it wasn't our own choice like history states. No, we were forced away and there was no way for us to stop it." She looks me up and down. "In all truth, Lianna, you should not exist as you are. An Omni

Goddess, brand new yet full of old magic. It should have been impossible for another Goddess to be born in this world, but here you are."

"How am I...*this*, then?" I ask her as we cross over the bridge to the Temple. Seeing it in its prime is everything I hoped it'd be and more. Every inch is shimmering in the sunlight and even without entering the building yet, I know there's a cascade of rainbows on every surface from the countless stained glass windows.

"Truthfully, I don't know. My sisters and I have our theories, but we can't be certain if any of them are true," she tells me. I'm about to ask her about their theories when a loud commotion sounds from inside the Temple. "Time for the show, Lianna. Prepare yourself. Some vile things happened this day and, though I have come to terms with it, it might be a little jarring for you." I nod my head as we enter the Temple towards the loud commotion.

As we walk into the building, we find ourselves at the edge of a large crowd gathered, all yelling and staring at the middle of the room. Some yell in agreement at whatever's happening, while others protest it loudly. Kaleen and I move through with ease, almost like we're walking straight through the figures around us. As we clear the crowd, I see what everyone is fixated on. Standing at the bottom of the alter are Kaleen, Odessa, and Lucienne.

Their wrists are bound together by thick pieces of quartz and there's some sort of fabric shoved in each of their mouths to prevent them from speaking or yelling. Odessa and Lucienne are both sobbing and panicking, while Kaleen stands in front of them with all the calmness in the world as a small child is being pulled off of her leg. *Holy shit, that must be Aris.* "What the hell is happening?"

"This is the day we disappeared. I told you, child, history lied. It was written that we chose to leave the Angel Fae, fae, and the humans to their own devices. We would have never left them if we had the choice. And, look," she points to her and her sisters in front of us. "We weren't given a choice."

We both stand in silence for the next few minutes as Kaleen allows me to watch their history unfold, the *true* history.

"You all know who stands before you now. The Goddesses, our *protectors*, our mothers," spits out the male in the front as he glares at the three Goddesses.

"And, for a while, they lived up to those titles. Until recently. They tried to tell us that Aislinn was killed by the humans, that they were rebelling against us, Angel Fae and fae alike. It was why they banished them to their own territories, because the *humans* killed their youngest sister."

"That's exactly what happened, Gaman. They were devastated, they did what was best and you know it," a female holding a sobbing Aris yells from the front of the circle to the male in the middle, Gaman.

"I thought I could trust them. I *thought* they were doing what was best for this realm. But, they were all lies. These three monsters killed their young sister because she grew more powerful than the three of them. The three who created this world who were supposed to be the most powerful beings in existence. Aislinn was casting a shadow over them with her abilities," Gaman hisses.

I whip my head to Kaleen who looks calm and void of emotion, but allows a single tear to run down her milky white cheek. "Tell me he's lying," I seethe. "Tell me you didn't murder your own sister because she was more powerful than you were."

Kaleen lifts her head higher and wipes the single tear away, her gaze still on the crowd in front of us. "We didn't murder Aislinn. She was the light of our lives. It is true, she was becoming more powerful, but we were so proud of her for finding her potential. Her untimely death brought darkness into our world."

"Then why does this Gaman seem so sure it was you three? What did he have to gain from it?" I demand.

"In the centuries that we have been trapped in our animal forms, we have learned the truth of it all. We have been waiting for the rightful heir to come along to right the wrongs that have occurred." Kaleen glances down at me, her garnet eyes sparkling. "You asked what Gaman had to gain from all of this. See that young boy behind him, ten years old, if that?"

"The one with the short black hair?" I ask and Kaleen nods. "Yes, I see him."

"That's Gaman's son. His name is Dion. *He* is the one that killed my sister and framed the humans for it."

"But...but why? He's just a child!" Surely she has to be wrong. There's no way this child killed an all powerful Omni Goddess.

"Because he has the darkness rooted inside him. Years prior to this, we began to notice that a very small amount of our offspring had a darkness in them that was far too dangerous for the world. We dealt with them and thought we rid the realms of their dangerous magic. We were mistaken. Dion was the last one with the darkness. It urged him to kill Aislinn because she was pure light."

I turn my head back to the middle where Gaman now has the three Goddesses on their knees. He pulls a book from inside his robes and turns to a bookmarked page towards the middle. "What is he doing?"

She points at the book he's holding. "That book is The Tome of Kaius, our mother." I gape at her and she huffs out a laugh. "Yes, it is shocking to discover that the original Goddesses had a mother. Though we were the original Goddesses *here*, we came from another world in order to begin this one ourselves. Our mother sent us here with her book of magic to help grow this universe into what it is now."

"I have so many questions," I mumble.

"I will answer them all for you, one day. But, now, watch carefully," she says. I turn back to Gaman and watch as he instructs three males to hold back their heads and remove their gags, all while pouring a dark brown liquid down their throats. Gaman begins to recite a spell from the book in a language I don't know, but it sounds similar to the language written around the arches to the tombs Desmond recited. When the spell is finished, a dark black smoke starts to seep from the bodies of the Goddesses, coming from every inch of them. The crowd panics and takes large steps back as Kaleen and her sisters begin to contort, their bound limbs darkening and transforming in front of us.

"Behold. The all powerful Goddesses, reduced to this." He motions towards the Goddesses with his arm, where three black panthers now crouch. The males that once held their heads back are now holding onto them with thick chains around their necks. Gaman stalks over to them, close enough to speak to them in a whisper, but far enough away that they can't reach him.

He huffs out a laugh at the sisters before him. "Your reign is over. The world will think you abandoned your children, your realms. Sure, they will worship you for creating this world, but the truth about you will never be the real truth.

The trench where your sister was murdered, it will be named after her. I'll make sure of it. History will remember *me* as the one who saved this realm when you disappeared." He circles them and stands behind their crouching bodies, raising his voice for all to hear. "These monsters will spend the rest of their immortal lives in the trench where they murdered their sister, now known as the Trench of Aislinn."

Cheers erupt from Gaman's supporters, while the protestors silently sneak out of the Temple, leaving behind their hope for the realm. I turn to look at Kaleen, but instead of coming face to face with her Goddess form, she now stands before me as a panther once more. Bound to this body for eternity. She bows her head to me like before, and I let my forehead touch hers and watch as the truth of her past melts away.

Chapter 34

Odessa and Lucienne are circling the rest of my group when we come back from the memory, keeping their eyes locked on them as they move. But, the moment they sense Kaleen's presence, their circling ceases and they make their way back to her side.

"Lianna," Wes whisper-yells at me as I stay glued to Kaleen's side. "Can you explain what the fuck is going on? And where the hell were you?" I turn to look at Wes and the others, all while Kaleen sits on the ground right next to me, wrapping her long tail around my feet.

I take a deep breath. "I realize that what I'm about to say is going to sound completely insane, but I need you trust me." I look between my siblings, Tate, and Desmond, the pit in my stomach deepening remembering Shay's not here. I gesture to the three Goddesses behind me in their panther forms. "These three are the original Omni Goddesses. Kaleen, Odessa, and Lucienne."

Silence stretches across them and they all give me quizzical looks. Please, please believe me. After a few moments, Desmond pushes to the front and speaks up. "You're sure about this?"

I nod. "I'm positive. You want to know where I was?" I point back at the Goddesses behind me. "I was in a memory that Kaleen brought me to. I was in there with her and she presented herself to me in her Goddess form. She and her sisters are bound to these panther bodies from a curse placed on them centuries ago. They never abandoned their realm, Desmond. They were forced to leave them." He starts to walk forward and a low growl sounds from Lucienne and Odessa. Kaleen silences them with a growl of her own, almost like she's assuring them that Desmond is safe and won't hurt them.

I wonder if she can sense things about others?

Desmond comes to stand in front of me and cups my cheek in his hand. "I trust you," he whispers, then moves to the side so he's directly in front of the Goddesses and drops down onto one knee. He bows his head and speaks to them clearly and without fear. "Goddesses, it is an honor to be in your presence." He stays low and doesn't raise his head as Kaleen stalks over to him. She sits down in front of him and nudges him with her nose.

He doesn't rise, but lifts his head to face her straight on, looking right into those garnet eyes. She bows her own head, just as she had for me, but Desmond looks between me and her filled with confusion. "She wants to show you a memory. Let her," I urge him. He looks a bit unsure but, eventually, lowers his head to hers and lets their foreheads come together. They disappear in a whirl of white fog and are back before I even have time to wonder how it's going.

Kaleen does this for Wes and Tate as well, letting them see the same memory about the truth of the three Goddesses. I stand quietly to the side as they all take their turns, trying to come up with a plan to find Shay. I'm starting to get anxious with how much time has passed between him disappearing and now, but everything with the Goddesses is just to important to walk away from.

Tate comes over to me while Marlene takes her turn, sitting on the rough ground next to me. "The amount of convincing it took to get Marlene to touch Kaleen's forehead was incredible," he says. He throws his arm around my shoulder and pulls me into his side. "We'll find him, Lianna. He's tough. He can handle himself wherever he is. But I promise, we will find him."

"I'm just afraid that we've wasted too much time here. We should've been out looking for him immediately."

"At the time, we couldn't. We were surrounded by what we thought were creatures that would harm us. And then, finding out all of this? This is way too important to not deal with, don't you agree?" Tate counters, voicing exactly what I just thought of in my head.

"Of course I agree, I'm just-"

"You're worried. I know, me too. Once Marlene gets back, we'll figure something out and go find him," he assures me. I nod and bring my knees up to my chest, resting my chin on them. Tate gives my shoulders one last squeeze and stands, walking back over to the circle to wait for Marlene. I let out a sigh and try to go back to planning when a strange whisper sounds from behind me.

My back is towards the South where we entered the trench and, when I look behind me, I can see the opening of a cave carved into the trench wall right next to the ramp down, almost three miles away. At this point, we've been walking for an hour and are halfway done the journey. Backtracking to the cave would add two hours onto the trip, one hour to get there and another to get back to this point.

But I can't shake this feeling that I need to get to that cave right now.

"Desmond?" I wave him over when he hears me call his name. He excuses himself from Tate and Wes and makes his way over to me, still sitting on the ground.

"What's up, kid?" he says, plopping down next to me.

"See that cave over there?" I ask, pointing to the one in the distance. He nods. "We need to go there. Now."

He looks at me dumbfounded and shakes his head. "No, Lianna, we have to keep moving."

"No. We *need* to find Shay and something is pulling me there and I can't help but think that it's our soulbond connection and he's in there." He looks at me with genuine worry on his face as I frantically spew this all out. "Please."

"Alright, alright. If you really think we have to go there, we'll go. As soon as Marlene gets back, we *will* go." He starts to get up off the ground, but pauses and looks back at me. "Maybe see if the Goddesses can come with us."

"I can ask them," I say, feeling hopeful. I stand as he does and walk back over to the group with him, letting Wes and Tate in on the new plan. Neither of them like the idea of backtracking and adding more time, but when I basically beg them to go in hopes Shay is there, they can't find a reason to say no. They know that no matter what *they* choose to do, I'll ignore them and go find my soulbond anyway, with or without them.

I debate asking Odessa or Lucienne to help, but seeing as I haven't really made a connection with them yet, I'm guessing Kaleen will be the best option. Lucky for me, she reappears with Marlene not even a minute later. I watch her stride back to her sisters and I take a deep breath and stand up straight, trying to build up as much confidence as I can as I walk over.

They're all standing in a straight line looking down at me when I get to them. I glance between the three of them as I speak, making sure to address each one. "I have a favor to ask all of you, and I would really appreciate if I could get your help." Kaleen tilts her head to the side to inquire about the favor, and I'm momentarily in awe with how the sun shines off her fur. I suck in a breath and spit it out. "Would you mind escorting us over to that cave?" I ask pointing behind them.

Their heads all turn in unison to the direction I point in at the cave a few miles back. A low rumble comes from Odessa and I bite my lip nervously, expecting this not to go my way. Odessa and Lucienne are the first to turn their attention back to me, but they don't give me any clue to their answer. When Kaleen finally turns back around, she stalks towards me and stands at her full height in front of me. Truthfully, it's a little intimidating. Even knowing who she is, seeing them in their panther forms is downright terrifying.

She lets out a hot blow of air through her nose and nods her head in approval.

"Thank you," I say on an exhaled breath, bringing my hand to lightly stroke the fur between her eyes.

When I turn around, they're all trying to make it look like they weren't just blatantly staring at the Goddesses and I. When I see Desmond still looking at me, I nod and he relaxes his shoulders instantly, relief flooding his features knowing that the Goddesses are going to escort us.

And we might not even need their help. But who the hell knows if there are other creatures we'll need to be on guard for.

***

An hour later, we're finally at the cave opening. The air coming from within is freezing cold and damp, sending shivers down my entire body. The smell of mold and rot fills my nose and I can't stop the bile that races up my throat. I'm able to hold it back but I can hear someone behind me spew theirs onto the rocky ground.

"Do we really have to go in there, Li?" Marlene whispers from behind me.

I turn to her and look around at all of them. "Listen, I'm not going to make you come in with me. Whoever wants to come is more than welcome to, but I won't blame you if you want to stay out here."

There's a long moment of silence filled with eyes darting back and forth. It doesn't surprise me that Desmond steps forward first. "I'm coming with you. I'm not letting you go in there alone." The Goddesses grumble from behind me. Desmond lowers his head at them. "No offense to the three of you, I swear it."

I huff out a quiet laugh watching Desmond feel embarrassed in front of the Goddesses. Though, my smile fades when Tate and Marlene walk up to me somberly. "Li, I'm sorry but I would feel a little better waiting out here. And Tate doesn't want to leave me alone, obviously," she says, seeming a little nervous. "I'm so sorry."

I feel the relief settle in me knowing that she doesn't want to follow me in. I walk over to her and take her hands in mine, rubbing my thumbs along her knuckles. "You have absolutely no reason to be sorry. I'd rather you stay out here where I know you'll be safe. We have no idea what's in there, and I'll have Desmond and the Goddesses for protection. I'll be fine," I promise, kissing her cheek.

"Uh, and me? Did you happen to forget I'm here?" Wes says with a scoff, clearly offended.

"No, of course not." I roll my eyes and drag my gaze to his. "But you're staying out here with Tate and Marlene," I state. Wes starts to object but I cut him off before he even has a chance to get his words out. "I know Tate can handle things out here, but I would feel a lot better knowing that Marlene has both of you."

"Lianna-" Wes tries again.

"No, Wes. I'm not changing my mind. I'll have more than enough protection in there. I have Desmond and three terrifying panthers with me." Kaleen nudges my arm right as the words leave my mouth. I turn to the Goddesses, seeing Lucienne sitting at the mouth of the cave next to Tate. "Is she staying with them?" Kaleen nods her head slowly and I feel even more relief knowing they'll have Lucienne with them.

"Well, that makes me feel better," Wes says. "I'll stay out here, but please try to hurry." He pulls me into a tight embrace and I let myself melt into his hug just for a moment. I pull away and start to walk into the cave with Desmond on my right, Kaleen on my left, and Odessa up front.

The light is swallowed up by the dark of the cave not long after we enter. "You don't happen to have any matches in your bag, do you?" I ask Desmond as I pick up a few small sticks in my path.

"Not exactly matches, but I have something that'll help," he says and a moment later, our path is completely illuminated. I look to Desmond in surprise, seeing a small ball of fire in his hand.

"I didn't know you could do that," I say in awe.

He shrugs. "I tend not to use my magic these days."

"Why not?" I ask intrusively.

"When I was living in Shal on my own all those years, I had everything I needed. There was never really any need to use it," he tells me, pulling me out of the way of a small puddle.

"Thanks," I say quietly, darting my gaze back and forth between the cave and Desmond.

One corner of his mouth turns up but I watch the sadness bloom over his features. "When I lost you, your mom, and Landon, I lost all hope. And after she disappeared, Drake was convinced it was my fault. He wanted me imprisoned or killed, and he didn't care which one it was, so I left. When I found refuge in Shal, it was utterly abandoned. There wasn't a trace of a single Angel Fae anywhere. I searched for years for your mom and came up empty every time. Which was already difficult because I couldn't leave the Angel Fae territories all thanks to Drake and his order to kill me if I stepped foot in his kingdom."

"I had no idea, Desmond," I sigh, and then realization rushes through me. "Wait, we're going to Meobith, though. Won't they try to kill you if you go there?"

He shakes his head. "No one in Meobith would dare. It's a small town in the middle of the desert and everyone who lives there was strongly against the Angel Fae executions back in King Ashton's day. It's safe there."

I open my mouth to ask more about Desmond's powers, knowing he has more being an Angel Fae, but I'm interrupted by Odessa's low growl ahead of us. She's stopped in the middle of the tunnel a few feet ahead in a very defensive stance, her head low to the ground.

Desmond stops me and leans close to my ear. "Unsheathe my sword and hold it in front of me."

I do as he says and, when it's directly in front of him, he touches his flame to the blade, igniting it instantly. "Shit," I breathe out, as he takes the sword from my grasp and holds it in front of him.

"Pretty fun, right?" he chuckles. "I would get those blades of yours out, just to be safe."

I nod, unsheathing my blades and holding them tightly at my sides. Kaleen stops next to us, waiting for Odessa to give any signal and, when she does, Kaleen starts forward, urging us with her.

I take a deep breath and follow to where Kaleen stands next to Odessa fiercely. I have no idea what to even expect but, as I get closer, I can see a small glint of light, like a small fire dying down.

I sidestep between Kaleen and Odessa to see what has them so on edge. It must not be too dangerous if they're letting me pass with this much ease. I follow their line of sight and, when I see it, I gasp and stumble back into Kaleen's soft body.

"What is it?" Desmond rushes up beside me and, when he sees what's in front of us, his sword clangs to the ground. "Oh, fuck." He swiftly pulls my head against his chest and turns me around so I won't have to see the devastating scene.

But it's too late. It's engrained in my mind already.

Lying in a pool of his own blood, chest rapidly rising and falling, is Shay.

Chapter 35

I rip myself out of Desmond's grasp and run over to Shay as fast as my legs will take me, almost slipping in the blood that surrounds him. I crash to my knees the second I'm next to him and immediately start looking for the wound that's causing all of this blood.

I find it quickly. There's a large slash across his stomach and his trembling hands are desperately trying to keep pressure on it, but failing miserably. I throw my own hands over his and put more pressure on the wound, pulling a groan from his bloodied lips. *A good sign, I think?*

"Shay. Shay, I'm here. I found you," I say, panic filling my words. His eyelids flutter at the sound of my voice but they don't open. He *needs* to open his eyes. "Desmond, come help me, please!"

Desmond's already at my side and I can't remember when that happened, but he's here and he can help me. "What do you want me to do?" he asks, eyeing the blood seeping from between my fingers.

"In my bag is a spare shirt and spare pants. Get them both and help me get this bleeding under control," I yell. He yanks the bag open on my back and rifles around until he finds the spare clothing.

"Alright, I have them but, I can't tie them, Lianna," he says. A momentary bout of anger creeps over me when he says that, and it's very quickly replaced with embarrassment. Of course he can't fucking tie them. He's missing a hand. I need to rethink my plan.

"I know, I will. I'm going to lift our hands and I need you to put the shirt over the wound. Then I'll put the pants on top and try my best to tie them around his middle. But you need to keep pressure on the wound while I do it, okay?"

He nods. "When you're ready, honey." I take a deep breath and look around the cave. *What the hell happened here?*

"Alright, on the count of three," I say, anxiously biting my lower lip. "One, two, three."

As soon as the word leaves my mouth, we're on the move. I lift both mine and Shay's hands from the wound and Desmond gets the shirt placed perfectly over the slash while I situate the pants right on top of it. Desmond holds pressure as best as he can without hurting Shay too much while I thread the pant legs underneath his back and around to his side, tightly tying a knot to keep it in place.

Only when I'm sure the knot will hold do I tell Desmond to move his hands to see if the makeshift bandage works. He's still bleeding but now he's not losing it in massive quantities. "Why isn't he healing?" I ask angrily.

"Just because his heritage allows him to heal quickly, doesn't mean it'll happen right before our eyes," he says calmly.

"I didn't expect it to! But fuck, this is a lot of blood. He has to have been like this for a while. Why isn't it working?" I seethe, snapping at Desmond. Regret fills me immediately at my angry outburst and I drop my head, letting out a sigh. "I'm sorry. I just don't understand."

"Listen to me. He will heal. But, with how deep that gash is, it might take a few more hours. We got to him in good time, Lianna," he says, bringing his arm around my shoulders. I lean into him and I can't help the sobs that come from deep in my chest.

"How the hell are we going to get him out of here?" I question out loud. I reach over to a nearby puddle of water to wash my bloodied hands and wipe them on my pants.

In answer, Kaleen strides over to us and gently nudges his feet. "There's your answer," Desmond retorts. He pushes himself up from the ground and helps me to my feet.

"You're going to carry him?" I ask her and, without hesitation, she nods her sleek, black head at me. Odessa warily stands back a few feet, but I peer around Kaleen to make sure she knows I'm speaking to her, too. "Thank you."

Together, Desmond and I lift Shay up onto Kaleen's back, positioning him so he won't slide off. It pulls pained groans from him and, as much as it hurts to hear him in pain, him making noise means he's alive. I start to back away from the Goddess after he's all settled, but she stops me with her paw and motions to her back with her head.

"I think she wants you up there, too," Desmond whispers.

"Help me up." Kaleen lowers herself more, allowing Desmond to help lift me onto her back right behind Shay, keeping him far more stable.

"Keep your pace slower, please. Without him able to keep himself up, it's going take a lot from me to be able to keep him steady," I say softly to Kaleen. She huffs out a breath and starts forward slowly with Desmond leading the way and Odessa following behind us.

It only takes a few minutes to get back out of the cave and, when we do, all hell breaks loose when they all see the state Shay's in. Tate's the first to make it to us as I jump off of Kaleen's back, panicking when he sees the bloodied mess of a shirt around his middle.

"What the fuck happened?" Tate yells, eyes darting back and forth between Desmond and I. He touches Shay's neck to feel for a pulse, but pulls away quickly. *Weird.*

"I don't know. Odessa found him like this. There was nothing else in that cave and no blood trail in or out. I don't know what happened, I'm sorry," I say, tears falling from my eyes. Tate's expression softens and he pulls me into a gentle hug, resting his chin on my forehead.

"It's not your fault," Tate reassures me.

"He'll heal soon. Give it some time," Desmond reminds us. Tate nods and breaks our embrace to pull Desmond to the side to talk.

I make my way to my siblings, but I can't help but eavesdrop on what Tate has to say to Desmond. "That is *not* Shay, Des. What the fuck happened?"

"Quiet, keep your damn voice down. I don't know what happened but, until we can figure this out, don't say anything to Lianna. Not yet," Desmond replies. I shake their voices from my head, pretending I didn't just overhear them voicing my own concerns. Because when I touched Shay in that cave, he *felt* different.

Wes and Marlene wrap me in a hug and let me cry into them, knowing that the tears I let out in the cave were not all of them. Marlene's hand comes up to move the hair out of my face as she holds me close. "We won't let anything happen to him, Li. You heard Desmond. He said he'll heal soon," she says into the side of my head.

"If we get moving now, we'll be out of this damn trench in a few hours and safely back on normal ground where we can make camp for the night. I guarantee he'll be better by morning," Wes adds, standing next to Marlene and I, holding my hand in his.

I nod and drop my head to try and regulate my uneven breaths. But the second my eyes make contact with the hem of my shirt, eyeing the blood that's soaking the once green fabric, I lose it. "Fuck." I furiously rub it on my pant leg, trying to rid it of Shay's blood, as I feel the sudden warmth of my magic welling in me again. "Not now!" I scream, urging the magic to disappear and keep itself inside.

I *know* how to control my Feeler magic. I've been keeping it in check for a while now. Even when I found Shay in the cave, I felt it coming but had been able to push it away.

But right now, I have no control. It's slowly creeping its way along my skin and a faint roar is sounding in my ears. The iridescent glow comes on much quicker than usual and the red mist is pooling at my feet where I'm standing.

I look up to Marlene and Wes in a panic. They're both far too close to me and screaming something in my face, but I can't hear them. I squeeze my eyes shut as the roaring in my body intensifies. I'm going to lose whatever ounce of control I still have. They need to move, why won't they fucking move?

Seeing his blood staining my clothes broke something inside me, even though he's right next to me on Kaleen's back. His breathing is far more normal than earlier and the bleeding is slowing with each minute that passes.

But, it's all too much.

"Lianna, you need to breathe," I barely hear Desmond say. I snap my eyes open just as he pushes my siblings to safety and stands right in front of me. He starts to say something else, but I can't understand any of his words. The magic is too overpowering.

Red mist is coating every inch of me and is dimming my iridescent glow substantially. The mist isn't its usual transparent color, but instead, more opaque which I don't think is a good thing. I'm barely able to see Tate and Desmond pull Wes and Marlene behind a large rock, the Goddesses in tow behind them with Shay still on Kaleen's back, before my emotions take control and the red mist erupts from me in every direction.

It doesn't just erupt, it explodes. Instead of just passing through everything it comes in contact with like it usually does, it hardens and demolishes rocks, creating cracks along the trench floor as it moves.

This. This is what Desmond warned me about when he taught me control. But what the fuck did he tell me about this part?

I push through the magic surging in me to search my memory for the first day Desmond started training me about control, desperately trying to remember what he told me about how to reign in wild magic.

***

"It's too much, Desmond! Help!" I scream to him. Sweat and tears are pouring down my face, mixing together in salty streaks through the dirt that cakes my cheeks.

He wanted to spark deep emotions in me to get my Feeler magic to come out, that way I can use what he's taught me to control it so I won't hurt myself or anyone else with it.

"I can't help you, Lianna. You have to be able to do this yourself. There will be times when your emotions will come on too strong and it will get dangerous. You need to know how to shut them off and get your magic under control," he yells from where he sits behind a large tree trunk, keeping himself from getting hurt if my mists get too wild.

"I can't do it!" I pant. The red mist that usually encases my body when my Feeler magic comes out is starting to become more opaque with each second and Desmond

warned me about this part. When it gets this way, the mists will become destructive to my surroundings and completely drain me. "I don't remember what to do!"

"You do, I know you do. Step one, breathe! Control your breathing, damn it!" he yells frantically, seeing the mist covering my skin more. I nod at him, feeling my heart race faster. With panic or because of my magic, I don't know, but I'm scared, which only fuels the magic more.

But then I remember.

Step one, breathe.

Step two, pinpoint where in the body the emotion is rooted.

Step three, cut off the emotion altogether.

I know that in a real fight, I won't have much time to get through the steps if I lose control so I need to be able to do it quickly.

I close my eyes tightly and let out the breath I'm holding. I take in a few deep breaths and let each exhale relax my shoulders, as I feel the calm wash over me.

When I feel a bit more in control, I pinpoint where the root of this emotion is stemming from and will it to leave. I have no idea if this is even the right way to cut off the emotions, but I have no other option. Desmond doesn't have this ability, so all the knowledge he has is going off of what he's read about Feeler magic.

At first, nothing happens. My emotions are still going wild and the mist is almost fully opaque. I take another deep breath and dive back into my mind.

This time, though, instead of just willing it to leave, I imagine the emotion as a physical shape in my mind and visualize it dissolving out of me.

Within seconds, I can feel my magic start to die down and I watch as the mists slowly become transparent once more.

"Good, Lianna. You got it," Desmond yells. "Now, before all of the emotion is gone, try to control it to your will, form it into something. You are in charge, not the emotions."

I close my eyes. I can see the dissolving emotion in my mind and, before it all fades away, I force it to stop. I picture my magic coming from my arms in controlled ropes of red mist, almost like I'm holding a whip of magic in each hand.

The sound of Desmond yelling my name has me opening my eyes, coming face to face with what I just imagined in my mind.

I am physically holding my power in my hands, like two trailing whips.

A grin spreads across my face as I lift my hands and watch in amazement as the whips follow my movements.

I'm in control now.

***

I open my eyes to someone screaming for me.

My mind can't decipher who the voice belongs to, but I can see that my magic is destroying too much down here. If it goes on any longer, I'm sure that the walls of the trench will come down.

Not only that, but I can feel myself draining substantially. My entire body feels weak and I'm getting more tired than I've ever been. This needs to stop.

Doing exactly what Desmond taught me, I search through my mind for the source of this emotion and take control of it, willing it to dissolve completely out of me.

I can feel as the mists slowly retract back to me and seep into my skin, disappearing within seconds.

I stumble slightly as the force of my magic comes to a halt, feeling lighter on my feet but far too weak. My limbs are too heavy, my eyes are stinging, and my head is pounding. I crumble to my knees, crashing down on them with incredible force, but I don't feel any of the pain. Later I definitely will. The sound of multiple sets of feet running towards me is too loud, and I clutch my hands over my ears as they get closer.

"Li, are you ok? Please tell me you're ok," the sound of Marlene's voice is comforting, even though her usual soft tone is now sharp and full of panic.

I smile weakly at her, finding I'm not able to use the muscles in my face all too well. That's probably not a good sign. "I'm fine, Mar. I promise. Just need a nap, I think." I use some of the strength left in me to stand and, just when I feel myself falling back down, a warm head supports my back.

I turn around to find the three Goddesses behind me, their unique eyes tracking my every movement, and now there's worry etching all of their faces.

Great, I've *worried* the Goddesses. Lucienne moves from where she caught me to stand adjacent to her sister, and she nods up to the sky.

The sun is getting too low. Our time with daylight is quickly dwindling and, if I'm catching on to what the Goddesses are hinting at, staying down here when it gets dark isn't the best idea.

I push the power draining exhaustion away and stretch out my limbs before attempting to walk over to Desmond. When he realizes it's him I'm stumbling to, he meets me halfway and grabs onto my arm to help keep me upright. I'm out of breath from just walking that small distance. How the hell am I going to make it five miles across the entire trench?

"What're you thinking?" Desmond asks, Tate close behind.

"I think that we're losing daylight and I don't want to be down here when the night creatures come out," I say in a hushed voice. Marlene doesn't need another reason to worry. "The Goddesses look on edge with the sun going down and I'm not taking that as a good sign."

"You think you'll be fine making that trip?" Tate asks, eyeing my weakened body up and down with an arched brow. I nod. It's obvious that Tate is far from convinced, but there's no other option. I *have* to be fine.

"At most, it'll be two hours. By the time we make it to the other side, the sun will be starting to set. An hour to climb out of this damn trench and we'll be setting up camp by dinner," I say, trying to find the strength in me somewhere.

"I don't think any of us believe you right now, Lianna, but I agree we have to keep moving. We'll get going if you promise us one thing," Tate says. I narrow my eyes at him and nod, waiting for him to continue. "If walking gets to be too much, you have to tell us. No pretending you're fine. We can all take turns carrying you on ours backs, and I'm just going to assume that Odessa and Lucienne would be willing to do that, too."

I glance at the Goddesses and they both give me low nods before bringing their gaze to me. They will. And I know all of them will do what they can to help me. That knowledge fills me with so many conflicting emotions, but I can't think about that now.

I have to think about getting out of this damn trench.

And I need to figure out what the hell happened to Shay in that cave.

Chapter 36

I made it about twenty minutes before I collapsed into Tate's back.

I tried to play it off like I was fine, but no one believed me. They all just stayed rooted to where they stopped until I agreed to let someone carry me. Desmond volunteered first but we quickly found out how hard it is to maneuver around his wings. And that's how I ended up where I am now, on Wes' back as he struggles to carry me.

We're halfway through the walk, which means I've been on his back for close to forty minutes out of the hour we've been walking. "Seriously, Wes, I promise I'm good to walk now. It's been long enough and you're probably exhausted from carrying me."

"Are you sure? I don't mind, Li," Wes says over his shoulder to me. I can see the distinct sheen of sweat lining his hairline and his face is as red as a tomato. I know for a fact that he got tired twenty minutes ago, but he refused to admit it and continued to carry me. Even with Wes being decently strong, I'm still inches taller than he is and I weigh a bit more than him.

"Yes, I'm sure. Besides, you look like you're about to pass out. I don't feel as drained anymore and we're halfway to the other side," I assure him.

He stops walking and gently puts me on solid ground. I stumble a little and Wes gives me a look, like he's about to pick me back up. "My legs are asleep, Wes. I haven't used them in forty minutes. Give me a break."

He watches as I stretch them out and take a few wobbly steps forward before he's convinced I'm telling the truth. And, once he's satisfied, we continue on.

Wes speeds up a bit and starts walking with Tate and Marlene, while I hang back with Desmond and the Goddesses, periodically checking Shay's injury.

He isn't fully awake yet but, every now and then, he opens his eyes for a brief moment before going back to sleep.

"When do you think he'll wake up?" I ask Desmond.

He looks over at Shay and shrugs. "If I had to guess, I'd say by the time we get camp set up tonight. Last I checked his wound, it looked almost fully healed and his breathing is back to normal."

I nod. It's a good sign and I should be ecstatic about it. But, I'm not. Don't get me wrong, I'm relieved he's coming around, but I know what I felt when I first touched him. And overhearing Tate and Desmond only confirmed what I felt.

I keep quiet for a few moments and stare straight ahead as the other side of the trench gets closer. The sun is much lower now and hiding behind the mountains, so we're cast in the shadows. The only source of our light, now, is the glow of the sun peeking around the sides of the mountain as it sets. So far, we've only run into some small snakes and rats, but nothing more than that, thank the Goddesses.

"I heard you talking to Tate about Shay," I say quietly, breaking the silence. Desmond turns his head to me and opens his mouth before closing it again as he tries to find the right words.

"Lianna, I-" he starts, but I cut him off.

"I felt it, too." Desmond stares at me in shock, trying to process what I'm admitting. "When we found him in the cave and I touched him for the first time, it felt wrong. *He* felt wrong. It's like half of him is the Shay I fell in love with, and the other half is something else. Something cold and vicious. I chalked it up to his injury at the time but, even still, I feel that same sensation now." My eyes dart over to Shay and, thankfully, his eyes are still closed.

"We'll figure it out. Once he wakes up and can tell us what happened to him...we'll figure it out," Desmond says, cupping my face in his hand. I lean my head into his palm and feel so grateful for him and everything he's done for me. The past few months of getting to know Desmond and hearing about his past with my mom has been a gift to me. For years after I started getting the letters from Drake and being told he was my father, I was so afraid to meet him and for my life to change completely. With him being the King of Odrera, I wasn't ready to step into this life of being a princess when all I've ever known is the small, quaint life of living in Peham.

But knowing that Desmond is my real father, and knowing the kind of life he has lived and wants to continue to live, I can see that's the kind of life I want to be a part of. Not a royal life in the city, but a simple life in the middle of nowhere.

"Everything ok, honey?" Desmond says, breaking me from my stupor. He's looking at me like I have two heads and I guess I must've spaced out for a few minutes.

"Yeah, I was just thinking, that's all." I smile at him before turning my attention back to the trench wall ahead of us.

"Not much longer now. Less than thirty minutes, if I had to guess," Tate calls back. Relief floods me as I daydream about getting to sit down and relax without having to worry about creatures attacking us.

***

Tate's right. Barely.

It took twenty-eight minutes to get to the other side of the trench, according to Marlene. I'm not sure where the hell it came from, but she conveniently had an old watch in her pocket that she says came from Tate's old bedroom in Shal.

We halt at the bottom of the path up, which looks like makeshift stairs carved into the side of the wall. Again, convenient.

"No use just looking at it," Wes says as he starts to climb up the steps. We all begin to follow, Desmond and I still in the back, when I feel a slight nudge on my arm. When I turn and see Kaleen directly behind me, while her sisters stand a few feet behind her unmoving, I realize that something isn't right.

"You're not coming, are you?" I ask, not all that surprised but still hurt. After all, they've been bound here by their curse. I should've known they wouldn't be able to leave.

Kaleen brings her head to mine and lets our foreheads rest against one another, a gesture that means far too much to me now. I throw my arms around her, reveling in the feeling of her silky black fur under my arms, as a small stream of tears runs down my cheeks. I faintly hear Tate and Desmond walk around us to get Shay off of her back, but I don't care. I'm doing everything I can to stay in this moment with her. The one true connection I have to my heritage. I have so much I want to learn from them and I don't know if I'll ever get that chance again.

Slowly, Lucienne and Odessa come to stand on either side of me. Lucienne rests her own forehead against my right side while Odessa stays on my left and, with the three of them surrounding me, I feel more at home than I ever have. These Goddesses are the only ones just like me and they've been lost to the world until now.

My skin begins to warm slightly and I know I'm glowing without even having to look. But, what I wasn't expecting to see is all three of the Goddesses glowing, too. But, instead of an iridescent shine like Shay said they had, they each glow their own color. Kaleen has varying shades of red shining off her figure, Lucienne has shades of citrine, yellows, and oranges, and Odessa shines bright green hues. And my rainbow iridescence shines through their colors like a beacon. When I lock eyes with Kaleen, I hear it.

In my mind, Kaleen speaks to me. "Speak to us when you need us. We will find you again, Lianna. You are the only hope for this world and for your kind. Do not give up." I nod at her as she finishes speaking, her glow dimming as she steps away from me.

Lucienne is the next to nudge me and, when I make eye contact with her citrine eyes, the same thing happens. Unlike the low, raspy voice of Kaleen, Lucienne has a soft, smooth voice. "Lianna, meeting you was everything I hoped. I am honored that you are the last Goddess." I bow to her as her glow dims, too, just as Kaleen's.

I turn to Odessa before she even has a chance to get my attention. I smile at her as she stares at me with her emerald eyes. "Be careful, Goddess. There is someone among you that does not belong, and there will be more. Do not let them fool you. *You* are what we've been waiting for." I swallow the lump in my throat as I glance sideways at Shay, now limply hanging between Wes and Tate.

When the Goddesses pull away, they bow low to the ground in front of me, letting out three deep growls as a goodbye to the rest of the group. We all stand at the bottom of the stairs as we watch them prowl towards the middle of the trench, back to wherever they've been since they were cursed. I close my eyes and take a deep breath, feeling as my glow dims to nothing.

With my back towards everyone still, I bring my hand in front of me and slowly open my fist, palm up. I felt something appear in my hand when the three Goddesses all surrounded me, but didn't dare ask about it or look until they left.

But, now, I see that there's a thin golden ring shaped into leafy vines sitting in the middle of my palm. I have no idea what it means or what it does, but if the Goddesses are leaving it with me, it has to be important. I slide it onto my left index finger, marveling at how perfectly it fits me.

I blow air out my nose as I huff out a small laugh. Of course it does. It's a magic ring gifted to me by the Goddesses.

"Ready, Li?" I hear Wes call from behind me. I drag my gaze towards the trench once more to see that the Goddesses are completely out of sight, now, and nod.

"Coming," I say, turning towards them. Marlene and I follow behind Desmond as he guides us, while Tate and Wes try to maneuver Shay up the steep stairs.

Before we know it, we'll be safely at the top and Shay will be awake soon.

But after Odessa's warning, I can't help but wonder if *he* is what we need to be afraid of.

Chapter 37

T he sun is filling the sky with hues of reds, pinks, and oranges by the time we get to the top.

Climbing up was surprisingly easy, considering Wes and Tate basically carried Shay the whole time, and I'm still running on fumes. But it took a little under an hour, which Desmond said he never expected.

Camp setup takes about twenty minutes and, not long after, we're all huddled around the fire Tate made and eating porridge from packets I shoved at the bottom of my backpack. It's not the best, and I'm sure it's so far past expired, but at least it's something to fill our stomachs until we can hunt for something in the morning.

I'm pushing my arms through my jacket for extra warmth when Desmond walks up to me. Tate and Marlene are already in their tent and snoring away, and Wes is closing the flap of his, giving me a tired smile just before shutting himself in. "You've got first watch, I take it?" I say to him, still struggling with my sleeves.

He nods. "You having some trouble there?" he asks with a hint of sarcasm.

"You've got a good eye there," I say, immediately regretting the words that come out of my mouth. I squeeze my eyes shut at the realization of what I actually said and as I look up at him, at the *one eye* that he still has, my face flushes bright red. "That was the stupidest fucking thing I've ever said." But he's not even phased. He just bursts into laughter loud enough that it wakes everyone else in our group, causing them to scream at him through their tents.

"Holy shit, that was incredible," he says through laughs. "Thanks, honey, I needed that."

The red on my face slowly disappears, and I look down at the ground in front of me, trying to hide my grin. I bring my head back up, smile still plastered on my face, and see Desmond looking at me smiling. "What?" I ask.

He shakes his head. "You look so much like your mother when you smile," he says, his smile turning sad. "Do you finally want to hear how I lost it?" He points to his eye and I straighten in my seat. In all the time I've known him, it hasn't come up. He always told me he'd tell me about it, but not until the right time. I guess there was never a right time until now.

"I do," I say softly, turning in my seat to face him better. "I don't know if I'm ready to see it, though."

"I don't blame you. It was somewhat gruesome," he admits. "I can *tell* you the shortened version, if you want?"

"I think that would be better, if that's alright with you." Having to witness him losing his arm was one thing, because I didn't know him yet. But now, with everything between us, I don't think I could handle it.

"It happened a few years after I lost my arm. When I told you that I spent years looking for you mother, I was also looking for Landon, too. And I haven't been entirely truthful with any of you."

I furrow my brows in confusion. "What do you mean? You've been lying to us?"

"Not exactly. It's a little more complicated than that." He lets out a breath. "Ten years after I lost all of you, I found a trace of Landon." The glow of the fire shines off of the tears streaming from his eye. He doesn't wipe it away, though, and he's not ashamed about it either.

"What did you find?" I ask carefully. I don't want to overstep at all, but my heart is twisting in knots hearing this because...that's my brother.

"I found a wanted poster of him, of all fucking things. I was hiding out in a dirty inn on the border of Meobith and Bayra, and it was being plastered to the bulletin in the lobby when I walked in one day." He reaches into his jacket and pulls out a folded up piece of paper and hands it to me. I take it from him so gently, feeling the softness of the paper in my fingers. He must unfold this multiple times a day for it to be like this. I unfold it and look down at the male looking back at me. He's so much older in this picture from when I saw him in the memory.

And he looks just like Desmond. Though Desmond has a thicker beard, Landon's thin one is halfway there in this picture. They both have the same exact eye and nose shape, but his lips are the same shade as mine. He has a similar silver eye color like Desmond and his hair is dark brown and is buzzed short in this picture.

I scan the words on the poster and I'm confused. "Wanted for kidnapping and murder?" I whip my head to look at Desmond. "This can't be right, can it? How the hell did he go from that young male in your memory to...this?"

Desmond shakes his head. "I don't know. But after he disappeared from Odrera, I questioned everyone that saw him. They said that he looked possessed and wandered off." He pokes his finger at the poster. "*This* is not my Landon. Something made him do these things. I refuse to believe that the boy I raised did this."

"I believe you," I tell him.

He smiles and folds the poster back up, replacing it in his jacket. "When I found the poster, I started asking around. Pretended I was a bounty hunter and got all the information I could. Turned out, he was quite elusive and no one has been able to find any trace of him. But-"

"But, you did."

"I did. I trailed him all the way to the edge of Bayra on a path towards Marsa. I hired a boat crew to take me there but, just as we got close to Marsa, we were attacked by Drake's soldiers. Turns out someone tipped them off about my whereabouts when I inquired about a crew and they were sent to kill me. My crew actually fought *with* me against the Odrera soldiers, even once they knew who I was. We were doing pretty well for ourselves until one of the soldiers snuck up on me from behind and stabbed me straight through the eye with a knife. I was immediately able to bring my sword back on him, but the pain of the knife stuck in my eye was unbearable. One of the other soldiers took advantage of my momentary lapse and pushed me over the edge into the ocean."

I let out the breath I don't realize I'm holding and wipe away a single tear on my cheek. "How the hell did you survive that?"

"I didn't think I would. I was in so much pain and I'm not the best swimmer to begin with for obvious reasons. It was a struggle to stay above the water, especially with how water logged my wings were. But, just when I thought I was going to have to give up, someone or something saved me. I was on the edge of consciousness so I have no idea what it was that saved me. But I felt something grab me and then I woke up on the shores of Eldolon, right outside of the Quartz Wall. My eye was sewn shut and I was all alone. That day, I figured it would be the best for me if I stayed inside the Angel Fae territories for my own safety. Especially if I wanted to be reunited with you and your mother one day."

"Did you ever find out what it was that saved you that day? Someone from Marsa?" I ask, my curiosity getting the better of me.

"No, never did. And no one lives on Marsa. Since the time of the Goddesses, that island has been unexplored and left alone. In the past, it was because the fae were afraid of the creatures that dwelled there and, over time, it just became common sense to stay away," he tells me. "But I have my theories about my rescue."

I resume putting on my jacket and slide into my sleeping bag in front of the fire, right next to where Shay sleeps in his own sleeping bag. I prop myself up on my elbow and look up at Desmond, who is now intently looking at Shay. "What do you think he'll be like when he wakes up?" I ask, changing the subject.

He shrugs. "I don't know. There might not even be anything wrong with him, Lianna. He just *felt* off when we got to him. But I could've been feeling some other presence in the cave that wasn't even connected to him."

I shake my head. "No. It's him. I felt it, Tate felt it. Something happened to him in that cave and we all know it." I roll onto my back and stare at the night sky. "I don't know how I'm supposed to feel when he does wake up. Obviously I'm happy we have him back and he's alive, but what if he becomes a danger to us? You can't expect me to leave him behind or, worse, kill him."

"We would never ask you to do that. And we wouldn't leave him behind, either. Worst case scenario, if he becomes a problem, we restrain him and keep a close eye on him until we get to Meobith." Desmond reaches over to grab my wrist. "We are all with you. We won't do anything that will hurt you in any way."

"I'm scared, Des," I admit, but the shock that spreads across his face isn't because I'm afraid. No, it's because I didn't call him Desmond. I used the nickname Shay and Tate use for him. "Is it alright if I call you that?"

He nods and I can see he's trying to hide the slight tremble in his lip. "Yeah, of course it's alright. Desmond was way too formal, anyway." He gives me a soft smile and walks to my side . "Get some rest. I'll keep my eye on you, too."

I stare at him as he bends over and pulls the sleeping bag up to my chin, tucking me in like I'm a child. Then, he brings his face near mine and kisses my forehead lightly, before standing back up and sitting at the fire. That simple gesture warms me to my core. I turn to lay on my left side so I'm facing Shay and watch as his chest rises and falls rhythmically, urging me to sleep.

I close my eyes and sleep consumes me almost instantly.

***

"Lianna, wake up," Des hisses in my ear, shaking me awake. I groan as I sit up and rub my eyes, forcing myself to wake up. Des is right in front of me and when I look to my left, I bolt to my feet. Tate has Shay on the ground on his stomach, his *injured* stomach, with his hands behind his back.

"What the fuck is going on?" I demand, anger boiling inside me.

"I don't know," Shay chokes out. "Ask *him*." He motions to Tate with his head.

"He woke up in a fit and unsheathed one of your knives when we tried to get close to him," Tate explains, looking distressed. "I'm sorry, it was just a precaution."

"And like I explained, I was just confused because the last thing I remember was being attacked in that cave and I was disoriented. I thought I was with *them*," Shay explains.

I glance behind Tate to where Marlene is tucked behind Wes' back, both with knives in their hands. *Shit. How bad was this freak out?* "Can you tell us what you remember?" I ask Shay, bringing my gaze back to him.

"Can we get him off of me first?" he asks. I bite my lip anxiously, reminding myself that this is my soulbond and not our enemy. That I trust him with my life and, unless I show him I trust him, we'll never find out what happened to him.

I bring my gaze up to Tate and nod. "Let him go."

His mouth drops open. "Lianna, I don't-"

"No, we're not debating this. It's Shay. He's been through enough and you're treating him like the villain. Let's cut him some slack, please?" I say, keeping my voice as steady as I can. I know they don't believe I'm convinced this easily it's Shay, and I'm really hoping they realize what I'm trying to do. That this is the only way to move forward.

"Fine," Tate says begrudgingly. But he lets go of his wrists and helps him to his feet anyway. Tate stalks away to where Marlene is and Wes takes his previous spot by Shay's side.

"Thank you," Shay calls after Tate. Then he looks at me. "Look, I'm sorry for how I woke up. Like I said, I was disoriented and my mind was convinced I was still stuck in that cave fighting off death."

"I know. Just, don't pull that shit again, Shay. Seriously. Because next time I'm going to let Tate keep you restrained for the rest of the trip. Understood?"

"Completely," he says, closing the distance between us. He takes my hand in his and a chill travels through me. I suppress it and try not to let anyone else see me shudder at his touch. But he still doesn't feel right. "I can tell you what I remember but it's all pretty foggy so just bear with me."

"It might be easier if I just memory walk, that way it's all right in front of us and you don't have to worry about trying to recall all the details," I offer, my eyes locked on Shay. If I wasn't locked in on him, I would've missed the nervous look that he almost lets slip. It's there for a millisecond and then it's gone.

What the hell does he have to be nervous about?

"Sure, go for it," he says. There's a slight tremble in his voice as he looks down at our joined hands. The second Shay isn't looking, I quickly glance back at Des, my eyes widening when our gazes meet. I watch his jaw clench and then he slowly makes his way behind me, touching my back with his hand.

Before Shay can realize Des has his hand on my back, I call for my magic and let it flow through me, as my glow lights up our small campsite. I've only ever brought Des into a memory with me once, and now I'm attempting to go into Shay's memory with both of them. I know I'll be drained a bit when we get back, but I need Des with me. I'm not very confident that I'd be safe alone.

When my magic reaches its full power, I will all three of us into Shay's memory of the cave and we vanish in a wisp of smoke.

***

We reappear in the bottom of the trench just a few minutes before we came face to face with the Goddesses in their panther forms. The gold winged butterflies float past my face and just the sight of them helps me breathe easier. I don't like the feeling I'm getting being in this memory and I know Des feels it too. We stand next to each other while Shay bends over trying to catch his breath and calm the nausea that comes with first-time memory walking.

I probably should've warned him about that.

Whoops.

I walk over to him as he stands to his full height. He smiles at me for a moment before it drops when he looks over my shoulder at Des. "What's he doing here?" He drags his gaze back to me. "You brought *him* with us?"

The tone of disgust in his voice puts a look of repulsion of my own on my face, so I can only imagine the look Des has. "I wanted someone else to see what happened to you."

He closes the distance between us and towers over me by at least a foot and a half. "Don't you trust me, princess?"

"I do." *I don't.* Especially after the word princess escapes his lips, a nickname he swore he'd never call me again. "I just don't want anyone to think I'm not telling the truth just because we're soulbonded. It's just Des, Shay."

"Fine. Come on, the panthers are almost here," he says, turning and heading for the memory that's playing out a few feet away.

I start to follow but Des grabs my arm, stopping me in my tracks. He speaks so quietly that I can barely hear him. "I don't like this. It's like he doesn't even remember who everyone is to him. I saw your face when he called you princess. We all know you hate that nickname."

"I know," I mumble. I shake my head and straighten up, speaking with a little less nerves. "Trust me, I don't like it either. But we have to just be on his side for now. Please," I plead. Des gives me a wary look but releases my arm and nods. We follow behind Shay to the group where the Goddesses have us cornered. "Look, this is right before Shay disappears," I point out.

In front of us, the panthers have us surrounded and, when past me has my back turned, I watch as Shay quietly unsheathes his knife and pokes the tip into his finger, drawing his own blood. And then he fucking *places* his knife on the ground before slipping away unnoticed.

"Wait, what?" I turn to Shay, angry tears forming. "You didn't get taken? You just left us?" A lump starts to form in my throat and it sits very heavily as I feel all different forms of betrayal surge through me.

"What the hell, Shay? Why'd you leave? We could've been fucking mauled and you just left *willingly*?" Des seethes. I do a double take when I glance at him. I can literally see the anger boiling in him as steam seeps from his skin.

"Des, are you ok?" I ask cautiously as I take a step towards him. He closes his eyes and takes a deep breath, and I watch as the steam slowly soaks back into his skin. The amount of control he has over his magic is so impressive, and it makes me wonder what other powers he has coursing through him.

"I'm fine, honey. Thanks," he says softly to me before turning back to Shay. He points his finger at him. "Get moving. We're following you."

We have to jog to catch up to past Shay who slipped off behind some rocks. As we get closer, I can hear him speaking quietly to someone but, when we round the corner to see who, the entire image is blurred, almost like the memory is tainted and changed so we can't see who it is. "Who were you talking to, Shay?" I ask, not taking my eyes off him.

"I don't-" he starts, but is cut off by sudden movement from the memory. When we look back over, past Shay is alone again and then he disappears into thin air not even ten seconds later.

"What the-" I panic, my eyes darting all around looking for him. "Where the hell did you go?"

He shakes his head, something like panic surfacing. Whether it's real or an act, I honestly can't tell. "This is what I don't remember. I don't remember walking away from you like that, I don't remember who I was talking to. I never would have abandoned you like that, Lianna. *Never.* From that point until the cave, I don't remember anything."

I look at him warily, wanting so badly to believe what he's saying. But whatever happened to him that makes him feel so different is also making it so hard to trust him. "Alright let's just...let's just go to the cave. Whatever made you disappear must have brought you there." I look over at Des with widened eyes and a furrowed brow, so in need of any sort of help from him.

He understands right away what I need from him, so he takes Shay by the elbow and physically starts to move him towards the cave in the distance.

I stay close behind them, keeping my focus on Shay and studying every movement he makes. He moves almost exactly like Shay, and the differences are nothing major that anyone would notice. But I'm not just anyone. Watching the way this Shay walks, I can tell instantly it's not right. Whether this is someone pretending to be Shay or something infected Shay's body, this is *not* the male I love.

Chapter 38

Even being in a memory, the walk to the cave takes us an hour.

Luckily, nothing unusual happens and we stay eerily quiet as we hastily walk towards the cave. It was at the start of our walk that Shay intertwined our fingers together, and we've been side by side the whole time. But it doesn't feel right and that's slowly destroying me. Our bond feels so forced now and it feels like I'm making myself pretend it feels normal when it's far from that. His hand squeezes mine slightly as my pulse quickens the smallest bit, and the feelings of his skin is smooth and cold and clammy. It's so unlike how his hands feel normally; calloused and warm at all times.

This is wrong.

When we get to the mouth of the cave, I can see the glow of a fire blazing deep inside. I turn to squint at the past versions of us, knowing that in a few minutes they'll be coming this way. So, whatever happens to Shay in this cave will be within the hour.

I drop Shay's hand and move next to Des. "We need to get in there now."

"Don't you feel it?" he whispers in fear, frozen where he stands. "That same feeling from my memory. It's here."

I pause and, sure enough, I'm overcome with that bone-chilling feeling. The hairs on the back of my neck and on my arms stand up, and a chill runs down the entire length of me. "It feels stronger here," I say, looking around the dimly lit cave in front of us.

"Well, I don't feel anything," Shay says, coming up behind us. "Come on. I can hear me up ahead." He starts to walk into the cave, leaving us to follow him.

I glance at Des as nerves consume me and I feel like my feet are made of lead. He takes my hand tightly in his and pulls me next to him as we follow after Shay.

The deeper we get into the cave, the brighter the light from the fire gets and the louder the voices ahead become. There are multiple different voices but it's near impossible to make out what they're saying at all. Their words are all garbled, like they're talking underwater.

It's not long until we get to the area in the cave that Des and I originally found Shay when he was injured, and just being back here brings a wave of grief crashing over me as the memory surfaces. I push it down as far as I can and focus on what we're here for.

As we reach the fire, we find Shay lying beside it, bound by rope yet uninjured, and surrounded by three figures. And, just like the figure behind the rock, these three are all blurry and unrecognizable. "Well, shit," I huff out, annoyance radiating from me. "I really thought this would be easier."

"I wish I could remember it clearer. I don't even remember them talking to me, let alone what they look like," Shay says, turning to me. "What now?"

"We wait. As traumatizing as it might be, I need to see how you got as injured as you did. You clearly remember being in this cave at some point, you said it yourself when you first woke up. So, between now and when Des and I found you, you remembered something."

"So what, we just sit and wait until he gets attacked?" Des asks as I sit down on the cold stone floor.

"That's exactly what we're going to do. We'll wait and keep our ears open in case some of these garbled words start to make sense." I gesture for Des and Shay to come sit with me. They look at each other tentatively before giving up and sitting on the ground on either side of me. "Perfect. Now, shut up and pay attention."

We wait for something to happen for forty-five minutes. I don't think I've ever been so bored in my entire life.

The three figures talk among each other constantly and after some time, one of them disappears, leaving Shay alone with the other two. I have to assume one of them is female because, even though I can't see or hear her, the garbled tone of the voice is far more feminine than the other two.

By now, our past selves will be getting close to the cave, if not already here. Yet, Shay still sits on the ground uninjured. With the extent of his injuries, whatever happens to him should've occurred by now.

"I don't get it, Des. When we found Shay, he was near death. Like he'd been sitting injured for a good amount of time," I say, avoiding eye contact with Shay.

"I don't get it either. There's no way he was attacked right before we got in here. We would've heard it and he would've lost far less blood," Des agrees. We both look over at past Shay, still sitting silently with the mystery figures, when all of a sudden the female starts to speak again.

Her words are still garbled but, somehow, a few words come through clearly. "...recognize...my magic...my castle...memories...concealed...job...kill him...betrayed."

I'm still trying to wrap my head around the string of extremely alarming words that come through the underwater garble, when I hear the heavy steps of the Goddesses in their panther bodies coming down the cave.

Des and I turn to look down the corridor to see just how close they are and, when we turn back, the other figure is gone, leaving just Shay and the female. But, now, he's unbound and standing in front of her calmly. And that's when I see it. The small smirk on his face as she prowls closer to him. And there's something different about this Shay, but I can't figure out what. She moves so quickly and, when she steps away from him a moment later, his stomach is slashed open and blood is pouring out.

I hold in a sob as a chill coats my skin, the goosebumps doubling and the hairs on my body standing taller.

Then, a small green light emanates around what I'm assuming are her hands, and she moves them back and forth from his stomach, inwards and outwards. With each pull, more and more blood pours out, setting the scene that he was injured for much longer than he really was.

Sneaky fucking bitch.

A low growl comes from behind us and I turn my head to see Odessa staring directly at this blurred figure. She continues to growl and I can hear the low whispers of Des and I with Kaleen not far behind.

I watch as Odessa pins the blurred figure in place with her glare as Kaleen moves beside her. A low huff of a laugh comes from the figure and, just before my past self comes pushing past the Goddesses, the figure disappears into thin air just as I burst through to find Shay.

"They saw her," I whisper, making to take a step towards where past me is tending to Shay. But I'm stopped by present Shay as he grabs my arm, taking all of us out of the memory as I hear myself cry to Des to help me save him.

***

When we reappear in our camp, Tate, Wes, and Marlene race to form a circle around us. But I can't stop the rising anger that's building in me. No, it's more than anger. It's fucking fury.

I break free of Shay's grip and stomp away from our camp, heading deeper into the mountain range. I don't stop until I'm far enough away from everyone, and only then do I fall to my knees and let my anger explode out of me.

I let my Feeler magic surge but I keep it as controlled as I can, not wanting to destroy anything. I'm just so desperate for a release. The red mist hangs close to me, never venturing farther than I allow it to, and my skin glows brightly, bouncing off the dew drops on the grass underneath me.

I let myself feel absolutely everything I need to for a minute, and then I will it all back in, locking it deep in my chest before I lose control over it. Fuck, I feel so much lighter.

"Impressive," Des' voice sounds behind me. I whip my head around, fighting the anger towards him for following me out here, but it quickly fades when I see just how far he's standing from me. Afraid I might explode again and lose control this time, or simply to respect my space, I don't know. My anger fades as I sink back down to my knees and drop my chin to my chest.

"They saw her, Des. Odessa and Kaleen, they fucking saw her and they didn't even try to warn me after we saved Shay," I say with a shaky voice. Hot tears are streaming down my face and there's no stopping them. "How could they do that? I thought they were *helping me*." I want to scream so loud that it turns my voice hoarse and destroys my throat, but I don't. I can't.

"Maybe in some twisted, fucked up way, this was their idea of helping you," he says, and my hands start to fist by my sides. How dare he? "Knock it off, kid. That doesn't mean I agree with them or think it was right, because I don't. *But* they are the Goddesses. They know what they're doing better than anyone and maybe there's a reason for it."

He makes his way over to me, despite my anger, and crouches in front of me, lifting my chin up with his finger. When my gaze meets his, he gives me a soft smile and I feel my anger completely melt away. He lets go of my chin and stands, extending his hand to me. It takes me a second to fully compose myself and, when I do, I take it and let him help me to my feet.

"I'm so angry, Des."

"I know."

"And sad. And heartbroken. And scared. And guilty."

"I know, and you have every right to feel all of that," he says, wiping away the tears that stain my cheeks. "Well, maybe not guilty, because you haven't done anything wrong here."

"If it wasn't for me, no one would have been put in this situation," I say, feeling so damn defeated. He doesn't say anything to that. Instead, he just glares at me and shakes his head. "You don't have to agree with me, but this is all so overwhelming."

"I'd be concerned if you *weren't* feeling overwhelmed. You've dealt with more than anyone your age should and it's only going to get worse," he says nonchalantly.

"That doesn't help, Des," I shoot back.

"I probably could've been a little gentler with that, sorry. But I don't want your mind to trick itself into thinking it's going to get easier from this point on. Because the reality is, it's going to get much harder and it'll take a toll on you," he says bluntly. "You might not believe it, but you're the strongest one out of all of us, honey. Sure, you're still exploring your magic and learning how to handle it but, once you do, you'll be unstoppable. And I'll be by your side as long as you want me to be."

"That's terrifying to hear you say that," I admit quietly. "This life is all so new to me and it's been thrown at me at full speed. I just need time."

"Honey, you don't have much more time to prepare. And, fuck, I wish you did. But we'll make sure you're as ready as you can be for whatever we come across. I promise," he tells me.

I sigh, letting my shoulders droop slightly. We look at each other for a moment and then I do something I've been too nervous to do for some time now.

I rush into Des and wrap my arms around his middle, tucking my head into his chest. I breathe in the scent of him; apples and bourbon. I didn't realize how familiar his smell has become to me, but, damn, it instantly calms me and eases my breathing substantially.

My sudden hug takes him by surprise, but once the initial shock of me tucking myself into him wears off, he wraps his arm around me and holds me as tight as he can. "I could get used to these. I've missed out on so many," he mumbles.

"Hopefully we can make up for lost time once this shit is all over," I say into his shirt, not quite ready to pull away. He takes a breath to respond when we're interrupted by Marlene coming from camp.

"Sorry to interrupt, but Tate has breakfast ready if either of you are hungry," she calls over to us. I reluctantly pull away from the embrace and look up at him, smiling wide. He brings my head closer to him and kisses my forehead gently, the warmth of his lips soothing my throbbing head.

"We've got this, I promise. We'll head to Meobith and get the answers we need about your mom and figure out what's going on with Shay. Someone there will be able to help us, alright?" he assures me. I nod and take a deep breath.

Together, we turn and walk towards Marlene, following her back to camp where everyone is sitting around the fire eating some sort of small animal out of the metal bowls from Marlene's bag. Shay strides over to me and pulls me to him, tightly embracing me, when I notice something I didn't before.

His familiar scent of vanilla and oak is gone and, instead, it's something else I can't place. Something distantly familiar.

Chapter 39

Shortly after we finish breakfast, we pack up camp and begin to walk again. Starting now, this'll be the longest part of our journey, according to Tate and Des.

From where we set up camp at the edge of the trench, it'll take us around three days to get to Meobith, once we factor in all the stops we'll have to make to eat and rest. Plus, we have no idea what we might run into on our way.

But there's another issue, too.

There's no guarantee that we won't get caught once we leave the Angel Fae territories and enter into the Fae realm. After what Des told us about Drake, I wouldn't put it past him to have spies everywhere. I have no doubt that he doesn't want us veering from our destination at all.

I stick with Shay for the majority of the morning, prodding him for more answers about the cave, but he still can't remember much. At least, now, he's starting to act a little like his old self again. Des and Tate are still wary of him, but as far as I'm concerned, it was the magic enhanced injury that made him seem off. And now that it's out of his system, it's our Shay again.

"How're you feeling?" I ask for the tenth time. He sighs and looks down at me. I know I'm annoying him, but I can't help it.

"Sweetheart, I'm alright, I promise. You don't have to ask me that every ten minutes." He squeezes my hand and kisses my temple. "I'm better now. My body just needed some time to heal. Whatever magic that female used on me must've been powerful enough to stall my healing but, I'm good now."

"I'm sorry. It was just so hard to find you like that and not know if you were going to make it. Everyone kept reassuring me you'd be fine, but it was scary.

And then having to watch it happen in your memory and *still* not know who did it...it's agonizing," I whine.

"Whining is definitely not going to help, love." He chuckles and wipes a bead of sweat from my forehead.

"Yeah, but it makes me feel a little better to whine about it," I counter, smiling up at him. He rolls his eyes and picks me up as we walk, flattening me against his chest, and giving me a quick kiss before planting me back on my feet.

"You make me laugh," he says, as his smile starts to fade from his face. He drops his head slightly and speaks to me in a low tone. "I'm sorry I made you all doubt it was me for a bit. I can't imagine how frustrating it must've been."

"It was. But, I kept reminding myself that if it wasn't really you, then this connection between us, our soulbond tether, it would have suffered somehow. But that never changed, so I just had to push through that small time frame where you didn't act like your normal self and just hope the real you would come back to us."

"I'll always come back to you," he promises. "Thank you for keeping faith in me. I don't know what I would've done if I had lost you."

"Don't worry, you won't," I say, leaning against his arm as we walk.

"Hey, hold on, lets stop for a minute," Tate calls up to Des and Wes, who took over the role of leading us through the mountains. At some point at the beginning of our walk, Shay and I gravitated to the back of the group for some privacy and no one seemed to mind.

We catch up to Tate and Marlene just as Des and Wes walk over to them. "Getting hungry?" Des asks them. Marlene nods quickly, eyes widening, and just the thought of food makes my stomach growl. We've been walking for at least five hours now and it has to be well past noon, and none of us have eaten since the small breakfast this morning. I'm actually surprised no one asked to stop until now.

"Let's stop. I could use a break, too," I agree. We divert from the dirt path we've been walking on to the vast grassy area at the base of the mountain and set our bags down. I bend down to run my fingers through the blades and almost sigh with utter happiness.

Since we entered the trench, we've been walking and sleeping on hard, barren ground. There's been some occasional grass patches, but nothing like this. This is soft and thick and lush. Without a second thought, I plop myself on my back in the grass and soak up every minute of this small luxury.

"Comfy over there?" Wes calls over to me, laughing slightly. I shoot up my middle finger directly at him, prompting him to throw a small dirt ball at my legs. It explodes into a cloud of dust but it doesn't even phase me. I'm way too relaxed as the warm sun beats down on me and, before I know it, I doze off.

***

I wake up to Shay gently nudging me awake. When I open my eyes, his smiling face is the first thing I see above me, blocking out the sun with his body so that I'm concealed in his shadow. With the sun beaming on his back, it looks like he's glowing around the edges. He looks ethereal.

May gaze travels down to the metal bowl in his hands and find it filled with meat and some fresh berries. Holy shit, I slept right through lunch. I was so hungry when we stopped, but clearly my body needed the rest more than a meal. Shay offers the bowl to me and I take it as I sit up. "How long was I asleep for?"

"Not long. I'd say thirty minutes, maybe? I would've let you sleep longer but Des just finished cooking the meat and I wanted you to be able to eat it while it was still hot," he explains. And there it is, the Shay I know and love, putting me first. I can't believe I ever doubted him.

"It's so peaceful here," I say, looking around me. There are birds flying high in the air and different types of insects closer to the ground, finding all the patches of wildflowers that grow along the mountains. I feel so connected to this area and it brings me so much joy. I really needed this.

"It really is," Shay says, sitting next to me, our backs to the sun, and stretching his legs out in front of him. He leans back on his hands and looks around at all I just admired, then points over past the mountain range to the West. "Over that stretch of mountains is the Chasm of Whispers. It's the ravine that separates Eldolon from Fahal. It's one of the most dangerous spots in all of Aphria." He must see the worry on my face because he adds on, "We won't be going anywhere near it, trust me."

"That's a relief, but I didn't realize we were that close to Fahal," I say, shocked by how far we've made it already.

"We are. But we're far enough in the mountains that they won't get to us. None of the Magicless ever leave Fahal. Even if they wanted to, the magical wall wouldn't let them."

"Good to know," I say as I mindlessly pick at the berries in my bowl.

We're quickly interrupted by Tate sitting down in the grass next to us. "So, we were all talking and we think we should set up camp here now and just recharge for the rest of the day. We can continue on tomorrow morning once we're all fully rested."

"I have no arguments there," Shay says, throwing himself back in the grass just as I had, and closes his eyes. Tate looks at me, then.

"Are you alright with that?" he asks. "I only ask because I know you want to see what answers Meobith has and this will delay us slightly, but-"

I cut him off mid-sentence. "Tate, stop. I am completely fine with that. I was just telling Shay how much I love it here so it'll be nice to get to relax and explore a little." I smile at him but he doesn't seem convinced. I nudge him with my foot. "I'm serious. We all need a recharge in a place like this."

Tate stands and smiles, looking back at where Marlene sits with Wes, braiding long blades of grass together and tying them around his wrist. "They both seem to like it here, too. They seem much more at peace around nature like this."

"This is how we grew up. Mom always said it was the best way to connect with the world and, if we took care of it, it would take care of us. I always thought it was just a weird quirk of hers, but now it makes me wonder if it was the Angel Fae in her and that she knew just how much the Goddesses would take care of us."

"That sounds like Amara to me. Out of the three of them, she was always much more connected to nature. It doesn't surprise me that she passed that along to you three," Tate says.

I nod towards my siblings. "Go. Enjoy nature with them. I'm going to explore a little while Shay naps. If I'm not back for dinner, come looking," I say. Tate chuckles and plants a kiss on the top of my head before walking away. I smile to myself, loving the joy this place brings me.

I can't wrap my head around how lucky I feel in this moment. The love of my life is back to himself, my siblings are safe, happy, and by my side, I gained a protective brother in Tate the last few months, and I'm getting closer and closer to my father as each day passes.

My entire body feels full of happiness for a small moment before it quickly drains out of me almost as fast as it came in. Sharp fear replaces the once warm feeling of happiness. Something is going to go wrong, I can feel it. No one can be this happy and have all of this good without something horrible happening to change all of that.

But what will it be? What will my undoing be?

Chapter 40

I try not to stray too far from camp as I explore, and I keep to the bases of the surrounding mountains.

These mountains seem to be shorter than the ones on the other side of the trench, which allows me to see all the way to the tops of them with ease. From everything I *can* see, it appears that all the mountains are covered in lush, green grass and peppered with wildflowers of all colors.

Butterflies of all shapes and sizes fly everywhere I go, and they seem to be drawn to me, following every path I take. A few have even landed on me; my nose, my finger, my shoulders, even the top of my head.

It feels magical and...*right.*

The farther East I walk, the closer I get to the portion of the Quartz Wall that's accessible from where we're camped. On either side of me is a mountain that the wall runs directly through, but doesn't have a clear path.

Which is fine.

Des briefly explained where we are and, according to the map he has, Hogarth Lake is right on the other side.

As I reach the gleaming wall, I throw my head all the way back, trying to get a view of the top. But, it's far too tall to see anything. The height of it towers significantly over the mountains around me.

I stare at the wall before me, studying the surface as I feel my magic rise up in me. I shouldn't do what I'm thinking, but *something* is urging me to, if only to see if I can.

I mean, I *am* a Goddess, I have all magic inside of me. Surely I'll be able to.

I close my eyes and concentrate on my power flowing to my hands, envisioning the wall opening a doorway when I touch it, just as Tate had when we first arrived in Shal.

I open my eyes and see my glowing hands encased with a pale blue mist. "What the hell?" I say as a surprised gasp escapes my lips, holding them in front of me and turning them around to examine them. Whenever my magic conjures a mist, it's always the Feeler magic red mist. This is new. And it feels calm.

It's beautiful.

I bring my gaze back to the wall and slowly reach my hands out in front of me, aiming for the flat surface. I'm a few centimeters from touching it when a voice sounds to my left.

"I wouldn't do that if I were you," she calls out.

I whip my head in her direction, my magic quickly transforming from the calm, blue mist to the hot, red mist of a Feeler. I lock eyes with a female lounging on the ground behind a berry bush at the base of the wall, completely hidden from view, using magic to levitate berries above her outstretched hand. How did I not sense her here?

"Who the fuck are you?" I seethe. I take some deep breaths and control my magic, pushing it down slightly so I don't lose control. But I keep it close, right under my skin, just in case.

The female stands, letting all the floating berries fall to the ground, and I'm able to get a good look at her. She's tall, about my height, and petite, with not an ounce of fat on her anywhere. Her skin is a warm tawny brown and her hair hangs down her back in loose waves with tiny braids tied throughout it.

Her eyes, though, are captivating. They're pale green, like a fresh bundle of sage, and her long, dark lashes frame them beautifully. Against her skin tone, they're a striking comparison. She is one of the most beautiful females I've ever seen.

The lavender cotton dress she has on comes down to her knees, with a thin white rope tied around her waist, keeping the floor-length cardigan around her shoulders closed. There are silver rings on almost every finger of hers and her ears are littered with piercings.

And they're pointed.

I try not to get my hopes up as I casually search for any sign of wings, wondering if another Angel Fae has survived, but I don't find any. So, if she's just fae, what's she doing in the Angel Fae territories?

She looks to be my age but, with the aging process of the fae, she could be hundreds of years old.

"I promise, I'm not here to hurt you. But, open a doorway to the other side, and you might come face to face with a royal guard. So, maybe keep the wall in one piece?" she says with a smile. She takes a step towards me and, when I shrink back slightly, she throws her hands up at me, and steps back again. "Like I said, not here to hurt you. Just to help."

"You still haven't told me who you are," I say cautiously.

She looks at me, confused slightly, but then her eyes widen as she giggles to herself. "Shit, I'm sorry. I'm Taluheh. And you're Lianna, right?"

"How the-" I start, but she just continues, like her knowing who I am isn't insane.

"Everyone in Odrera knows who you are, silly. You're King Drake's missing daughter. How could we not know you?"

"Right...I guess that makes sense," I say timidly. The whole idea of everyone knowing who I am kind of freaks me out, and I guess I never stopped to think about how many fae will recognize me when we enter the Fae realm. I'm about to ask more about her when something hits me. She knows who I am, just by looking at me. The last anyone saw of me in the Fae realm was when I was an infant. How the hell does she know me *now* as an adult? "How did you recognize me? I haven't been here in over twenty years."

She looks at me dumbfounded and then answers me. "Do you know what the King's power is?" she asks. I shake my head and her eyes widen. "He's a Metamorphoser."

"A what?"

"A Metamorphoser. It's a group of fae that can transform their appearance into anything they want. Basically a shapeshifter. It's a crazy magical gift to have and not many fae possess it. But the King does and he definitely uses it," Taluheh explains.

"But what does that have to do with knowing what I look like now?" I ask.

"Well, because he's been using his magic to keep an eye on you all these years." My jaw drops at her words and I stumble back a few steps. No. That can't be right. There's no way he's been watching me and I haven't noticed something like that. Surely I would've noticed. My heart is racing so fast and it's taking everything in me to keep my emotions controlled and safely tucked away.

"He's been watching me?" I choke out, the lump in my throat rising and tears rimming my eyes.

Taluheh nods. "Honestly, no one ever sees him anymore. He stays locked away in the castle due to his grief of losing you and the Queen. Your older sister is the one that makes all of the appearances. But, every year on the day you disappeared, he transforms into the same male and one of his guards with a transporting power takes him to where you lived with your Aunt. And every time he returns, he brings back a picture of you to make posters so everyone knows what you look like currently. Honestly, I've always found it a bit creepy, especially since you weren't technically missing." I let out the breath I was holding. Taluheh stops explaining when she sees how much it upsets me. "I'm so sorry."

I shake my head furiously at her. "Who did he disguise himself as? What did he look like?" I'm seething with anger, fresh tears coming from my eyes every second.

"It was always the same. Male, red hair with gray streaks, a really long beard. I think he went by-"

"Nicolas," I say, sobbing now. The merchant man I always took time to go see and buy trinkets from. Once a year, always the week of my birthday. He was *always* there.

"Yes, that was the name he used." She looks at me and I know she can see the devastating sadness that's consuming me. "I take it you knew this form?"

"I did."

"Listen, I get if you don't want to trust me seeing that we just met and all, but I promise I'm not lying to you when I say this. Don't trust the King. He has ulterior motives to bringing you back to Odrera and we all know it."

"We? Who's we?"

"All of us in Meobith. None of us truly support the king, but we keep it quiet."

My ears perk at that. "You're from Meobith?"

She nods. "Kind of. That's where I've been staying. I left a few months ago and I've been traveling the Angel Fae realm since."

"Why'd you leave?"

"To find you," she says simply and my breathing starts to quicken again.

"Me? Why?"

"I get visions, that's another little power of mine. I had one a while back about you and your group traveling through here and, well, I wanted to warn you of him. I'm sure you already have an idea of who he is but, I had to make sure."

"Well, thank you for that," I say to her. She sucks in a deep breath and takes another step forward. Before I know it, she's untying the rope around her waist and lets it fall to the ground around her. She holds onto the openings of her cardigan and pauses as I speak. "Uh, what are you doing?"

She smiles at me and keeps her eyes locked with mine as the cardigan drops to the ground, revealing sage green wings protruding from her back.

"Holy shit," I breathe out, my eyes bulging out of my head.

"Surprise. We're not all gone."

***

I spend almost two hours sitting with Taluheh talking about who she is and how she survived. She explained that, when King Ashton executed the remaining Angel Fae, she was in hiding in Meobith for a few years already. The fae that reside in Meobith disagreed with the Angel Fae killings and hid all they could in an underground town they created for the refugees.

She was twenty when it happened, making her 178 years old now. Young for an Angel Fae.

I start explaining who and what I am, too, and when I tell her I'm not Angel Fae, but an Omni Goddess instead, she almost weeps. "I'm sorry, I don't mean to cry. But there are stories that have been passed down through generations about how one last Omni would come back and save us all. One that begins as one and becomes two. I've never understood that part of the prophecy, but it has to be you, Lianna!"

"Those are just stories. Maybe it means one of the original Goddesses will come back. I mean, I have no idea what I'm doing. It can't be me that saves everyone," I argue. I push away the intruding memory about when Shay told me for the first time that I'm an Omni. He talked about a prophecy and that I was the last one to ever exist. Could she be right? Is it my destiny to save everyone?

"You never know," she counters, bringing me back to the present.

"Do you wanna come back to camp with me?" I blurt out. I don't know why, but embarrassment floods through my body. Even though she said she came looking for me, she might not want to stay with us. "You can travel with us if you don't want to stay here alone," I offer. She takes a few minutes to think it over as we sit cross legged in the grass, knee to knee, but eventually, she agrees.

Her cardigan is back around her, concealing her wings, as we walk back to camp. We both agreed that she should introduce herself first and tell them everything about Drake and Meobith first before revealing what she really is.

"I'm nervous, Lianna. What if they don't understand?" she says as she plays with a small braid between her fingers.

"They might not at first but, I know they will eventually," I assure her. "Don't worry, I won't let anything happen to you." I take her hand in mine as we walk the remaining distance to camp. I don't know if she feels it, too, but there's a connection between the two of us. Not like Shay and I, but something about her and her very being feels familiar and I can't help but feel like I *know* her.

There's no way, though.

I can hear all of their voices as we get closer, the smell of the fire wafting in the air heavily. It's nearing dinner so I know someone will start making food soon.

As we come over the small hill blocking camp, all eyes fly to me with relief. Those expressions quickly change to fear and nervousness when they see I'm not alone.

Everyone's on their feet in an instant, their hands flying towards any weapon that's close by.

"Lianna? Who the hell is this?" Des says as I walk forward with Taluheh.

I look at her and nod, and she takes two steps ahead of me, keeping our hands interlocked. She takes a deep breath and glances at everyone standing before her. "My name is Taluheh and I'm here to help."

Chapter 41

Everyone intently listens as Taluheh explains everything to them like she had for me. She leaves out the part about me trying to open a doorway in the Quartz Wall, thank the Goddesses. I would've heard it from all of them if they knew I was less than an inch away from trying.

When she finishes explaining everything, she looks over at me once more. Her hand is hovering above the rope around her waist, waiting for me to let her know it's the right moment for her big reveal.

Everyone has their undivided attention fully on her, and I can see the understanding and acceptance start to bloom. I look back at Taluheh and nod, giving her a reassuring smile. She draws her bottom lip in with her teeth and grins, placing her hand on the tie of the rope.

She undoes it with ease and I watch everyones faces as the cardigan drops, revealing the gorgeous wings hidden underneath.

Every single jaw drops as they unfold and spread to their full length behind her, adding on to her beauty and uniqueness.

Des is the first to speak up, which doesn't really surprise me. "How?"

And, so, Taluheh goes on to explain how she survived the Angel Fae executions. Des sits down on the log by the fire in a daze. I can't tell what he's feeling, but his breathing hitches a few times as he sits in silence, taking it all in. Shay pulls Tate to the side, away from the group, and talks quietly to him. His eyes dart between Tate and Taluheh, but I ignore them, keeping my focus on her and Des.

"I'll tell you what I told Lianna. I'm not interested in betraying or hurting anyone. I truly just want to help," she says to everyone. She looks over at Des as he disassociates in his seat, then looks to me. "Is he ok?" she asks quietly.

"I think it's just a lot for him to take in. He's had a lot of new information sprung on him in the last few months," I explain. I glance back over to Tate and Shay talking quietly to each other. When they notice I'm staring, they make their way back to our circle around the fire.

"She can stay," Tate says. "If everything she told us is the truth, then we have no reason not to trust her."

Out of the corner of my eye, I see Taluheh relax her shoulders and squeal slightly in excitement. "Thank you so much, you won't regret this."

Des snaps out of it and stands, walking over to Taluheh and I, as a smile grows on his face the closer he gets. "Come on ladies, let's sit down for some dinner." He nods towards the roaring fire in the middle of camp, then looks at Taluheh. "Don't expect anything too fancy, just some rabbit and vegetables I found. But, it'll keep you full until breakfast tomorrow."

"I'm grateful for anything, honestly. Since I left Meobith and have been on my own, it's been mainly fruits and vegetables. And the occasional fish when I can catch one," she says. Listening to the diet she's had for the past few months explains why she's so skinny.

We sit down around the fire as Des passes around bowls of food, along with the filled water jug. I watch curiously as Taluheh waits until everyone else starts to eat before digging in herself. And after just one bite, her face lights up like she's never eaten something so good before.

I smile down at my bowl at her appreciation and feel my insides warming. The past few years, even months, I've been surrounded by family of varying sorts. Adding Taluheh, someone who genuinely just wants to be a friend, is such a different feeling of happiness.

But I can't erase the unease and nervousness that festers deep down at the thought that this female I just met, a literal stranger, has the ability to betray me. And I already know, if that happens, it'll break me.

***

Not too long after we finish dinner, the sun begins to set quickly.

When it's time to settle in for the night, there's not much discussion on where Taluheh's going to sleep. At first, she tried to convince us that she'd be fine sleeping in the grass.

I was not having that, though. And neither was anyone else, which surprised her a bit.

Instead, Shay and I unzip each of our sleeping bags fully and lay one out to its full length on the ground. We all fit on the extended sleeping bag pretty well and the other one is thrown over our bodies like a blanket. It's actually pretty spacious and warm, especially since I'm sandwiched between Taluheh and Shay.

After tonight, we'll be on our way to Meobith and will have to cross through parts of Eldolon. Des says it's an abandoned city just like Shal, and there'll be plenty of homes we can explore and sleep in. The thought of getting to sleep indoors again and potentially on a bed instead of the ground is keeping my mind far too awake.

I lay on my back, staring into the starry sky as anxiety creeps in out of nowhere. To my left, Shay is sound asleep on his side facing me with his arm draped over my middle and, to my right, Taluheh is also asleep with her back facing me.

I sigh and slowly inch my way out from between them and tiptoe over to where Wes is sleeping. He opted to sleep under the stars tonight since it's a bit warmer than previous nights have been.

"Wes. Are you awake?" I whisper, nudging him with my toe.

"I am now, thanks to your toe." He sits up in his sleeping bag, rubbing sleep from his eyes. "Is everything ok? Did Shay do something? Or was it Taluheh?" His glance darts over to their peacefully sleeping forms, assessing them carefully before turning back to me.

"They didn't do anything, relax." I sit down on the ground next to him and cross my legs in front of me. "Can I admit something to you?"

His eyebrows come together as his look turns serious. "Of course you can, Li. Always and forever, remember?" he says, shoving me gently.

I huff out a small laugh and tilt my head back, blinking back tears. "I'm worried. And not about Taluheh joining us, before you say anything. That's the least of my worries, honestly."

"Do you want to list them for me? And then we can go through them all?" he asks. A small bit of relief hits me. This is what I know I can always count on. Him. From a young age, he's always known the best ways to pull me from my anxious thoughts and how to keep me grounded. It's exactly what I need right now.

I sigh and drop my head. "So many things, Wes. I'm worried about *so many things*. Like, what if there's something wrong with Shay? Or what if the answers I need aren't in Meobith? What if Drake finds us even before we can get to Meobith? What if we run into others that want to hurt us? What if there are more creatures we don't know about? What if something happens to you or Marlene or Tate or Des or Shay, or even Taluheh? What if something happens to me?"

Wes raises his eyebrows and lets out a sigh, taking in all I said to him and trying to figure out the best way to approach all of my pent up worries. I'm sure he's regretting having me list all my worries after I just woke him from a very peaceful sleep. But after a few moments, he unzips his sleeping bag and gets out, coming to sit right by my side. He wraps his arm around me and guides my head down onto his shoulder, hugging me close.

"Here's what I'll say to all of that. Some of us might get hurt along the way," he starts and I choke back a traitorous sob as a tear slips free. Wes wipes it away quickly and continues. "I know it worries you, but you have to remember that we all chose to follow you and be by your side. We all knew what that meant. You mean so much to all of us in so many ways and all we want to do is keep you safe," he says with his cheek resting on my head.

"But that's the problem, Wes. I don't know if I'll be able to live with myself if anyone gets hurt because of me." I need to control my breathing, or else I won't have control. *Deep breath in. And out.*

"You'll be able to, trust me. You're not someone that gives up easily. I know you'll want to and, Goddesses, I know you'll try. But, you have something inside of you that won't let any of that stop you and it makes you stronger. And, yeah, Meobith might not have the answers you're looking for but, they might have answers to questions you didn't even know you had. It might seem like a failure at first, but everything will all be worth it eventually."

"Why do you think I'm that strong? You've seen me almost give up. You saw me sink so low that I didn't think I'd ever surface again. Why would it be any different?"

"That's exactly why, Li. You've almost given up but you're still here. You *did* surface again. Because you knew your story wasn't over yet and you had so much more living to do. Especially now, you have far more than you ever thought you could have. Look around you. Your family has doubled in the past few months alone. You've found your soulbond and your real dad. You've found more power in you than you knew was possible and learned that you're a fucking Goddess, the *last* Goddess for that matter. You will never give up because now you have too much to live for," Wes says, pulling me away from him so he can face me. "And don't think you're getting rid of anyone that easily. You're stuck with us all for a long ass time."

Tears threaten to spill down my face again, but I wipe them away before they can leave my eyes. "I don't know how you do it. Every time, without fail, you pull me out of my anxious thoughts and make things so much better. I couldn't have asked for a better brother."

"Yeah, remember that the next time I piss you off somehow," he says, chuckling. "Go get some sleep. We have a long day ahead of us tomorrow."

I stand, brushing the grass off my pants as I turn back to Wes. "Thank you for letting me disturb your sleep."

"Anytime, Li." He sinks back down into his sleeping bag and zips himself in, closing his eyes as he gets comfortable. "Now, I love you, but go to bed so I can go back to sleep."

I laugh softly and go back to my sleeping bag, where Shay and Taluheh left my empty space in the middle open. I dust the dirt off the bottoms of my feet before I slip back into my now cold spot and let my eyes close for some much needed rest.

Chapter 42

"L ianna. Wake up, quickly," Taluheh hisses as she nudges me in my side with her elbow.

I open my eyes to see her staring at me filled with worry and it immediately has me on edge. I bolt upright and notice pretty quickly that Shay isn't next to me anymore. The space where he slept is barely warm, but cold enough that he's been gone for at least an hour.

I look at the sky. Dawn is just beginning to break, and the cloudy sky is a masterpiece of various shades of blue, bronze, and orange. I look back at Taluheh as she scans the rest of the campsite. I follow her gaze and land on the spot where Wes' sleeping bag is set up.

But it's empty.

"Where the hell are Shay and Wes?" I ask her quietly enough to not wake everyone else.

She shakes her head. "I don't know. I heard some mumbling coming from the edge of camp and, when I opened my eyes, I saw someone leading them away from us to the West. It was too dark to see who the mystery figure was, but they both followed behind them willingly, " she says in a panic.

I slip out of the sleeping bag cover and pull my thigh holsters on, making sure all of my knives are strapped in place before putting my boots on. I unsheathe one of the daggers I found in Shal and give it to Taluheh. "Here, just in case."

She takes it from me hesitantly before nodding and holding it by her side. "Do you want to wake everyone else?" she asks.

No, I don't. But I know having backup is the smart choice, because I have no idea what we're going to find when we follow the path they took. "Yeah, let's do it."

We go around to each one of them and gently shake them awake, explaining what happened once everyone is coherent enough the understand. After a few minutes, everyone is dressed and strapped with as many weapons as they can carry. Des even makes Taluheh a makeshift strap for around her waist for the dagger I lent her.

"Listen, I don't know what the hell is going on. But we aren't taking any chances. Be ready for anything," I say in a hushed tone to the four of them standing around me. I'm trying so hard to stay positive and make myself look confident but, even with my little speech, I can't shake the feeling that something terrible is about to happen.

Because I can't think of a good enough reason for both Shay and Wes to be gone and headed towards the one place Shay warned me about just yesterday as we laid in the grass together.

Who were they with and why the hell are they going towards the Chasm of Whispers?

***

We walk for almost three hours with no sign of Shay or Wes.

At this point, the sun is high in the sky and beating down on us hard. When we first started walking, we had no idea where the hell to go, so we just kept going West. But, a few minutes into the walk, we noticed small droplets of blood every few feet on the dirt path. It looked like someone was unknowingly dripping blood as they walked.

Or was purposely leaving a trail.

At some point, the trail veered to the right slightly, changing our direction to head Northwest, instead.

Des catches up to me and walks besides me as we all continue to follow the path. "I have a really bad feeling about this. I don't like the idea of heading towards the chasm to begin with but, now, we're heading in the direction of the bridge that takes you right to Fahal. I don't want any of us going there. It's not safe."

"I know. I don't want to go there either. But what if Shay and Wes are there? What if they're in trouble?"

"What if *Shay* is the trouble, Lianna? Did you think about that at all? Don't you remember the bits of the memory we saw? There were three other figures there with him. What if one of them lured them out here? Or..."

"Don't even fucking say that. I know what you're thinking. Shay did not lead Wes out here. Wes *and* Shay were taken here, they're both in danger," I seethe.

"I don't want to think that either, but he hasn't been himself since we found him in the cave. I just want you to prepare yourself just in case."

"Yeah, I'll remember that. Thanks," I say through my teeth, ripping out of his grasp and quickening my pace to walk next to Taluheh. I can feel his stare on my back and the guilt starts to rise inside me.

Because he might be right. And it's something I don't want to breathe life into because it can't be true.

"Stop," Tate hisses from the front of the group. He halts abruptly and ducks behind a group of large boulders at the edge of the mountain pass. We're more out in the open now and I can hear the rushing water ahead of us.

The Chasm of Whispers.

The water far below sounds just like hundreds of whispers all at once, and it makes me wonder if that's how it got its name. Or for a far more gruesome reason.

"Lianna, come here. Quietly," Tate calls back to me in a hushed tone. I slowly make my way to where Tate's crouched and kneel down next to him, peering around the rock slightly to see what he's staring at.

My eyebrows come together in confusion. Because I know what I'm looking at, but it seems so wrong and this feeling has the hairs on my body standing straight up. I whip my head back to Des, who has the same look of confusion and understanding on his face.

The feeling that's thick in the air is the same feeling we had in the cave and in the memory when we saw the Caviax. But, fuck, it's never felt this *heavy*.

And it's the same feeling I have now as I look at Shay standing at the edge of the chasm alone, staring right at us with his arms by his side, sleeves rolled up to his elbows. And covering his skin, from his fingertips to the crooks of his elbows, is deep red blood, dripping on the ground.

Right onto the discarded hatchet by his feet.

***

There is no part of me that wants to run up to Shay right now.

Because that is *not* him.

Since we found him in the cave, I've been trying to convince myself that he's still the same Shay we all know. But, looking at him now, I know something awful happened to him in that cave. And feeling this hair raising magic coming from him, I'm certain that the love of my life, my *soulbond*, is nowhere in there.

"Tate. What do we do? Do you see Wes anywhere?" I whisper in a panic.

He shakes his head and pushes Marlene further behind him, keeping his grip on her tight. "I don't see him. But, Lianna..."

"The blood, I know." I can feel my magic surging inside me, begging to be released. "I need to get closer to Shay."

"Lianna, no. That's the stupidest fucking idea I've ever heard. That's not him. He might hurt you," Tate says, holding me back. But I rip my arm from his grasp and step out from the safety of the boulder into clear view.

"Shay," I call out. His eyes are already tracking my every movement, and he has a blank expression filling his face. Other than a sinister grin, there's nothing there. No emotion at all. I swallow the lump in my throat. "Shay, it's me. It's Lianna. Are you okay?"

At the sound of my name, his eyes blink rapidly and some strange haze comes over him as he tilts his head to the side slightly. "I was just taking care of a problem, love," he says coldly. Even his voice sounds wrong, like there are two separate voices fighting to come free, twisting together with each word.

I take a few steps towards him, and two figures appear out of thin air by his side. They're both shrouded from head to toe by a black mist, concealing them completely.

Only one of the figures emerges from the shadows, a female, while the other stays hidden in the mist surrounding them. She comes up beside Shay and links her arms through his, kissing him on the cheek and pulling herself far too close to him as she nuzzles his neck.

The sight of it makes my magic rear in anger and jealousy, but once again, I push it away. I can't look like a threat. Not yet.

"Lianna, it's so nice to finally meet you, dear," the female says in a low, sultry voice. It takes everything in me to not stumble backwards when I realize just who stands in front of me. At how similar she looks to her sisters. Her black curls hang around her face perfectly and her emerald green eyes glow with terrible power.

"Izara," I hiss through my teeth. "You're Izara, aren't you?"

She lets out a breathy laugh. "You catch on quickly. What was it that gave it away? That you've heard so much about your dear auntie Izara from my loving sisters? Or do I look too much like your precious mother and aunt?"

She untangles herself from Shay and takes a few steps towards me. I withdraw two of my knives, keeping them by my sides as she stops in her tracks, making a clicking noise through her teeth at me. "Where's Wes?" I grind out.

"Oh, we'll get to him soon. But first..." she trails off as her gaze moves behind me to Des and Tate who are now protectively at my back. I risk a small glance behind me, making it seem as if I'm looking at the males, but I look to the boulders instead. Marlene and Taluheh are still crouched behind them with Taluheh's wings wrapped around them tightly like a shield. A small wave of relief washes over me seeing them safely together, clutching onto each others hands in fear. I hate seeing them so terrified, but at least they're protected.

I turn back to Izara as she eyes up Des and Tate. "It's been a while since I've seen either of you handsome males," she purrs. Neither of them speak a word, but continue to stand behind me unmoving and seemingly unfazed. Though, I know this is putting them on edge. "Tate, you were a naughty one, letting Shay here take your place. Though, it did work in my favor." She turns to Des, then. "And Desmond, you healed nicely."

"Don't fucking talk to them," I snap, allowing some of my magic to rise to the surface. I allow myself to glow faintly, but I keep my mists concealed, making sure to keep my emotions under control. Yet, none of it seems to faze Izara at all. She looks...happy.

"So, you did get the powers, hmm? I knew I scented it on you when your wretched mother birthed you. I knew she'd waste all the potential you have, potential I can help you reach."

"She *saved* me from you."

"You can continue to think that, but one day you'll see she was wrong." She turns to the figure that's still concealed in the mist and waves her hand in front of it, wiping it all away to nothing to reveal a male armed from head to toe in weapons of every sorts.

His stare is menacing and it's directed right at Tate, who is quickly moving to my left side. "Long time no see, brother," the male says in a deep voice.

I glance up at Tate, and his face is filled with dread and betrayal. "Caz," he spits out, glancing sideways at me for a split second.

Caz. He had been Izara's guard when they were younger, and was Shay and Tate's friend for so many years.

"Didn't think you'd see me again, did you?" Caz laughs.

"Considering we watched you die, no I didn't," Tate says angrily. "Who the hell brought you back?"

"Wouldn't you like to know," Caz sneers, stepping forward slightly, but Izara stops him.

"As beautiful as this little reunion is, I really have a lot to do, so..." she nods at Caz who disappears from where he stands, and then reappears a second later right next to Des. I whirl around in shock, reaching out for Des, but Caz is too quick. He grabs onto Des' arm and, in a split second, they both disappear into thin air.

"Dad!" I scream, diving forward to the spot where he was just a second ago. I'm too late. Izara's gasp echoes from behind me.

"Well that's an interesting development," she says, smirking. She looks over at Shay, who tenses slightly, before turning back to me. "I'll be honest, I genuinely didn't know that. Naughty, naughty Flora." She laughs and then turns to Shay once more. "Alright, I've had my fun. Get it over with and make it quick." Shay nods at her as she takes a few steps and then disappears once more.

Shay then turns his head to me slightly, a mix of remorse and betrayal coating his face. Then, a black mist covers his hands as he raises them slowly in front of him, never breaking eye contact with me. And what rises from the depths of the chasm brings me to my knees.

This is my undoing.

Wes.

Chapter 43

The sound that comes from me is a guttural scream that turns my throat raw.

I vaguely notice Tate turn and run from me to Marlene, who's shrieking behind me. I barely hear the faint sound of bile hitting the grass between screams. The magic I pushed down starts to seep out of me as I try to regain control. I *need* to stay in control, or else I might not come back from it.

I want so badly to look away from the devastating scene in front of me, but I can't tear my eyes from him. Wes is suspended in mid air above the chasm by tendrils of black mist, blood dripping from him in so many places. I fall forward onto my hands as the full image of him registers in my mind, breaking my gaze from him and dropping my head down to keep my own bile from coming up.

There's a reason Shay is so blood soaked with a hatchet at his feet. My brothers limbs are barely attached to his limp body, as if Shay started to saw them off but gave up halfway through. Now, they just hang there, bone completely exposed and the skin around each saw mark bruised and blood stained. The worst part is, he's alive. The tendrils are supporting him around his middle and lightly around his neck, and his eyelids are fluttering rapidly. The amount of pain he's in because of *him* makes me sick.

"What did you do to him?" I cry out, turning my attention to Shay, still a few feet in front of me. He keeps his hands raised, keeping Wes suspended, and looks at me angrily.

"I did what I needed to do. *He* was a problem. *He* was holding you back and babying you. You were never going to succeed with him in the way."

"He's my *brother!* All he's ever done is support me, not hold me back. How could you?" I seethe. "How could you do this to me? *You* betrayed me. In every way possible." I let some of my mist seep out and focus it to wrap around my hands. "Stop this, now. This is over, Shay."

He looks at me then, confusion falling over his face. "Betray you? No. I was never on your side to begin with. I just needed to get close to you to help *her*." His face lights up as he continues to talk. "She has so much she has planned for you, and we needed you to be completely focused. Wes was one of the distractions, Desmond was another. And look, both distractions are being taken care of."

"You...lied to me? But you're my soulbond. You love me," I stutter, backing into Tate who's once more behind me and steadying me with trembling hands. I have never felt so betrayed before. Even Luke never did anything to this extent.

"Soulbond? No, absolutely not. Just simple magic. Only took finding the right spell in Kaius' Tome to create a fake soulbond connection to make it all believable," he says, uninterested.

"How the hell did you get the Tome?" I say through my teeth.

"Funny story. When Gaman originally took it from the Goddesses, he entrusted his son, Dion, to keep it safe. Turns out it was a good idea, because Gaman was murdered and, when they came for Dion, he was no where to be found and the Tome was gone. Turns out, he's a Metamorphoser so he was able to elude his own murder easily. He became a very powerful fae ruler, King Ashton to be exact, and he continued to kill the Angel Fae just like his father taught him to."

I whip my head around to look at Taluheh and her eyes are wide in fear. Judging by the look on her face, she's come to the same conclusion I have about Dion the Metamorphoser. I give her a slight nod and motion towards the bridge with my eyes, and her and Marlene nod their heads quickly, ducking behind the boulder and picking up all of the discarded weapons around them.

I turn back around to face Shay, trying my best to hide the shock erupting in me. Beside me, Tate is breathing heavily and gripping his sword so tightly that his knuckles are turning white.

"King Ashton is dead, Dion is dead. How'd you get the Tome?" I say, trying to keep the conversation going long enough for Marlene and Taluheh to sneak around to the bridge to grab Wes. He's suspended just by the bridge and he's close enough that the two of them will be able to grab him, especially with Taluheh's levitation magic. She'll be able to bring him closer and they can get him down so Tate and I can go for Shay. I just need to keep him distracted.

"Ashton's death was a sham. Just a show so that Dion could turn into someone else. And he's still very much here," Shay taunts.

"So, what, you think I'm just going to willingly give myself over to you? So Izara can use me for her own selfish reasons?"

"Oh, sweetheart, you won't have a choice," he huffs out. And then he spins around towards the bridge Marlene and Taluheh are racing down. He shoots his right hand towards them and sends a black tendril out, letting it wrap around Taluheh's ankle to pull her back off the bridge, leaving Marlene alone.

Tate drops his sword to the ground and starts to sprint to my sister, while I keep my eyes on Shay. He laughs to himself and lets his hands drop, calling back the tendrils to his body.

I leap to my feet quickly as the tendrils release Wes from their grasp, sending him into a free fall into the chasm. I run to the edge and watch in horror as he gets closer to the bottom, and I start to panic. I try to focus my Elemental magic to bring the ground closer to him or to conjure soft grass at the bottom to soften the blow. I have no idea what I'm doing, but I need to do *something*. I have to save him. I close my eyes to imagine something rising to catch him and...

A choking sounds distracts me. And Tate's screams fill the air. *No.*

I turn to see Marlene being held against Shay's body in the middle of the bridge and I...I don't understand what's happening. When did Shay transport to her? I didn't even know he could do that but, then again, I don't know him. And then I see it.

Red drips down her neck and stains the front of her shirt. The hatchet that was just a few feet from me is now in Shay's hands at her neck. She drops to the ground limply as he disappears from behind her and reappears on the other side of the chasm, watching me. And...

And then I hear the deafening crack in the chasm down below. Of Wes' body hitting the hard surface my magic brought halfway from the ground to save him. I take slow steps to the very edge and force myself to look down.

Tears are blinding me, but I still see it. Wes' body is completely mangled on the small square of earth I conjured. I squeeze my eyes shut and stumble backwards, trying to erase the image of not only his broken body a few feet down, but Marlene's lifeless body on the bridge ahead.

No.

The magic in me starts to turn to fire inside.

No.

Wes is dead. My best friend. My protector. My big brother.

No.

Marlene is dead. My biggest fan. My angel. My little sister.

No.

Shay killed them both. The male I was tricked into loving betrayed me.

No.

It's all my fault.

No.

My fault.

No.

My...

"No!" I scream, magic erupting from my hands as I throw them out at my sides. Intertwining mists of red and blue come from the center of my palms and my skin is glowing brighter than it ever has before. The ground around me starts to shake as I release my Elemental magic. I'm surrounded by every element I can conjure, shielding me like it did the day Luke attacked in Shal. Earth, fire, water, wind...it all materializes around me as I feel myself levitate in the air.

Without even seeing myself, I know I look like power come to life, eyes ablaze from the fire inside me.

I lift my gaze to Shay, who now looks at me in fear. Fear of what his actions unleashed. Fear of what I've become. Fear of what I've always been.

And it's aimed at him.

I speak in a low whisper that my magic carries to his ears only. "I am power and you will pay."

Then, focusing all of my power directly at Shay, I turn up the corner of my mouth as the flow of tears continue. Smoke is coming from my skin and I can feel the fire inside me burning way too hot, but I can't stop. Not now, not for anything. This is all for my siblings and the lives they lost for me and because of me.

I bring my hands back and send a stream of concentrated magic directly at Shay. He stares me down with a grin on his face and, just as the magic is about to hit him head on, he vanishes into thin air and doesn't reappear.

"Fuck!" I yell into the air, throwing my head back as a shriek rips from my throat, sending more magic pulsing out of me. I bring my head down with determined anger and scan the area for him, but he's truly gone this time. There's no trace of him.

And, yet, my magic continues to surge.

It's finally happening. I'm losing control and I can't reign it back in. I bring myself back down to solid ground, and the moment my feet hit the earth, my magic enters the ground and bits of dirt and rock explode upwards in a fury, my magic tearing apart the land around me.

Footsteps sound behind me and I spin around defensively, fueled by the magic coursing through me, and come face to face with Taluheh.

She looks at me with tears flooding her eyes and shakes her head at me. "Lianna, don't do this to yourself."

But I don't know how to stop it. My mind is empty, nothing matters anymore, nothing but getting this anger and devastation out of me. Tears spill from my eyes, streaking my dirt coated cheeks, sizzling and steaming as they go.

Taluheh reaches out and grabs my wrist, my skin smoking at the contact. She winces at the pain my burning skin causes, but she holds tight. She won't let me go. "Tate needs you," she pleads, and I look up to see him cradling Marlene's bloodied body in his lap, rocking her back and forth. He's sobbing uncontrollably and there's nothing anyone can do because she's gone. *His* soulbond, the love of his life, gone. "And Desmond needs you to find him," she adds on. My dad. Taken from me.

I muster all of the strength I can and squeeze my eyes shut, begging myself to remember anything he taught me to reign in my control. I can almost hear Wes' voice in my head, reminding me of the conversation we had just a few hours ago. That I have too much to live for. And, even with half of those reasons gone, I still have to hold on. For Tate, for Taluheh, for my dad. My mom is out there somewhere, and my parents in Peham will need me.

I let out a cry of pain and force myself to pull my magic back inside. Every drag of that power feels like I'm being stabbed over and over.

But, it's working. I'm calming the storm of my magic.

Slowly, my magic subsides and the shield of elements drops from around me at the same time the mists seep back into my body. It's almost gone, almost pushed down.

"Wait," I breathe. I halt my magic from reeling in and use the rest of my energy to stumble to the edge of the chasm. I force myself to look down at Wes' body once more, another hole tearing in my heart, and use the last bit of magic I can afford to levitate him from down below and place him on the ground in front of me. "I'm so sorry, Wes. I couldn't protect you or Marlene," I whisper through sobs. "I hope Sierra's waiting for you. I hope you find Marlene. One day I'll find both of you again. I love you. I love you so much."

I let out the breath I've been holding and the rest of my magic snaps back inside. I collapse on the ground next to my brother, reaching out to grab his hand one last time.

***

I don't feel the fire inside me die down. I don't feel when Taluheh rushes to my side and wraps my charred skin in a damp cloth or forces me to drink water to ease the burn in my throat. I don't feel when Tate lifts my drained, limp body off the ground away from my brother, while Taluheh uses her magic to levitate the corpses of my siblings behind us.

I don't feel anything.

No more tears come, now. Either I've cried them all or the fire that burned too hot in me has dried them all up. I will no longer get to feel the warmth of Wes' hugs. Or hear his deep laugh ever again. I'll never get to smell eucalyptus and citrus on him again, or have his shoulder to cry on when the anxiety overwhelms me.

I'll never get to sit and watch Marlene bake in the middle of the night when she can't sleep. Never get to climb in bed with her when the nightmares get too real. I'll never see the way her eyes light up when she talks about a new book she read or get to experience the smell of fresh bread on her when she comes home from work.

Because they're both gone. And Shay killed them.

Anger festers inside me again, only this time, nothing comes with it. My skin is glowing faintly, like it's been dimmed to the lowest setting, but I can't *feel* the magic. It just feels used up and dry. It feels gone.

My breathing starts to quicken and the panic rises in me, but Tate holds me close to his chest and smoothes down my hair. "It's called burnout, Li. You lost control and used up all of the magic in your body. It's not gone for good, but it'll take some time for it to replenish."

"Time," I say in a hoarse voice. But I don't have time. I need to find my dad and bring him back before I lose someone else I love. And I will not let that happen. I've already lost too much.

I reach up and take hold of the garnet around my neck, cursing it for not protecting us from this. Why didn't it protect them? "Close your eyes, Lianna. We'll be back to camp in a few minutes and then we'll get you cleaned up," Tate says, still clutching me to his chest. He's trembling and I know he wishes he was holding Marlene. Not only did I lose my little sister, but he lost his soulbond and it was the betrayal of his best friend, his *brother,* that's causing his pain. And he's keeping it together for *me.*

I don't deserve any of his kindness. Marlene would still be here if she had just stayed in Peham, safe and sound. But she wanted to protect me.

But no one protected her.

I let my eyes flutter shut and before I know it, sleep takes over.

***

I don't know how long I slept, but when I wake up, it's dark out. I look around and realize I'm not in the sleeping bag that me, Shay, and Taluheh shared last night, but tucked in someone's sleeping bag and zipped inside Tate's tent. Outside, I can hear Tate and Taluheh talking softly and the crackling of the fire close by.

I sit up, which takes an awful lot of effort, and rub my eyes with my hands. I wince at the contact and look down to see that they're wrapped in cloth, and there's a hint of charred skin peeking through. Why am I not healing faster?

I pull on a sweatshirt that's placed on the ground next to me and slip out of the sleeping bag to tug on my boots. I scoot over to the tent door and unzip it, letting in the cool breeze of the night. I shiver with the sudden temperature change and step into the fire lit night.

When I stand fully, I feel just how sore I am. Even my bones feel bruised. It's a struggle to walk the short distance to the fire where the two of them are sitting, but I manage to get there without any help. Goddesses, it fucking hurts.

Taluheh is the first to notice me as I step into the light. She jumps to her feet and basically runs to my side as I stagger over to them. She grabs me around the waist and helps me the remaining few feet to sit me down on a log around the fire.

"How're you feeling?" Tate asks quietly, concern lining his face.

"I should be asking you that," I say sadly as a cough follows my words. Taluheh hands me the jug of water and I drink it down greedily. It's so cold on my throat and soothes it almost immediately. "Thanks."

"There's some food saved for you, too. You've been asleep all day, so whenever you're ready, I can heat it up for you," she says, her hand gripping my wrist lightly.

I look around camp, the lack of *everyone* weighing heavily on me, when my eyes stop on something tucked at the edge of camp. Two large wooden boxes sit underneath a sleeping bag and my eyes widen when I realize what they are. I point a shaky finger towards them, and both Tate and Taluheh exchange glances, not even needing to look. "Are those-"

"Yes," Tate says quickly, letting his head drop as tears fall from his eyes, his hair falling long around his face. "Earlier, when we all got back to camp and we got you situated in the tent, I went out and did some damage in the woods. Anger and sadness...it all hit me and my magic destroyed a lot of trees. When I saw how much wood came down, I got the idea to make those."

"You made that for them?" I ask Tate.

He nods and looks back up at me. "I couldn't leave them...out. They're in there, now."

"My...my parents are going to want to-" I start, not even able to get the rest of the words out.

"I'll find a way to get them here. We can go back to Shal and have a small funeral for them. Honor them."

The thought of backtracking now when we're so close makes it feel like there's lead in my stomach, but it might be the smartest thing to do considering everything that has happened. I nod at Tate, swallowing a lump low in my throat. We all sit in silence for a few minutes, the only sounds coming from the crackling fire and the night life around us.

Taluheh is the first to speak. "So, what's the official plan, then?"

We all look at each other for a moment, and then I speak up. "We go back to Shal, pay respects to Wes and Marlene. Then, we need to find my dad." I clench my teeth together, the absence of Des squeezing my heart tightly. Then, a wave of anger floods over me. *He fucking murdered them.*

"Li?" Tate lightly touches my shaking hand. I look at him, the fire returning to my eyes. I want revenge.

"And then, I'm going to kill Shay."

Afterword

Hi there!

I want to take this moment to really thank all of you, as readers, for taking a chance on *Dawn of the Forsaken*. This is my debut novel, and the first book in the Lost Fae Lineage series. It is my hope that those of you that read and enjoyed this book stick around and continue with your incredible support.

I have been dreaming of being an author of some sort for pretty much my whole life. Reading and writing has always been such a huge passion of mine, and I can't even count how many times I started a story and let it fade into nothing because I was too afraid to follow my dream. I was in a writing slump for years after the last book I attempted to write back in 2018. But, something snapped inside of me and I had this idea for this book right here, and I went with it. I spent countless late nights writing and rewriting, getting into slumps, having incredible ideas at 3 a.m. scribbled down incoherently in my notes app. And now, it's all finished and in my hands. Everything about this book makes me so proud of myself for, not only writing it, but following through with it. And I couldn't have done it without that constant love and support from my friends and family, and everyone I've come across on social media.

To my Eli. You made me realize my dreams were worth chasing. You supported me through every single process of this book, from letting me explain plot points and characters you didn't understand to watching me create and edit my world map countless times. I don't know if I could have gotten this far without you. Thank you for everything. Your love and support for me and my dreams means more than anything to me, and I love you endlessly, soulbond.

To my sweet daughter. Though you don't understand fully what I have accomplished, you have supported me in your own way through it all. You are my own personal cheerleader, and you make me proud to me your mom every day. Thank you for watching me follow my dreams, and I can't wait to be your cheerleader in everything you do. You are what I follow my dreams for. I love you more than anything on this earth.

Thank you all for your support now and for times to come.

Lots of love,
Kyle Michelle

About the author

Kyle Michelle was born and raised in Pennsylvania, where she still lives now. Growing up, Kyle has always had an intense love for books, both reading and writing them. She was always writing short stories in her notebooks in class and even submitted multiple poems to eventually be published in poetry books.

After what felt like an eternity in a writing slump, the idea for *Dawn of the Forsaken* came to Kyle and, after a year of writing, her debut novel was finished, with ideas for the rest of the series already planned and plotted.

Kyle lives in a small commuter town in Pennsylvania with her other half and daughter. When Kyle isn't writing, you can find her waitressing at her day-job or playing Barbies with her daughter.

www.ingramcontent.com/pod-product-compliance
Lightning Source LLC
Chambersburg PA
CBHW030241120726
47903CB00005B/1567